Dating
by the
Book

A Romantic Comedy

By

Paul Ekert

1st Edition Paperback Published in 2019 by PaulEkert.com

Copyright © Text Paul Ekert

1st Edition Paperback

ISBN: 9781086524574

The author asserts the moral right under the Copyright, Designs and Patents Act 1988 to be identified as the author of this work.

This novel is a work of fiction, and any resemblance between characters living or dead is purely coincidental.

All Rights Reserved. No part of this publication may be reproduced, stored in a retrieval system, or transmitted, in any form or by any means without the prior written consent of the author, nor be otherwise circulated in any form of binding or cover other than that in which it is published and without a similar condition being imposed on the subsequent purchaser.

PaulEkert@PaulEkert.com

www.PaulEkert.com

Dedicated to Liz, Phil, Deborah, Carl, and Jan whose wonderful acting breathed life into the characters of the original stage play.

And to the unsung heroes of Steeple Aston Players; Alan, Mike, Marian, Will, Peter, Sue, John plus many, many others who worked alongside me to overcome all the myriad 'issues' that occur when staging a play.

This book is for you all.

"There is only one way to avoid criticism:

Do nothing, say nothing, and be nothing."

Aristotle (*possibly*)

Chapter 1

Juliet

London

Late March

Around lunchtime…

First dates fail for a variety of reasons; incompatibility, mutual boredom, conflicting politics and in extreme cases, death. Only the latter failed to visit Juliet's lunchtime rendezvous with Ron, a man whose brash tie screamed travelling salesman just a little louder than the Jaguar key fob he'd flung on the table.

He was twenty minutes late and at least five stone overweight, although surprisingly nimble, kissing her on the cheek before she had a chance to evade what appeared to be a ritualistic slobbering. After confirming her name, he elected to call her 'babe', eased her into her chair by gently patting her arse and in that crucial moment of a first impression, managed to violate both her physical and mental state in a single stroke of misogynistic loathsomeness.

The date had gone downhill from there.

It was no small relief when Juliet's phone beeped.

Will hunt U down & kill U, Juliet tapped into her spotlessly pink phone in reply to the seemingly innocuous text message; ***how's it going?*** She finished her own message with a *Scream* Emoji and realised that Ron had stopped talking and was staring at her phone with evident annoyance.

"Who's that, babe?" He asked, his face clearly telegraphing the sulk emoji.

"My sister, Tina," Juliet said, politely resisting the phrase; *mind your own fucking business.*

"Ah Tina," Ron said with far too much suggestive wetting of his lips. "And how is our little… Cupid?"

"Not yet dead."

"Sorry?"

"I said, she's up to her neck. In work. Needs me. Back at the office." Juliet forced herself to stop talking, aware that she sounded like the verbal equivalent of a telegram whenever she lied. "Sorry. Have to leave. Now."

"But you've not ordered." Ron's practised nicotine-stained smile slipped slightly, but only slightly.

"I never eat lunch."

"Really?" Ron's searching eyes played downwards over her body like the worst kind of evasive airport body scanner. "No wonder you're as thin as a …. No wonder you have such a gorgeous figure."

Juliet had thought the final straw of this implausible date had been the pat on her arse, but it was fascinating to see this straw resurrected from the grave, given a full bill of health, only to be once more broken in two.

In truth, it wasn't Ron's fault that his compliment had fallen on ears that were not just unreceptive to such remarks, but positively hostile.

Juliet simply wanted to be seen, not just as a powerful businesswoman, although that power of late seemed to be draining away before her eyes, and not just as a woman who had taken control of her life, even though that control could be described as sporadic at best. No, Juliet just wanted to be seen as an actual person. Someone who could exist in this world without being told how lucky they were to have beautiful hair, or good skin, or a waistline that didn't get jammed in revolving doors.

And honestly, she didn't regard any of this as a big fucking ask!

Aside from all of that, compliments were enjoyed by Juliet with the same enthusiasm as toothache, and with as much faith in these non-life changing, and often empty affirmations as believing in the tooth fairy. She regarded her looks as a functional part of her life. Albeit as a literary agent, her life consisted mostly of echoing equally empty affirmations to disappointed writers, who by definition she regarded as people most definitely somewhere or other on the autistic spectrum.

And yet there was a side of Juliet, a hated side, a side that liked to hear such nonsense. That her figure was indeed slim, that she retained her narrow hips from youth, along with a flat stomach and small boobs that were, if not pert, at least looking as though they were still paying attention. Most of all she enjoyed the thought that there was actually a point to the constant fitness studio visits she found so numbingly dull; more so than reading a first draft novel from a talented creative writer with an MA in talented creative writing.

And yet...

Compliments for Juliet were fickle creatures. Some days, it didn't hurt to hear them. Even if, as a feminist, it hurt to hear them.

That being said, Juliet felt confident that she most certainly did not pine for such speculative attention, especially when that attention came wrapped in a sandwich of overt leering with a side order of smarm.

"Thank you," she said, managing to avoid blurting out a lecture on the pros and cons of accidentally joining the ranks of #MeToo offenders with unnecessary pats in the direction of her arse. She managed this via the realisation that another moment of conversation with this man was more than she could stomach.

Juliet gave herself a moment to breathe and remember the durable, reliable, internal power all women carried. At the same time, she tried not to choke on her glass of water when she noticed Ron had begun rubbing his nipple through the material of his stained nylon shirt.

"It was my pleasure," he said in apparent breathless appreciation of Juliet thanking him for his compliment. He seemed to lose confidence, however, when he became aware of Juliet staring at his nipple rubbing hand and dropped it unceremoniously into his lap.

"My pleasure is complimenting women. I mean. That's where I get my real pleasure. In fact, I think you should know, it's the main reason I get out of bed in the morning."

Juliet stared at the hand that had transferred to Ron's lap, praying nothing down there was going to get rubbed, and tried to remember why it was she hadn't yet left. Not finding a thought at the end of that particular panic tunnel, she gathered her things and stood with what she hoped looked like dignified finality, rather than abject fear from the possible onslaught of public masturbation.

"Ron, I'm leaving, right now."

"Oh?" His ruddy rounded face was a flustered period under a flagging question mark. "Can I… Walk you back to your office?"

"Oh, don't bother."

"It's not a bother."

"But my office is just over the road. Look, I can see the door from here."

"Yes, I know, I wanted to see you across the road."

"You do realise I mastered the Green Cross Code when I was a teenager."

Ron's eyesight softened to the mid-distance, a hand unconsciously returning to what appeared to be his favourite nipple.

"I bet you were a beautiful teenager."

"Ron," Juliet tried not to mentally vomit. "Did you just mentally travel in time to perv' a teenaged-me?"

Ron snapped back to the here and now with an almost audible twang.

"Ummm.... No?" He said with a conviction that defined the word insignificant.

"I am most definitely out of here," Juliet said, leaving her chair with enough speed to avoid any further conversational deviances from Ron that she would find either revolting or disturbing or both. Such was her panic to reach the café door, Juliet blindly collided with something substantial, unrelenting and male.

"Ms Raphael," the French accent belonging to her collision of fortune instantly lifted Juliet's mood. She took a step back and looked up into the rugged and not entirely unhandsome face of the café owner, Pascal Noir.

"What a wonderful surprise to see you here in my humble café at..." He glanced at his watch, the curious expression in those emotional eyes leaving Juliet a little more breathless than her expectation of feminine fortification had expected. "A wonderful surprise to see you here at lunchtime."

Juliet laughed, loudly, and for a prolonged length of time, and then realised that Pascal probably hadn't said anything remotely funny. In the silence that followed, she tried to think of something to say. Anything really.

"Oh, has it been that long?"

"Regrettably," Pascal said, his French accent making this single word sound like an eroticism of missed opportunities. "I believe it has been many weeks, Ms Raphael."

He stopped talking, his grey eyes boring through her, and making her wonder if she had applied enough foundation before stepping into his radiant gaze.

"I hope," he said. "That you have not forgotten my policy on food?"

"No," Juliet said with care, her mind jumping back to the here and now. "When one of London's top chefs refuses to cook food anymore, it is…"

"Regrettable," Pascal suggested into her trailing sentence.

"I was going to say, perplexing."

"I have my reasons," he said. "But they are too dark to share."

If nothing else, Pascal could do enigmatic as though it were an Olympic sport.

"Ms Raphael," Pascal said, drawing suddenly close to her and raising her heartbeat in an improbably short amount of time. "May I ask you a question?"

"Yes, Pascal?" Her voice sounded unnaturally high, as though she had decided to wear a G-string several sizes too small.

"Are you here with that man?"

"What man?"

"The fat one," Pascal motioned with a brief nod that caused his head of partly grey curly hair to flick backwards and forwards across his face with distracting ease. "The one who keeps waving at you."

"Oh, *that* one!" Juliet said. "Yes, I am, in fact, here with that man."

"Really?"

Juliet couldn't decide if that word was judgmental or pitying, or which one she would prefer. In her moment of mortification, she began to hear a whiny voice babbling on about interfering sisters and blind dates, and then with a shock, realised the sound was her own voice, and she still hadn't finished talking.

"…and when I say, *with that* man, I mean, *was with*, as in leaving now, due to… Not wanting to be here anymore, and often I think, that's best, don't you, not to prolong the agony, but just end the date, kill it stone dead, before it has the chance to hope for something that can never be. You see what I mean… Pascal?"

If Pascal was alarmed by her verbal equivalent of running out of the café and screaming loudly at the pigeons, he didn't show it. Instead, a knee-weakening twinkle filled his eye.

"Oh, so your beautiful sister is being, as you English say, a pain in the back of your side."

Juliet took a moment to appreciate how the French could describe any woman as beautiful without sounding slimy. It was a gift.

"Tina is being… Tina! Should I say more? Problem is, I don't really have time for her games, not right at the moment. However well aimed her good intentions might be."

They both looked back at Ron, who had pulled an enormous dirty hanky from his pocket and was blowing his nose with all the enthusiasm of a lighthouse in thick fog.

"Although in this case," Juliet said. "I feel the phrase, good intentions, may not be entirely appropriate."

Juliet glanced at her watch, her eyes widening at the sight of the actual time. She really should get the actual fuck out of here. Her business, such as what remained of it, wouldn't run itself, and her sister was, in Juliet's opinion, the definitive chocolate teapot when it came to administrative duties.

She reached for the door and was stopped cold by eight words delivered with the soft ease of Pascal's Parisian accent.

"Juliet, do you have time? Time for me?"

Juliet felt her conflictions have conflictions.

"Ordinarily, yes, but I'm not joking. I have to get back. Between you and me, I spend all my time just keeping my agency afloat. How the mighty have fallen, eh?"

Pascal regarded her with a sombre expression.

"Perhaps it has something to do with the quality of your clients? No?"

Juliet bit her tongue.

"I assume that barbed remark is a reference to your brother," she said carefully.

"He is no longer my brother; he is just some bastard I once knew."

The bastard bit Juliet could empathise with as Jacque's ambitions in the publishing world were rampantly hindered by the man's refusal to do any redrafting, attend meetings, or really do any work on the book whatsoever since he had submitted the final text. He was without a doubt the worst client her agency had ever sought to represent and considering her clients were mostly actors, politicians or sports personalities with wildly self-aggrandising biographies to flog, this was truly saying something.

"Can you not find another client?" Pascal continued, still in brother hating rant mode. "You are a woman of remarkable talent and beauty. Are there no other books for you to publish?"

Juliet tried to think of a way to backtrack the conversation to the point where Pascal regarded her as a woman of remarkable beauty, but she failed to see an in, or indeed, an out. There was this odd feeling she had, whenever in Pascal's presence, that something more should be going on between them, even though, despite being in each other's close orbit for years, they seemed to barely know each other.

"Sadly not," she said, remembering with a shudder all those unsolicited novels Tina was currently forcing her to read; even though Juliet's agency had minimal experience in dealing with fiction of any shape or size. She only capitulated now to her sister's demands because biographies, her previous line of literary satisfaction, had run aground for a variety of reasons. Countless of which she resentfully believed were not of her making.

Pascal regarded her with a stare that would have been unfathomable to a highly trained interrogator. Somewhere in the past, she had thought, perhaps wrongly, that Pascal was more than a little interested in her. This had changed, though, almost overnight, when Juliet took on Jacque as a client. Now it seemed this moment of them was never to be, and if ever there was an obstacle between Pascal and her that could seemingly never be overcome, it was the fact that she now represented a man Pascal hated for reasons that were entirely unclear, but very possibly, thoroughly French.

Pascal moved subtly, a small shuffle of his feet, and a slant of his shoulders placing him well within her personal boundaries. In fact, she had to rock back slightly on her heels in order just to look him in the eye.

"Ms Raphael... Juliet! I need to talk to you. I need to tell you something, something urgent, something I have wanted to tell you for a long time. Something of great personal importance to me, something that…"

"What do you want to say, Pascal," Juliet said, trying to keep her patience in check for once in her life. It wasn't easy, apart from being famous for his incredible food, Pascal was doubly renowned for being a man who very rarely got to the point without a gun to his head.

"Yes, of course, you are a busy woman, I will tell you this thing I need to tell you, for it is an important part of my life, and I need to share it with you Juliet, and with you alone. You see I…"

"Pascal?" A youthful high-pitched voice called out as a spindly teenage girl with an improbable amount of long dark hair appeared from the kitchen of the café. "I have a telephone call for you."

"Oh, can it wait," Juliet snapped, and the young girl instantly burst into tears and ran back to the safety of the kitchen.

"Sorry," Juliet said. "I forgot that she doesn't actually work for me."

"Do not worry," Pascal said. "Yvonne has been a little highly strung since she graduated."

"Yvonne?" Juliet did a double-take towards the empty kitchen door. "That's Jacque's daughter?"

"I prefer to think of her as my niece, it causes me less pain."

"My, she has grown up… I don't suppose she knows where her father is?"

"If she did, I would not ask her." Pascal's hair had flopped across his eyes, and he brushed it back, the dark hairs on his arm, dancing a few tantalising inches from Juliet's face. "Now, if you will excuse me, I have to see to her, she is emotional since her loss."

"Oh, a death in the family?"

"No, I mean when she works here, she has lost the internet connection from her phone. She finds this very distressing."

"Oh."

"But still, I must speak with you. Juliet! Will you wait for me?"

Juliet stared back at Ron, who had stopped blowing his nose and was now using the handkerchief to dab at spots of perspiration on his forehead. If she waited, she would have to sit with Ron, she was far too English to just stand here by the door. And she really wanted to hear the end of Pascal's sentence. Assuming he ever got to it.

Needs must, she thought as Pascal vanished from her side, leaving her with little choice but to re-join Ron at the table.

"Oh hello," he said with apparent surprise when Juliet returned to her seat in front of him. "Where did you go then? Little girls' room? Hope you remembered to wash your hands?"

Ron laughed at his own attempt at humour. Loud and nasally, his large framed glasses sliding down his greasy nose, and the few strands of hair he possessed, moved to cover ears that certainly did not lack hair.

For a long moment, Juliet weighed up the prospects that Pascal had something to tell her that would make it worth her while sitting here with this awful man for one second more. The moment must have lasted longer than she realised and she became increasingly aware that Ron had stopped talking and was sitting staring at her as though waiting for her to drop dead, face down on the table. Briefly, Juliet wondered how many of Ron's dates had feigned death in order to escape the encounter, or indeed how many of them had actually passed away from the sheer boredom of talking to the man.

"Do you mind me asking a personal question?" he said.

"Is there any physical way of stopping you?" She said, eyeing the kitchen door and willing Pascal to reappear.

"I was just wondering, is this your first date since your husband left you to be with another man?"

"How the fuck do you know that?"

"Tina told me."

"Did she now!" Juliet made a mental note to beat her sister about the head with a copy of Vogue as soon as this lunch-date from hell was over. "Look, Ron, wouldn't you rather talk about politics?"

"Don't really follow it."

"What about sport?"

"Don't really follow it."

"Fine art and/or literature?"

"Don't really..."

"...Follow it. Yes, of course. Got it."

Ron huffed a bit, sitting back and staring at the hair that covered his short stubby fingers. Juliet had the horrifying feeling that this passed in Ron's world for profound thought. His next words confirmed that she was partially right. He had thought, just not very profoundly.

"If you find it difficult or embarrassing, or even demeaning that your husband left you because he decided he was gay after ten years of marriage, I can understand that."

"That's very magnanimous of you Ron."

"You see, I knew you'd be clever, using words like that. Minute I laid eyes on you, I could tell you were an intelligent woman," Ron said, weighing these last words on his tongue as though in itself, the concept was an oxymoron.

A silence settled over the small table, crowding out the possibility of avoiding an answer, but at least conversation seemed to keep Ron's hands away from his nipples, so for this reason alone, Juliet decided to play along.

"Technically, yes, I suppose this is my first date."

"Technically?"

"Well, if I don't include all the dates where men stood me up, then I suppose, yes, this is technically the first I've had since my husband came out of the closet."

"Why on earth would anyone stand up a good-looking bird… Woman, I mean, like yourself?" Ron shook his head as though all the woe of the world had been presented to him for condemnation. "It makes no sense to me."

There were, Juliet had come to realise, many, many things in this world that probably made no sense to Ron. Although in this case, she had to agree, it made no sense to her either.

Juliet considered herself to be an intelligent, reasonably good-looking woman who looked after her figure. She spent a lot of money on clothes and make-up and knew how to combine them in ways that were not likely to cause anyone to mutter anything about Mutton. And yet, many times of late, she had suffered the indignation of being stood up on a date.

"Oh well," she said, attempting to deflect with platitudes. "You know, people have complicated lives."

Clearly, platitudes were a mistake as Ron at first looked confused, then, in apparent desperation to think of any reply, fell back on a compliment.

"You have stunning eyes," he said which would have been bad enough if he had not added; "although they are a little crooked, honestly though, that would never bother me."

Juliet felt a small note of panic whistle through her mind and wondered if this was in some way Ron proposing a future life together where he would valiantly ignore her wonky gaze in the name of love. The panic settled down and became resentment, which Juliet decided was enough justification for outright honesty.

"Sorry, Ron," she gave him her best condescending smile. "This isn't going to work."

She swapped the smile for a look of sympathy and prayed to whichever god was listening that he would become so offended as to leave, in a huff, hopefully never to be seen again.

Ron, though, was unexpectedly made of sterner stuff.

"What isn't going to work?"

Juliet took a deep breath.

"This... This date, Ron. You see..." Juliet decided to press on with honesty, partly because she wanted to remain true to herself, but mostly because she was out of any other ideas. "The thing is Ron, I'm afraid I just don't..."

"...Find me attractive," Ron finished, as though he had heard those words many times before. Quite how often Juliet was loathed to guess, but it was probably a number which would never be described as insignificantly small.

Faced with this, Juliet found herself squirming under the critical eye of self-reproach. She attempted to row the situation back a little.

"No, no, it's not that."

"So, you do find me attractive?"

Juliet's eyes became saucer-shaped as she realised her row back, had rowed so far back, they were now at the crest of Niagara Falls.

"Actually, it's a no to that as well. Look, it's not you, it's me, I'm just swamped right now, and I don't want to string you along, so it's probably best if..."

"But what about your little problem," Ron said, breaking into her clichéd ridden sentence with an obscure comment that for a moment made her wonder if her blouse had popped open.

"My little…"

"With the awards ceremony," Ron said, leaning in close to her and whispering this part in the empty café for reasons that were not entirely clear. "And your sister telling me you didn't want to go alone."

"She said what?"

"And also, this apparently has more than a little to do with your husband coming out as gay, and you still finding it difficult to live it down, but need to go to this award ceremony in case you bag a prize for best literary agent, what you've been tipped to win." Ron paused for breath, which after that sentence, he clearly needed, before adding. "Which will give you some keenly required publicity to rescue your ailing business from its death throes."

"Just how long were you talking to my sister?"

"About ten minutes."

"I am… Going… Kill... Her…" Juliet said, shuddering as her voice began skipping and fading in a most alarming fashion.

"Oh," Ron said. "Tina did mention that you had a bit of a funny voice. I just thought she meant high-pitched, you know, like David Beckham, or Punch and Judy."

For a second, the mixed images of David Beckham being swept away by a small hand puppet with a large nose was so jarring Juliet became lost for words while at the same time suffering the inability to actually speak. A very disconcerting feeling.

"I do… Not… Have… Funny voice," She managed to croak and took a sip of her mineral water to recover a little of her vocal prowess.

"Sorry?"

"I said…" Juliet paused, bereft of ideas for what she could say to suddenly hearing all the problems of her life listed back to her by a complete stranger. The problem with her voice had emerged about the same time she discovered her husband was gay. It was, her therapist eventually informed her, purely psychological and a direct result of being exposed to unexpectedly high levels of stress. Juliet glanced up at Ron, who had for some unknown reason, began rubbing his nipple again, and figured that if this didn't count as unexpectedly high levels of stress, then she didn't know what did.

She took another sip of water and recovered enough vocal ability to speak. Albeit slowly.

"Thing is Ron, while all of that is, mostly, true, I am not sure that I want to go any fu…"

"Juliet," Ron said, thankfully breaking into a sentence that Juliet realised was heading only to bad places. "Let's not waste each other's time. Let's just be honest. Can you be honest, Juliet? Can you be honest with me?"

Oh, I can do that, thought Juliet, in response to Ron inadvertently waving a red conversational rag in her bullish direction. Within a heartbeat, she felt her voice return to normal.

"Oh yes, Ron, I can… Do that. In fact, let me be… Frank. Do you mind if… I am frank?"

"No, no," Ron said, a look of faint alarm on his face. "You can be anyone you want to be."

"I want to be honest… Ron… Honest and frank!"

"Right, sure," Ron said his face a mask of relief. "I knew that."

"Great, so, here is my honest appraisal of this date, Ron." Juliet began, the problems with her voice dissolving away as her confidence returned. Folding her arms across her lap, she met his watery gaze head-on. "And I don't want to appear as though I am overly negative, but it has to be said, that by and large, I would rather be run over by a heard of horses, multiple times, with my hair on fire and matchsticks under my fingernails, than ever spend another moment in your company. And by ever I do mean for the rest of my life or yours, or whichever one of us dies first, which hopefully won't be me, but if it is the only way I can escape this date from hell, I am willing to give it a fucking go."

At the back of her mind, she became aware that her voice may have moved up the volumetric scale a tad, this being confirmed by Pascal and Yvonne appearing wide-eyed at the kitchen door. They both looked from her to Ron, and their shocked expressions grew wider still.

Juliet glanced back at Ron and was horrified to see the man had started to leak tears from his tiny eyes, a steady stream that trickled down his face, ending in damp patches on his shirt collar. Amid this horrifying scene, Ron took out his dirty hanky and began to howl his grief into the stained material. His cries caused Yvonne to once more start sobbing and Pascal to look at Juliet with reproach.

Juliet looked from one expression to another, and then finally back to Ron, whose face had become a version of the saddest cabbage patch doll ever made.

"Oh, for fuck's sake," she said, causing Ron to howl even louder.

Chapter 2

Tina

The office window from which Tina observed the final stages of Juliet's apocalyptic date was a grand affair. Something of an oddity in their small compact office above a kebab shop. The window itself was large and angular, stretching upwards to the ceiling and outwards towards each corner of the room; its subsequent size flooding the room with enormous amounts of sunshine when sunshine was bestowed on London. The window also offered an envious uncluttered view down Essex road towards Islington Green; a small triangle of trees and grass and park benches in the smoggy distance.

Away from the window, the rest of the office offered a sense of grandeur somewhat less enchanting than the view. It was functional at best, with the main office occupied by Juliet's large desk, a sofa that no one ever used, and a couple of client chairs that, sadly these days, were also seldom used by anyone other than Tina.

A partition wall with a single door separated this main office from Tina's tiny work area beyond; a small closet type room with an entrance to the stairs, and another to the toilet, and a cramped corner that passed for a kitchen area. It was enough for Tina. She was happy with her little desk that served as a reception area and doubled up for drinks and snack making.

Or at least she had been happy, in the grand old days of yesteryear when the business, *Juliet Raphael - Literary Agent to the Stars,* was awash with celebratory biographies. Those early memories of the business Tina held forever as precious, but if they were ever forced to leave this office, it would be this window, in Juliet's office, with its unique picturesque view of the London skyline that Tina would miss the most. She dearly hoped they wouldn't have to leave, or give up this dream, but after watching the fiasco that was Juliet's latest lunchtime date, Tina wondered if there really was any hope at all.

From the office window of *Juliet Raphael - Literary Agent to the Stars*, Tina watched balefully as Ron emerged from Pascal's Café, his face a contorted mess of uncontrolled emotions, tears visible even from this distance. This gave Tina no other choice than to assume the blind date with her sister Juliet had been less than successful. She watched, mesmerised, as Ron stumbled into his car, flogged the starter motor to death, then ground the gears, before setting off down Essex Road in a series of lurching gear changes and squealing tyres.

Such a shame.

Tina had high hopes for this particular romantic matchmaking. After all, she considered Ron to be quite the catch; in that he was single, sort of, mid-divorce, but that was close enough these days, and he had an actual job. One that paid well and included a car. A job that required Ron to wear a tie. In fact, if Tina hadn't been so intent on solving her sister's romantic issues, she might have taken a shine to the man herself.

She continued watching as Ron's variable driving skills took him into the path of a cycling vicar. The well-known local chaplain and former army captain had just signalled a left turn when his military-trained instincts alerted him to the close proximity of Ron's car; in that, it had just impacted with his back wheel. The jolt sent him in a slow arc through the air that ended on the bonnet of Ron's sleek looking Jaguar.

The vicar had just a few seconds to admire the superior paintwork when Ron braked, sending the man of the cloth in another slow arc that terminated on a bakery stall, fortuitously piled high with hot cross buns. Notwithstanding his age, the vicar performed an enthusiastic parachute roll across the crusted buns, something hammered into him during his years of service with the Paratroopers.

Tina watched Ron lean out of the window and presumably ask the man he had just run over if he was feeling okay. The vicar gave him a double thumbs-up as he was helped on his feet by those concerned onlookers who weren't filming the whole thing on their mobile phones. Safely back upright, the vicar reached down for a handful of hot cross buns and held them upwards to the heavens. Over the sound of traffic, Tina could hear the words; *saved by the body of Christ, saved by the body of Christ.*

Ron stayed until the vicar offered him a hot cross bun, which Ron took with a brief nod, before biting into it and then leaving the vicar to his religious fervour, which most of the onlookers also decided was the best course of action.

A short while later, the police turned up, which Tina found out was only on the instance of the baker who was happy the vicar was okay but would be really pleased if he could sod off so she could get back to making a living. Apparently, all that talk of the *body of Christ being invested in the dough of the bun* was suppressing sales a tad.

Tina would have preferred to watch for longer, but the sound of the outer office door opening and slamming shut was advanced warning of the whirlwind that was her sister. Juliet would be full of accusations; Tina knew this for sure. When anything ever went wrong, she was the one to get the blame. She braced herself, and belatedly remembered a supply of chocolate hidden in a much-underused filing cabinet under E for Energy, or possibly, in this case, Emergency. Chocolate was Tina's answer to many questions, even those questions she had never really asked herself.

Before Juliet could finish fighting with the partition door between the office areas, Tina found time to grab several chocolates from her secret stash to steel herself against the inevitable recriminations. Fortunately, Tina was not Juliet's primary focus of anger. As was typical in these situations; Juliet was more concerned about Juliet.

"Please tell me the vicar isn't dead," Juliet said, rushing into the main office with what appeared to be a concerned expression, a concern slightly muted by her next uttering. "The last thing I need is bad publicity. This sort of thing could ruin my business."

Tina sighed, popped another chocolate of courage into her mouth, followed quickly by a third just to keep the other two company. When she spoke, the chocolates nestled into her cheeks, giving her the look of a happy hamster, but with short blond curls and glasses.

"No, don't panic, he managed to jump off the bonnet of Ron's car before it got to close."

"I think you will find," Juliet said with acid dripping from her angered expression. "That having to jump off the bonnet of a car is a clear indication that it is in fact too fucking close."

With a practised deft movement, Tina collected a small tin from the top of a dust-covered filing cabinet and rattled it under Juliet's nose. A motion that widened Juliet's eyes with a delightful amount of alarm.

"Possibly," Tina said, shaking the swear box again under her sister's nose. "And that will be a pound please."

"A pound? I thought it was 50 pence?"

"I've adjusted the prices because the previous ones were clearly not enough of a deterrent."

For a moment, the two women glared at each other, although Tina, with her superior height, was also able to look down her nose at Juliet, which often was enough to win the argument. After a short time, in which the air all but blistered, Juliet dug around in her bag for a pound coin, and placed it, less than graciously in Tina's tin.

"Thank you," Tina said, feeling a little more in control of the situation, then seeing Juliet's ire rise towards utter rage, decided to follow up with an attack. Attack being the best form of sibling defence.

"I think the real issue is," Tina said, "why he drove so badly?"

"Oh, that's easy, it's because Ron is a total cretin who probably shouldn't have the vote, let alone a fucking driving licence."

Tina rattled the tin under Juliet's nose again and watched as her sister nearly went apoplectic, before caving in and fishing for more change in her bag.

"Or to play Devil's advocate," Tina said as Juliet deposited more money in her tin. "Perhaps he drove like that because… You made him cry!"

Juliet's mouth slammed shut with an audible crack as she stood looking at Tina with the frustrated rage that only younger sisters can muster for their older siblings. She edged a little to look around Tina's reproachful stance and out towards the street. In the distance, the vicar was now wheeling his damaged bike off down the road, giving out hot cross buns to anyone unwise enough to make eye contact.

"I did not make him cry," Juliet said. "I simply pointed out to him that we had different... Life goals, and that... that we were unlikely to see a mutually invested emotional connection at any near or indeed, distant, future point."

"You said all that?"

"I said words to that effect, yes."

Tina allowed her face to indicate a certain sense of disbelief. Her tongue, along with the depleted chocolate, pushed one cheek out in order to emphasise the likelihood of Juliet's scenario to be less than credible.

"Look," Juliet said. "I'm the victim here."

"Really?" Tina said, with a telling look towards the distantly limping vicar.

"Yes, I am the victim of a nipple rubbing salesman who cries at the drop of a hat and is entirely too helpful with his hands on my arse."

"Sounds awful."

"Yes, thank you, at last, it bloody was."

Tina rattled the tin and Juliet looked at her with barely concealed rage.

"How much?"

"Fifty pence."

"For bloody?"

"Now it's a pound."

"What? That's not fair, I was just..." Juliet trailed off under her older sister's stern gaze. "Oh, for God's sake, here you are, and that's the last of my change."

"Then you had best keep your mouth out of Potty Street then?"

"Seriously, who says Potty Street?"

"I do! Now, tell me, what exactly you said to make poor Ron cry."

"I was just being honest with him."

"Honest?"

"Yes, and then I did my level best to let him down gently."

"Gently?"

Tina watched as Juliet mentally replayed her conversation with Ron. She knew from bitter experience that Juliet's memory for things that were said and done was legendary.

"I may," Juliet said with all the care of a politician speaking to an unusually intelligent BBC news reporter. "Have put it a tad forcefully."

"You shouted!"

"I did not SHOUT!"

"You're shouting now," Tina said with triumph and popped a victory-chocolate into her mouth, savouring the taste. However bad the blind date might have been, Tina's part in its inception had now been erased by the confession of Juliet behaving badly. That was, at the very least, something to be proud of today.

"Yes, I'm shouting now, but that's because you are being..." Juliet's voice trailed off in a croak that clearly infuriated her.

Tina tactically decided to not deploy the swear box at this sensitive moment. There were few times she allowed leniency when dealing with Juliet, but the sporadic loss of her voice was indeed one of those sacred moments. She surveyed the younger sister in front of her. Fists in tiny balls of frustration, and tears brimming at the corners of her eyes. Hardened executive that Juliet was, it always appalled Tina how easily she could make her sister cry. Tina was also a keen judge of mood and decided that while she had the moral victory in her bag, it was probably prudent to take that bag and be somewhere else.

Anywhere else.

Discreetly she poured Juliet a glass of water and gave it to her, in silence, her own eyes now starting to fill with tears.

Two could play that game.

"I was only trying to help," Tina said, cementing the fact that Juliet alone now totally owned this blind date failure. "But I will now get out of your way and do some work. Let's hope I can at least get that right. And hope that I avoid being *Bloody Annoying* anymore today."

She managed a small emotional sob on the last word, just before she flounced out of the office, ignoring pleas from Juliet to wait a moment, and pretending not to listen to affirmations that Juliet *hadn't meant it like that*, and so on.

These were the usual apologies that Tina received once she had successfully turned the tables on her younger sister. She gave one last withering look at Juliet, a small tear in the corner of her eye, magnified by the strong lenses Tina needed in part to stop her walking into buses, but also to make sure everyone could see her tears when required.

Tina's sense of victory she felt closing the office partition door was slightly tarnished when she saw a note on her desk in her own handwriting. It was an urgent reminder that Juliet needed to contact the somewhat tiresomely passive-aggressive Emma at Prized Publishing. This was a phone call Juliet would not enjoy making. It would be about Jacque Noir and his problematic cookbook. Problematic in that Jacque never seemed to spend much time working on it.

Diplomatically, Tina decided to forget she had taken the message and called Emma, before putting the call through to Juliet and making it sound as though Emma had only just phoned. She then crept to the partition door and tried to listen in on the conversation. It didn't take too long before the air on the other side of the wall developed a severe blue tinge, and although Tina was itching to break in with her swear box, she considered that now might not be the best time.

Without warning the phone call ended, and Juliet snatched open the door, leaving Tina to pretend she was dusting the frame. Her sister regarded her with a moment of suspicion before shrugging it off.

"Shit storm," Juliet said by way of explanation, pointedly ignoring the swear tin. "I have to go and see Emma, see if I can sort it out."

"Can't you just send Emma an email?" Tina said. From experience, she knew Millennials preferred most forms of communication other than face-to-face ones. Plus, with Juliet's... ... Voice Issues, it was much better for her sister to not actually speak to people unless necessary.

"I can't," Juliet said. "My F... My stupid laptop has gone wrong."

"Again?"

"Yes, I tried to do something with something else, and then this box came up asking me about something or other that I'm pretty sure I didn't ask it to do and... Well, then it stopped working."

"I see," Tina said, wondering vaguely how much damage her sister's random mouse clicks had done to her laptop this time.

"Yes, and now I think the laptop is totally confused."

"Right, of the two of you, it's the laptop that you think is confused?"

"Well clearly," Juliet said while checking her bag for phone and purse. "Can you sort it out for me? Please?"

"I will try," Tina said.

"Thank you. And if Jacque should happen to turn up, make sure he stays here until I get back."

Without waiting for an answer, Juliet left the office, the door slam echoing around the room for several seconds after she had gone. Tina crossed to the window and watched Juliet flag down a cab. She dearly hoped her sister would be able to sort this out; Jacque was pretty much their last client and if this publishing deal went wrong…Well, that would be the end of *Juliet Raphael - Literary Agent to the Stars*. However much Tina loved beating her younger sister in an argument, she really hated the thought of her failing.

At anything at all.

Desperate measures, Tina thought, demand desperate solutions.

Picking up her phone, she clicked through the contact list until she found Ron's number stored under *U*, for *Unexpectedly Hunky*, and called him. She hated to do this to the man, but Juliet was running out of options.

.

Chapter 3

Ron

It wasn't the actual presence of tears that upset Ron; it was that these rivers of upset had poured out of him at such an inopportune moment.

In his opinion, Juliet could have been perhaps a tad more tactful in the way she rejected his... advances. She could have, for example, not karate chopped one of her hands into the other to punctuate each and every dagger of a word that laid out, in no uncertain terms, how little enthusiasm she had for the idea of seeing him in a romantic capacity. Or indeed, as she had clarified, seeing him in any capacity whatsoever, except perhaps in the obituaries.

It was a relief when Juliet's voice had started to go wrong. Again.

Even so, Ron had been particularly wounded by this last remark. He had, after all, only attended this blind date on the insistence of Juliet's sister, Tina. In this he had assumed, given Juliet's tragic romantic history, his position in this particular part of her life to be that of a gallant knight.

A White Knight at that. Charging into the rescue, whisking Juliet off to some highfalutin awards ceremony that she apparently feared to attend sans-partner. In short; he saw himself as the hero who would save the day. In this alternative version of reality, Ron also saw a vision of them dancing together, a fast, reckless dance, one that would cut the rug, and smash the house, or whatever it was that dancers did when they flabbergasted all and sundry with their dashing dancing skills.

The last part of this fantasy was something Ron chose not to dwell on. In truth, his dancing abilities came with various limitations that had much to do with his considerable girth, his lack of any musical timing, and two very fat left feet. All this was complicated by a brain that sent commands to his body, just a little later than it should.

Still, even if this part of his fantasy had been, well, pure fantasy, he had at least expected to attend the evening as Juliet's handsome mystery man. And bag a free meal. And possibly fill his trousers at the free bar. To have this dream of perfect excessive consumption decapitated by a small feminine hand chopping through the air, and through his self-esteem at the same time, was too much to bear.

Hence the tears, which had flooded endlessly out of him; embarrassing himself, Juliet, and that snooty French waiter. A tall, hulking man who insisted Ron pay the bill, even though he had eaten nothing at all. That perhaps had been the final indignity. Paying a Frenchman for something he had never even got to eat. It's no wonder so many people backed Brexit. He had abstained, but that was mostly because he couldn't be arsed to vote.

After that, blinded by his emotional outpouring, Ron had staggered out to his car, reversed it through several traffic cones, and then had what he chose to think of as a religious experience with a frantically pedalling vicar. Having deposited the man of the cloth face first in a hot cross bun stall, where he lay still on the doughy mattress of crushed bakery products praising the wonder of Jesus, Ron decided not to question divine intervention and drove off at the first opportunity. He left behind a scene of open-mouthed wonder as he hurried away to find the nearest place where he could stop and examine his car for any apparent damage.

A quiet carpark near a crematorium provided a likely spot where he could pull over and look, heart in mouth, for any scratches to the expensive paintwork, or worse still, a dent in his pride and Jag. It wasn't that he loved his Jaguar XE; flash motors were not Ron's thing, not even when they came with an exclusivity that Jaguar had bankrolled for several decades. He did, however, find it a handy tool in his trade. Demanding customers, people who were resistant to Ron's charm, could often be swayed towards bumping their order numbers a little higher, just with the offer of a quick shufti at his Jag. Particularly troublesome clients could be taken out to lunch, in his Jag, and those that were considered a very tough sell would even be allowed to have a drive, in his Jag. It was the sort of tactic that was meaningless in a Mondeo or even a well-spec'd Passat.

Of course, his boss moaned about the leasing costs and the insurance, so accidental run-ins with cycling vicars were not the sort of thing Ron wished to write down on an insurance claim form or indeed on a police report.

In this case, though, it appeared as though the vicar had left no visible marks, although there were some black scuffs on the bumper, which may or may not have been the by-product of ramming a bike back wheel into a cake stall. Mostly though, Ron felt as though he, and his Jag, had escaped the incident with barely a scratch.

Such was his joy at finding his Jag unharmed, Ron punched the air with delight and let out a loud whoop just as a coffin was being slowly pulled out of a hearse. Jumping at the unexpected sound of Ron's glee, one of the pallbearers lost a moment's concentration, and his grip, and the wooden box exited the back of the car with a lot less decor than could be considered respectful.

The baleful stare of mourners standing around a coffin that now lay on its side on the tarmac helped Ron realise this might not be, as his younger sales colleagues might say, a positive optic. He mouthed a quick *sorry* before exiting the crematorium carpark at speed.

In his Jag.

He was at any rate late for his next appointment at a hulking squat warehouse in the middle of other ugly squat warehouses in Park Royal industrial estate. One where the manager of a trade store for electrical supplies was particularly tardy with his order of knurled spacers and Ron had been sent to find out why. Awful human being though he was, his boss understood that Ron was also a damned good salesman.

On the drive up the Westway, past the queues for Madam Tussauds, and through the snarling traffic that looped around the exclusivity of the congestion zone, Ron hit every red light possible, and spent a great deal of time avoiding eye contact with the endless stream of windscreen cleaners that loitered under each glaring red eye. This constant stop-go of slug-like traffic left Ron's mind free to replay the events of the last hour, mostly the bit where Juliet had rejected him.

The flying vicar he chose to suppress.

Once or twice, he considered ringing Tina to find out why she had sent him on what now appeared to be, in hindsight, the dating equivalent of a suicide mission. Had Tina set him up? He found that hard to believe, she seemed to be the sort of person that would never do such a thing. A real honest woman, with a beautiful rounded body and a smile that cheered his day, although, he couldn't help but be reminded of his mother, and the distance that had always existed between the two of them.

With these memories flowing through his unguarded heart, and with the experience of the lunchtime date from hell still fresh in his mind, it wasn't long before the tears once again started to flow down his blackhead-potted nose. This, in turn, fogged up his glasses, causing him to miss one set of light changes completely, and earning him the wrath of a black cab driver whose grasp of profanities was clearly insightful.

Ron hadn't always been this way.

He had cried precisely twice in his adult life; once when he found out how much his wedding had cost, and once when he found out how much his divorce would continue to cost. Ron's emotional landscape, however, had forever been changed after a brief visit to *Tears Before Bedtime*, a company based in the New Forest that stylised themselves as *Personality Adjusters*. Ron considered them emotional vandals and blamed this quasi-cult/encounter group for this sorry state of unexplained sobbing that he now endured.

It hadn't even been his idea to go. He had been, as far as he was concerned, press-ganged into attending by an over-enthusiastic Human Resources department. Most people thought HR was there to protect the employees from the more ruthless thoughts of the Employer, whereas Ron fully understood their job was to protect the Employer from possible lawsuits. And that's pretty much how Ron ended up in the dark, in the New Forest, sitting around a campfire, drinking warm beer, waiting for food to be served, and having to listen to a bunch of soft talking

Personality Adjusters knacker on about owning personal responsibility. They described themselves as *Personal Development Assistants* but talked exactly like most do-gooding counsellors that Ron, from time to time, had to deal with for various reasons, mostly work-based misunderstandings.

The particular misunderstanding that brought him to the attention of *Tears Before Bedtime* had been, in Ron's view, a small, perhaps even insignificant incident. A simple blunder. It was nothing really. Well, not much. Well, in the wrong light, Ron could understand that delivering flowers to the same woman, Trudy, on an irregular basis for a little over three months could be seen by some closed minds as less of a romantic gesture and more the initial gestation of stalking.

This had all started after a brief snog Trudy had unwisely capitulated to under the mistletoe while being very drunk at the office party. In the cold light of next day, Trudy attempted to let Ron know that he was not the one for her, but she wrapped the meaning in subtle words designed to let the man down gently, and as such, had been more or less wasting her time.

Trudy's attempt to move Ron to the Friends-Zone having failed to gain any traction, she had taken to sitting on the toilet for a prolonged length of time to avoid Ron whenever his roving sales duties required him to visit the office. It was during one of these enduring sessions on the lavatory that Ron had decided to rise to the challenge Trudy was clearly placing before him and delivered a bunch of petrol-station flowers by sliding them under the partition from the next cubicle. It was the only time Ron had ever seen the advantage of unisex toilets.

The scream from Trudy had not only roused the first aid officer from the warehouse floor but also caught the attention of every tyre fitter who worked in a shed nearly a quarter of a mile away. It had also piqued the exacting curiosity of the HR department who, despite Ron's lengthy explanation, appeared determined not to see the funny side.

HR, a department that consisted of one woman, Brenda, who was currently going through a messy divorce, had at first all but insisted Ron be fired or she would have to leave on principles that could not be bent or broken. However, as the boss wasn't overly keen on having to listen to Brenda's private life being broadcast across the office every time she went for a tearful cup of herbal tea, he was just fine with the idea of her leaving so she could maintain her principles. Or really, just leaving. At this point, Brenda had backtracked and decided to think out-of-the-box, and look towards solutions rather than confrontations, and disappeared into her office for a prolonged session with Google.

After an extended dive into the less profitable areas of company-management, she chanced on an Encounter Group that had an exciting program that seemed to suit this situation; or at least one that was within the companies minimal Personal Enhancement Training Budget.

Within days Ron found himself travelling to *Tears Before Bedtime*, a company that appeared to have based their entire business plan on watching one Channel 4 documentary, *Men in the Woods*, which focused primarily on how men could be helped to deal with their feelings by getting them to cry a bit. The founders of *Tears Before Bedtime* chose to largely ignore the bit about it being filmed in America, where emotions are always a little more touchy-feely and often tinged with the apprehension that comes with unrestricted gun control.

Nevertheless, they stole the idea wholesale and then went on to charge companies a small fortune with the expectation that *troublesome men* could become once again, or perhaps for the first time, a dynamic part of the corporate machine. Or at the very least, they could trim some emotional anger from the worst cases and allow HR the *Get Out of Jail* card of actually having done something should the person in question ever turn violent.

When Ron arrived, a man who went by the unlikely name of Doctor Peace, did a quick search of Ron's Jag and appeared unsurprised to find most of the items on the prohibited list hidden in a box, under a blanket, stuffed toward the back of the boot. After a short confiscation, a somewhat sulky Ron was introduced to his key worker.

"Hello, I'm James, I will be your Personal PDA during your visit to TBB," a young man had said to Ron with as much friendliness as he could manage for a man who had just witnessed a Jag parking on top of his expensive E-Bike.

Ron had then been introduced to the other P-PDA's who were either all taking their names from the Gospel or had a very well organised and specific recruiting process. Once he saw the staff were male only, and there would be no Mary Magdalenes turning up to bring some light to his life, Ron realised his upfront decision not to enjoy the weekend had been on the money.

Despite this assessment, Ron had the time of his life.

At first, it had been all the mortifying embarrassment Ron had come to expect from such courses; introductions, trust exercises, and some inevitably long-winded PowerPoint presentations on the process of emotional understanding. All the usual bullshit, bracketed with a sandwich lunch that barely coped with the ravenous demands of bored men, not to mention the obviously student-based P-PDA's who ate like this was their only meal of the day. Or possibly the week.

Then things had started to get down to the intensely mortifying meat of the whole weekend. The bit where everyone was encouraged to share their inner traumas, to speak with the voice of their inner child, and to generally bring all the inner stuff to the outer. In Ron's view, most inner stuff was inside for a very good reason and bringing it to the outer could only lead to the raking of old memories and the opening of old wounds. However, embarrassing though he first found it all, eventually, sharing personal pain around a campfire, along with a good supply of beer, had a relaxing effect on him.

For want of anything else to do, Ron had been forced into listening to the other men, to their stories, to their sad little tales of woe, most of which seemed to consist of complaints that life hadn't worked out quite the way they thought it should have. And then something truly remarkable happened. Ron had actually begun to understand, to empathise, and to hear their pain.

Most of the stories were predictably similar; wannabee sad people talking, at length, about their First-World-Problems of trying to be a nice person in a non-nice world. Often failing to see a causality between lack of effort and lack of success, and at the same time wondering why White Male-Privilege hadn't seemed to amount to very much in the long run.

In between the tears and the occasional howl of grief from his new fire-sharing friends, Ron had a startling moment of epiphany, a word he had read in a Christmas cracker joke but failed to understand. These people, these emotionally stunted and trembling few, these men who told, in a couple of cases, some reprehensible life-stories, were his kind of people.

They were, without Ron wanting to be overly dramatic, his soulmates, and after just a short time of listening, he started to believe that he too had a story to tell, that he too, had something to share, something that he needed to get out of his system.

It would be something that Ron's P-PDAs later described in a memo to HR as *'some pretty dark and disturbing shit'*.

About that point, on his third beer, and with just ten minutes to the BBQ being officially declared open, his tears had unexpectedly begun to flow. And flow, and flow! It was as though a dam had been broken. Ron hadn't even noticed them at first, he assumed it was raining, and his face was getting wet from the drizzle. Then, when he saw the truth, the tears came thicker and faster, leaving him a blubbering mess that was so overpowering with raw emotion, a few of the group felt compelled to edge away from him, and start conversations about the weather, and the roadworks on the North Circular.

Despite his doubts on the validity of *Tears Before Bedtime*, the entire weekend, for Ron, had been a revelation. The fact that he cried all through his first night in the bunk room, leading to several members trying to sleep on the toilet, only strengthened Ron's need to cry some more. He left the camp, a changed man.

However, following that weekend of emotional revelation, it seemed tears were only ever a moment away. In fact, now Ron only had to think of a Lassie film, and he started blubbering, and he dare not even contemplate the plight of small children in Africa for fear of ending his life in a fiery tear-stained car crash.

In truth, Ron often wished he could go back to *Tears Before Bedtime*, have a talk with someone, maybe another little cry, and perhaps get it out of his system every other weekend, so that he could be his old self during the week. However, the weekend had ended with a sour note, when during the burning ceremony, Ron, whose glasses were still steamed up, had accidentally pushed Doctor Peace into the fire, and the arrival of the ambulance, and a police car, had rather put a damp sponge on the whole weekend. It also led to the company refusing any attempt by Ron to attend any sessions in the near future, or as Doctor Peace had put it; *'any fucking time soon'*.

The red lights of the A40 gave way to side roads that eventually led to the industrial parks and Ron's destination. He straightened up, determined to solve this case of lower than optimal order fulfilments. Ron was salaried, and well paid because he was actually pretty good at his job, but divorce had taught him that his salary wasn't nearly as all-encompassing as he thought it was. Mostly, he survived on his commission fees. With this in mind, he strode purposefully towards the office, making sure his usual cheerful demur was once more back in place.

Ron's target sat at his desk, head in hands, staring with a lost look of apathy at his telephone. Ron seized that moment and closed for the sales pitch kill.

"No need to wait on my call," Ron said, "I am here to solve all your Electrical hardware needs. Let's not beat about the bush on price, let's take it straight up to discounts, and if you need to squeeze me for blood and percentages, so be it."

Getting no response, Ron closed on the desk, flopped down in a chair opposite, and then slapped his hand on his thigh.

"Come on, mate. Don't look so down, it might never happen."

The man opposite looked at Ron, seemingly to notice him for the first time.

"I just found out," he said, his voice cracking with emotion. "That my father was hit by a bus. He died instantly."

Ron paled, sat up, and straightened his tie.

"That's awful," he said. "And I just want to say, in these situations, I am authorised to give an extra five per cent discount."

A few painfully awkward moments later, back out in the carpark, and with his ears still burning from the massive bollocking he had received from his, presumably now lost, customer, Ron noticed several missed calls from Tina's number. But when he thought of the lost commission, he began to blubber again and decided now was not the ideal time to call her back.

He did wonder what she might want and hoped it had nothing to do with the flying vicar.

Chapter 4

Pascal

There were days when Pascal regarded working in catering as being an activity that was both woefully underpaid and lacking in any real genuine joy. Possibly, just short of the feeling he might have if he were ever to be waterboarded for information that he couldn't possibly have. Such as the reason why he had failed, once again, to have a meaningful conversation with Juliet.

This time he had tried, really tried, and it seemed as though this time, fate, rather than his lack of effort in that general direction, had been to blame. Having missed his chance to speak with Juliet, again, he was left with just the bitter memory of what can only be described as an endlessly awkward drama of dealing with her blubbering blind date, Ron. With that finally cleared away, and deliberately ignoring the sounds of car chaos from the street outside, Pascal felt drained and unprepared to deal with the dishevelled pile of weeping emotions that was his niece, Yvonne.

He found her sitting on the floor near the kitchen bins, her voluminous hair piled over her face and body so that she looked like a small dog trying to sleep. She had retreated here after Juliet snapped at her a second time, apparently for *looking at her funny*. To be fair, everyone was looking at Juliet in a funny way after she had made a grown man cry, and then started to shout at him about it! Halfway through her rant on overt patriarchal abuses of power, she lost her voice and left the premises as though her pants were on fire.

"Yvonne," he said in what he hoped was a voice that contained enough empathy for the complex emotions that no doubt raced through this teenager's hormonally infested body. "Isn't there a funny cat video that will cheer you up?"

Yvonne spent many an hour in this part of the café, one that she had identified as being within the occasional range of an unguarded Wi-Fi signal. A signal she spent most of her time desperately trying to ensnare.

The sullen young girl stood slowly to her feet, avoiding Pascal's concerned look, but gracing him with a sad, dark-eyed nod, before wordlessly typing a search for just such a video of feline fun. As she tapped, she juggled the phone through the air, changing the angle and height every few seconds in an attempt to strain a full bar out of the half a bar of Wi-Fi she currently received.

Just before the display updated to one of furry fun, Pascal noted her last search had been *how to deal with assertive women*. He wondered briefly if she had found any decent hits, or smashes or impacts, or whatever internet answers were called, and if so, would she share them?

Yvonne climbed up onto the counter in search of a stronger connection, her black leggings slipping on the Formica surface. Pascal decided that perhaps now was not the time to bring up the hygiene requirements of a public food service area. He'd just wipe that down later when she had finished her shift, which he hoped would be fairly soon.

Yvonne working at the café was a favour Pascal had been pressured into by his brother's ex-wife, Rose, who Pascal still kept in touch with for various complicated reasons that were mostly to do with family. He liked to think it was more than just habit, or that Rose was a highly skilled accountant and as such, fundamentally useful to someone like Pascal, whose grasp of the catering business world tended to end at the cool end of a cooking pot handle.

It was though, more than that, and less than anything else.

As well as being handy with figure work, he also liked to have Rose round for a coffee and a chat. He found her easy to talk to, level-headed, sensible, someone with whom he could share his thoughts. It was perhaps a relationship that worked well because neither was physically attracted to the other, for those complex reasons that had nothing to do with sex and everything to do with something else, but no one really knew what.

How Rose ended up with a daughter of such high emotional stakes had much to do with Jacque being the father, of this Pascal was certain, although of course, daughters often differed from their mothers. If he needed evidence of this, surely, he need only look at the remarkable physical differences between Yvonne and her mother, Rose.

The daughter was a strange combination of looks and intelligence, borrowing most of her physical traits from Jacque, possessing a paler skin than her mother's Nigerian heritage, her fine hair that drew looks of stunned appreciation wherever this beguiling teenager went. Despite the angular cut of her chin that made her look so much like her father,

Yvonne stole back femininity with those dark soulful eyes of her mother. Eyes that were most days prone to leaking.

Yvonne had worked at Pascal's café for the last three weeks, although this seemed in many ways much longer, and the definition of what actually constituted *work* seemed to be something that Yvonne regarded as a problem that had yet to be solved. On day one, she had announced to Pascal that she would take charge of all Social Media relating to the café. Something that Pascal readily agreed to, as mostly he didn't really know what that meant and assumed it was some kind of hobby she would partake in during her own time. It soon transpired that updating Social Media to keep it *fresh & current* and other buzzwords that meant nothing to Pascal involved much staring at a laptop screen and mentioning things like digital cameras and asking if he knew any celebrities.

But still, credit where it was due, Pascal's café now featured a Facebook page, an Instagram account, something to do with Tumbler that he totally failed to get his brain behind and a Twitter account that appeared to be more trouble than it was worth. There was even an entry on LinkedIn, which Yvonne said was probably a waste of time, but she did it anyway just to give the café maximum exposure.

From Pascal's point of view, maximum exposure to Social Media had so far failed to bring in a single new customer, and the only person who was actually active on their internet presence was Yvonne herself. Actual help in running the day-to-day motions of the café, like buying milk or doing the washing up, seemed to be the main thing Yvonne was incapable of providing. Pascal had assumed that she would want to do all the things that youngsters did back in the day when he started in his father's kitchen in Paris. Yet, a simple request to perform any menial task would earn him a thirty-minute lecture on the symptomatic abuse of patriarchal power in the workplace. These lectures tended to be of such complexity, he rarely asked a second time.

Rose had popped by once, noted his plight, with what seemed to be the vaguest of sympathies, and suggested Pascal just simply *wait her out*.

"She's a Millennial," Rose had said from behind expensive sunglasses. "She'll get bored of all that Twitter nonsense soon enough, then she will be begging you to let her do the dishes."

Pascal, whose ears were still ringing from a lecture on what constituted *personal misogynist behaviour* after requesting she not leave her laptop bag near the door and thus nearly kill him whenever he walked in, was sceptical. In fact, he began to believe the whole point of finding Yvonne a place in the world was nothing to do with teaching her valuable life skills but had simply been to get her out of Rose's hair for as long as was humanly possible.

Today, treading carefully as he now did, Pascal regarded the doe-eyed twenty-something, whose smeared mascara gave her a slightly sinister look, with near exhaustion. True to say, Yvonne had not interrupted Pascal and Juliet on purpose, and the phone call had indeed been an urgent one, from a debt collector chasing Jacque, who had somehow managed to list Pascal as a loan guarantee without his knowledge.

But…

The moment to talk with Juliet had been there, his courage, frequently somewhat vague in her presence, had been stuck to the sticking place, and then… And then the moment had evaporated, and the fat man had started crying, which had at least stopped Yvonne crying as they both came out to stare at Juliet, verbally disembowelling Ron. Juliet, multitasker that she was, had also managed to find time to snap at Yvonne, catapulting the sobbing ball of emotion back to the locked toilet from which she had been removed only with considerable persuasive effort.

While Yvonne sat peacefully digesting furry video fun on her phone, it gave Pascal a few moments of personal peace to think about how his life had arrived at this point. Namely; sitting in a small café, with no customers, and occasionally trying to talk his only staff member out of the loo before her sobs alarmed the neighbours, and they called the police.

There had been a time, before all of this, just after his father decided to uproot the family and bring them all to London to seek his fortune as a famous French chef, when Pascal believed he had it all. That nothing could stop him and his family, the family Noir, from the greatness they deserved.

Back then, everyone seemed young, even their father who married late in life a woman half his age, and became a parent in middle age. Back then, Pascal was in his mid-twenties; his brother Jacque, just entering early thirties and a tower of inspiration to a younger brother who looked up to him and treated him with reverence, following his shadow no matter where that path took them.

As the years passed, the gold sheen of Pascal's admiration for his brother tarnished, and resentment replaced adulation, and now Pascal, himself in the middle of a divorce to an American woman he should never have married in the first place, found himself wanting to be more than a man living in the shadow of his older brother.

In the midst of all this drama, there was Juliet.

A woman he first met while she was sitting next to her talented and handsome husband. A woman who looked so incredibly happy in her own skin, in her own life, a life that did not and could never include him.

A woman he fell in love with at first sight.

Where did that emotion come from? That overwhelming feeling that she was the one? Pascal had no idea. He had at first hand dismissed it. A fancy. A lost thought. A random instant that could be ignored as he continued his day-to-day running of a restaurant with Jacque and their parents.

He had turned his thoughts to his cooking, to creating meals that his mother approved to the point where tears of joy appeared in her eyes. And without noticing, slowly, the fractured indifference of his own marriage that had fizzled and died before the honeymoon had finished, troubled him less and less.

Despite this slavish duty to his own art form, those thoughts and feelings for Juliet never went away. No matter how hard he tried, whenever he met Juliet, it was as though he saw her again, each time, for the first time. As though he fell in love with her all over again, a moment of blissful torture he would hate as much as he desired.

Then came the day Jacque told him, full of excitement, extolling the airs and graces of a man who had found fame, that Juliet had asked him to write a cookery book. One to be represented by her Literary Agency, one that would mean they both would be spending a good deal of time with Juliet as they wrote and then published their book.

"This will make us very rich," Jacque had said, opening a bottle of very expensive brandy, and offering Pascal a glass.

He had taken the bitter liquor, drank it even though it was still early morning, and he had enjoyed the guilty thought of having a reason to be near Juliet as the fiery liquid drained through his soul.

Jacque was still talking, rambling, excited chatter about turning them into household names, letting them create a chain from Restaurant Noir, he even envisaged them becoming a global presence.

Restaurant Noir in New York, Hong Kong…

Even in Paris!

The sky and the stars were achievable targets, the start of something so great, that perhaps even Jacque himself did not fully understand it. Yet, all Pascal could think about was being near to Juliet, a woman now divorced from a man who inexplicably turned out to be gay.

Pascal himself was still married, and as a man who took the tortured soul of the self to new and unparalleled depths, he worried endlessly over this. He agonised over this as much as he thought about the chance to be with Juliet.

And then it all went wrong.

Something had to give. Family Noir had a reputation for bad luck and tragedy, so much so, Pascal should have expected that in this moment of potential success, something would drop on them from a great height and kill dead their dreams.

Something did. An old grudge emerged when Jacque gave Pascal a laptop and told him to get on with writing the book while he was busy creating publicity for it. Jacque hadn't spoken to Pascal for weeks after signing the book contract, largely leaving the running of the restaurant in the younger brother's hands. Good cook though he was, Pascal couldn't handle the day-to-day stress of staff management and customer relations, so when Jacque appeared with a laptop and a demand that Pascal simply do as his brother wished, the atmosphere had darkened. After the last customer left that evening, for their professionalism forbad such arguments while the restaurant was open, they had begun a row that had dwarfed the viciousness of previous disputes and had only ended when both men became totally drunk.

The next day, still mostly drunk, they had avoided the argument by continuing to drink, which at least allowed them to work together. There, in the middle of that singular unsuccessful method to solve their disputes, they had attempted to deal with an OAP Christmas special. A day that would forever remain in Pascal's memory for all the wrong reasons.

In the moment of being drunk with his brother, Pascal had regressed, as had Jacque, and they began to dare each other to alter food. A little too much pepper to cause a sneezing fit, a little too much spice to cause a cry for water, a bit too much garlic just to see what the reaction would be. All relatively harmless stuff, unless you were the unfortunate recipient of such a prank, but the dares got out of control and tragedy was their reward for such irresponsible behaviour.

The next day they were hardly able to believe how quickly they sobered up when tragic news reached them.

A customer had died.

Pascal was devastated, Jacque a little more pragmatic. He covered their trail, made sure no one knew what had happened, kept their reckless action out of the public view.

He had saved them both.

Of course, there was a cost.

The damn book.

Pascal had little choice now but to write it, and it broke him to transcribe family recipes, secrets passed on by each generation of Noir parents, into a format that would be seen by other people. Strangers. Unworthy cooks who would treat the measures, the ingredients, the small and insignificant methods within that amounted to culinary genius with less reverence than he cared to imagine.

It wounded him.

It ruined him, and in a moment of irrational anger, he took in his hands the opportunity to betray his brother. An act of drunken revenge that he pursued without thinking of the consequence to anyone else involved in the project.

Without thinking of the consequences to Juliet!

In turn, that moment of revenge became a burden of guilt towards his mother's recipes, his mother's memory. A burden that one day saw him put down his cook's knife, discard his whites and walk away from Restaurant Noir, never to return. From that moment on, he swore never to cook, never again to create food that would delight.

He could not. He was unworthy. He was broken.

Within a few months, his life had changed. His wife finally left him and returned to New York, and having foreswore cooking, Pascal found a small café where he could live out his days, serving coffee, and making the occasional handmade croissant. A café that just happened to be opposite Juliet's office. One with a small studio flat above that featured a window looking in the direction of where Juliet worked every day.

Finding a café so close to Juliet wasn't a deliberate act, but a moment of fate that Pascal considered to be his punishment. To be near the woman he loved, to be able to see her, but now never allowed to give way to his feelings, to reveal to her his true inner passion.

It would be his penance. His self-determined incarceration.

Life, Pascal mused, was sometimes so shit, it hurt.

Chapter 5

Jacque

Jacque sat slumped in a darkened corner of a table booth, far from a tiny stage on which a slightly overweight middle-aged woman gyrated to a beat outside of that which permeated the air around them. He watched her dance with disinterested quietness, noting the plastic earplugs that lead to a cheap phone gaffer taped to her bare upper thigh. Her eyes remained closed, shutting out the room and its depressing population of inebriated men. Men lured here on the promise of exotic dancers; men who now stared with vague disappointment in her barely clothed direction. Her thoughts were closed from them, even the music she danced to remained private and inaccessible.

For Jacque, she represented his life; once young and vibrant, full of hope and promise. Possibly once lithe and athletic. Maybe with a pretty smile that had been worn away by the passage of time and the brutality of merely living. Where once this gyrating woman would have summoned lust and excitement by her mere presence, she represented now a placeholder, a moment in time to fill this part of the day, this part of a sordid existence that belonged to those men who watched without desire but never left.

Where would they go? There were no places left to run, no appointments to keep, no adventures to be had. No one to love, or love them. Strip clubs in the early afternoon were the graveyard of humanity.

Jacque glanced at his wrist to check just how much of the afternoon remained to be wasted. The space on his arm was barren and empty; a faded tan line was all that endured to remind him of a Rolex he had received from his wife, on a birthday he could barely remember. An expensive icon he had worn with pride. A badge of honour that said: I have arrived.

The watch had been gambled away a few nights back. Maybe it was last week. Jacque wasn't sure it mattered. He couldn't even remember the face of the man who won it or the cards he held. The pain of loss, though; Jacque could remember that. Remember its bite. Remember the soulless gaze of the faceless player scooping up Jacque's chips, his watch, his IOU's.

With no cash for a cab and no money in the bank to draw, he'd walked home from that game. Cash machines were no longer his friends, where once they seemed perfect starting points of limitless entertainment. Jump-off-points to a life that was exciting, demanding, draining... Perfect.

Stocks and shares had been sold the day after he lost his Rolex, sold at a fraction of what he could have earned from them; he knew this with a perceptive pain all of its own. Jacque had many faults but he was, at least, a canny businessman. He knew the value of everything, and he knew to a penny how much he had left of his squandered fortune. It was an amount of money he chose not to think about too carefully.

How had it come to this?

He traced his life backwards; skipping over the bad decisions he had made and focused instead on those people who had let him down. Proportioning blame in random values to random faces on the complex path of his life. His ex-wife, his brother, the many one-night-stands and more durable lovers, and finally, the blank faces around the soft green felt of a poker table. All had contributed to his current lousy luck by failing to be the people he needed them to be.

The dancer with the phone attached to her leg began to finish her routine, scooping to pick up her now discarded underwear and hold these items across her body. Protectively. She was done! They were not to watch her anymore, not even as they gave her their muted applause.

Jacque wanted to show his contempt for such attitude by throwing money at her as she walked by, but he feared this would leave him with nothing left in his wallet, so he watched her go with a dark look on his face, his mind adding this nameless stripper to the list of people who had wronged him.

He watched her leave, disappearing behind a cheap plastic beaded curtain, heading for the sanctity of not being near men. Another quickly replaced her, the DJ announcing they should give a *'big hand for Jezebel'*, a large black woman with an even larger afro and a purple bikini that strained around her generously sized breasts and a G-string that largely remained hidden from view.

As Jezebel passed his table, she unwisely made brief eye contact, and Jacque unwisely spoke to her.

"Excusez-moi Madam," Jacque said. "Do you have the time?"

She stopped for a moment, leaning over the table, his expensive drink contacting with a nipple that failed to be contained by the flimsy material of her bikini.

"If you've got the money darling, I've got the time," she said with a girly giggle that sat at odds with lines etched into the corners of her eyes.

Jacque tried to think of something equally witty he could shout back above the now thumping disco beat, but while he pondered, his glass succumbed to the dancer's swaying breasts and was swept off the table. An almost full glass of overly priced and excessively diluted gin deposited itself over his already stained white trousers.

Jacque leapt from his seat; several explicit French swear words surging from his mouth as he searched the table for a serviette to wipe away the soiled stain. It was in this moment of swearing nonstop at the cowering woman, while aggressively rubbing his crotch with a damp hanky, when the club's doorman and bouncer chose to appear from the gents.

"What's going on Jez?" said the large man as he approached the table with unhurried ease. A man, Jacque could see, of an age that could no longer be considered middle, but whose demeanour left no doubts to his levels of confidence.

"This… Customer, Barry, calls me over and then goes ape shit on me."

"Jacque Noir does not go ape shit, as you so poetically put it," Jacque protested while dabbing at the spreading stain on his trousers.

"Jacky who?" Asked the confused looking Jezebel. "Who's this Jacky Moor then?"

"Jacque Noir is this bloke," Barry explained. "He's referring to himself in the third party."

"Oh," Jezebel said with a dawning realisation that made Jacque wonder if he was a little too drunk for his own good. "You mean like that

Illeism stuff we talked about in book club last week."

"Exactly Jez," Barry answered with a balanced amount of surrealism. "In that case, we referenced Illeism to express humility as a literary device, and as you've probably seen on TV, that's not the case with our French friend here."

As Jacque listened to this conversation unfurl itself in unlikely directions, like an earthworm recently run over by a large lorry, he now began to wonder if he was in fact not drunk enough.

"TV?" Jezebel blinked in the subdued lighting of the club and tried to take in Jacque's face. After a long moment in which Jacque felt more naked than the exotic dancer before him, her eyes widened in recognition. "Oh, ain't you that bloke what does stuff with food?"

"Jacque Noir is a master chef," Jacque blustered, the effort giving him a mild case of drunken dizziness. "And when he does *stuff* with food, it is to create a taste sensation of unparalleled sophistication."

"Right," Jezebel said, clearly wishing Jacque was Phillip Schofield. "So, do you want a lap dance or not?"

"No! What Jacque Noir wants is to be pissed off that you have poured gin down a pair of hideously expensive made-to-measure trousers, and you have done this because you are quite clearly an idiot."

That earned him a slap round the back of the head from Barry and Jacque became aware he had morphed into the centre of attention for all the other punters. Especially those men who seemed silently amused to see someone creating a little bit of drama in their otherwise placid afternoon.

"Please, I am not a man who believes in violence," Jacque said.

"Not a problem, I have enough belief for the both of us," Barry said, moving closer and cracking his knuckles. He seemed mildly relieved to have something to do in what appeared to be a very quiet day. "Now that we've sorted out your modern usage of third-party reference, do you want a lap dance with Jezebel or not? I can recommend her; she has beautiful nipples."

"Oh, thanks, Barry."

"No thank you, her nipples have already caused me enough problems."

"Then why are you bothering her?"

"Bothering? I only wanted to know if she could tell me the time."

"Does she look like she's wearing a watch?"

"Yeah, where do you think I'd put it, love?"

Jacque surveyed her enormous cleavage and glanced at an arse crack large enough to park a bike, but decided now was not the time to mention any of this. Jezebel, however, seemed to interpret the silence as rudeness.

"Fucking French, all the fucking same," she said, proving to Jacque that if nothing else in the universe was true, at least racism could be nonexclusive to nationality or skin colour.

She moved away, swaying towards the stage, getting a larger round of applause than she might normally have expected. There she began her routine, and the men in the room began once more to mentally shut down.

"Come on you," Barry said, reaching out with a hand that looked like a side of ham, only with various disturbing tattoos running across it. "Time you went home."

"Really? How do you know? How do you know this is time for me to be going home when we don't know what the time is?"

"I don't have to know," Barry said and smiled, revealing a row of yellow stained teeth with the occasional gap. "That's the beauty of my job. I just do shit anyway."

Jacque sighed and resigned himself to being propelled at speed from the club, with, of course, a quick stop at the cashier to pay an eye wateringly large drinks bill. He used the credit card he thought most likely not to be rejected. The Frenchman's hands shook slightly as he punched in a pin code that he hoped was not incorrect while Barry loomed over him, close enough that Jacque could smell stale tobacco smoke emanating from his leather waistcoat.

After an age of one technically challenged device talking to another, the machine gave a soft burb, then spat out a receipt. The barman ripped it off, noted that no tip had been given, then slapped both it and the credit card down in a puddle of something sticky on the bar. Something that Jacque hoped was a liqueur and not actual bodily fluids. Considering the establishment he stood in, it wasn't a certainty either way. Jacque scooped up both receipt and card and plunged them deep into his pocket.

"Please," he said, remembering now his motivation for interrupting Jezebel's swaying walk to the stage. "Jacque Noir just wants… I want to know the time; I have a meeting…"

"Look," Barry said, towing him firmly towards the exit. "I don't have the time, and even if I did, I probably wouldn't tell you."

"Oh," Jacque said, a wave of drunken heroism breaking unexpectedly over his inner dissatisfaction at the high bill, the low-grade strippers and the watered-down booze. "I suppose then a blow job is totally out of the question."

Barry it seemed wasn't really into beating up small drunken French men, and that was probably the only reason Jacque found himself propelled out of the club door, rather than the customary habit of being taken around the back for a short and succinct conversation.

The strip club door closed behind Jacque as his body sprawled face down on the small red carpet outside on the pavement. Here Jacque became slowly aware of the glaring sun, the ordinary street around him, and the faces of people gawking at him as he lay there, outside a strip club, dishevelled, a dark stain on his crotch. He pulled a crumpled hat from his inner jacket pocket, jammed it down over his ears, and staggered away.

A sullen beep sounded from his inside pocket, and he took out his phone and was rewarded by the site of the correct time. Why hadn't he thought of that? The notion brought back memories of his lost Rolex, of the moments when he would look at it, not for the time, but simply to look at it, the moments when people would ask him the time and he, with great flourish, would reveal the gaudy Rolex on his skinny pale wrist.

The time on his phone was displayed over a message from Tina. A reminder of a meeting and a request not to be late. AGAIN! The last word, in capitals and larger font size, was followed by a lengthy tirade of Emojis whose hieroglyphical meaning was lost on Jacque. The meeting was timed for thirty minutes ago, and Juliet's office was a twenty-minute cab ride away. Beside him, the traffic was at a standstill.

So, he'd be an hour late. So what?

A quick search of his pockets, mostly unnecessary, but just to be sure, revealed them to be bereft of cash. Briefly, he attempted to cross the road to a cash machine, but a Jaguar being driven by a large man sobbing into a hanky sounded its horn with such ferocity, he quickly gave up on the idea.

He needed to see Juliet today, try to persuade her to get another advance royalty payment from the publishers. It was a short-term fix, but it would be a start. Of course, he had a reputation as an arrogant

Frenchman to uphold, so arriving a little late would be fine, but he needed to be there. If he played things just right, and often he did, especially with women, it was a chance to turn things around.

Make them great again.

Make them Rolex-wearing great again.

There was, he felt, just this one chance left, and he couldn't afford to fuck it up.

Regardless of his lack of cash, and physical appearance, Jacque hailed the first black cab that would stop for a man who looked to be either homeless, drunk, or possibly both. Sinking gratefully into the wide cool seats, he gave the address, and then covered his eyes with his hat, partly to sleep, but mostly to obscure the cab driver.

"Hey," the driver said. "Didn't you used to be that French cooking bloke on TV?"

"Yes," Jacque said, and his mind hovered around the myriad of abusive comebacks he could deliver to the ears of this unfortunate driver. But exhaustion overtook him and a snarky remark died on his tongue before it could truly be born. "Please… Just… Just drive while I sleep."

His body still felt the soulless beat of the strip club music pounding through him, and with it, he could still taste the isolated loneliness of just being there.

Chapter 6

Juliet

The phone call that occurred immediately after Juliet lost her blind date argument with Tina had not been a pleasant one. Or indeed one that Juliet had been expecting, but it had at least given her a cast-iron opportunity to escape the frosty atmosphere. It also offered the chance for her to use some choice swear words without fear of going broke while doing so.

As far as Juliet was concerned, no one deserved the F-word more than publishers.

Juliet had time to mull over her argument with Tina on the cab ride to the publisher in question, but for the life of her, she still couldn't figure out how she had lost, yet again, an argument with her big sister. Had she not endured enough at the hands of the walking nipple rubbing festival that was Ron? Had she not suffered the epitomical lunchtime date from hell? Why then was it, when she protested to Tina about setting the whole thing up, did she, Juliet, end up being the bad person. Again!

It beggared belief.

At least the phone call from the publishers had come at an appropriate juncture to allow her to escape and regroup her morale, although truth to be told, the phone call wasn't exactly great news. In fact, it was pretty shitty news, which tended to be the case when publishers contacted her. Either something was terribly wrong and about to fall apart, or she never heard a peep from them.

Surely there had to be a middle ground, she thought fuming with such intensity, even the black cab driver refrained from talking to her.

Arriving at the publishers' sleek and swanky building, Juliet found herself remembering a time when she had worked in such a place. Not quite like this, perhaps less bright curvy wood everywhere, and a touch more chrome in her day (everywhere), but, architectural changes aside, entering the office area gave her an uncomfortable feeling of unwanted déjà vu. It took her straight back to a moment in her life that was just after Uni, just when the fun stopped. A moment when she waltzed, innocent and naïve into her first job. One of many with a long string of publishing companies on whom she would base her career.

Having joined university a little later in life than planned, Juliet had just turned twenty-five when she left. Determinedly single then and walking around with the kind of ridiculous swagger a double-first affords recent graduates. Education had been mercifully free in those days, so apart from a crippling credit card bill, a sizable bank overdraft, a car loan that she would be paying longer than the car lasted, and a personal loan from her father to secure the deposit on her rented flat, she was debt free.

These were, to this young and inexperienced Juliet, mere details on the journey of life. Soon she would be promoted and make real money, and then, well then, she could buy those fancy new tights that everyone was talking about, the ones that made your bum look pert.

The present-day Juliet shuddered at the memory of wanting to have a bum perter than it could possibly be at just twenty-five. Women, she had decided long ago, worried far too much over their appearance and anyway, it was all to please those degenerates of the world known as *men*. How her younger self had longed to see the world changed, to see women at the forefront of every industry, to see the world become a place where all could earn a decent living; especially women.

Or, if Juliet were to be honest, especially her.

Today, standing here, older and wiser, and looking around Prized Publishing's modern-day hot-desked office, Juliet wondered if all of those aspirations should be filed under *be careful what you wish for*.

There was, it had to be said, a dearth of men in this antiseptically open-plan office. Occasionally she would see one scurrying out of the photocopier room, or an IT support bod kneeling beside a printer, fishing out whatever was jammed in there and shaking his head. Apart from that, the place was predominately female and very young, and despite her feminist-self railing against such thoughts, Juliet couldn't help wondering how many of these bright young things got their jobs on merit alone. Or how many rode the feminist wave, surfing into employment on the back of Equality of Outcome, rather than, you know, being the best at what they did.

Juliet announced herself at the receptionist, one of the few men in the room. He sat behind a barebones desk, resplendent in a bright pink shirt with matching nails and managed to talk to Juliet as though she wasn't actually present.

"Emma knows Juliet Raphael is here," he said with something approaching a soft Welsh accent. "Please take a seat."

"Thank you, any chance of a coffee?"

The receptionist glanced momentarily her way over his half-rimmed glasses. It was a glance that suggested Juliet had just asked him to suck her toes.

"Not my job," he said eventually, and when Juliet tried to apologise, in that very English and upper-class way, he held out his hand and touched it to his ear.

"Prized Publishing, how can I... Please hold. Hello Fiona, call for you..."

Juliet slunk away and had a quick scan of the office to see if she could locate a coffee percolator. Eventually she located a kettle and decided to just help herself, but the cupboards were frustratingly free of anything vaguely caffeine-related. Mostly they contained tea bags in brightly coloured packets, each adorned with terribly twee hand-drawn images of herbs and fruit. She sorted through, looking vainly for English Breakfast.

"Hello Juliet," a voice behind her said, nearly making her jump out of her shoes and bang her head on a cupboard door. "Not here to steal the tea bags I hope?"

Juliet turned to find Emma standing resplendently behind her. It was difficult from Juliet's point of view to understand how Emma ever got any work done, there seemed little chance that anything approaching a productive day could be managed while presenting oneself to the world as a flawless human being.

Hair perfectly in place; check.

Make up perfect to catwalk standards; check.

Clothes wrinkle-free and fitting perfectly to Emma's somewhat androgynous body.

Check and check, thought Juliet while attempting in vain not to grind her teeth.

Juliet managed a hearty laugh at Emma's half-hearted tea-bag-stealing joke and reached out to shake the woman's hand, but Emma had already turned and began walking back towards her office on heels that looked, from Juliet's experience, impossible to balance on.

As she followed Emma past her colleagues, Juliet noted they were all, every single one of them, incredibly beautiful, even the very few men present. These metrosexual men were either rugged and well kept, or effeminate and well kept.

Juliet speculated how she would compete in this new world where every woman was allowed a chance at success, but in reality, only the beautiful ones tended to get past the winner's tape. Juliet had never been an ugly duckling, by no means. She regarded herself, at least when she was younger, as having been quite the head-turner. Not unusually tall or well endowed, but there was a certain something to her face that seemed to make men, and some women, want to take a second glance whenever she entered the room. As she aged, of course, the stress of work, late-night projects, red-eye flights, and the sheer will-power to have a social life had etched irremovable history into her face. Now she felt she was still a looker, but older, less likely to cause a man to turn and stare, as he walked into a lamppost. It still happened, but not as often, and when it did, she found this person had questionable eyesight so that probably didn't count.

Emma's perfect pace, on her perfectly polished shoes, led to her glass-walled office at the end of the building. Here it surveyed in one direction all the underlings working on tasks set presumably by her, and in the other direction the River Thames swirling off into the distance, passing the Millennial Bridge and the majestic dome of St Paul's Cathedral, before swishing off to the excessively expensive Docklands beyond. It was a view that captured her heart whenever she visited Prized Publishing. Juliet's office had a less than stunning view of some flats built on top of shops, one of which Pascal's Café resided in. Most of the apartments bore heavy net curtains over their windows, so their occupancy was a daily mystery. This was probably for the best as the only window she could see through contained a view of a large bald man who liked to walk around in nothing but a black G-String. Occasionally, when she stood at her window seeking inspiration, she would spy his hairless body lifeless and prone on the bed, lit by the glow of his 50-inch TV.

Tina was always knocking on about the size of their office window, and how they could see Islington Green at the end of the road, which Juliet thought was a bit optimistic as all she could see was a bit of green that might be *The* Green, but equally, could be a parked delivery van. One day, she thought, one day when she had regained her place in this industry, when she had reignited the story of her success, she would have a view like this.

All she needed was a string of hits from those fuckwits she worked with called writers. How hard could that be?

"It's bad news I'm afraid," Emma said, proving her passive-aggressive training day hadn't gone to waste, despite the rumours of her having a minor breakdown in a group hug session over unresolved daddy issues.

"Yes, you mentioned on the phone," Juliet said, trying to tread carefully until the situation could be fully understood. "But what exactly is the problem?"

"Right, okay, so, Juliet, here's the thing," Emma said, her smile indicating that she saw no reason why this meeting was taking place or why she had to repeat everything she had said on the phone. "As I mentioned on the phone… Some of the early pre-reviews of the book, sent to us kindly by the papers before publishing, have taken a less than positive stance towards Jacque Noir's recipes."

"Yes, this is the part I didn't fully understand as the actual publish date isn't until next month?" Juliet tried to phrase this partly as fact and partly as a question, and realised she came across as someone trying to defuse a bomb with chopsticks and good intentions.

"Right, okay, so, Juliet, here's the thing," Emma tended to add Juliet's name to every sentence, and Juliet felt her blood pressure increase every single time. "Our test focus groups were giving us mixed messages, so we decided to ask for some early feedback from the press?"

"What are you talking about? Focus groups? When did *that* happen?"

Juliet observed Emma's (perfect) eyebrows shoot up in alarm at Juliet's raised voice. She moved effortlessly to the office door and closed it, ignoring the raised heads that had appeared above the sleekly styled monitors beyond.

"Right okay, here's the thing, Juliet."

Juliet steeled herself. Talking to anyone in an office in London was now something akin to entering the Twilight Zone where everyone was trained to repeat the same phrases over and over until everyone either went mad or freelance. Which in the long-run, was pretty much the same thing.

"Now, I want you to understand that everyone here has the greatest respect for you," Emma said, with precise and careful eye contact.

Juliet felt a pang in her stomach. Words like this were always going to be followed by bad news, or worse news, and sometimes even apocalyptically lousy news wrapped in a sandwich of even shittier news.

"Here's the thing, Juliet, everyone here was so excited about the book," she paused to glance over Juliet's shoulder. Juliet fought the impulse to follow the glance; instead, she studied the reflection behind Emma, which revealed a worrying interest from the office staff beyond. "And here's the thing, a few people got carried away and took draft copies home and wanted to try the recipes first hand, you know, impress their parents at a special occasion, ruby wedding anniversary, that sort of thing."

This last example was so weirdly specific that Juliet could not help suspect the person Emma was talking about was in fact, Emma.

"And here's the thing, the recipes," Emma held up overly dramatic jazz hands and went comically wide-eyed. "They no work mademoiselle."

Her last words were said with a faux French accent, which Juliet could only assume was an attempt to break the tension with humour. But as the word *mademoiselle* referred to a single woman, and Juliet was still to deal with the mental shrapnel of divorce, she steeled her look to one of severe displeasure. It was time to get serious.

"Perhaps," Juliet said, leaning forward in an aggressively aggressive manner. "Perhaps the person in question just didn't know what they were doing!"

This time, she pointedly removed the question mark from the sentence and Emma's perfectly lined lips formed a thin red wall of hard resistance.

"No, the... The person in question is very accomplished and adept at pretty much everything she does."

Juliet dialled her aggression down a notch and decided not to open that particular can of worms again. She had overextended herself in this meeting, email would have been better, find out what the issue was, and then have an answer ready for a problem that may or may not actually exist. The fact that her email, along with her laptop, was totally bolloxed, and probably at her own hand, was neither here nor there. Regardless of this, she was here now and on the defensive, fact-finding and firefighting at the same time. A precarious situation, even at the best of times.

"Fair enough, but one person's... Issues... Shouldn't cause that much alarm."

"Right, okay, thing is, Juliet, I did mention earlier, you know, focus groups."

Fuck. Emma had just mentioned that, and in her blind panic, Juliet had managed to forget a conversation thread that had occurred only minutes earlier. She endured a sympathetic look from Emma, who was still so young she no doubt regarded anyone over thirty-five as old, and anyone nearing their fifties as almost dead.

"Yes, okay, but..." But what? Juliet took a leap in the dark. "But, focus groups can also create results that are not indicative of an actual paying audience."

"So, here's the thing, Juliet, we did actually think of that as well," Emma paused, presumably waiting for a round of applause for merely doing her job. "That's why we asked for some early pre-reviews before publishing. I also did mention that... Ermm. Earlier."

Juliet closed her eyes and took a deep breath. Patronised by a Millennial who possessed both perfect curls and all the facts was not how she enjoyed spending her afternoon. She wondered briefly if she should have stayed in the café with Ron, and then shook herself free of that thought. It didn't even have the sense to qualify as a last resort.

Juliet must have done more than mentally shake away the thought of

Ron's nipple rubbing habits as Emma lost a moment of calm repose and sat back with a sharp look. The sort of look Juliet herself used when confronted by a drunk on the bus.

"And the reviews are coming in a tad negative?" Juliet asked if only to prove to herself that she was slowly catching up.

Emma handed a USB stick over to Juliet, who looked at it with incomprehension.

"It's a data stick, it has all the reviews. In PDF format." Emma said, then when Juliet failed to take it, she added for clarity; "you can read them on your computer."

"Thank you," Juliet said, instead of *I know what a fucking data stick is and how to use one*. Right now, she wanted the floor to open up and swallow her whole, preferably dumping her in the Thames so she could flow out into the sea, then perhaps make a brief escape to Finland on the back of a friendly Dolphin. "Do you have any printouts I could read now?"

"We are a paperless office, Juliet."

"A paper-free publisher?"

"Yes, that's right. Just doing our part to save the planet."

"I'm sure."

"Thing is Juliet," Emma said, setting a new record for the number of times Juliet had ever heard her name mentioned in a single conversation. "As the reviews are a tad negative and as personal... as the experience of my staff seems to indicate a lack of... proper error checking in the recipes themselves, we are going to restrict the print launch run in anticipation of a... soft sales situation."

Holy fuck! Juliet thought and tried not to look like she had just allowed panic-stricken swear words to cross her panic-stricken mind.

Restricting the print launch run would, of course, directly impact sales, and in turn, directly impact her commission that relied heavily on high volume sales. A commission deal she had brokered in the belief it was the best way to return her agency to solvency. Juliet prepared a confident smile, but it was disintegrated by Emma's next ninja-level passive-aggressive retort.

"Perhaps, Jacque simply got the recipes wrong?"

"Got them wrong?" Juliet said, struggling to get her voice to work correctly. "He's an internationally renowned chef, how can he…"

"Our initial thoughts as well, Juliet, however…" Emma trailed off, her eyes on the USB stick still on the desk.

"Focus groups, yes, got it." Juliet picked up the data stick and held it tightly in a clenched fist that she imagined ramming down Jacque's throat. Her own throat felt as if a bucket of razor blades had just been deposited somewhere near her tonsils.

"Anyway, thing is, I've another client to see Juliet," Emma glanced at a timepiece on her wrist that looked as though it had escaped from the land of the giants. "So, if there is nothing else…?"

Bad reviews. Poor reception from focus groups. The initial print-run to be restricted. Soft sales leading to less money for her agency. Nope, thought Juliet, that was enough to be going on with, until she found Jacque and cleaved his ineffectual and offensive head from his equally offensive and in all probability ineffectual body.

"Oh," Emma said, causing Juliet to pause halfway between sitting and standing, her body frozen in a position of someone trying to take an uncomfortable shit. "One last thing, due to these issues, we may have to, and I do stress the word, *may*… We may have to use the clawback option on the large advance we have already paid to Jacque."

"Clawback?" Juliet's voice cracked slightly, and she struggled to finish the word.

"Oh, you poor thing, do you still have that thing with your voice?"

"I do not... Have... A... Thing with my voice," Juliet struggled to say, her voice all but an inaudible whisper.

"No, no, of course not. I didn't mean to suggest any mental incapacity... We are, of course, equal opportunity employers here. I mean I wasn't implying that you have... Mental issues..." Emma stopped talking, aware of the hole she was digging for herself. "In any event, the clawback clause is in the contract, but as Jacque's agent, you're probably already aware of this. After all, you have been in the business for ages and ages." Emma said, proving to Juliet, there were hidden depths to this woman that she had yet to discover and loathe.

Emma filled the silence between them by uselessly realigning the phone on her desk, presumably with magnetic north. Juliet filled it by allowing herself to stand and then holding out her hand to Emma, who took it with what can only be described as overt caution.

"Thank you for your time, Emma," Juliet said, through the pain of her voice skipping words like a record player with a dull needle. She found a small bottle of water in her bag and took a long gulp from the fizzy contents, ending with a burb that widened Emma's perfectly mascaraed eyes. "And for bringing these issues to my attention. I will, of course, look into them and get back to you ASAP."

"Of course," Emma said, with a smile that said, *Clawback.*

Outside the office, Juliet's voice had not recovered enough for a phone call, so she sent a message to Tina asking if Jacque had been seen or heard from recently. Tina's reply reminded Juliet that she was in fact supposed to have a meeting with Jacque an hour ago, but as he was always late, she still had time to get back to meet him.

"If he turns up before I do," she wrote, "Do not allow him to leave under any circumstances!"

Tina's reply was the screaming emoji, which baffled Juliet, but she spared little time on the issue. Working with Jacque had revealed him to be a slimeball, and now she had found out he was a useless slimeball. Why wasn't she surprised?

She caught a cab and presented her business card to the driver by way of giving the destination. He took the card and decided that if she was mute, then his theories on why Brexit hadn't worked out quite the way the Leavers thought it should, was just the sort of thing she probably wanted to hear about. Without the will to protest, Juliet, who had been a lacklustre Remainer, dutifully blanked out the standard diatribe of protectionist Rule Britannia propaganda. One that came bundled in its usual ball of fluffy white middle-class racism.

Just as they passed Kings Cross, her phone beeped with an email from the pristinely annoying Emma. An email that Juliet was relieved to see did not start with the words, *so here's the thing, Juliet*. Instead, there was a more ominous three-letter acronym in the title bar; FYI.

The email was blank, apart from that somewhat distractingly unhelpful comment, and it took Juliet several moments and opening the email twice to realise it contained a PDF attachment. She opened the document and squinted at it on her phone, before giving up and fishing around in the vastness of her handbag for her often mislaid reading glasses.

When she was finally in a position to read the text, she did so rapidly, and then did so again, a little slower, then a third time, at which point she was able to focus on those words that most worried her. Which were most of them. At this point she swore, so loudly and vehemently the cab driver stopped in mid-Farage and jumped in his seat.

"Everything alright, luv?"

"Yes... No... Take me to Soho."

The cab driver looked perplexed by these answers, so she followed it up by glaring at him and reissuing the command, but this time with a little more coherence.

"Soho, please. Compton Road. Fast as you can."

"No worries," the cab driver said, as though he was used to this sort of thing all day, which he probably was.

They moved into a sickening U-turn, earning many toots from the following cars as the black cab performed its party trick of turning in a small circle, and then they powered back past the National Library, heading once again for the West End.

With a little more time to hand, the cab driver decided to expand on his theory of how Brexit could have been better realised; if only the politicians had the wit to listen to the true will of the people. Juliet once again phased his voice from her life and instead focused her hatred on one small piece of Europe.

The bit represented by the one and only Jacque Noir.

Chapter 7

Tina

Having done her dutiful duty as Juliet's office assistant and placed in envelopes all those novels Juliet had this week rejected, which was sadly everything they had been sent, Tina was free at last to leave the office. To shake off the moment of work, and engage with the world around her. To see with relaxed eyes the buzzing back and forth of Islington High Street, taking in the heady mixture of the hyper-expensive wares displayed, sans price tag, in reinforced shop windows and the less intimidating mobile phone repair shops with their special offers handwritten on cards of orange and green.

As she walked down Essex Road, noting the closed sign on the door to Pascal's Café, she shrugged away for the moment the worries of the office and of Juliet's impending doom, choosing instead to absorb the feeling of being on the street in London, possibly the most exciting city in the world.

It had to be said though, that London in not yet Spring tended to look less exciting than it could. Having lost the magic of Christmas some months earlier, and still awaiting the warmth of summer, the atmosphere under the grey clouds was best described as subdued. Even the air around Islington hung rather than sat in a damp mist of in-betweenness. March had not yet given up her grip on winter and was yet to relinquish to the hope of warmer, dryer summer days. Now, on this dull and overcast Thursday morning, life was a palatable conveyer belt of discontent and random acts of human kindness.

Amongst the latter, Tina moved silently, attending her rounds, doing what she could for those that had no hope to do for themselves. Gliding through the crowds to see her usual people in their usual places. People who sat invisible to the majority of Londoners.

Near Islington Green, close to what had been a local cinema, sat a hunched figure whose thinning hair and an alcoholic's ravaged face left a man whose age could only be guessed at. Sightless eyes that had seen too little and experienced too much looked at nothing.

Tina stopped and gave him a sandwich and a small cup of coffee and offered a few words of comfort against the weather. She didn't get a verbal reply, she never did and his eyes never met hers, but there was a nod, a sway to his manner that changed when she approached. A sign that he had acknowledged her, had seen her, had been, as far as possible, comforted in some small way by her caring.

Cardboard coffee tray in hand, a plastic bag containing food, Tina moved around the streets of Islington, dishing out small mercies to the invisible. Near the Angel tube station, she found a young woman trying to sell copies of The Big Issue, but her manner was aggressive, her face contorted with the pain of rejection. Her open cry, '*please… will someone, please buy something from me… please*' had drawn Tina from across the road where she had been heading towards Chapel Street market. Nearing the distressed young woman, Tina took hold of her hand and gently prised a copy of the magazine from her grip while pressing money into the other. The young face, tear-stained and bleak, managed a smile as Tina lent into to whisper, *'you'll sell more if you smile'*.

Tina leant back, away from the young woman, careful not to register the heavy odour that peeled from the other's clothes in waves of unpleasantness. Tina smiled her happy smile and walked away, hoping and praying to a God she didn't really believe in, that the young magazine seller would find an inner calm, a way to escape the person who had become trapped on these streets.

Tina knew better than to give her any extra money, but still, as she crossed back towards the market, she paused to wipe away a single tear. It was no wonder, Tina thought, that people walked on by these street dwellers. It was always sad to interact with them, to be momentarily part of their sorrow. And yet, try as she might, she could not help but get involved in some small way.

Tina opened the door to the local post office and was appalled, as always, at the queue. She joined the endless line and attempted once again to find her happy place.

Since the agency had been forced to change its business model after Juliet's divorce and celebrity biographies had dried away like spilt water in the desert, Tina spent most of her lunchtimes in the post office. Here she dropped off all the rejected manuscripts, sending them back to disappoint people around the country, and sometimes around the world. It was the part of her job she disliked the most and had balanced it by feeding and providing hot drinks to a few on the street that she saw every day, on her way to and from being the unfortunate bearer of shattered dreams to so many eager writers.

Tina had started with just helping one man. She had given him a cup of hot chocolate when he had berated her for not coughing up fifty pence so he could make an urgent phone call to his dying brother. Tina had read better plotlines in those books they now received from small villages in Kent, Sussex and Norfolk. The staple home of the dreadful romantic novel, the dizzyingly complex Science Fiction epic, and the depressingly unerotic collection of erotic short stories. So, in the middle of his tirade to her on the oppression of the less well-off by the much better-off, she had given him her heavily sugared cup of hot chocolate, and a doughnut with a pink covering that she had really been looking forward to eating.

The man had been so surprised; he had smiled, and then wished her a pleasant day with plenty of luck. Weeks had followed where their paths crossed more and more, drinks and food exchanged for a few words of aspirational good fortune, until one cold winter's day his sleeping bag sat empty on the pavement, a dried vomit stain on the pavement beside it, the only remaining signs of his existence. At some point, the sleeping bag vanished, to be replaced with another similar, but sadly younger man who rarely talked or looked at people, but just rocked backwards and forwards on the balls of his feet.

Tina often wondered what happened to that original homeless man. She suspected he died, maybe from his drinking, perhaps from the cold, and she would sometimes sit alone in bed and wonder if there was more she could have done. Or, if there was anything at all she could have done that would have made the slightest bit of difference.

She forced her thoughts away from this and attempted to lift her mood as she finally left the post office and made her way to Chapel Market. Here she was determined to enjoy the buzz of the place, the diversity of the people, the smell of food from a hundred nations, the sound of languages from around the globe. The street took maybe ten minutes to stroll down, if you walked slowly enough, with stalls every few feet that covered the scope of humanity's needs, from nappies to loo rolls, bread rolls to soup, socks to hats, Tampax to balls of wool.

Men and women of all sizes, shapes and colours mixed here, including those whose gender was in flux, and those who decided not to decide. Tina came here for the atmosphere, for the cheap tights and the fresh fruit, and a lunchtime menu that was as diverse as it was confusing. She settled for a Thai curry that came in a small plastic cup with a lid and a not so small portion of spiced potatoes in a paper bag. Her free-trade cotton bag-for-life soon became weighed down with all of the things she anticipated needing to get through the rest of the day, chocolate being the main ingredient.

Shopping complete, Tina headed for the triangular green space between the two main roads. Islington Green; the place where the A1 began its epic journey up the geographical spine of England, with Essex Street splitting away and catering for traffic that seemed for various reasons less frantic. In the middle sat this tree-lined oasis, surrounded by a black cast iron fence of spiked top poles. Sitting there was a small luxury in her day, a moment to enjoy the pleasure of eating alfresco while fighting off the evasive persuasions of the local pigeons.

Avoiding the throng of Upper Street, Tina varied her route towards the idyllic green in order to take in the small, almost quaint shops that ran along the grandly named but oddly insignificant Islington High Street. By chance, she glanced down a side road and caught sight of the now darkened windows of the now-defunct Restaurant Noir.

She stopped for a moment, to pace towards the silent door, and press a palm against the cold glass in the act of quiet remembrance. She cupped that hand on the pane and tried to steal a glimpse into the shadows of the closed shop beyond. Furniture still occupied the room, but it was randomly piled to the side. Tables and chairs where she had sat… Where they had all sat… Now nothing more than dust collectors, awaiting a final journey to the tip to be crushed or burnt.

It was all so unfortunate.

Back, not so long ago, back before Juliet divorced Clive, before the Noir boys fell out and closed this place for good, back then, this restaurant had been the very centre of their existence. A place they had discovered the day Juliet opened her Literary Agency.

Having signed the contract to the new office, and taken possession of the keys, they, Tina, Juliet and Clive, Juliet's handsome actor husband and financial backer, had rushed round to view the barren, empty office, and proceeded to do all the ceremonial stuff. Turning on the office lights to see if they worked, testing to see if the phone actually rang, checking the loo to see if it flushed (it didn't), opening windows to let in the air. Heady stuff! The inception of the new had all seemed so terribly exciting. And then, there they had sat, on the dusty office floor, drinking at least two or three bottles of reasonably cold bubbly and dreaming rosy dreams of the future.

Everything had been different then. They were so full of hope, fuelled by the enthusiasm of the new, untroubled by the problems posed by an uncertain future.

The office was a modest affair, just two rooms and a toilet with what could be described as a kitchen; so long as one thought kitchens began and ended their usage at tea and toast. Or whatever evil could be persuaded from a microwave. This second room, really an entrance hall to the main room, created a reception area to Juliet's office and had become Tina's place of work. True, the view from Tina's office/entrance hall or even Juliet's more extensive window could never be described as a vista of the imagination, but their location was just a short walk from the Northern Line. It was also a quick cab ride past Kings Cross to Russel Square, where literary agents of wealth resided. More importantly, as far as Tina was concerned, they were just a short bus ride from Oxford Street and the West End.

Pretty much perfect, and all without costing a small fortune. True to say the rent was more aptly described as a tiny fortune, but tiny was smaller than small, and if they had moved even further out to the fringes of London, things probably wouldn't be much cheaper. At the same time, they would have to endure putting up with clients ranting about travelling to Croydon, or Romford, or (God Forbid) Pinner!

The office, the new business, Tina's wages, the whole adventure, had been funded initially by a combination of Juliet's savings, and a sizeable loan from Clive, an actor she met and then married while working at a publishing house who dealt with such high flying, high earning clients. Some of those clients had been persuaded to make the journey across to Juliet's agency and become their early stream of revenue and so, to begin with, on that first day the potential for this new venture looked to be engagingly diverse. Which was another way of saying, no one had a clue how much they might actually make.

Or lose.

Eventually, they became hungry from a diet of bubbly alcohol and had gone in search of what lunchtime delights their new working location could offer. With the excitement of the moment still in their blood, they had explored Islington, looking for something a little bit special to celebrate this dizzying dive into the unknown. Tina knew Clive liked to have a good time, that it was his favourite thing to do, but even she was surprised when they ended up, just a short walk from the new office, at Restaurant Noir, a venue infamous for being hideously expensive. Clive had waved aside Juliet's objections, and that afternoon lunch had been lavish, opulent, and so much fun. Such was their spending power that afternoon, combined with the amount of ruckus the three of them created from their own good-humoured mood, the head chef himself had joined their table.

At first sight, Jacque Noir appeared to Tina as a charming middle-aged man, much of the charm springing from his beguiling French accent and a twinkle of charisma beyond anything she had previously encountered. Every time they tried to leave, Jacque produced one more delicacy to try, one more wine they had to experience. One more liquor to taste with one last speciality cheese. It had carried on to the point where Tina thought she would explode. Or pass out. Or both.

At some point, Jacque's moody brother, Pascal, had joined them, mainly at Jacque's insistence, and the drink had flowed again, the table reinvigorated by fresh, conversational blood.

Kind of. If you considered Pascal's single syllable answers as a conversation.

This celebration lunch had been the time of her life. A moment Tina would look back on and smile, warmly, deeply. It had become something that she thought about while giving out coffee and hot chocolate to the homeless. Nothing to do with guilt, but more the self-assurance that if she could have such happiness, it was only right that her future self should distribute that joy, in whatever small way she could.

At the end of this legendary lunchtime session, when they were so drunk, they had almost drunk themselves sober, taxis were ordered, and Clive had produced his credit card, as he usually did, only to be waved away by Jacque.

"No!" Jacque had said standing dramatically on the table and ripping the somewhat lengthy bill in two. "Next time you can pay, but today, today we celebrate the opening of Juliet Raphael, *Literary Agency to the Stars*. We celebrate the future."

In amongst this chaos, where Clive had again attempted, not too strongly, to pay, Tina had seen Pascal looking ominously at his brother and at the torn bill. A complex flow of emotions lit the younger man's eyes; anger, frustration; finally, capitulation. He caught Tina staring at him and looked away, quickly making his excuses to leave and prepare for the evening menu.

Peering now through the darkened door at the piles of dusty furniture, Tina watched him go in her memory. A ghost of a time when they had few thoughts towards the uncertain future. Tina still did not fully understand why the brothers had split so acrimoniously, why they had closed their wonderfully successful restaurant, or why indeed they no longer spoke. She only knew that missing this place and the memories it invoked, had become a point of personal pain for her, and she wished it could just all come back to being.

To being there.

Nothing though was the same now. Juliet had divorced Clive, for wholly understandable reasons, and the business of being a literary agent had begun to suffer without Clive and his circle of contacts. His indisputably high level of networking. Juliet was struggling to keep the wolf from the door, and the one grace of fine weather on the horizon had been Jacque and his recipe book, but even that had proved problematic.

Deadlines had been missed, the Christmas market was forsaken for Easter, and this in turn rescheduled for a summer release that would give them plenty of challenges to think about. Tina hoped there would be better times ahead, but as she turned her back on the closed restaurant, she couldn't help but wonder if they had already seen the best of times.

Tina weaved her way back to Islington Green and found a park bench that was empty, apart from a small Chinese student who really wasn't taking up too much room. Taking out her Thai curry and spicy potatoes, she sat and ate quietly, and thought once more about the pressing problems of the present, rather than the absence of a happier past. She thought instead of Juliet's upcoming award ceremony. An event Juliet wanted to attend but felt, for her own reasons, she couldn't attend alone.

So strange to think of Juliet, the most independent woman Tina knew without looking in the mirror or visiting her mother's grave, as being dependent on a suitor to accompany her anywhere. And yet, this thing had got into her sister's head, that if Juliet couldn't find a date while in the judgemental company of her peers, then she couldn't hold her head high; couldn't put to rest the corpse of a messy divorce. Tina knew better than to argue with such faulty logic.

Once Juliet had made her mind up about something, changing that course was an unlikely scenario. Juliet had acted like this from pretty much the moment she had been born. Tina had been ten, and so excited to get a younger sister, at last, and then as the years wore on, realised that siblings could be a burden as much as a joy.

So, if Juliet couldn't be persuaded that attending a gala dinner on one's own was not a clear public display of some kind of existential crisis, then she needed to be found a date.

It was as simple as that.

Thus far, despite Tina's best attempts, Juliet had failed systematically at this task of securing a Plus-One.

It wasn't that Juliet was unlikable, although, yes, sometimes she was… Unlikeable. And it wasn't that Juliet was blunt, rude, and occasionally arrogant, although, yes, she could also be these things, as well, on occasion, that is to say, during her waking hours she could be all of these things and more without even ever seeming to tax herself. It was just that Juliet was Juliet, and men either liked that sort of woman, or they didn't, and at the moment, the didn'ts were seemingly easier to find than the dids.

The list of available suitors was also getting shorter with every passing request. Tina had thought about Pascal, who Juliet clearly liked, but who was impossible to get into a conversation about anything much at all. Particularly it would seem any conversation that had anything at all to do with Juliet, so that seemed a non-starter.

The obvious answer was, of course, the least appealing.

Jacque Noir!

Yes, that would take some persuading, thought Tina as she popped the last spicy potato in her mouth. Unless she could coax Juliet with the ploy that perhaps this could generate some extra publicity for the book. If Juliet attended with Jacque as a kind of ruse, something to get the gossip rags writing about… Stuff. Then this could, perhaps, be good for business.

That had to be a winning argument with Juliet. Or at least an argument that Juliet would not be able to instantly dismiss.

Tina began to spoon away her curry with more enthusiasm, gaining a look of concern from the Chinese student, whose lunch seemed to consist of half a tomato and a bit of lettuce. She closed the lid on the plastic cup and folded the greasy potato bag. Time to get back to the office; she needed a cup of tea and some chocolate so she could formulate her arguments as to why it would be an excellent idea for Juliet to attend the Gala dinner with a man she loathed.

Plus, Juliet would never ask him herself, her pride would not allow it, so Tina would need to persuade Jacque, a walking example of why excessive narcissism is terrible for the soul, to ask Juliet if she would accompany him to the Gala.

And he had to ask it in such a way that it sounded like a business proposition and not another type of proposition.

And he had to do it nicely.

And soon.

It was Thursday afternoon, and the Gala was tomorrow evening.

At the same time, she would need to be there, in close proximity to oversee the whole Gala evening, just to make sure things didn't go totally pear-shaped. For this she was going to need her own plus-one in the shape of Ron, another man who would need to be manipulated into the right course of action, in this case, asking Tina if he could accompany her to the Gala.

And like Jacque, Ron had to think it was his idea in the first place. It would mean Ron having to endure an evening of Juliet's weapons-grade sarcasm, but he seemed to be made of stern stuff. Spontaneous crying aside.

All she needed to get her plan rolling was Ron to answer his damn phone and Jacque to finally crawl out of whichever dark pit he had hidden away in.

Tina took a calming deep breath. She knew from bitter experience that manipulating others, in particular men, could be a slow and drawn-out process. Today, however, was stretching her patience towards the sharp edge of thin.

Tina checked her bag. She was going to need a bigger box of chocolates if she had half a chance of sorting all this out in such a short time frame.

With that in mind, she was up and heading towards her favourite sweet shop, when she heard her name called out, loudly, urgently, and with a French twang to it. In the distance, Jacque was standing outside the door that led to their office. Behind him loomed a cab driver, standing, it seemed to Tina, close enough to the Frenchman to grab him, should he decide to do a runner.

Quickly she checked her purse for cash, then with a sigh, walked slowly towards the urgently beckoning man who was dressed in what appeared to be very soiled trousers. Not a particularly auspicious start to phase one of her plan to save everyone from themselves.

Chapter 8

Pascal

Pascal sat on the floor of his café, his long legs hugged to his chest, not in any kind of trauma, but simply to hide his feet from the man currently banging on the locked front door.

"Brother," the voice implored and then continued in rapid-fire French. "Pascal, please, I must talk to you. Please. I am begging you, is that what you want to hear? Is it? If it is, I am doing it. I am doing it now!"

"Well," Rose said from her position next to him on the floor. "My French is a little rusty since I split with Jacque, but it does sound like he is desperate to attain your forgiveness."

Pascal glanced at her, allowing one of his famous dark looks to say more than words ever could. He did not care if his brother was desperate, but he did not care to confront him about it either; hence he and Rose now hid on the floor of his own café, behind the counter, like a couple of school kids bunking off school.

He had been fortunate enough to glance out of the window in time to see Jacque paying a cab driver, or rather, directing Tina to pay the cab driver. After a brief discussion, which Pascal hoped would end with Tina pushing his brother in front of a bus, a slow-moving one that would only cause him harm rather than be fatal, Tina had opened the door that led to Juliet's office and ushered Jacque towards it. His brother, however, had glanced across the road, and presumably having seen his brother peeking through the blinds, had scurried over, narrowly avoiding a collision with a fast-paced messenger bike.

The cyclist had aggressively blown his whistle at Jacque who had stopped dead, given a rude gesture, then hurried off when the cyclist stopped and stared at him through mirror-shaded sunglasses. All of which had given Pascal enough time to lock the door, grab Rose and drag her to the floor behind the cake counter.

"What the actual fuck?" had been Rose's immediate reaction to this, but once she heard the banging at the door, and the shouts of Jacque, she sighed in realisation. "So, you two are still doing this then?"

"Oui, we are still doing this, we are still doing this until one of us is no longer living."

"Right," Rose said, through a long drawn out sigh. "So long as it's not overly dramatic or anything, that's the main thing, eh?"

Pascal ignored this provocation and sat back, quietly waiting for the noise outside to go away.

"Okay," Rose said when it became clear Pascal wasn't going to get up or comment further. "I guess we can carry on with our meeting then. Although I would just say, for the record, that if you really wanted to avoid the man, perhaps opening a café just around the corner from your old restaurant and just across the road from his literary agent would seem to lack… Forward planning."

"Noted!" Pascal said, resting his head back on the comforting cold surface of the cupboard door and closing his eyes to the world around him.

In this self-imposed darkness, he heard Rose sigh, again, and the faint rustling of something being pulled from a bag. A laptop beeped, and soon she began to list the various results of various spreadsheets that apparently showed various predictions for various nasty ends for Pascal's café. Despite her welcoming personality, Rose could be, when doing her job, one very effective buzz kill.

Pascal refused to release his eyes to this reality, but regardless, Rose talked on about income to expenditure shortfalls, until Pascal finally capitulated and turned to stare at her with animated seriousness. It was difficult sometimes to match the businesswoman she had become with the younger woman he met by chance on a sunny day in Monaco. Many years though, had passed since that fateful day. Many rainy days and much water had flown beneath the bridges of all their lives.

Back then, just before he met Rose for the first time, Pascal had just finished Cookery College and was helping at his father's restaurant in Paris. Working all the crap kitchen jobs, but learning, always learning. Dedicated to being good enough to make his parents proud. To be their legacy. Focused as he was, even his unwavering dedication could not always work in tandem with Pascal's natural youthful feelings of wanderlust. The need to see the world. Or at least, to find other places, other dishes to cook, to taste, to learn from.

To placate the wanderlust, Pascal would travel away from Paris, to areas that gave him a fresh view of life. To stay true to his passion for learning all things cookery, he tended to travel in a direction that brought him, at one point or another, back to his grandparents' home in the South of France. They were both renowned cooks themselves, now retired, but

Pascal could spend weeks here, learning, relaxing, and for the most part, being himself. Time could pass so quickly when he stayed with the older couple in their little cottage on the hillsides of a village that Pascal viewed as being beyond beauty.

Nestled into the hillside of Pinella, on the South Coast of France and overlooking the glittering Mediterranean, the house was just a brisk walk to the town of Menton or a short, but expensive cab ride to Monte Carlo in the other direction. The village itself sat just outside the scope of tourism, but close enough to the coast for Pascal to buy fresh fish and lobster directly from the few boatmen still operating off the beaches.

Throughout his life, Pascal thought of himself as being at his happiest here in this moment. Walking the many steps down to the beach each day, never tiring of the multi-coloured doors that littered the pathway down, or the procession of hungry cats that begged for attention, or ignored him completely. And then, on the beach, before the tourists could arrive, he would buy Sea Bass, or a Skate, perhaps Mackerel for a change. This he carried back up past the coloured doors and cats of furious curiosity until he arrived at the small red garden door that led to a tiny courtyard, where he could gut the fish and prepare them to be cooked.

His grandmother would appear at this point, not to interfere, as much as an older woman can resist not interfering, but to guide, to help, to illuminate Pascal in all those forgotten ways of infusing the best taste from these simple fish. Everything he had ever needed to know about cooking fish had come from this one woman during those idyllic summer days.

Occasionally, rarely would be more accurate, and only when he needed money, Jacque would join them. He would appear out of the blue, often requiring someone to pay his cab fare, and insisting they eat out, even if Pascal had almost completed the meal for the day. Jacque was the apple of their grandfather's eye, the man of the family who was most admired, the one everyone saw as a torchbearer for the family's legacy.

How wrong they had all been!

Outside Pascal's Café, Jacque's demands and banging got louder and louder until he finished with a rapid tattoo, a lot of swearing in French, and then silence.

"And now," Rose said, "I really am glad I don't remember much of my French."

Pascal found that Rose, like most English people, spoke other languages with a grudging lack of enthusiasm that comes from having the whole world understand your native tongue. It wasn't that she couldn't speak French, it's just that her accent was so terrible and her pronunciation so varied, that most French people she interacted with wondered if it was some kind of example of this famous English humour they kept hearing about.

It was in this manner that Pascal had first met Rose.

Jacque had been in town to raise money for his latest and greatest sure-fire money-making scheme. Something to do with spices and suppliers who had no vision of the future, and he was well placed to take advantage of this unique opportunity. And so on…

It wasn't mentioned directly, but Jacque hinted that their father's parents, who remained forever in Paris, had passed on the opportunity of a lifetime, and so here he was, in the South of France, talking to their mother's parents. Both of whom were considered far more approachable to the idea of lending money than their Parisian counterparts, who were much older, and much less likely to be mesmerised by Jacque's charm.

Pascal had turned off in the first few minutes of the conversation. He had no money and would never be asked to help, so all this talk, all this nonsense, all this was just a distraction from his enjoyment. His moment of culinary creation and peace.

He had left the chatter of money and golden opportunities, and stood outside the red wooden gate, at the very top of the stone stairs that lead down towards the town and the beach. Here he could see the houses and gardens laid out below in a tapestry of colour. Beyond, on a clear day, Italy was somewhere in the shimmering distance. In the other direction, much closer, the opulence of Monaco and the distant fake yellow of the beaches at Cannes.

Standing there, in the still of the afternoon, with the sun peeling away towards the distant Mediterranean horizon, he would be at peace, his dark moods, his worries of the future, of the present, would fade and he would recall again the most recent recipe imparted to him by his grandmother. Reciting the details in his mind, hard coding his brain to remember every single tiny significant detail that lifted a fish dish from palatable to mouth-watering genius.

Jacque had appeared silently behind him at that moment, his cigarillo smoke announcing his arrival before he spoke. He wanted to go into Monaco, take in the sights, wanted his brother's company, he wanted to do it right now.

To Pascal's mind, this translated as; Jacque had spoken to their grandfather about the business idea, and the old man remained unconvinced, and Jacque knew better than push too far, so wanted to make himself scarce. Give his grandfather time to think it all through. As with most things, Jacque hated to do anything alone, hated to be without an audience, and so they both ended up together in the grandeur of Monte Carlo.

At first, they had been content to wander aimlessly, marvelling at the sports cars outside the casino, and wondering at the cost of Fabergé eggs that were for sale in the heavily plate glassed shop windows, but without a price tag. Somewhere along this route of playing tourist in a neighbouring country, they had stumbled across Rose as she sauntered along with a friend, map in hand. The two young women were glancing left and right, walking a few paces, and then stopping. They might as well have worn a T-shirt that said, *Tourist*.

Rose had been wearing red shorts and a red bikini top, with some kind of red blouse that flowed around at the whim of a summer breeze. It was an outfit that perfectly showed off her angular hips and flattened stomach, and a skin so dark it almost absorbed the bright sunlight. Her large wide sunglasses emerged from a short afro in such a way that when she smiled, even Pascal couldn't help smiling. When she had smiled at them, without knowing it, she drew them into her world.

Jacque took control, of course, first offering directions to the two women, then offering coffee, then lunch and then suddenly, out of nowhere, Pascal found that he was actually enjoying himself. Enjoying the moment of being with people he didn't know, enjoying something outside of cooking and the kitchen. This was always the secret of his brother, his ability to charm anyone, even Pascal.

Sitting in his café, on the floor, with Rose next to him, listening to his brother ranting outside the door, Pascal tried to remember the other woman in Monaco, the one who travelled with Rose, but who clearly had other things on her mind. Things that kept her smile from fully opening. For the life of him, he could not remember her name or even her face.

There was half a memory of a cropped T-shirt that displayed a tattoo, words that ran from under the belt of her blue denim shorts, and over her skin before disappearing again under yet more material.

Jacque had, of course, asked about it, even asked if he could see the whole sentence, just out of curiosity of course, but he had been denied, and when she explained it was something to do with poetry, he had lost interest. Pascal's focus at the time had been on Rose, but as was the way with beautiful women, her focus had been on Jacque.

All the pretty ones liked Jacque, liked his roughish humour, his bad boy demeanour, his lust for the exciting and the instant. Few had time for Pascal and his dark creative moods. It had been the story of their upbringing, something Pascal had resented, but over time, had learnt to live with.

Lunch with these two young women had morphed into an invite by Jacque to their grandparents' place for a fish supper; a fish dish that Jacque proclaimed to be as near to ecstasy as one can have; outside of bed.

The remark brought a flirty response from Rose and then, all of a sudden, they were walking up the stone steps towards their grandparents' house, Rose and Jacque already hand in hand, Pascal and the tattooed denim-shorts girl sauntering along behind, feeling like the spare parts that they were.

When they arrived, Pascal's world changed.

In the blink of an eye.

Some people may wonder forever where and when their lives zigged when they should have zagged, or when things started, inexorably down the road to the way they were. Pascal was not amongst them. He knew exactly that moment. It was in a small courtyard, behind a bright red gate, under a crimson, scarlet Mediterranean sunset. Here their father had appeared unexpectedly from the house, a sight that startled Pascal, as he usually loathed to visit his in-laws, and then he saw his mother behind him, a slightly worried frown creasing her otherwise beautiful features.

"Good news," their father had said without preamble. "Good news, the best."

He went on to explain that a restaurant had come on the market in London, one that offered them access to top-class clientele and a pathway to greater recognition. A place where their father could be recognised, at last, as one of the most celebrated chefs of our age. A recognition he struggled to attain in Paris, amongst the incredible competition of the self-proclaimed culinary capital, but one that he felt in London, was perhaps more... Realistic.

"Eventually," his mother had cautioned. "We hope eventually this will come to pass."

Their mother was so much younger than their father but, in many ways, years older. She stood there in that moment, shoulder to shoulder with her mother, who quietly held onto her daughter's arm in a supportive way. The older woman's hair was tied back in the same way as her daughter, only the grey strands in those long locks separating them as mother and child rather than sisters.

"Of course, it will come to pass," his father had said. "Of course, it will. What can stop it? We are the family Noir."

It was easy, sometimes, to see which parent Jacque took after.

"What's happening?" the denim wearing poetry tattooed woman had asked as the excited French dialogue flowed over her head.

"We are moving to London," Pascal could remember saying. "We are moving there next month."

"Oh really," Rose had asked, turning to Jacque for the answer. "Whereabouts?"

Jacque had shrugged the name at her. "A place called Soho?"

"Wow, that's not far from where I live," she said. "Fancy that."

"Yes," Jacque had replied, standing close to her, "I do fancy that."

And so family Noir, much to the disappointment of both sets of grandparents, moved to a Britain where Brexit remained just the fevered dream of various gammon faced men. A fallacy yet to be invoked.

"Do you think he's gone?" Rose asked, dragging Pascal's thoughts into the present.

She turned to peek over the counter.

"Honestly," she said, with one hand on her back. "I think I'm past caring. If I sit on this floor any longer, my designer trousers will never forgive me."

She pattered away on her small heels to the door, smoothing away the non-existent creases on her expensive looking red trouser suit and cautiously peeked around the blinds. After a short moment, she gave the all-clear and returned to the counter where she dragged Pascal to his feet.

Placing her laptop on the white surface, she pointed at the latest Excel sheet that been had summoned, apparently, from the Cloud!

"You see here," she pointed at one red line. A line that seemed to start high and then climb to even greater aspirational heights. "This is your fixed costs, which because of the location, the rent, business rates, and so on… Well, they are somewhat high."

Her well-manicured red nails danced across the keyboard, and a friendlier green line appeared to overlay the red line. In comparison, this line started life near to the bottom of the graph and mostly stayed there, looking like the brain scan of a coma patient.

"And this represents your overall takings so far, which, as you can see, are largely pathetic."

"That is a little, as you English say, on the side of strong."

"On the strong-*side*, we say strong-side. And no, it is not." She turned to Pascal, tilting her neck upwards to stare into dark eyes that loomed above her and smiled. A sad little smile. "It's very simple. You are just not bringing in enough customers, and the customers you are bringing in will not sustain the future of this business. In fact, if you were anyone else I would recommend you shut up shop today."

"Things cannot be that bad, why only yesterday I had two new customers in a row."

"Really? I was unaware of this sudden upturn in your fortunes. What did they buy?"

"One bought a latte, the other wanted to know when the dry-cleaning place that used to be here had closed down."

"So technically, not actually a customer. And I think we can both agree the sale of a single latte every day is going to make a difference of approximately fuck all to your takings." She turned off her laptop by closing the screen and let out a resigned sigh. "Your choice is simple, Pascal, either close down now or find yourself filing for bankruptcy in three months. Possibly less."

Pascal turned away, eyes closed, his hands gripping the counter in front of him as though it were the bridge of a ship in a stormy ocean.

"These are my options?"

"Pretty much. Unless you have an undisclosed amount of money somewhere that I don't know about."

"I do not."

Everything, all his savings, his inheritance, had gone into the lease and refitting the shop! And his divorce. And paying some debts that he had been partially responsible for while running Restaurant Noir with his brother. Not to mention a nasty addiction he had to expensive red wine.

"Or," Rose said slowly. "You have a hidden talent you could exploit."

Pascal laughed; a bitter bark of a noise that made Rose jump slightly. "Perhaps I should learn the juggling. Is this your suggestion?"

"Maybe, or maybe... Maybe you could... Write a book?"

Pascal turned from the counter and glared at Rose with such ferocity that she actually took a step back. Appalled at her reaction to him, at his part in that moment, he looked away, at the cappuccino maker, at the dirty cups in the sink, at anything other than her concerned face.

"You are speaking with the wrong brother." He said carefully and clearly.

"Am I?"

Despite himself, he looked again at her, this time with a mixture of surprise and perhaps even fear.

"Oh, come on Pascal, everyone banged on about Jacque being the Master Chef at Restaurant Noir, but every time I visited the kitchen, there you were, covered in all sorts of stuff from cooking and preparing and serving. And there was Jacque, in his spotless chef whites."

Pascal remembered that too. Jacque, always with a drink in his hand, drifting through the kitchen, occasionally barking orders, sometimes firing people, often out front, with the public, taking a bow for whatever meal he had just taken credit for. Pascal never objected, never fought this hierarchy. For him, the truth was in the food, the taste, the moment, the delight of the meal.

Nothing else mattered more to him. Nothing. When an order was completed, when the challenge was accomplished, the best had been obtained from the ingredients, it was time then to start the next meal.

Onwards, ever onwards.

"I remember the same thing when I first saw your mother and father working together, your mother covered in various ingredients and your father…" She stopped as Pascal's face darkened. "I'm sorry Pascal, I forgot that you… That your mother's memory is still… That…"

"It's okay Rose, sometimes it is good to remember…"

A silence stretched between them, and he could see she regretted mentioning his mother, regretted bringing back the pain of recent times. She packed away her laptop, walked over to him, and on tiptoes, planted a single dry kiss on his cheek.

"Think it over Pascal. You either start serving food in here or…" She looked about the tiny café. "Or you write a book about food, or…"

He looked at her questioningly.

"Or you find something else to do," she finished.

Without further words she left, the small door ringing its bell as she exited onto the busy London street beyond, leaving Pascal to dwell on his future in the fading light of a late winter's afternoon.

Chapter 9

Jacque

Jacque rushed up the stairs to Juliet's office with a furious stomping of small feet and fist balled anger, a childish display that left him breathless and slightly dizzy by the time he reached the second floor. He stopped for a moment to recompose himself, leaning on the door and gripping a sign that said; *Juliet Raphael, Literary Agent to the Stars*. Jacque sneered at the wording, just as he always did. He was the only star she now represented, something perhaps for both of them to think about.

He barged in, almost knocking Tina over who was bending over to fetch milk from the fridge.

"Goodness, Mr Noir, you took me by surprise."

"Jacque Noir has asked you many times to use his first name, has he not? And also, you should not be surprised when I take you by surprise. You are a woman; it is only natural you should be surprised at the strength of your feelings for such a man as Jacque Noir..."

Jacque paused as this outburst, plus the recent stair stomping left him with small stars shooting about his field of vision. He closed the door behind him and stumbled forward, ending up in Tina's wide-eyed embrace.

Jacque stood holding her for a moment, mostly in an effort to maintain his balance, then lunged in close to her, enjoying the smell of her perfume and the feel of her womanly curves pressing into his own body. He turned on the charm, the smile, the power of Jacque Noir, the man loathed by husbands of beautiful women and loved by the wives of men less charismatically powerful than himself.

Jacque knew he wasn't the best-looking man in the world. He took that from his father, while Pascal inherited their mother's otherworldly beauty, albeit in a rugged male form, and of course her dark moods. Jacque wished that at least he could have inherited his mother's hair or her height. Instead, he was short, slightly plump, and with white hair that was always edging towards a somewhat suboptimal comb-over. Yet all of this Jacque overcame with diligent use of radiant blue eyes, and his megawatt enhanced, some might say X-rated smile.

People who met Jacque for the first time, knowing his reputation for womanising, for continually referring to himself in the arrogance of the third person, often set out in a determined fashion to hate him in person as much as they hated him from the close-up distance of a TV screen. Yet they were nearly always becalmed by his charm, frequently becoming a fan for life, and in many encounters, leaving with his sperm in one orifice or another.

Often it was both.

"Oh, Mr Noir," Tina said, squirming under his unexpected embrace. "I think your belt buckle is sticking into my hip."

"Ma Cherie, I do not think that is Jacque Noir's belt buckle!"

Jacque watched Tina's eyes go wide, and with a series of sudden eel-like squirming movements, she was free from him, leaving him clutching at empty air and almost falling flat on his face.

"Mr Noir!" Tina seemed on the verge of saying something, but then an inner calm appeared to wash through her. "Juliet is out of the office right now, but I do know that she wants to see you. Urgently!"

"Jacque, please, Jacque Noir wants you to call him Jacque."

"And Tina Raphael is happy to call you Mr Noir, and happier still if Mr Noir were to keep his hands to himself."

Tina remained an elusive conquest for Jacque. One of particular interest, partly because of this elusive nature, and partly because Jacque had often indulged in idle fantasies over the exact size and shape of Tina's breasts. These were, in contrast to Juliet's modest bra size, very much on the generous size, her summer blouses often suffering a certain button straining whenever she laughed.

Jacque smiled his most engaging smile, a slight tilt of the head, and an almost, but not quite, apologetic look in his twinkling blue eyes.

"Of course, ma Cherie, of course, Jacque Noir is your humble servant in all things."

He gave a short bow, then stood, hands in pockets, looking about the office as though he had just got here and nothing untoward had ever occurred.

If the movement seemed practised to Tina, that's only because it was; a highly coveted and superior tactic that Jacque pulled out of his charm offensive when needed. He enjoyed the seduction of women, all women of any kind, all body types, all skin colours, all types of personalities and behaviourisms. Of all the things that could be said of Jacque Noir, he was, without a doubt, bipartisan in the extreme when it came to the purist of a good fuck.

However, and this was as important to his ego as the air was to his lungs, these women needed to desire Jacque, they needed to want to be seduced, they needed to be needed. It took time to seduce the difficult ones, but in the end, all succumbed to his charm, but they had to succumb willingly, there had to be that delicious moment, where they desired him, as much as he needed them to desire him.

There had been a time, in Restaurant Noir, when he came across a lower-ranking chef in the alley outside the restaurant, back when his father still ran his place. Back before his mother...

Back then!

This... Chef! What had been his name? Adam something? This Adam was involved in a conversation with a young waiter, an attractive young man at least half the age of the balding pot-bellied Adam who loomed in front of him. He stood, aggressively blocking the younger man's way, and although Jacque had not heard the whole conversation, he had heard enough. The promises Adam made, and indeed the threats he uttered to this young man had not been implicit, merely implied. Suggested scenarios on what could happen for the best, and what might occur for the worst. It all depended on whether or not a certain cock was sucked, right there and right then.

Jacque had pulled back into the shadows, vanishing before either man could see him. He tried to forget about it, but days later he got into an argument with Adam, one Jacque perhaps manufactured, he couldn't be sure, but it was a roof lifter. Had Adam *whatever his name* not resigned on the spot, Jacque would have fired him.

After this incident his father had shrugged, sitting in his office, sleeves rolled up, his usual sporting paper held loosely in one-hand.

"I'll make some calls," his father had said without emotion. "Get a replacement for tonight."

His mother had been a little more visceral regarding the whole matter, but kept her remarks to a simple; "I'm glad he left. I did not like this man. He was bad with the staff."

Jacque and his mother had exchanged looks that seemed to indicate they both knew what *bad* meant.

Years later and the incident remained in his mind, and at times like this, it came back to haunt him. Returning to remind him that while Jacque might play with few rules when it came to the opposite sex, he did have one golden rule that he never broke.

No meant no.

Jacque failed to understand men who used their position of power to obtain sex, either with promises or threats, or a combination of both. Where was the fun in that, he would muse, often while thrusting into a woman bent double over wherever they were, screaming with the enhanced pleasure that came from an illicit fucking.

For Jacque, the simple act of seduction was so much fun, often more fun than the actual sex.

"Juliet will be with you shortly, she's just messaged me to say she really needs to speak to you," Tina said while reading from her phone.

"Oh?" Jacque tried to sound unconcerned, but he was far from convincing even to himself. "And how is our preciously beautiful Juliet? You know. After all that she has been through."

He could see Tina melt at the thought of him being concerned for another human being. Concern and sympathy, he found, were always clean and efficient methods to bed a woman. Females were, by and large, caring creatures.

"Well…" Tina said hesitantly. As though she was giving each word careful consideration before their utterance could prove to be a mistake. Jacque knew this wasn't her strong suit. It wasn't even a suit she preferred to play. It was, in fact, a suit in opposition to that of how her soul linked itself to the universe.

"Yes?" Jacque prompted, preparing to say something else that was designed to manipulate Tina on an emotional level, to get her guard down and set her talking. In the event he didn't need to bother as the damn in Tina's reserve had broken, and she began to spill out the problems of Juliet's world, as seen from her perspective.

Jacque listened attentively, perched on the edge of the desk, his face impassive; a father listening without judgement to the worried child about the non-existent monster under the bed. When she finished, he sat for a moment, digesting all of the various problems, First-World though they were, and allowed his mind to search through the information given and find a way to turn all this to his advantage.

"I believe, ma Cherie," he said eventually, aware that his continued silence had begun to concern Tina. "That Jacque Noir may have a solution to all of these problems that trouble you so."

"Oh? Oh, that's great. Really great…. Only…. What are they?"

"Well, it is obvious, is it not? Juliet needs a date for the awards ceremony and Jacque Noir is, as it so happens, able to be her consort for that evening."

"Oh, Mr Noir, I had assumed you were already going with someone, you know, one of those young dancer types I see you photographed with in the papers."

"Of course, I have several women who call me incessantly to see if they can be, as you English say, my Plus-One." Jacque lied with the barefaced ability of someone who had worked for years in catering. In truth, he had not even considered going.

These award ceremony dinners were almost exclusively filled with self-ingratiating backstabbers who liked the sound of their own voices and had become obsessed with the importance of their own importance. He had, of course, received many awards when Noir Restaurant had still been open, collected them with Pascal as his silent shadow, and gave yet another speech that thanked everyone involved for the splendour of the team effort. This year, his book would not even be released until long after the awards, and Restaurant Noir was closed, so there seemed little point in attending. Even the thought of a free bar was not enough to tempt him.

Although...

If he were to do Juliet a favour, then perhaps she would get off his back on the delays to volume two of the cookery book. A book that in truth existed in title only.

Yes, that might actually work, and who knows, perhaps under the influence of enough champagne, Juliet would, at last, become a conquest. If that should happen... The playing field would be a different place the next day and if he didn't get the chance to sleep with her, if she refused, yet again, then perhaps he could persuade her that sex had not occurred because of his heightened chivalry. That he alone had been the one to decide against the possible risks of mixing business with pleasure.

Basically, it was a win-win opportunity that was simply too good to miss.

"But if you have all these women wanting to go with you," Tina was saying. "Won't they be disappointed if you attend with Juliet?"

"They will be crushed and probably never sleep... I mean, speak with me again. But for you, Tina, to help you, and of course to help your emotionally damaged sister I am willing to…"

"Juliet is going to take a lot of persuasion to attend with you." Tina interrupted. "Especially after the last time."

"Last time?"

"Yes," Tina said, with a knowing nod, which remained opaque to Jacque.

"Trust me, Tina," he said to cover his confusion. "I will talk to her. I will… Create a moment that is an everlasting truth in the story of us all."

Tina sat back, mouth open, clearly she didn't know how to respond to this crescendo in the conversation. She looked left and right and finally fled to the safety of the mini kitchen.

"Coffee?" she asked, holding out a jar of instant.

Jacque stared at it with the eyes of a man who had been presented with an extremely shitty end of a very short stick. He continued staring until she put the jar back on the shelf.

"Maybe I should pop out and get you a real coffee, I'll go see if anything's still open," Tina said, grabbing her bag and flew from the office before Jacque even had the chance to pretend to offer her some money.

Alone in the office, he sauntered through to Juliet's inner chamber and approached the expansive window. From here he watched Tina's progress down the street and over the road to Pascal's. There she read the closed sign and carried on walking. A few moments later, the blinds at the café door were pressed apart by an unseen hand and then disappeared just as quickly.

"Merde," Jacque muttered to himself. Pascal had been there all the time. That damn brother of his, stubborn was not the word he wanted to use. Just like his mother, *their* mother. Strong and silent, but when offended, that strength, that silence, it could turn a minor slight into a family feud. A simple family lunch could seem eternal under such circumstances.

However, there was nothing to be done. Jacque knew this. Only time would bring Pascal back to him, although right now, time was something of a precious commodity. As he watched from his vantage point, a familiar woman, dark of skin and dressed in red, emerged from Pascal's shop door, laptop case forever over one shoulder, and Jacque experienced an unfamiliar pang of jealousy. He shook it off as fast as it tried to invade his brain. There had been a time, perhaps, when Pascal might have tried to be with Rose, but that was long ago, way back when they first met. A time that was mixed within so much history, so many women, that Jacque even struggled to remember where he first met Rose.

Had it been in Paris?

Perhaps.

He remembered it was shortly before their father had moved the family, lock stock and cats, to London, seeking fame and recognition. The sort of stardust that was not part of the busy Parisian restaurant scene. Or at least, it was, but there were too many chefs, spoiling the broth of greatness; and blocking the true celebrity status their father sought.

And so, to London it was, where a Frenchman could be a celebrity through the grace of being exotically French, even if Paris, which was rammed with Frenchmen of a similar calibre, was a mere few hours away by train.

Yes, he thought, it had been around that time he first met Rose because she had been his initial contact here, his grounding into a city he knew from visits, but did not know intimately enough to take it by storm.

Rose had been his local guide, she helped him at first simply to understand the bizarre English customs of queuing, and being polite, and holding open doors for people one did not know and would never meet again. He even began to understand how to apologise for things that were not actually the fault of those who said these apologies, although, in the several decades he had lived here, he had rarely used this knowledge to any significant effect.

And then, somewhere along the line, Jacque had decided Rose was the one. Partly he suspected because Pascal was always sniffing around, waiting to take second servings from his cast-off females, and for some reason, this time, it bothered him, even though it had never bothered him before. On a whim, he married Rose and loved her, and adored her. He gave her a home, a child and lavished her with all that he could think she would need.

Everything except fidelity.

Eventually, the only thing she was missing was a divorce.

They separated when Yvonne was twelve and old enough to understand what it all would mean, and what it all wouldn't mean. In fact, their only daughter had been stoic about the whole thing, less damaged than apparently relieved they had *finally allowed their broken lives to be an open book to themselves* or something along those lines. There were times when Jacque could see the disadvantages of lavishing an expensive poetic education on their daughter.

From the semi-darkness of Juliet's office, Jacque watched an indelible fragment of his past walk away, watched as Rose glanced at her phone as she went, and waved a cab down with her free hand. Of course, two cabs made a beeline for the black beauty dressed in the expensive red business suit, and Jacque suppressed a smile as the winning taxi whisked her away.

He glanced back at the café and locked eyes unexpectedly with Pascal who was staring up at the office window, his face unreadable in this darkened cloudy afternoon. Jacque stared back at his brother, until the younger man disappeared into his domain, the lights flicking off and announcing that to run over there now would be a waste of time.

He turned to the office and gathered his thoughts. Juliet would be due back soon, and he needed some pretty strong arguments if he were to convince Juliet that he could help her in this moment of need and become her Plus-One. Despite his bravado with Tina, he knew this would be, as he once heard the long-gone English Brexit Prime Minister say in her faltering voice; '*A tough sell*'.

It had been as much of a flagrant understatement then as it was now.

In deeper thought than lunchtime alcohol usually allowed him, Jacque moved about the office, looking at the books on the shelves and playing with the chairs, until it came to him that Tina always kept a bottle of something or other in the filing cabinet. Jacque's search was rewarded with an unopened vodka bottle filed under P for reasons that were not entirely clear.

He cracked the seal on the bottle and sat in Juliet's chair, feet on the desk, drinking liberally from the bottle. He didn't bother with a glass; it had been that sort of a day. He'd just have a little drop, just to steady his nerves for when Juliet arrived back at the office and he made his play.

Jacque glanced at the space on his wrist where his watch had been and swore. He took another swig and wondered when Tina was going to get back with his coffee. And when his life was going to get back to being wonderful. Rolex-watch-wearing-wonderful.

Chapter 10

Ron

Ron parked his Jag with such excitement, it was a moment before he realised he'd blocked in a police car by parking across the entrance to the police station car park. Fortunately, they saw the funny side of it, which in Metropolitan Police terms meant they didn't breathalyse him, and just stared balefully at him until he corrected his error.

On the second attempt, Ron parked successfully, although not too cheaply. A rough-looking man, who emerged from the world's smallest portacabin, charged him twenty quid for the privilege of parking in what appeared to be the last remaining bombsite in London.

"But I only want to park for an hour, maybe two at the most," Ron had protested.

"We only park cars for the day, and it's twenty for the day," the short, stocky man with an obvious black eye and a name badge that said *Harry*, explained carefully, as though speaking to a child. "You can take it or leave it. Up to you mate."

Ron checked his watch and realised all this dithering was going to make him late for his meeting with Tina. He decided to take it.

Tina's phone call a few hours earlier had been the one bright spot in an otherwise depressing day and he wasn't going to jeopardise the chance to hear some good news for the sake of twenty pounds. Although she hadn't explicitly said there was any good news, he rather assumed that must be the case, otherwise, why call him? He parted with two fresh ten-pound notes and hoped his logic was not faulty.

On the way from the car park to meeting Tina, Ron considered the other phone calls he'd received throughout the day.

Brenda, from HR, rang about one of Ron's clients who weren't happy with the way Ron had treated a recent bereavement. Also, Ron's number plate had been reported to the police in connection with a vicar's damaged bike, and there was another report from the council about some inappropriate behaviour in the car park of a crematorium.

'Could Ron pop into the office for a chat about it tomorrow?'

Following on closely from that, Desdemona, his ex-wife, had called almost as soon as he'd hung up on Brenda, complaining that his phone was always busy and that he had no time for his kids, or her. To which, Ron had to explain, again, that seeing as Desdemona and he were now divorced, then traditionally, in these situations, couples tended to see less of each other, not more. That hadn't exactly poured oil on heavy waters. In fact, it was more like pouring aviation fuel on a forest fire in a high wind; only with Desdemona, it was a good deal more life-threatening.

Finally, she'd hammered him over the phone about something or other the kids had done wrong, and blamed him in some way for the unseen actions of his son, who was thirteen, but acting out, or acting up, or something. Ron promised to have a word next time he saw his son and then asked when that would be, to which Desdemona had said she and Billy, her new love interest from Ireland, were planning a nice getaway to Dublin this weekend, so Ron would get to see his kids then.

Ron had bit down on the remark of wanting to be an actual father rather than a babysitter for her weekend piss-ups. Instead, he promised to pop round early Saturday morning so Desdemona could get away to the airport on time.

Once this call had finished, and desperate to escape a world of endless telecommunicated hurt and pain, Ron had taken the unusual step of turning his phone off so that he could drive back to his small flat in relative peace.

And hopefully not cry on the way.

Not that he found much peace in the London traffic at rush hour or in the East End tower block where he now lived. Having been booted unceremoniously out of a house that he had paid for, technically, was still paying for, he'd managed to find a small two-bedroom flat in Tower Hamlets. Ron didn't earn a bad salary, and his bonuses from various sales drives were healthy enough, but the up-keep on two homes, plus paying for his kids, and paying Desdemona a monthly maintenance was proving an expensive endeavour.

He'd thought, when he first moved into this flat, overlooking the never sleeping East India Dock Road, that he could begin his bachelor days again, that he could become a singleton about town. A few weeks into this new lifestyle and lack of money combined with being dead tired after each working day put a damp squib on dreams of re-treading a youth that Ron remembered with sporadic accuracy.

Where had he found the energy when he was younger? True he had lived with his elderly mother in those heady days of being twenty-something, which meant the niceties of life, such as doing the washing or the shopping, were invisible to his younger self, but still... Did being nearly fifty mean, in some way, that he was almost dead? That simply popping down the pub for a pint of an evening felt like too much of a faff.

Often, after each working day, he ended up on his cheap Ikea sofa, the horror of a microwave meal on his lap, a second can of beer on the go. And a TV blaring out some crap that he would forget before the end credits had finished rolling. Sometimes, from the vantage point of his eighth-floor living-room window, he would just stare out at the city skyline.

The flat wasn't much to shout about, but it was the first place he had ever had on his own, having moved directly from his mother's to marry (the heavily pregnant) Desdemona and settle into the daily chaos that passed for domestic bliss. Ron knew the flat wasn't really his, he didn't own it, never would, but while he lived here, and paid the eye-watering private rent, he enjoyed the feeling of having somewhere that was his and his alone.

His one joy, the reason he loved this tiny flat so much, was the narrow balcony that clung precariously to the building and allowed him an evening smoke while overlooking the bustle of East End London. Here he could enjoy the illusion of isolation the eighth-floor gave him, right in the middle of this busy metropolis.

At the stub end of this personal nirvana, with the noise of the traffic starting to grate, and thoughts of his dinner not far from his mind, Ron had remembered his phone was still off and retrieved it. The warbling ring tone (*Welcome to the Jungle* by Guns and Roses), went off the second he powered it up.

Oh great! More complaints, he thought as he answered the call. In fact it had been Tina, asking to see him, straight away. She wanted to meet in Islington, *if it wasn't too much bother*, unaware that Ron was already running out of his flat door and heading for his car before she had finished asking her question.

After a short walk from the mildly expensive car park to Upper Street, Ron all but ran into Tina outside a Pret A Manger, such was his eagerness to meet her. His happiness evaporated somewhat under the dry gaze of her worried look.

"What's up, Babe?" He asked, kissing her cheek and patting her arse as he always did with members of the opposite sex in an attempt to put them at ease.

Tina didn't answer directly but suggested they go to a pub and not any of the poncey ones that littered Islington High Street. A real pub, Tina suggested. One that sold real beer, and for a moment, Ron wondered if he had fallen asleep smoking on his balcony and this was all a dream.

By the time they reached the sanctity of the bar, Ron was red in the face and slightly winded from Tina's fast-paced walk. He was also dying for a smoke, but he managed to forego the right to pollute his own lungs at the sight of a dark pint of ale being placed directly before him.

With the first quarter of a pint sliding down his gullet, Ron was able to relax and perch his generous behind on a barstool that was screwed to the floor. He rotated left and right to take in his surroundings. Tina had mentioned that she knew a pub that held its charm, that still had not succumbed to the mighty High Street Brewery chains. Ron liked the concept, but he wasn't too sure if *charm* was the right word to describe this pub. It certainly held an authentic tone, one that reminded him of pubs from yesteryear, when they were a bit crap, smelt mostly of piss and vomit, and the most exotic food they could muster was a packet of prawn cocktail crisps.

Ron looked around the room. In one corner sat a blinking slot machine, occupied by a thin, emaciated woman whose age could only be guessed at, and who held on to a pint of cider with a one-handed death grip. Her other hand relentlessly fed the unsympathetic machine. Every now and again, she would pick up a packet of cigarettes, look towards the door, then glance around at the room and decide, no, she wouldn't risk leaving her machine unguarded. Anyone could play it if she left, anyone could win. Win her money.

Ron recognised that fevered look; he had many colleagues suffer the same, with machines, horses, dogs, cards, or whatever. In the end, gambling could be about two flies crawling up a wall, just so long as there was enough money in the pot to make it exciting. He made eye contact with the sad face woman for a split second, and they both seemed to know, to understand, that more than money was at stake here.

"I thought about owning a pub once," Ron said, hardly realising he was speaking to someone who was actually listening to him.

"Oh? Where?" Tina replied brightly, the question taking him off guard.

He'd never really thought about it, other than to imagine it would be somewhere in the country, somewhere locals would come and chat with him, somewhere he could feel at ease, but somewhere near enough to the city, so he didn't feel cut off from the world. Somewhere, in all probability, that did not exist.

Ron refocused on the here and now, taking time to enjoy the sight of Tina sitting on the next barstool, sipping elegantly at an unidentified white wine that was served in a glass that probably wasn't the cleanest in the entire world.

"I don't know really. Kent maybe?"

"Have you thought about where in Kent?"

"Not really, guess I am just waiting for the right opportunity to come along." He said and realised this had been the story of his life. Only, the right opportunity never had come along, or when it had, it was an opportunity that turned out to be the wrong one. They lapsed into an embarrassed silence, which Ron broke by asking for a packet of crisps.

"Nothing in stock," the barmaid said, her tattooed arms resting on a Sun crossword from which she did not bother to look up. "Next door is a newsagent, he sells crisps."

"Does he sell beer as well?" Ron asked, feeling a little embittered at poor customer service, especially when it had to do with his stomach.

"You can please your fucking self," the barmaid retorted, again without looking up from a crossword that Ron noted she had nearly completed. So saying the barmaid wandered down the bar to greet an old man with his dog who had just sauntered in.

"All right Sid? Usual?" The barmaid took down a pint glass and started the slow process of pumping out a pint of ale, finding time for the occasional glare in Ron's direction.

"So," Ron said to break the next embarrassing silence. "If I understand you correctly, you're hiding in here because of some French bloke who can't keep his hands to himself?"

This was, from what Ron could hear over the noise of the traffic on the short, fast-paced walk here, the gist of it. He glugged at his pint, reaching the halfway point and feeling another pang of hunger. His stomach was noting the absence of its usual evening microwave meal with loud grumbles of disapproval.

"That's about right," Tina was saying while glancing in the direction of Ron's rumbles. "I mean, not that I have anything against the French…"

"I have," announced the frail voice of Sid from the other end of the bar. "Bleedin' let us down in the war, didn't they?" Beside him, an ancient grey whippet yawned and lay at his feet.

"Don't forget they took a hit too, French resistance and all that. Remember," the barmaid pointed at a TV on the wall that had a nasty crack running straight across the middle. "We saw all that on the history channel. You know, before Bill lost his rag and broke the TV with a shot glass."

"What about that French fucker, Tusk? He shafted us over Brexit."

"He's Polish Sid. We've talked about this mate."

"That's the problem with Europe, to many fucking foreigners. And also because of that, umm, what's it called?" Sid said, sipped from his light ale and then looked thoughtful before lapsing into a silence of presumably trying to remember what it was about Europe that he hated more than it not being Britain.

Ron and Tina waited, staring at Sid for a few moments before it became clear he wasn't going to remember anything at all, or speak again.

"So anyway," Tina continued. "This French bloke…"

"Fucking Treaty of Versailles," Sid muttered. "Fucking disgrace."

Ron glanced around, but Sid was back in his own world, staring out the window, his pint resting on the bar beside him, the dog asleep at his feet.

"Maybe," Ron said, "You should avoid the F-word."

Tina nodded.

"This man from… Continental Europe… his name is Jacque, he's that celebrity chef from the TV, you know, the one who's always talking about Fre… Foreign food?"

Ron shrugged. He never watched cooking programmes, partly because they were on when he worked, but mainly because they didn't feature any nudity. The thought of watching such a show did reawaken his slumbering stomach, which growled once again its displeasure at drinking beer without consuming food. Ron wondered if he could sneak out to the shop next door and grab a packet of pork scratchings, or something.

These thoughts were suppressed by the living fear of leaving Tina alone. She was a woman who had voluntarily decided to spend time with him, and he didn't want to chance her vanishing away while he was distracted by pork scratchings.

"Don't think I've heard of him," Ron said when it became clear Tina was waiting for some kind of recognition of who Jacque was, or is, or however it worked with celebrities that were no longer very popular.

"Oh?" Tina said, clearly disappointed. "Anyway, he's a big thing in the food world, or rather, was, and Juliet is representing him for a recipe book he has written."

"Is this the same bloke that runs the café opposite your office?"

"No, that's his brother, Pascal."

Ron drained his glass and thought about that a bit. He had really hoped this was the French bloke they were talking about because then he could have followed the rest of Tina's story with a little more ease. As it was, he remained confused.

And hungry.

"So, this is the bloke that Juliet has been trying to get hold off all week, and now he's in her office, she's danced off somewhere else?"

Tina nodded, and Ron realised he had once again described the story of his life.

"I got a message from her," Tina said. "Saying she was on her way back to the office, then while I was out buying coffee for Jacque, she sent another message saying she had something urgent to do and I should entertain him until she could get back."

Ron watched Tina place the word *Entertain* in quotation marks with her fingers and raise her eyebrows as if to suggest that this explained her problem. Ron thought carefully about those air-quotation marks and decided it was best to ask some follow-up questions.

"So, he's in the office…"

"Right now. Yes."

"And you don't want to *Entertain* him," He made the quotations marks with one hand to avoid putting down his beer. "Because…"

"…the man is a human octopus with a minimal understanding of personal boundaries."

Ron, who had been about to place a comforting hand on Tina's thigh, redirected the motion to his own, which migrated against his own sensibilities to the soft comfort of his left nipple. Realising, from the look on Tina's face, this wasn't the thing to do right now, he put down his pint and pretended his glasses needed cleaning, but his hanky was beyond this task, so he used his tie, which just made them even greasier. In the end, Tina took sympathy on him and gently cleaned them with a disposable hanky (clean). When he put the glasses back on, they were, he realised, the cleanest he had seen them for weeks, perhaps months.

The thought broke a wave of emotion over his shoulders, one he tried to hold back, but it crashed over his bruised soul, and he began crying, darkly and intensely, right there in the middle of the pub. In front of everyone, even Sid and his dog.

"Oh, you poor man," Tina said, appearing to take this all in her stride. "You must be starving. Let's get you some food."

Quietly she bundled him up and propelled him out of the door at such speed, his tears dried up on their own volition. Within a few minutes, they were sitting in a fast-food restaurant, a tray of burgers and a mountain of fries sitting before his startled teary gaze. Tina indicated that two of the burgers and most of the chips were for him, and it occurred to Ron that this really was what love should feel like.

"Sorry about that," he said between and also during mouthfuls. "There was this encounter workshop I did and…"

"Yes, poor you, must have been dreadful, but going back to *my* problem," Tina said, and Ron, with food delivered to his body, and more to come, felt able at last to give her his full undivided attention.

Except that…

"I don't want to seem disagreeable," Ron said, perhaps to the broader universe. "But is this really such a big problem? I mean you did say you wanted your sister to have a date for the award ceremony, and now this Jacque has agreed to do it… Well. Problemo sorted."

With food inside him, Ron was feeling more alive by the second. The sobbing Ron of a few moments ago had been vanquished by a robust intake of complex carbohydrates and the promise of more empty calories in the shape of over salted French fries that were yet to be fully consumed.

"Ron," Tina said, her tone of voice putting a dampener on his newfound confidence. "I wanted an *ideal* date for my sister; Jacque is far from that description."

"I see, is that why you picked me first?"

"It was one of many reasons Ron, but you need to hear the whole story to understand the whole problem," Tina said and laid out the complicated life of her sister and those she consorted with.

While he ate, Tina explained that since her sister divorced a husband she discovered to be gay, Juliet had become somewhat anti-men.

"I tried asking everyone I knew if they would go with her to the awards," Tina said. "Friends, friends of friends, people we barely knew, and yet it was always the same reaction. I mention Juliet's name, a light of recognition floods their eyes, then whoosh."

"Whoosh?"

"Yes, whoosh, off they run. Sometimes, literally."

"Are you saying that no one you know will date your sister?"

"Yes. Actually, even people who only vaguely know her tend to have the same reaction."

"But I still don't understand, if Jacque will take her, isn't that okay then? I mean, at least for the awards ceremony."

"There was sadly an incident in a limo," Tina said carefully, as though revealing the full details could in some way be too gruesome a story to be heard over food. Although, of course, moments later, she did reveal the full details, and in very gory specifics. So much so, the table next to them started eavesdropping with undisguised delight.

"He tried to do that?" Ron said, his mind attempting to get behind the logistics of such an act inside a car, even one with exceptional legroom. "In a limo? Were there leather seats? Because that's very hard to clean."

"I don't know, all I remember is Jacque's nose wouldn't stop bleeding for a long time, and the driver kept insisting he should call the police." Tina stuffed a handful of chips in her mouth. "Daddy had to get involved in the end and use his connections to keep it quiet. After that incident, and with Juliet in such an emotionally challenging place, I can't possibly leave her alone with Jacque for an entire evening at the awards ceremony and... Is everything okay Ron? Are you having a stroke?"

"No. I'm thinking."

"Thinking Ron? Is that a good idea?"

"Yes," Ron said, sitting back in what he hoped would be a dramatic and assertive fashion, his breathing laboured as he tried to bring together the full picture of the idea forming in his mind. "I think that we should go to the awards ceremony as well."

"Me and you Ron? That is a surprising and unexpected suggestion."

"Yes, exactly. I can be your Plus-One. Both of us there together but, you know, not necessarily as a couple... Just these two people in the same place at the same time who can then keep watch over your sister, and the Fre... And that bloke. And make sure nothing happens to her, what-do-you-think?"

He delivered the monologue as one garbled outburst, his smoker's lungs beginning to give up the ghost towards the end of this lengthy speech.

"We still need to persuade Juliet, but I do think," Tina said, glancing down at the food tray, Ron followed her gaze to note that all the chips had now been eaten. "I really do think, Ron that you've had a great idea."

"Oh Tina, you won't regret it," he said aware that he had started to cry and try as he might, Ron couldn't ignore the look in Tina's eyes that indicated she might already have arrived at a place called regret.

Chapter 11

Rose

Jacque was not going to turn up.

Rose reached that painful conclusion as she waited patiently outside the office door to a very important and influential investment banker. A man that very few people knew existed, and those that did often had very little chance of meeting. He was a Sir, his father a Lord, and in some vague way related to the Archbishop of Canterbury, and was, without a doubt, an insufferable snob.

Possibly, Rose mused, the most offensively posh person she personally knew. Although she had to admit to having never met Jacob Reece-Mogg.

Rose was, however, prepared (pronounced: *desperate*) to overlook most of these issues in pursuit of securing financial backing for Jacque, even if it meant spending time with a Knighted arsehole who made her skin crawl. Which made Jacque's absence even more perplexing and very much a screaming annoyance.

She glanced at the closed door to the office beyond and wondered, again, if there wasn't a better way to solve these problems? Class, the persistence of the upper class to behave as though they were the ruling class, was a terrible thing in London. It pervaded every avenue of the city's existence, reminding those on the lower rungs of the ladder that social mobility was a dangling carrot hung on a twanging piece of elastic.

Thoughts of this nature were easy to conjure as she sat waiting, and finding herself constantly stared at, the result no doubt of being one of very few black women in the entire building, and possibly one of the few women of any colour on this entire floor. If it wasn't for the fact that Jacque needed money to stay afloat and in doing so, retain valuable assets that would eventually go to their daughter, Rose wasn't sure she would have ever voluntarily stepped into this building.

Being with Jacque had always been a roller coaster of dubious pleasure, and like most rides of this nature, eventually, they left everyone concerned feeling sick and dizzy and wondering why they rode it. Even if it was a ride that ultimately benefited their lives.

Despite herself, Rose smiled at the memory of meeting Jacque for the first time and falling, almost straight away, for his persuasive charms. From there, it had seemed almost too simple to plunge into a whirlwind that was a beautiful moment of them; a love story that became her life story.

Rose felt sure that she would have made a life for herself without Jacque. She would have made herself into something beyond that which was expected of a Comprehensively educated kid. With Jacque in her life though, she had undeniably been propelled up into a social level she would have found difficult to access alone. She knew that and was never stupid enough to deny it. Through Restaurant Noir, Jacque had amassed contacts that would embarrass leading politicians and often, in answer to the question, *who have you met that was famous*, he had replied, *'anyone that wasn't dead before Jacque Noir was born.'*

It was no idle boast and this list of contacts was a resource Rose had not hesitated in using to enhance her own professional life.

While married to Jacque, Rose had been, mostly, enthralled by a world that was beyond anything she had dreamed of while growing up on a Peckham housing estate with her single mum. Her father had been out of the picture for a long time, by the time Rose was a teenager, she rarely thought about him, and her mother seldom mentioned his name.

Walking to school down roads where kids her age could end their days on the sharp end of a blade, Rose had seen a different path for herself. She had been smart, smart enough to know the right careers to follow, to know the good degrees from the bad Uni's. And those early years in the rough and tumble of a South London's education system had given her a thick skin. Thick enough to survive a university system populated almost entirely by the suffocating patronisation of the guilt-ridden white-middle-class.

At her first year in University, Rose had tried but failed to be amused as this strange tribe of well-spoken white faces who fought amongst themselves to be her friend, frequently, Rose suspected, so they could say they had a friend who was black. Often, they were disappointed to discover that it was pretty much the same as having a white friend, except maybe borrowing her foundation makeup was problematic.

University for her had been the University of Bath, a place that she initially assumed was on the coast, for some reason, and was the furthest from London she had ever lived. It was also an excellent university for anyone wanting to enter accountancy at a higher level, and one where she was never short of invitations to dinner, or cinema and sometimes, when she found a rare working-class male, to a pub. Despite this, she passed through her whole three years without a single boyfriend to encumber essential studies.

Her one true friend had been Roberta. Slender tattooed Robbo of the many face piercings. Robbo, the rock of reliability. A live wire who liked to drink a lot in a short amount of time.

Rose and Robbo had struck it off from the very first day and stuck together through overdue essays and regretful hangovers. At the end of the final year, not wishing to face the inevitable parting as they went to their future lives, the pair had packed a rucksack each and flown, pretty much on a whim, to the South of France.

In years to come, whenever anyone asked her what she attributed to her success, her standing in accountancy and business manager circles, and her small, yet lucrative collection of clients, she would say *'Easy Jet last minute flights.'* Well, sometimes she would say that, mostly she would say something about hard work, having ambitions, the importance of risk-based planning and blah blah blah. And then end with the joke about Easy Jet, which of course, was perhaps nearer to the truth than she liked to admit.

A last minute, cheap flight with Easy Jet had landed her and Robbo in the South of France. Between them, they had about 100 Euros, which in Cannes lasted around an hour and a half. Their mistake had been wandering from Cannes to Monaco and stopping to have lunch without scanning the prices first. For two newly qualified accounts, this was, to say the least, somewhat embarrassing, but they managed to pay the bill and had worked out that one or other of their parents would probably have to send them money. The fact that Robbo's mother was never contactable, due to an ongoing substance abuse problem, and Rose's mother had no idea her daughter had even left the country were mere details in this moment of madness that both girls decided to find hilarious, rather than worryingly tragic.

On route to finding a cybercafé to send an email to Rose's mother, they had run into Jacque and Pascal. The two brothers had been walking along the beachfront, talking animatedly about something or other. Rose spoke approximately five words of French, Robbo significantly less, but she could sense in some way, these were the men to approach for help. They looked genuine and helpful, and not likely to jump down her knickers at the first opportunity. At any rate. Pascal seemed harmless, Jacque had a certain predatory look in his eye, but he had a handsome smile, and when he spoke to her for the first time, she found his appeal incredibly beguiling.

Rose clicked with Jacque almost straight away. Not at the very first word, his stumbling English and heavy accent took her a short amount of time to acclimatise to, but quicker than she thought possible, she became interested in this man. Very interested.

Robbo, on the other hand, never showed any curiosity for Pascal, and as far as Rose knew, never thought of him again beyond the time they spent in France. In fact, Robbo had been somewhat suspicious, which for a woman who never turned down a free drink in Uni, no matter which dodgy male had bought it, was surprising.

"We don't know who these people are," Robbo protested when they arrived at Jacque's grandparents and had been offered a guest room for the night. It meant the girls sharing a double bed, and the boys sleeping in a single bed (Jacque) and on the sofa (Pascal), this decided apparently on the toss of a coin, but it was better than the alternative, which given their monetary woes would literally have been sleeping on the beach.

"I don't mind," Robbo said, almost wistfully, as though she had been looking forward to it. The reality, of course, looked very different. They had seen homeless people gathering on the shingle beach before sunset, and the police keeping an eye on them, and in some cases, moving them on and putting out fires.

In the end, Rose and Robbo stayed a whole week in the little house nestled on the side of a hill, at the top of what felt like 5000 steps down to the beach. At some point, Jacque and Rose had ended up in that single bed, quietly making love, or as quiet as they could, which in her case, was often not terribly low volume.

"Sounds like you had fun last night," Robbo said after breakfast, and Rose blushed, burying her nose in a giant wide rimmed glass that contained freshly squeezed orange juice and a dash of champagne.

Champagne had been flowing at a constant rate of knots since the family announced their plans for moving to London. It had been like something from a soap opera, when Jacque's father, Miguel Noir, had first broken the explosive news. He had of course spoken in French and when she heard London being mentioned Rose worried for a moment, fearing news of another bombing or other act of fate that removed loved ones suddenly from the world. Their manner convinced her she was wrong, but it was also a private time, the conversation, excited and earnest, with questions being fired from Jacque, while Pascal spoke quietly with a stunningly beautiful woman that turned out to be his mother, despite the fact that she was clearly so much younger than their father.

It all left Rose and Robbo feeling as though they were intruding.

"Shall we just go?" Robbo asked, and for a second, Rose was tempted to say yes. Then she thought of all those steps that led back down to the beach and decided against it.

"Let's hang for a bit," she said. "I want to see what they are all excited about."

At that moment, Jacque had remembered them again, brought them over, and introduced the two girls to his parents. It was all a little heady, finding a man she fancied, and then being introduced to his parents less than an hour later. And then in short order, being introduced to his grandparents, and discovering the grandmother was almost as beautiful as Jacque's mother. But Rose decided to go with the flow, although she wondered on the wisdom of this decision when Jacque introduced her directly to his mother.

As Rose shook hands with Jacque's mother, a small soft gesture that lasted barely the beat of a heart, she was forced to look upwards into this tall woman's eyes, craning her neck to see a woman that looked back at her as though she knew Rose's story from start to finish. It was unnerving, being so close to the mother of a man she barely knew, watching herself being studied, and judged.

Ariel was and possibly remained the most stunningly beautiful woman that Rose had ever personally known, and through Jacque, Rose had met stars of film and theatre! Yet, here, in this one graceful woman, Rose felt her breath almost literally taken away as she stood so close to such perfection and failed, despite looking hard, to find a fault in her face or in those endlessly cascading curls of dark thick hair that framed it. Hair that Ariel would try to tame with impatient one-handed gestures; motions that were doomed to failure as the hair flooded back, an unstoppable force of nature.

"Charmé," she had said to Rose as they first met, her eyes widening somewhat when she took in the tattooed and pierced features of Robbo.

"Pleased to meet you," she said to Robbo, with a brief look at Pascal that spoke of instant disapproval. "I will find you a coffee, sit."

"Oh, there's no need to ..." Rose had attempted to say, her English manners jumping to the fore.

"Sit," Ariel had repeated, this time fire rising to the bubbling volcanic surface of her personality, and Rose and Robbo had sat with the speed of well-trained police dogs.

Over coffee, Jacque had mentioned the family were moving to London, and the restaurant would be in Soho. Rose had blurted out that she lived in London and not far from Soho at all. It was a white lie, and as a tall black person, she didn't feel bad about it. A return to London, to live and work, was her intention, although she was determined not to end up back at her mother's South London maisonette. After three years of relative freedom, Christmas, Easter and Summer holidays aside, Rose clung fiercely to her independence. It would break her mother's heart, but it was something that Rose was determined to do, even though she had no idea how she would do it.

At the end of the week, Jacque had borrowed his grandparents' Mercedes and taken Robbo and Rose back to the airport in style. Pascal had not joined them. In fact, he had not been seen very much at all, tending to be up early for the walk down to the beach to buy fish, and then spending the majority of his time in the kitchen with his grandmother.

Jacque had also been busy, on the phone and on a slow, continually crashing computer, which he used to research London, but he always found time in the evening to show Rose the sights. Even Robbo would begrudgingly admit on the flight back, that Jacque had made their time in the South of France unique; the holiday of a lifetime. At least, for two young women at the start of their adult life.

On returning to the UK, Robbo and Rose had said their goodbyes at Bath train station. Robbo could not be tempted by the bright lights of London. In truth, Rose knew she despised big cities and Bath had been, despite its relative charms, more than enough for her. She would return to the North of England. Back to Yorkshire where she had a job lined up with a bookmaker chain as Junior accountant. Robbo needed a job quickly so she could rent a place for her and her mother, who had once again been evicted.

Rose asked her before they parted ways, why she tried so hard when her mother kept letting her down time and time again. Robbo had shrugged and muttered something about family, and they had hugged and parted tearfully. Rose to go back to her near perfect, albeit suffocating and controlling mother. Robbo to a mother who needed to be rescued that very weekend from a methadone overdose.

They kept in touch, and Rose would witness, at a distance, Robbo's fight to the bitter end. Only when Robbo's mother had invariably succumbed to her addictions and died, would she find peace and normality in life. They still spoke on Facebook, commented on each other's photos, and shared on Mother's Day a moment of quiet contemplation that only they could understand.

In London, as a graduate with a double first, Rose was looking forward to reaping the rewards of her studies. However, she soon found that having a double first was not particularly unusual in the square mile, but being female and being black was apparently a problematic combination in the finance world. As such, finding that top job she thought had to be merely waiting for her to take became just that little bit tougher. Naturally, renting her own place in London if she didn't actually have a job proved to be a notch above impossible.

Two things happened to rescue her from the future precipice of being a small-time self-employed accountant for other small-time independent sole traders. Firstly; Jacque got back in touch with her, and secondly, he helped her get a foot in the door of a job with actual prospects.

They had met in the West End. She was on her way to an interview when he phoned, and they agreed to meet afterwards for a coffee and a chat. She kept the conversation brief and to the point, trying to remain in the zone for her impending interview, but secretly she was excited about meeting Jacque again, eager to hear not only about the restaurant in Soho but also excited to meet him, period.

After leaving Uni, her life had been, she had to admit, a little grey. The return to her mother's maisonette had reduced her status from an independent newly qualified woman to that of a 15-year-old who wasn't allowed to bring boys back to her room. She even found her TV usage, which had been virtually zero at Uni, was now restricted to what her mother wanted to watch, and sometimes, what her mother thought was suitable.

Yes, Rose no longer needed to do her own laundry, and it was nice to eat food that wasn't out of the packet or can or takeaway box, but the call of independent living had already been answered at Uni. Now, Rose could hear its nightly wail for her to return to a freedom she had known as she lay there, looking at the Pop Posters that still adorned the walls of her teenage bedroom.

Much of this was on her mind when she exited Piccadilly Circus, frantically pushing through the crowds and trying to find the right exit. No matter how many times she came here, she usually ended up on the wrong side of Regent Street. This time she was successful and bounded up the stairs two at a time, only to collide with a grinning Jacque Noir.

"Excusez-moi, ma Cherie," he enthused. "You have said where your interview was to be, and Jacque Noir could not help himself but meet you earlier and wish you Bon Chance."

He kissed her, and she went all cliché, standing on tiptoes, even though she was the same height, maybe slightly taller. For a moment, she even forgot about the interview. Fortunately, Jacque seemed to be a little more focused.

"Come," he said, pulling away from her, but still holding her arms in a soft passionate grip. "We walk to this place, you will get the job, I will celebrate with you. It will be a night of wonder and happiness, and… Bliss."

He kissed her again, and almost before she could regain her breath, Rose found herself whirled around and pretty much marched off towards the back of Regent Street and her impending interview. They talked animatedly on the way, about that week in France, about Robbo, some chat about the Noir restaurant plans, which Jacque mostly deflected, and then they were outside a lacklustre office block shortly before her appointment.

"Listen," she said to him, taking a moment to stare into a plate glass window and use the muggy reflection to adjust her hair and makeup. "I love the idea of a drink after the interview, but bear in mind, it might not be much of a celebration. This is the… God knows how many interviews I have had this month."

"But why? Do you not have the… Double one?"

"Double first, yes, the real problem is…"

"Hello, can I help you?" A voice behind had them both whirling around from the door Rose was about to enter.

"Oh hello," Rose said, recognising the man in front of her. "You must be Mr Peterson."

"That's right, and you are?"

"Rose Green, I'm your 2 pm interview?"

The smile on Mr Peterson's face froze in place for a bright moment in time. Half a second later, he recovered. Mostly.

"You're Ms Green?"

"Yes, that's right." When Mr Peterson continued to stare at her without replying, she said, "is there a problem?"

"Problem?" The very word seemed to alarm Mr Peterson, and he glanced almost guilty at Jacque, a slight red tinge to his cheeks. "No, absolutely not."

It was a reaction Rose had encountered many times in her journey through life in a country of prevailing whiteness. Her surname, taken from the errant father, and never changed by her mother, combined with a girl's name so evocatively English, had evidently conjured up in Peterson's mind a face that was a lot whiter than the one Rose possessed.

Peterson's reaction created an embarrassing silence into which Jacque jumped feet first.

"Jacque Noir, apologies for the intrusion. I was stealing some time from the wonderfully talented Rose." He shook hands with Mr Peterson. "Yes, we are swamped at the moment, overseeing the opening of a new restaurant in this fine city of yours, but these UK tax laws, and VAT, it is all so horribly complicated."

"Yes, yes it can be," Peterson said, a lot more interested now than he had been. "Can I ask, are your accounts professionally represented yet?"

"Noh, sadly, I have not found anyone suitable. Someone who can handle the large volume of cash we anticipate moving through our business."

Peterson's business card came out of his pocket like a ninja death star.

"If I can be of any help sir, this is my number... Sir!"

Jacque took the card and stared at it, as though a secret meaning could be deciphered from the tacky font and bog-standard logo.

"Merci, Steven, we will be in touch." He placed the card in his pocket, his movements being tracked hungrily by the man in front of him. "But it has to be said, Jacque Noir is already impressed by the quality of staff who you are interviewing. Bon Chance Rose."

And without warning, Jacque was away down the street, talking loudly into his phone about some expensive caviar he wanted to order. A phone that Rose could plainly see was off. As he rounded a corner, Jacque waited until Peterson was in the building before pointing Rose to a café where he would wait. She nodded once and mouthed a silent thank you in his direction.

Needless to say, she got the job, and the celebration afterwards, with Jacque, had been epic. Legendary in fact. Even if the bollocking she got from her mother for returning at three in the morning had been equally proportional.

A few days later, after signing a contract with her new employer, she met with Jacque and discovered the true scope of Family Noir's problems. Since they arrived in the UK, not much luck had befallen them...

Via the ruthless beauty of Gazumping, the Soho premises they originally sought had fallen through and they were now opening a restaurant in a less than optimal location in Islington. A place that included a flat above that was much smaller than they had anticipated living in, indeed, one where there was apparently no room for Jacque to sleep. He had however found a small room in a shared house nearby, but the let was only for a professional couple.

"You want me to move in with you," Rose had spluttered. "Look, I am grateful you helped me get this job, really I am, but don't you think this is moving a little fast?"

Jacque simply shrugged, in that Gallic way of his, and explained, with his undisputed charm, that it was just an arrangement. Yes, they would share the same bed, but his hours would have him arriving late at night, and asleep as she left for work. She would hardly notice he was there.

Rose wasn't sure that this was the perfect way to start a relationship, but she also thought back to the rows with her mum and about the curtailed freedom she had experienced since leaving Uni. Finally, Jacque had persuaded her with his own brand of logic.

"And it will be just for a few weeks, perhaps a month or two at most, then I will have money to rent somewhere better, and hopefully, by then, you will decide to remain with me."

He had also added that if she didn't want to join him, he would help her find her own place, and no harm done. In the meantime, it was just an arrangement of necessity. One made less complicated by the fact that he enjoyed making the sweet love to her.

This last point had left her choking on the last bite of a chocolate éclair, which she ate guilt-free, being one of those women who could consume calories without putting on weight. He had a point, though. She really did enjoy the sex, in the French bungalow overlooking the sea, and a few nights ago, in the disabled toilets of a local nightclub, which had seemed a little random at the time, but still left her smiling when she thought of it. And she figured, if it didn't work out, she could always run back home to mum.

It had worked out though and in the beginning, it had all been so wonderfully carefree and simple.

A few weeks had dragged into six months in the shared-house, but Jacque was busy, and so was she, and when they met, their relationship was still so new that sex could solve every problem. At the end of those six months, Jacque made good on his promise and found a delightful flat near Kings Cross that was all lofty ceilings and exposed brickwork. It made Rose feel very bohemian just to come home to it, and she found herself inviting old friends round just to show off her cool pad, although predictably her mother was not impressed.

"Why don't you wallpaper this room?" She said, and then made some comment about how a man of Jacque's age should probably not be going up a ladder anyway.

The age difference was something that remained a constant source of criticism from her mother, and even from some of her friends. Some people saw it, others did not. Rose was exactly twenty-two years younger than Jacque, but he had so much energy and passion for everything, in and out of bed, she rarely thought of it. Perhaps at birthdays, and when he spoke of music that she had never heard of, but in the main, it was the least significant problem in their whole time together.

The main problem had been his infidelity, and that enduring problem had been their ending.

A predictable end perhaps, if her mother had still been alive, she probably would have said a big fat *I told you so*, and she would have been fully justified in doing so. Indeed, if her mother hadn't been taken so early by cancer, she might also want to know why Rose was still managing Jacque's finances *after* they had been divorced. Rose explained it to herself as her way of keeping an eye on the interests of her daughter's inheritance, even though of late, that argument had begun to seem less than sound. Even Yvonne snorted derisively when Rose proffered this defence.

Today, for example, they had an appointment, one that had cost her a good deal of favours to secure, one that might see Jacque through his current rough patch. All he had to do was turn up.

And yet...

She flicked on her phone and sent yet another message, hoping it wouldn't land in the hands of someone who had won Jacque's phone at a poker game. She also tried a phone call but refrained from leaving a voice message, who knew the ears that were listening in a building like this. It was creepily quiet here, sitting on a wooden bench, under a stained-glass window that was God knows how many hundreds of years old. The floor looked to be genuine flagstone, and probably pre-dated Christ, with the walls being made from some kind of ancient stone that had been lucky enough to survive the great fire of London. At any moment, she expected Shakespeare to pop round the corner, in deep conversation with Henry VIII or Thomas Becket.

"Sir Geoffrey will see you now." The voice belonged to the whitest woman Rose had ever seen. The remark was followed by a tilt of a blonde head atop a pale slender neck, followed by a perfectly polite smile; all aimed at getting her to move without actually asking her to do so.

Posh people, Rose had concluded at length, could be total dicks around non-posh people.

The meeting with Sir Geoffrey lasted a full three minutes, during which Rose spent two of those minutes explaining why Jacque was not there and one frantic minute trying to arrange an appointment for the following day. Incredibly Sir Geoffrey agreed, and Rose began to realise he was a secret Jacque Noir fan and actually, just wanted to meet Jacque, for... Whatever reason! That was fine by her, his slavish devotion to collecting another celebrity to tell his posh friends about had bought her a second chance, a second appointment. Now all she needed to do was find Jacque.

Outside she rang every single number she could think of, but it was after five. No one in the publishing business was picking up because they had long gone home. No one in the catering business was picking up because they were busy preparing for tonight. It was just a bad time to find someone to talk about Jacque.

Rose tried Juliet's office in desperation, but Juliet's mobile was giving the busy signal. In the fading evening light, Rose wondered what else she could do. In the end, she went for a coffee and a doughnut in order to have another think about it all.

Life, she decided, was easier to cope with when one had sugary calories coursing through one's veins.

At a small café table, Rose flicked the phone to Juliet's number as she sipped her vanilla latte and was pleasantly surprised when it began ringing.

Chapter 12

Juliet

Juliet's diverted cab stopped, at her request, a few yards short of the entrance to Old Compton Street. She needed a few moments to prepare herself, both physically and mentally for what she was about to do; namely, confront someone she disliked and ask them for a favour.

She paid the fare and within seconds the cab driver had a new passenger and was on his way, leaving Juliet staring at a churchyard to her right and a backstage door to her left, and wondering if this in some way was symbolic of the sham that had been her marriage.

Her phone rang, jumping her from her reverie and she glanced at the display, expecting to see Tina's name, anticipating her cries for help with Jacque. Instead, she was surprised to see another name, one from the recent past.

"Hello Rose," Juliet said pressing the phone to her ear to hear the response above the hum of passing traffic.

"Hey Juliet," Rose's voice was always bubbly, a voice you wanted to listen to, a voice that made you happy just by hearing it. Today, there was an edge to that voice. "Do you have a minute spare? I'm not far from your office, and I wanted to pop by."

"Don't go to my office," Juliet snapped, perhaps a little too urgently.

"Problem?"

"Jacque is there."

"Well actually, it's him that I need to see you about."

"Okay, but can you give me an hour before you go there?" The last thing Juliet wanted was Rose tracking down Jacque to her office, having some kind of domestic and then him buggering off before she could get her hands on his unspeakable hide. "Listen, I'm kind of in the middle of something right now, can I call you back?"

"I do really need to talk to him, fairly urgently. But…" The line went quiet and Juliet waited impatiently for Rose's thought process to finish. "Listen, maybe I should talk with you first, put you in the picture."

"That doesn't sound good," Juliet said. All she needed right now was more Jacque related fuck-ups!

"To be honest with you, it's not good, but it's best if I explain in person. Where are you?"

Juliet gave her location and then realised how that might sound. The pregnant pause at the other end of the line, followed by a long *riiighhht* confirmed this.

"Do you mean the gay pub, in Old Compton Street? There isn't another Compton's that I don't know about?"

"Probably, but right now, I am outside the gay one."

Another silence followed in which time Juliet failed, by a hair, to explode with impatience.

"Any particular reason?"

"Yes, yes there is," Juliet said, somewhat testily, her courage was ebbing with every syllable she spoke. "But I really don't have time to discuss it."

"Okay, I'll... Leave you to it," Rose's voice sounded as though it was making a massive effort to stay neutral. "Listen, there's a café called A Real Cup of Coffee, should be just down from where you are now?"

Juliet glanced down the road and saw the café in the distance, a black sign outside was advertising lentil soup in colourful chalk with various smilies around it.

"I'll jump in a cab and meet you there in half an hour, okay?" Rose's voice was as insistent as Juliet remembered.

"Sure! Though it will have to be a quick meeting."

"Absolutely, see you then."

The line went dead, leaving Juliet to wonder why, in these days of modern communication, no one ever said goodbye at the end of a phone call.

Around her mingled the lunchtime trade that was Soho. That is to say, a mixed bag at best, but the atmosphere was light on this cold sunny afternoon, with the low winter sun spiking long shadows down Old Compton Street.

Despite its reputation as the epicentre of all things sexual in London, Soho was now a tame affair. Juliet could remember a different place back when she had just started working in London, during the mid-'80s, under the iron rule of Thatcher. The area then had been far seedier, with street workers lurking in the shadows, politely asking businessmen if they were *looking for a girl*. In those days, every other shop sold VHS flavoured porn, or sex toys, or had been an actual strip joint.

Now, Soho was all vegan restaurants and fair-trade cafés. Tiny places serving a wealthy and distinct clientele an expensive menu that came with lofty aspirational morals. The new Londoners hailed from such gentrified areas as Hackney and the Docklands. Areas that once were poor, until the poor could no longer afford to live there and were cleansed away.

Some of the *old* Soho remained. There was a street, not far from where she now stood, more of an alleyway, that featured Raymond's Review Bar and a host of sex shops. It was more touristy than debauched, a hangover from the previous incarnation of Soho, one the area seemed reluctant to let go.

Juliet once had a meeting at Raymond's Review Bar, a celebrity meeting, of course, when she had celebrities to meet. This one wanted his life story ghost-written but apparently couldn't spare the time away from his lavish lifestyle to visit Juliet in her office. She recalled Raymond's Review Bar being disappointingly small; almost a living room with a tiny bar, and of course at one end was a stage, more of a raised platform, with glitter marking the entrance. Through here exotic dancers would emerge and dance to music that blared out far too loud for such a tiny venue.

Despite all this, the meeting had gone reasonably well and a deal had been struck. The celebrity in question, a football legend in the making, had turned out to be a profitable addition to her client base, until his temper on and off the pitch saw him serving a five-year prison stretch. After that, bookshops had withdrawn their support, as had the publisher, and that line of revenue had been brought to an unexpected close.

All part of the fickle fate of being a Literary Agent to the Stars!

Another part of Soho that remained unchanged to the past was this pub; Compton's. Nestled between trendy fish and chip shops and those cafés Juliet hated so much. Compton's had been a gay pub for as long as anyone could remember and was in all likelihood the location of the man she now sought. A man from whom she needed a favour.

Her ex-husband! Clive!

Clive had been drunk the first time they met. They ran into each other, somewhat literally, at an expensive party for an outlandish celebrity, an actor who would later reach such heights of superior acting that he would soon be a total bore about it all. Most, in fact all of the people at that party had been of some boorish quality or another; all smiles and business cards, half an eye on the door for the next networking opportunity.

Clive on the other hand, who was mildly famous for his TV work and some film stuff that Juliet had not seen, had been something different. Polite and apologetic after he bumped into her, his calm words and genuine smile a small island of normality in amongst the fakery and snide remarks.

Juliet felt old at parties like these, even then, at just turned 40, she felt ancient amongst these pretty young things. It left her feeling awkward, out of place; an alien from another world. Clive had rescued her from this social awkwardness by bumping into her, then giving her a hug and saying with a grin; *'if you write my life story, you must say the first time you saw me, I was sober, and naked, and had a body of a Greek god'*.

Juliet had replied something along the lines of not knowing any Greek gods with an expanded waistline, a short put down that sprang from her lips in the normal way she defended herself against the unknown. Secretly she was somewhat flattered that Clive knew about her work with biographies. Juliet had edited many famous tomes for a variety of publishers over the years and was now at the point in her career where she was in charge of commissioning such books herself and choosing who should edit them. It was warming to know her work was acknowledged by more than the board of directors at the dry and dusty publishing house where she worked.

If Clive was put off by her opening retort, he did not show it. Instead, he spent time talking to her and, although he was drunk, Juliet noted that he was also charming, and soon she forgot she was surrounded by a kindergarten of tomorrow's talent and began to actually enjoy herself. In truth, she too became a little drunk, and later, when they decamped to a small café in Soho, not far from where she now stood, Clive and Juliet had talked and talked and talked. Clive announcing that he was hungry and they should order breakfast had startled her. Glancing at her watch, she wondered how long had it been since she had done an all-nighter? University? Maybe? Probably. But since then it had been all work and no time to party. This sacrifice had not been without reward; she had a position in a publishing house now, the career point she wanted so much from day one, but…

"Why aren't I happy with that?" She asked a man whom she had met for the first time just 24 hours earlier.

"Maybe," Clive had said, tucking into a breakfast that went a great deal towards explaining his ample girth, "it was never really what you wanted."

And just like that, a flashlight went off in her head.

He had been right, it wasn't what she wanted and she came to realise, over the next few months, that working inside the corporate structure was something with which she would never be happy. There were too many compromises, too many decisions made by too many people looking to avoid controversy and Twitter shit-storms, and career-ending interviews on breakfast TV. It stifled her and at the back of her mind was the question, if I had been making *all* the decisions, could this project have been better? Would it have been a deeper, more profound look at the subject?

Would it have made more money?

Several months after she first met Clive, the answers to those questions still burnt in her soul. Once that thought had been planted, an acorn in her mind, it was difficult not to judge every meeting, every situation, every email, without looking at them through this critical lens.

By then, Clive and Juliet were an item. They had slept together only after their third proper date. His treatment of her, his gentleness, his respect had been as much a part of his appeal as his humour and his broader view of life. Dating was erratic, because of his job, and because of hers. He spoke fluent French, the bonus of having a French mother, and so was often crossing the Channel to make yet another costume drama, often where he played an overweight comical figure. Despite his cynicism for such films, he never seemed to mind, and enjoyed the money and the chance to work, although he once commented that perhaps the French should have hung on to their aristocracy if they were so fascinated with them. A remark that Juliet hoped he never uttered on a French film set.

"You should go independent," Clive said as soon as Juliet had told him of her doubts, of her feeling that publishers were not doing what they should be doing to create biographies that could be… Better. And that sounded wonderful…

But!

Money, money and money, she had protested to him. Not to mention the problem of money.

She had, of course, already considered setting herself up as a literary agent that specialised in biographies, she would still need to interface, as they said in those days, with publishers, but with more control over the finished project and the ability to set terms for preferred clients, she might have more leverage. It all sounded so idyllic. There was though the small matter of saying goodbye to her monthly salary, of her pension-pot no longer getting bigger via the bonus of employer contributions. Not to mention no holiday pay either, not that she took holidays, and no sick pay, not that she had time to be sick, but all of these things weighed on her mind. She wanted to make that leap; she just wasn't sure she had the faith to take that first important step.

It was nearly a year later when Juliet had been invited to join Clive at Cannes when that leap of faith became more palatable to her risk averted self. Clive was a much sought after star at the festival, having been in a French farce based on a famous politician who had dallied with several young women, and men, before finally being caught up in an international spy ring. It was a hilarious film, but also intelligent and captured a fleeting zeitgeist of the moment, so much so that awards started to find their way to both the film and Clive.

After that, nothing could stop his career. Hollywood came knocking, and in the space of a few years, he starred in several blockbusters, small cameo appearances at first, then building up until suddenly he was the villain in a Bond movie.

It really was a whirlwind and one evening, in a hotel in Las Vegas, just after a film premiere that Juliet had flown out to see, they sat drinking and idly playing the slot machines built into the bar, trying to recall how this had all happened. How all this fame had come from seemingly nowhere, and all at once.

"I'm stinking rich you know," he said to her. A typical Clive remark that from the mouth of another man might have sounded arrogant, but from him, it sounded wistful, as though he didn't quite believe it.

Juliet had to agree with him, he was indeed a rich man, but she explained in drunken earnest, even if he was poor, she would still love him. The remark had meant to be equally wistful, and possibly a little humorous, but the moment between them, the moment of them, had changed and without warning, they were deadly serious, staring into each other's eyes as though the continued existence of the fabric of the universe depended on it.

Inevitably, they married that very night. Right there in Las Vegas. Tina cried when Juliet phoned to tell her and then gushed how happy she was for Juliet, and then in the same breath, berated her for not allowing Tina the chance to be a bridesmaid.

When they returned to England, travelling in the wonders of First Class, the papers had been waiting at the airport, snapping away, placing their tired red-eyed faces on the pages of the gossip columns. Placing Juliet for the first time in the limelight.

"Now's your chance," Clive said as the cameras snapped. "It's now or never."

And she saw he was right.

Using money borrowed from her father, a loan that unfortunately came with strings attached to employ her sister, and with some cash Juliet had saved up, and a sizable donation from Clive's bulging bank account, she finally took that leap of faith.

The office in Islington had been so easy to find, so ideal for them, that it was almost as though it had been waiting for her to arrive and claim. As though it was all preordained.

This whirlwind of luck had endured for some time.

With her picture in the paper next to the *actor of the moment*, the Bond villain of the day, doors that had stubbornly remained closed to her became instantly wide open. Sports stars, politicians, actors who she would be introduced to via Clive, became her clients, became books on shelves. The superior *interfacing,* she hoped to achieve with the publishers had turned out to be slightly trickier, most in the publishing business appearing to assume she had retired now that she was married to a rich actor. However, she persevered, she adapted, she overcame.

These were, Juliet would later realise, the halcyon days of her business. The list of well-known people filing through her life was one thing, the decent percentage she earned from working yet again all hours, was more than enough reward, but her best memories were always at Restaurant Noir, where she, Tina and Clive would take lunch until midnight, or dinner until 4 am. Where Jacque would join them for a nightcap and try to insist on ripping up the bill, and he and Clive would have a mock argument, often in French, over payment. So many wonderful conversations, jokes and laughter, and then one day…

It ended.

Juliet wasn't sure if she suspected. If she just turned a blind eye to it all in order to preserve the perfection of her life, or if she really thought about it at all. A lot of men in the theatrical industry were extravagant when it came to their sexual preferences, but Clive had been such a wonderful lover, so considerate, so passionate that it shocked Juliet to the core when she discovered her husband with another man.

She had returned home early, unexpectedly, a headache at the office, one of many she was enduring as a series of scandals from clients she represented were breaking left right and centre. Breakfast TV had even suggested her agency seemed to be, if not a focal point, then a magnet for those men who were falling foul of the crushing, scalp hungry #*MeToo* movement.

Entering the house through the backdoor, Juliet found a local builder doing much the same to her husband.

They froze in that position, the two of them, naked and entwined, sweaty and near the peak of passion, their faces two naughty children with their hands caught in the sweet jar. Motion happened, the two separating, the builder lurching backwards, revealing an enormous erection shrouded in a condom.

At least they used protection, Juliet could remember thinking, in a somewhat isolated way, and then remembered internally screaming at herself to stop being so bloody logical about it all.

Once the builder left, there had been plenty more real screaming to be had as accusations were made, fingers pointed, blame apportioned. In his defence, Juliet remembered that Clive did not seek to justify or defend himself, instead he quietly dressed and listened to Juliet's tirade; calm and undismissive. He said sorry, once or twice, he tried to explain that he felt this way about men, but it didn't change how he felt for her. He tried to get her to see this as something she could perhaps, if she didn't think about it too hard, simply accept.

She couldn't. She thought about it, but she couldn't. She had no problem with him being gay, or as he said, bisexual, but she didn't want to be a part of a relationship that wasn't exclusive. If he couldn't offer her that, he would have to leave.

And so he did.

Afterwards, when she sat in the half-assembled conservatory that the builder had been employed to construct, she thought about the hourly rate he charged and wondered how long they had been at it before she arrived. It seemed puerile to think like this, but a steady stream of sherry and the abject surrealism of the situation lead her with ease down such paths of logical self-destruction.

The next day, it turned out that not only was the builder a bit of tart, sleeping with his customers when given half the chance, and still charging the full rate, he was also a blabbermouth who sold his story to the papers.

And he still charged Juliet his full rate.

Juliet awoke to a crowd of reporters and photographers outside her house, all asking about her husband. Tina, always one to have her thumb firmly on the pulse of celebratory gossip, had found out and came visiting wearing a black scarf and wide-brimmed sunglasses, looking like a somewhat weightier version of Jacky Onassis. She parted the assembled paparazzi like Moses, wading through them to the front door with the occasional slap to the back of a head for anyone not quick enough on the uptake. In the house, she was all herbal tea and warm blankets. A non-judgmental version of her older sister that appeared in times of crises. Then, presumably in an attempt to ease the pain, Tina made a bad joke.

"So, looks like the new conservatory wasn't the only thing getting erected," she had said looking at the half-completed structure, and then her face had become the very picture of regret when she saw the pain on Juliet's face. "But still, you mustn't blame yourself."

Which was an odd thing to say, because up to that point, of all the people that Juliet blamed, and the list was long and varied, her name had so far never featured. Tina's words though found a crack in such armour and burrowed inwards, tearing at Juliet's weakened defences, shredding what remained of her dignity, and reducing her to tears. Quiet tears that ebbed rather than flowed, drifting down her face and splattering on the blanket Tina had tucked around her.

Tina had tried to backtrack, speaking in a hurry, unguarded, digging the hole ever deeper, and explaining to Juliet that it was unlikely her marriage to Clive had sent him gay. It had been the final straw, this imaginary act of kindness, this constructed explanation that men can in some way post themselves to the land of gayness due to the inattentions of a cruel or unfocused wife.

Juliet hadn't blamed herself for what had happened, until Tina said she shouldn't, and then she couldn't stop blaming herself, over and over again.

Eventually, the silence between the two women became more than either of them could bear and Tina left, the photographers outside receiving a few more slaps than was perhaps strictly necessary.

Over the weeks, this stillness, this quiet anger, continued between two women who became collateral damage in someone else's mistakes. As separation led to divorce papers, and the dividing of wealth, the gulf between them widened, as though the sisters were being divorced from each other.

Time passed. Papers were served. Lawyers were paid. Juliet was too proud to take Clive's money, but the house was sold and Juliet used her half to buy a small two-bedroom flat near Hampstead Heath. Here she would walk, and think, and look down on London, and feel like a bird that was gliding above a troubled land.

And then, one spring day, Tina who had been keeping their conversations firmly on business, which by then was firmly in decline, had mentioned a memory. She spoke, almost in single word sentences about the daffodils their father loved to cultivate, in pots and on borders, turning the winter landscape of clay soil into the herald of spring, the announcement of better days ahead. Juliet had joined Tina by the window, looking down at the flower shop opposite, the shop next to what would become Pascal's café, and enjoyed the vibrant colours on display, and spoke too of those shared memories.

In that moment, that time shared in past seasons, they forgave each other for something that had never been their fault. That wasn't the end of the ice age, but it was at least the beginning of the start of the possibility of a thaw.

Clive had not appeared in either of their lives for some time. Occasionally they would see him from afar, at parties or events they were obliged to attend. Clive was now entirely out of the closet, his gayness actually increasing his popularity. His waistline became trimmed, his somewhat rank hairstyle metrosexualized, and mostly via the Pink Dollar, he moved from star to megastar. Clive had ridden this wave for some years, until a moment of drunken indiscretion had him photographed in California with a young man who turned out to be seventeen.

Juliet heard that work dried up for Clive from that point onwards. Projects he had been attached to were suddenly unattached from him, and offers for new jobs began to vaporise. She also heard how he now spent most of his time in a pub, this pub that she now stood outside, waiting for the courage to enter.

Juliet became aware of a familiar tune pulsing through the doorway of the pub. A song Clive had fallen in love with and played endlessly on the CD player in their car, repeating it over and over, and making her laugh with his attempt to sing the high-pitched lyrics. Gravity! Some of those words now floated out towards her, dragging her down into a memory of when Clive and her seemed unbreakable.

She listened, mesmerised by the moment of regressed happiness, unsure now if the path she trod was the wisest, or even the only one available. Then the music changed, the soft swirls of *Tut Tut Child* replaced by *Dexys Midnight Runners*, and the spell was broken.

Juliet realised she had stood here for too long and some of the smokers outside Compton's, were starting to give her weird looks. On top of that, Rose was on her way here, presumably to divulge details of Jacque's latest fuck up. There was no more time, she realised, to prevaricate. The moment was now.

Now or never.

Dropping her phone back into her pocket, she surged forward on a wave of renewed bravery. The fact that she had to be in and out in less than half an hour gave her a much-needed shove to actually get it done at all. Without another moment of hesitation, she entered the pub and was swallowed almost at once by a sea of bald-headed men who looked at her with a mixture of surprise and suspicion.

The place was packed with quiet talking men, rowdy men, men on their own drinking beer at the bar, looking left and right, or staring straight ahead at their mirrored reflection behind the bar, vacant and alone in their thoughts. No women were here. None at all, apart from Juliet, which made her feel like a freak of nature.

At the very back of the pub, surrounded by a bevvy of good-looking young men, she found Clive holding court! He was slumped in his seat, a bottle of vodka beside a short glass, a bottle that was nearly empty. As Juliet approached, a young man whose hand was gliding up and down Clive's thigh, jumped when he saw her, a light of recognition on his face. He turned and whispered a warning in Clive's ear.

Clive's eyes widened and he snapped to look in Juliet's direction. Alarm changing to curiosity, to one of mild amusement. The sight of Juliet weaving her way between the leather jackets and the bald-heads must have been a surreal sight, but the look of determination on her face appeared to sober that amusement.

"Juliet? Is everything okay?" His voice was slightly slurred, but not beyond comprehension. If nothing else, Clive could hold his liquor.

"I need to ask you something," she said, keen to get this out of the way as quickly as possible. Being around gay men did not make her feel uncomfortable, but being the only woman in a crowded pub did.

"Sure," Clive looked left and right to his company at the table. "Can you give us a moment please?"

The young men swapped a look between them, and then silently filed away from the table, pushing past Juliet as they made their way towards the bar. One paused in front of her for a split second, the look on his face a mixture of resentment and perhaps even jealousy.

"I need to find Adam Russel. Urgently." Juliet said, sliding into the booth on the opposite side of the table to Clive. There was no point beating about the bush. What else would they talk about?

"Adam Russel? The food critic guy? Why on earth would I know where he is?" Clive asked, and then a moment of realisation bit into his tired expression. "Ah, because he's gay."

"Yes." It seemed pointless to deny.

"You must realise that I don't know the location of every gay man in London."

Juliet bit down on a remark that sprang quickly to mind and instead reached over to the bottle, poured herself a measure into the empty glass and downed it in one go. The sudden action sobered Clive and he looked at her again, closely, with something that might have resembled concern.

"Again," Clive said with care. "I have to ask, is everything okay?"

"Look, can you help me or not. This Adam Russel, he's been tied with your name in the past…"

"The distant past."

"And I need to find him, urgently. Very urgently."

Clive sat and watched her for a moment, the noise around them seeming to swell into the pain and the hurt that would always exist between the two of them. He took the bottle from her and poured them both an equal measure, finishing the contents.

"You don't want to believe everything you read in the papers, you of all people should know that."

During the scandal, Juliet's past, her university days, people she had argued with years ago had all come to the fore. Even her sexual orientation had been questioned until she took some of the papers to court and won settlements that barely covered her legal fees, and received apologies on page nine of newspapers that had used lurid front-page headlines to increase their sales.

"I had some… Dealings with Adam," Clive was saying. "But I found the man to be, let's just say, somewhat more revolting than even I could stand, and I'm in show business."

"I don't need to know the details; I just need to know where he is."

"The details are, I have not seen him for some time." As Juliet's face dropped, he sighed and took out his phone. "But I can make some phone calls and see if anyone knows where he can be found, okay?"

"Thank you."

"I don't know how long that's going to take. You want another drink?"

"No," said Juliet. "Call me when you find out anything."

Clive's face for a moment seemed to fold in on itself, perhaps with the memory of the hurt he had unleashed on her. In that second of her life, for reasons she perhaps did not herself clearly understand, she felt the need to be kind to the man who deserved so little kindness from her.

"I'm glad to see you happy," she said with a nod towards the group waiting at the bar and was surprised how genuine those words tasted as they left her mouth.

Clive froze for a second, perhaps suspecting a trap, that her words were simply a preamble towards a greater insult. A single eyebrow rose in what might have been surprise.

"Thank you," he said, a simple response that almost choked her on the spot.

Juliet gave a single nod in reply, standing suddenly; a sense of urgency to leave overtaking her, to be far away from this man who used to be her husband. This man that had said he loved her and in doing so, had betrayed her and even worse, himself.

A man who she was glad to see happy.

The conflicting emotions crowded in on her more than the sweat-stained T-Shirts that pressed down on her from seemingly every direction.

"I have to go; I have to meet..." Clive's hand on her arm stopped her flow of words and her motion of flight. She paused, a bird of prey resting on the arm of her trainer. Trembling in anticipation of flight. Of freedom.

"I am sorry," he said. "Truly sorry. I hope you know that. I hope you believe it."

They stared at each other for a long moment, until, under the weight of his own guilt, Clive dropped his hand away and sat, defeated and deadened under her gaze.

"What I know," Juliet said. "Is that nothing has ever been the same since you came into my life and since you left it. And yet... I am still glad, to see you happy."

Clive opened his mouth, his hands lifting from the table, the animation in his eyes stirring, the moment of the monologue close at hand. The moment he would say, and do, and be the actor; create the illusion of the man he wanted people to see.

Juliet stopped him in his tracks with one upraised hand. She had seen this act many times before and had little stomach for a repeat performance.

In that moment of silence, she turned and fled, barging through a montage of pint glasses and tattoos, focusing on the rectangle of light in front of her, the exit and salvation away from the crushing defeat that was her marriage to Clive.

She reached the street, the choking smog-filled air and breathed it deeply, like a field of flowers.

Like a moment of first life.

Chapter 13

Pascal

Pascal had been sitting motionless and deep within his own dark thoughts since Rose had delivered her damning verdict on the future of his café. Leaving him here alone, to contemplate the fate of idiots such as himself.

She was right, of course, about the future viability of this thing he laughably thought of as a business. She was right about what he needed to do. And at the same time, she was wrong about it all.

He could never again work with his brother, failing a miracle of a kind unlikely to occur. It would require Pascal to forgive his brother for what had happened that fateful night in Restaurant Noir. To forgive him for the actual death of a customer. A victim of one of Jacque's stupid pranks, a prank Pascal had been unwise and drunk enough to partake in. One man had paid a high price for their idiocy. It didn't matter how much Jacque argued that this man had been old and nearly dead anyway, Pascal felt the guilt every day and was convinced the only way to avoid anything like that ever happening again was simply to avoid Jacque for the rest of his life.

Pascal sighed, picked up the small cup and saucer, taking them through to the kitchen, carefully washing up and drying both items before replacing the crockery safely on the shelf. Once done, he returned to the darkened empty room that was his café.

Pascal's Café.

On the opening day, he had felt such bravado. Here he was, free at last from the shackles of his brother's restraints. His own man with his own business. A café where he would enjoy making small items, croissants and cakes, served with coffee. Real coffee; the sort of coffee you could only get in Paris, with actual cream floating on the surface, not this thick milk the English fooled themselves into thinking was cream.

He had it all planned out, in his mind, how the population of London could be re-educated into drinking coffee as it should be enjoyed, how it was meant to be consumed. He would be a *disrupter*, as they loved to say on the news; a game-changer.

In the end, the only game he changed was a slight variation in his daily routine. Instead of preparing for a punishing schedule of a sophisticated lunch menu followed by an even more complex evening menu, and enduring a day of shouting at staff to prepare vegetables, instead of all that, he created some basic pastry products and sometimes shouted at Yvonne who mostly cried and went home.

Pascal knew the truth. No customers meant no profits. He was not a simpleton, he understood this much of business, even if, at Restaurant Noir, Jacque had done all the heavy lifting when it came to the commercial side of life. What Pascal needed to know was how to change things for the better, not acknowledge how much debt he was in. What good did that do?

He tidied away the few things that needed tidying away, after another quiet day these were very few things indeed, and in doing so, was reminded of all his many duties in the kitchen of Restaurant Noir. All the thousand and one things that needed to be done before he could even think about going to bed.

Pascal knew this was one of the many reasons, Candy, his wife of just a few short years, had left him. The prolonged strain of providing high-quality food in such large quantities, day after day, had affected his mood and even his health. It even affected his performance in the marital bed, and this probably hadn't helped the survivability of their marriage. Or perhaps, as he suspected, she just got bored of being the wife of celebrity number two in the Noir Brother dynamic.

Candy had been passed to him by Jacque, like a baton in a race that only ever featured the two of them. She was very chatty, which Jacque never liked, and also American, of which Jacque also was not so keen. Otherwise, she had been what Jacque was usually keen on; tall, with long hair, a figure a little on the thin side, but with legs, which were always displayed in the tightest of jeans. And, it had to be said, she had the most beautiful smile.

When she remembered to use it.

Who knows why Jacque decided on that day to forego this beautiful woman? Maybe it had something to do with the responsibilities of being a father to Yvonne, who seemed to grow taller with every passing day, or perhaps he just wanted some kind of stability for Pascal, something to settle him into the day-to-day running of what had become a brutal kitchen regime.

For Pascal, Candy was a type of woman he had little experience with, although it had to be said, he had little experience with any kind of women. He heard others describe Candy as a force of nature, and although she was indeed a force to be reckoned with, little of her seemed to be an actual product of nature and more to do with a surgeon's scalpel.

Did he love her? Pascal wasn't sure. Looking back under the scrutiny of pain that was a breakdown of a marriage, everything tended to look different. Jaded. He was pretty sure he had loved her, in his own way, but had it been simply because Pascal could not have the one he truly loved?

Juliet entered Pascal's life a day before he met Candy. Eating a truly epic lunch at Restaurant Noir that stretched onwards to the evening, one of the many legendary lunches for which Restaurant Noir had become famous. She was with her sister, the irresistibly likeable Tina, and Juliet's effortlessly charming husband, Clive. They had been celebrating the opening of Juliet's new business, a literary agent that served only to bring to the public those autobiographies of the famous, celebrity memoirs that Pascal had no interest in at all.

The lunch had stretched on through to dinner, with Pascal still taking orders from the same table, for the same people, until curiosity got the better of him. Typically, front-of-house was an antithesis for him, a place he rarely ventured. That was Jacque's job, meet and greet, ask after wives and children, or if the customer was there with a lover, to find a darkened corner and tip them off if the paparazzi came sniffing. That evening, Pascal broke his own rule and came out to see who was eating all this excellent food he had been busy creating.

Emerging through the kitchen doors, dodging a fast-moving waitress laden down with gravy stained crockery, he had glanced around the near-empty restaurant, almost near to closing time, his gaze drawn to the sound of laughter, and there he had seen Juliet for the first time.

She had looked around at that precise moment, and for a second their eyes had locked across the room, like all those clichéd love stories that

Pascal had read as a romantic teenager. Her look had been one of…
What? Curiosity? Possibly. Interest? He wasn't sure. He only hoped that
he wasn't staring at her with an open mouth and looking an even bigger
idiot than he thought he looked pretty much all of the time.

Jacque had spotted him straight away, amazed at Pascal's presence in
the land of mere eating mortals, and dragged him over to meet the table,
to be introduced. There Pascal learnt Juliet's name, touched her hand,
locked eyes again, and forgot, for a moment, there were other people in
the room, in the city, in the world. Of course, at that point Jacque
introduced Pascal to Juliet's famous and rich actor husband, and Pascal
had thought; *of course, she's married. Of course, he is someone special.*

He had been forced to sit and drink brandy, and to enter into small
talk, which the people at the table would soon work out wasn't his most
favourite thing, and move on to talk with someone else.

Jacque had done his bill-ripping thing again, a marketing strategy he
called *A-loss-leader*. The company took a hit on one meal, one
celebration, and then the customers would be loyal forever. Pascal hated
the tactic, as much as he hated that it worked so well.

The next day, with Juliet's smile, her eyes, the soft grip of her hand,
the smell of her perfume still fresh in Pascal's mind, Candy had walked
into his life. Pascal allowed that moment to govern his decision-making.
He had fallen in love with Juliet at first sight, but she was married, so it
seemed only logical to find someone else, and right here, right now, was
Candy.

She was from the East Coast, as she liked to announce, without really
being specific. Pascal would yet learn this was a general euphemism for
being a New Yorker. A hardened soul who could order a bagel
containing twenty different ingredients while maintaining a deeply

personal phone conversation and warning anyone who invaded her personal space that she packed Mace in her bag. It was a startling combination.

He hadn't fallen in love with her, not at first sight, but eventually, she had worn him down, until one day he woke up next to her, stared at her sleeping form on the pillow, and made a decision.

They were married a few months later in a small church near St Paul's Cathedral, which Candy's mother mistook for St Paul's Cathedral and told all her friends via Instagram. No one corrected her, and to this day, as far as Pascal knew, she still believed it to be true. The honeymoon had been in Paris because Candy had never been there, and Pascal was keen to show off his new bride to friends of yesteryear, people who by and large asked him why he had married an American when there were so many beautiful French women in Paris.

'Well she doesn't smoke, for one', Pascal would reply in a rare attempt at humour. A joke that to anyone who knew the family Noir history would force them to lose their smile and change the subject.

He also wanted to introduce Candy to his father, who now spent most his time at the hilltop house once owned by the grandparents of his mother. Ironic that he had spent so much time avoiding this house, avoiding the company of the In-Laws when Ariel was alive, only to retire there. Albeit many years after their passing.

His father had refused to come back to England for the wedding, citing old age, and a cat that could not be left alone, and the fact that it brought back too many memories, too many bad memories.

Taking a break from Paris, Candy had been propelled southwards by the power of a French train travelling at speeds she apparently found hard to believe. As they shot through green and pleasant countryside, past distant snow-capped mountains, she was unusually quiet, still talking of course, but often lapsing into moments of thoughtful silence.

"Trains in America go much slower," she said after a prolonged time spent watching the countryside zip past.

Pascal wasn't sure if that was a compliment or a criticism of the French TGV, and so he kept his own counsel, and just smiled and nodded in return. Without realising it, he had set the standard of his behavioural responses for their entire future marriage.

At the train station, they were met by his father and Candy was gushing in that American way, welcoming his father's hugs and kisses as though she had known him all her life, and then apologising for being so forward. It was a dichotomy of thought and manners that Pascal found challenging to deal with; a very un-European way of acting.

After moments of swapping pleasantries, where Pascal's father made some faltering compliments in English, a language he seemed to have largely forgotten since he left London, an uncomfortable silence had settled onto the group. In this silence, Pascal became aware of how distant he had grown from his father, and he questioned the wisdom of visiting this place. He considered at that moment just shaking his father's hand and getting back on the train to Paris, but Candy, who seemed to sense a tension in the air, spoke to soothe that unease, and in a few careless words, doubled a conflict she knew nothing about.

"I can see Jacque takes after you," she said to the short balding man in front of her, before turning to her much taller thinner husband. "I guess Pascal must take after his mother."

"Oui," his father said suddenly staring at Pascal as though seeing him for the first time. "His Maman. Oui. His Maman. Her spirit lives in him."

Again, they were silent, Candy now visibly uncomfortable, crossing her arms and looking at Pascal as though he really should do something about it.

"Shall we get something to eat father?" He suggested, but his father held up a hand and with a soft charming smile, visibly dissolved Candy's fears and rid her of any lasting discomfort.

His father spoke a few words, his English gathering strength. He explained there was a taxi waiting to take them to his home, that they would be his guests for as long as they cared to stay, that he had a full lunch prepared and had ordered champagne be chilled and served on their arrival.

"My," Candy said. "You have gone to a great deal of trouble."

"Noh. It is… very little I do. I wish to welcome Pascal's beautiful bride with… Humble hospitality." He smiled, took her hand and lead her away.

"Monsieur Noir," Candy said, mangling the first word beyond recognition and the second beyond humour. "How can we ever thank you?"

"*Mon fille*, your smile and your… Being here. It is all the thanks an old man… requires. And you will call me Miguel."

"Miguel? Isn't that a Spanish name?"

"My great grandmother, she escaped Spain, escaped the fascist Franco."

"Oh my, that sounds like it should be a film."

"Oui. Maybe you should…" His father made squiggling writing motions in the air and Candy laughed, her arm ensnared now in the crook of his own, as the old man and the young bride walked free and easy under the bright sunshine of another beautiful Mediterranean afternoon. Any tensions drifted away behind them both, while Pascal followed with the cases, watching as his father effortlessly charmed Candy with a smile and a few simple faltering words of English.

Oh yes; Jacque took after his father.

They stayed here for a week, Candy enjoying the undivided attention of Miguel. The constant flattery sat well with her, left her at ease, she even looked to have gained a little weight, despite many an evening walk with Pascal down the hundreds of steps to the beach, past all those coloured gates he adored in his younger life.

At this house where his father now lived, where his mother's parents used to live, it felt odd to not be cooking, to not be thinking about work. Candy had not forbidden him from phoning and finding out if everything was okay, but she had suggested, quietly and directly, that it would be more romantic if he did not. He glanced at his phone, saw there were no messages, and placed it back in his pocket. His new wife sat, as she had done every evening, with Miguel, listening to another of his celebrity stories.

Pascal wondered then, had he made the right choice? Had he married Candy too soon? A woman he barely knew. Or was he just running from the thought of loving a woman who was already married? Glancing out at the sun setting over the sea, he shook the image of Juliet from his mind and focused instead on the moment of now.

Of being married to Candy.

When Pascal looked across at the two of them, he locked eyes for a moment with his father and he saw that dark shadow pass over the older man's face. That remembered pain. That moment of sadness, which would never leave. He knew that whenever his father looked at him, Miguel saw the image of Pascal's mother and that every moment they spent here would be another moment of pain in this old man's life.

They left the next day, Candy's protests diminished by the promise of travelling to Italy before they journeyed back to London. Within a few days the weather changed, even Italy has rain, and they flew back early, ending their honeymoon prematurely to begin their married life together. To begin to enact all those plans they made together.

None of the plans had worked out.

Pascal thought all that hard work in the kitchen would amount to something, that by effort alone, things would get better. Become perfect in some unfathomable way. In truth, a relentless work ethic left him burnt out and tired, just as it had left him little time for married life, and for charming an American wife whose views on the quaintness of English life soon became jaded.

When he had told Candy about his decision to stop cooking, to leave Restaurant Noir and lease the café, she had argued with him, said he was mad. Then, when Pascal mentioned his new café just happened to be opposite Juliet's office, Candy had grown quiet and sat unspeaking for the longest time before she said simply; *'opposite Juliet's? Go figure.'*

The next day, when he returned from signing the lease, he found Candy's wardrobe empty, a case missing, and a note by the table that said merely, G*oodbye Pascal. It was fun, now it isn't.*

All of this Pascal blamed on Jacque.

On that one moment of madness in Restaurant Noir that had changed all of their lives. A moment that haunted him to the core. A moment that would continue to haunt him until he confessed. He realised that now. He had to unburden his soul and tell someone about that night in the kitchen, about what he had done, what Jacque had made him do.

Not exactly forced him, but…

Pascal stood in the darkened room of his own mortality, staring into the shadows, starkly alone with his soul. His mind trapped by guilt could see only one way to release himself from this torment.

Confession!

It was, he realised in a blunt moment of realisation, the only way to find peace, the only way to move forward with his life. Reaching such a conclusion, in such a manner, left Pascal with little choice but to act on his instinct.

He would do it now, while he still had the nerve. While he still could not think of a single reason why he should not confess. He would admit everything to everyone, and he would start by confessing to Juliet.

He would do it now or he would die trying.

Pascal looked out across the street. Juliet's office light was on. Good, he would go to her, tell her everything. Bear his soul to her and hope she saw enough love in his eyes to forgive him.

He ran out of the café, crossing the street with barely a glance in either direction, narrowly avoiding cabs and buses, and pulling open the entrance to Juliet's office before bounding up the stairs, two at a time.

Once there, Pascal threw open the door to Juliet's office, strode past Tina's empty desk, entering the main office with a declaration of truth ready on his lips. The sight that greeted him as he slung the door eagerly open, stopped Pascal dead in his tracks, killing his confession in his throat.

Behind Juliet's desk, slumped and asleep in the chair sat the hateful spectre of his brother. Resplendent in a soiled white suit, an empty bottle of vodka still in Jacque's lifeless grip, his brother's head was tilted backwards, mouth open, loud snores emanating from within.

Pascal stood in the doorway, staring at his snoring nemesis, wondering why it was this man could be everywhere he was not needed.

After a moment, he walked up to Jacque and thought about kicking the man's feet from the desk, and then bawling into his face all the wrongs this brother had laid at his door. Pascal thought of doing many things in this moment of exhausted rage, but in the end, he settled on a black marker pen, and with careful but deft strokes, inscribed four clear capital letters on his brother's forehead.

Once finished, he replaced the pen and let himself out, closing the door quietly behind him.

Confessions to Juliet would have to wait. But confessions must be made. Sooner or later. Now that Pascal had made this tremendous decision, confession was the only option.

Come what may!

Chapter 14

Rose

Rose watched Juliet as covertly as she could from the opposite side of a tiny round bistro table. Juliet was trying to order a latte that she apparently didn't want, while fending off attempts by the barista to up-sell her towards a cream cake. He was young and brash, and despite his strong Spanish accent, doing an okay job of pronouncing the names of various sad looking end-of-day pastries. Unwisely he ran aground when his friendly manner crossed the low-water mark of unwanted flirting.

"I don't mean to be rude," Juliet said, rudely shutting the young man up in mid-compliment on the beauty of her eyes and comparisons to shooting stars. "But instead of providing me with a second-rate Patrick Moore and a list of things I don't want to eat, I would rather you just brought me a latte as quickly as humanly possible."

It wasn't clear if the barista knew who Patrick Moore was, or in this case, had been. Considering his spindly frame was probably equal to one of the late Moore's packed lunches, the link seemed tenuous in the extreme. He glanced to Rose for help or possibly support, neither of which Rose felt willing or able to give.

"I'll take an orange juice," she said if only to break the awkwardness of it all. "Nothing to eat."

As the young Spaniard sauntered off, the missing spring from his step obvious by its absence, Juliet looked at Rose and gave a heavy sigh.

"Why does this keep happening to me?" She said, rolling her beautifully bright blue eyes. "Am I fuckwit magnet, do you think?"

Without waiting for an answer, Juliet dived into her bag, rummaging around until finally she found her phone in a jacket pocket. With impatient eagerness in her eyes, she scanned the device for messages.

Her question had, in all probability, been rhetorical, but on the off chance it hadn't, Rose had a fairly definitive answer. Simply put; Juliet was beautiful. A beauty that was hard to define, but nonetheless a beauty that sprang from something more than Juliet's distinct good looks.

Yes, Rose considered as the waiter received a verbally garrotting for enquiring if Juliet wanted a small biscuit with her drink, it could be argued that Juliet didn't have a classic profile, that she wasn't particularly well endowed in the breast department, nor was she unusually tall or long-legged, or the many things that filled the lists of the sexual dreams of an idle mind.

And yet...

There was a certain something to Juliet. A combination of poise and a relaxed smile that had heads turning wherever she went. It was almost impossible to pin down, this elusive quality. Rose would often attribute it to a strange aura, a secret energy source radiating outward from Juliet's soul, energy others, such as this hapless barista, could feel, even if they could not fully understand.

So long as Rose had known Juliet, she had seen the way men looked at her, had been enthralled by her, and Rose had been, for the most part, as happy for her as any woman could be when sitting with someone who effortlessly turned other females in the room invisible. At the same time, Rose didn't envy the constant attention that Juliet's beauty afforded her, the consistently negative comments that were delivered, mostly from women who liked to backbite for no other reason than dissatisfaction with their own lives.

Occasionally it could be funny, this beguiling power that Juliet had, and they both could laugh at the absurdities of biological imperatives. Frequently though, far too regularly, it was merely an annoyance. Catching a bus, grabbing a cab, walking into a bar without a man in tow, standing in line to buy a simple loaf of bread, all of these things became so much harder when one was afflicted with beauty.

Rose, witnessing these moments first hand, had sometimes been glad that her own beauty was a little more subdued. Sure, she had suffered at the hands of men who thought making comments on the shortness of her skirt would make her day, even casual racists whose half-whispered comments she was supposed to hear, tinged their vile remarks with overt sexual reference points. These were though the everyday burdens of a woman living in a society that struggled to come to terms with what female equality actually meant. Let alone what it meant to a woman of colour.

Juliet's issues though were in a class of their own. Not only did she have to cope with the attraction of the instant, the moment of fascination that seemed to arrive the very second a man, and sometimes a woman, laid eyes on her, but also, she had to cope with the affliction of fame. Or perhaps, in this case, second-hand fame of being attached to those who were famous.

Juliet was 47 years old and in the soft shadows of the cafe, she looked a little younger, not much, enough to keep people guessing. Rose didn't need to guess, she knew Juliet's exact age because it had been plastered over every lurid news story that concerned the indiscretions of her husband, Clive. Every rancid newspaper story about Clive always ended with a short terse paragraph *Juliet Raphael, Literary Agent to the stars (45), was not available for comment.*

That had been two years ago, and as far as Rose knew, Clive and Juliet had spoken very little since the divorce had been finalised. Yet here they were, waiting for Clive to contact them with vital information that Juliet needed to save Jacque's reputation, and her business.

Rose had listened intently on arrival at the tiny café. Pressed up against the wall, her laptop bag on her lap because there simply wasn't room on the floor. The seated area of this café was really just a passageway between the wall and the serving area. Most people were encouraged to take their drinks and consume them on the move, those that did not, had to fight for one of only three tables that ran the gauntlet of the miniature passageway. Here you had the opportunity to see the drinks being made, and to view, with close detail, each backside that queued up to order their coffee.

It wasn't exactly relaxing, but Juliet's tale of intrigue had been so engrossing, Rose soon forgot that her personal boundaries were being impeached by a string of random strangers every few seconds. As they received their drinks from a barista, who this time said nothing, Rose outlined a summary of what she had just heard. She was an accountant and business manager; she couldn't help doing this.

"What you are saying is; this reviewer…"

"Adam Russel."

"Thank you... Adam has written such a bad review of Jacque's cookbook that it will sink sales before sales can even get going."

"That's about it, and if that happens, I will lose out on my agency commission, which I tied to book sales to try and get a cash boost from my business, and which has already been spent on last month's rent."

"I hadn't realised things were quite that bad," Rose said and realised she was having a day where this sentiment applied to lots of people close to her.

"Since..." Juliet paused and made a motion with her eyes, Rose took this to mean the whole *Clive being gay thing*. "Since that earlier problem, I've experienced a certain... Reluctance, shall we say, from other celebrities to work with me."

Rose nodded. It could happen. A friend of hers had a very successful accountancy operation in the city. During the bank crisis of 2007, he became a scapegoat for all those problems the bankers had created with their greed. Even when the dust had settled and fraud investigations came to nothing, his name remained tarnished. The bankers who bankrupted the country with their ravenousness need to accumulate obscene amounts of wealth had also seen to it that businesses around them carried as much of the blame as possible. In the end, Rose's friend had resorted to working for Russian Oligarchs, who in turn, made him a wealthy man.

Rose wasn't sure this story had the right moral ending; the fact that it was true also troubled her.

"Did you know?" Rose said carefully during a lull in the conversation. "That Jacque is also in trouble?"

Juliet paused from stirring her coffee.

"When isn't he? How much this time?"

"Juliet, I am a professional account and business manager, it would be unethical to tell you he is about up to… here in debt." Rose made a motion around neck level to indicate the depth of shit Jacque was sinking into.

"Got it."

"And if this book deal goes bad, it'll probably be this deep." She indicated a point some distance over her head.

"Bankruptcy?"

"It's a possibility. He owes money to the tax office," Rose added, a fact that she had found out just after the aborted meeting with Sir Geoffrey earlier today. If the Taxman didn't get his money, they would raid Jacque's private pension fund to get their pound of flesh.

They lapsed into silence. Rose didn't want to see this happen to Jacque, he was her ex-husband, a man who she sort of cared for, in a vaguely familiar way, probably because he was the father of her child, but… Well, if he went under, she would just be put in charge of his bankruptcy case, which in turn would earn her money, and then she would have some free time that could be filled by another client.

Maybe a Russian Oligarch this time.

It was almost win-win for Rose. It would leave Yvonne a little bereft in the inheritance department, but they would manage.

Juliet, on the other hand, was clearly out of options and relying on sales from Jacque's book. If Juliet didn't get this, she would go under as well, and that would be a damn shame.

Pascal, Jacque, Juliet. All in trouble at the same time, mostly, it had to be said, due to the actions, or inactions depending on how you looked at it, of her ex-husband; Jacque Noir.

The thought filled her with the associated guilt of having known someone that was, generally speaking, fucking things up for everyone.

Against her best self-advice, Rose felt compelled to speak.

"Juliet," she said and took a sip of orange juice for courage, one that she wished contained vodka. "You do know about the brothers, don't you? About the cooking? About…"

Rose tailed off… She wanted to help Juliet, and right now, she didn't owe Jacque diddlysquat, but this still felt like a betrayal. She knew a lot of Family Noir secrets, some she would take to her grave, this one she knew only because she had been there, in the kitchen, watching how things worked. Who did what. And who didn't! She had assumed others could see the big picture just by what happened in the recent past. From the puzzled look on Juliet's face, it seemed as though this may not be the case.

"Oh no, what have Pascal and Jacque done now?" Juliet said, clearly misunderstanding Rose's meaning. "Is it bad? Will it be in the papers?"

"No, it's not that, it's just…"

"Yes?"

"Well, in the kitchen, you see… It's really … It was always…"

Rose was cut off by a loud beep from Juliet's phone. Juliet silenced Rose with an upheld hand so she could urgently dedicate her attention to the display.

"It's Clive… He's got something for me." She said, hitting the screen with her well-manicured fingernails, scrolling and then sitting back with a slight look of disappointment.

"What is it? What did he say?" Rose asked, somewhat relieved that she had been spared from divulging one of the Noir Brothers' less well-known secrets. She wanted to help Juliet; she just wasn't sure that it should be her who informed Juliet of the stuff she needed to be informed of in order to be fully informed.

"Clive says he can't find Adam, but he knows someone who can." Juliet put the phone away, biting her lip and looking at Rose in a very odd way.

"Well," Rose said, intrigued. "Who is it?"

"Polly?"

"Polly? Polly who…? Oh. Polly!"

"Yes, Polly!"

There was a moment's silence, during which time it was clear that Juliet was giving Rose the chance to bail out and leave this unfolding drama well alone. Rose decided not to take that option. Secretly, she had to admit, this was shaping up to be the most fun she'd ever had as an accountant and business manager.

"Then we should go find Polly," Rose said. "And as chance would have it, I know where she is likely to be at this time of day."

"You do? Rose, thank you." Juliet stood and moved the ten centimetres necessary to reach the café bar. "Hey, you! I need this to go."

"Yes, yes," the young Spaniard said, sprinting the short distance to her. "And señora, have I mentioned how…"

"…Beautiful my eyes are? Yes, we've covered that. Now if you truly want to impress me, let's see if you can achieve putting this coffee in that cardboard cup without spilling a drop."

Out on the street, Rose hailed a cab and gave the driver the address of a pub near Vauxhall Bridge, to which Juliet gave a questioning look although Rose refused the opportunity to explain herself. Juliet was probably wondering why Rose knew the location of a woman that Rose had every right to hate.

Polly!

In truth though, Rose did not hate Polly, mainly because Polly was just another woman in a long line of women that Jacque had secretly, and not so secretly fucked. The way Polly had acted afterwards though and the way she attempted to profit from Jacque's indiscretion had marked her as different from the rest.

Jacque's indiscretions (*plural*), as they became referred to in family circles, had been something Rose chose mainly to ignore, to forgive, and then to indulge. The latter occurring as she found her own life in the bloom of turning thirty-something. Like most things in their relationship, it just seemed to happen. Very much like their marriage day.

Their wedding in the South of France, a magical day that people still talked about in her social circle, probably would not have happened if Rose hadn't become pregnant. She had been on the verge of leaving Jacque, at the end of her tether and appalled at how Jacque's *indiscretions* seemed to be getting younger and younger. They were, in fact, about the same age as they had always been, the age Rose had been when she first met him, but as she aged, their youth became an exaggerated focal point. Salt in the wound.

At the time, mentally, her bag had been packed for months; she even caught herself looking through property adverts, trying to figure out if there was something she could afford that was less than an hour's train journey from London. Then without warning, a baby was on the way, a product of make-up sex after an argument about unfaithfulness that he swore never happened, and even if it did, meant nothing, and even if it didn't, would never happen again.

Everything changed when Jacque found out about the baby. He proposed to her on the spot, swore to change his ways, and Rose had, possibly for self-interested reasons, believed him. Although it had to be said that he was always so persuasive. So charming. So easy to believe.

Marriage felt like the perfect answer to all their problems. Of course, it was no such thing.

As motherhood enveloped her life, she became her own boss, moved into her own office and took on her own clients, even a few from her original employer, Steven Peterson, who had made some unfortunate racists remarks on Twitter and been hounded from his profession. He now ran a fish and chip shop in South End on Sea, which apparently did a really nice saveloy.

Through the force of her own will, Rose's fortunes moved forward at the pace she set, which was frantic and hard. Eventually, she had to admit that motherhood and a career were not mutely compatible, and sent her daughter off to finishing school in France. Something that Yvonne had at first argued against, but when she heard about riding lessons, a lake where one could swim, and mountains that one could gaze at while writing poetry, she was pretty much gone on the first plane out.

At that point, Rose decided it would be prudent to take stock of where she was in her own life, and whether or not she was happy continuing to ignore Jacque's dalliances. Despite this inward marital navel-gazing, Rose did nothing until one morning fate tipped her hand. While emptying Jacque's trousers before taking them to the dry cleaners she found a phone number. She emptied Jacque's pockets on a regular basis as his chaotic personality often left him with hundreds of pounds in tips stuffed into a back pocket. That was a lot of money to give to the dry-cleaning lady, so Rose always checked.

Phone numbers were not an uncommon find either, Jacque liked to network as much as he liked to flirt, but this one was written in pink lipstick and it had a little love heart drawn next to it. Her interest piqued; Rose visited Restaurant Noir that very lunchtime to find the kitchen in the usual chaos. The Noir brothers were in pandemonium so often, it was relatively simple for her to slip in unnoticed and dial up the pink lipstick number.

A few seconds later and she saw a young waitress, barely a woman in Rose's eyes, take out a phone and answer it. As she spoke, the younger woman's eyes tracked towards Rose, saw her standing there with the phone to ear and a knowing look on her face, and the young waitress had gone several shades of scarlet. This was the first time Rose even remembered seeing Polly, but it was a face that would become familiar in newspapers and magazines, on TV and even once in a film.

It had not been the first time that Jacque had slept with the staff, but so appalled was Rose at the age of the young woman, Rose had demanded, to her future shame, Polly be sacked. Jacque, without a thought, had done Rose's bidding to keep the matrimonial peace.

Polly, young in years as she might be, had a certain knowledge of Social Media and also, rather crucially, a few good contacts in the print media. One contact, in particular, was Adam Russel, her uncle, a chef Jacque had once fired for reasons that were never made clear. A man who had failed to make a career in cooking and instead became a food critic, much to Jacque's continued amusement, and occasional resentment when Restaurant Noir did not receive the praise he thought it should, from the man whose career Jacque had ruined.

Adam got the last laugh, getting his niece's story published in the gossip columns as an explosive *Kiss & Tell*, and an insight into the frenzied working of Restaurant Noir. The last bit had been cut from the article due to legal pressure from Jacque and Pascal that cost the restaurant a good deal of money. The *Kiss & Tell* though had been printed unedited and left Rose utterly humiliated. Within a year, Rose and Jacque were divorced. Still civil, mostly for the sake of their daughter, who ironically rarely saw her parents, or came home.

Catapulted into the world of gossip columns and lads' mags, Polly became a topless model, and here she earned the name *Perky Polly*. All of which would have been fine if she hadn't piled on the pounds via the excessive nature of simply being famous. It wasn't long after a beach holiday in the canaries that her name became twisted into *Porky Polly*. Around this time a sex tape surfaced. Not of Jacque, fortunately, but something she had created with a boyfriend a few months before she even started work at Restaurant Noir. A video in which she was doing all the stuff adults do, which was fine, but during sex, she made remarks about people of colour that inflamed Twitter; the home of rigid intolerance.

On mass, the internet mob decided to punish Polly for the sin of being an imperfect victim. As she had been the archetypal *Other Woman*, female press pundits, and the usually vocal feminist Twitterers had been less than swift in her defence. Finally, as her 15 minutes of fame faded, Polly ended up on Reality TV as an E-Rated Celeb in the Jungle wearing bathing suits that now did her plus-size figure no favours. To cap it all, under the spotlight of 24/7 TV, she let slip some personal views on multiculturalism that most people found repulsive and was voted off straight away. Not even interesting enough to be the nasty one who usually beats the rest.

Now Polly worked behind the bar in a pub that few people had heard of, and apparently still signed autographs for anyone that still remembered who she had been. Rose knew the pub because she'd read about it in gossip columns of magazines that she only read in newsagents without actually buying a copy. As though doing so made Rose less complicit in the exploitation of those people being dissected in print.

Rose took no joy from knowing Polly had ended her fame in such a fashion, that she had restarted her career as a waitress, or in this case, barwoman. In some ways, like most people who came in contact with Jacque, Rose felt, in a way sorry for Polly.

Now Rose and Juliet were in a cab, barrelling through rush-hour traffic towards a pub where Polly worked. Rose figured that if anyone knew Adam's location tonight, it would be his favourite niece. Although exactly how Juliet intended getting him to change his review was anyone's guess. She dearly hoped that Juliet had a cunning plan.

As the pub came into sight, Rose gathered her bag and her wits. This would be no easy encounter as Polly was unlikely to be best pleased to see her, or indeed Juliet. Apparently, Juliet had turned down the chance to represent Polly who, at the grand age of 23, wanted to sell her autobiography to the highest bidder. In the event, publishers and agents had failed to show any interest whatsoever in documenting what had so far transpired of young Polly's life story. As one wit had snidely remarked in reference to Polly's sex tape; *the best bits were already on the internet.*

With all this in mind and with some trepidation, Juliet and Rose entered a pub that from the outside looked to be exactly the sort of place they had spent their whole adult lives avoiding. Inside was no better, in many ways, it underlined the stark warning the outside had attempted to give them.

There were a few punters at the bar, a few at tables eating their fish and chips, but mostly the place was empty, almost destitute. If this pub had a motto it would be, *our best days are behind us.* A fitting place, Rose thought, for *Perky Polly* to have ended her reign of fame, and then dismissed the thought when she remembered she was supposed to be feeling sorry for her.

Polly wasn't behind the bar when they came in; she was standing by a half-open fire exit, through which she blew smoke, half her attention on the bar and the vague possibility that someone might order something. The two women locked eyes the moment they spotted each other; Polly's widening slightly, but she seemed to mentally hold her ground. She'd been through Twitter taunting hell and back and now was a woman who knew no little fear. A fact that in some ways frightened Rose more than she cared to admit.

She had aged, Rose could see. Polly had always looked younger than her years, now though fame had left a scar that ran deeper than her rough complexion and the darkened rings under eyes. Her figure, which had previously been top-heavy but trim at the waist, was now lumpy and undefined. Even her hair, once shiny and blond was now artificially white and straggly.

Some women, like Juliet, were blessed with an enduring beauty that simply increased its intensity with age; others had a brief moment in time when their beauty was at its height, and then, like a flowering orchid, the moment was all too quickly gone. A fleeting moment that Polly clearly attempted to recapture using hair dye, false lashes and fake nails, and makeup that hindered rather than helped.

Rose approached the bar with as much ballsiness as she could muster and Polly flicked her fag out into the night air, closing the door and turning to face the two women with fearsome bluster.

"Is there a reunion I don't know about?" Polly said, with a smile that defined the word nasty. "For women who've fucked Jacque Noir."

This took the wind out of Rose's sails somewhat, and she stood for a moment, trying to reorganise her thoughts.

"Actually, I've never been fucked by Jacque," Juliet said, her posh voice ringing out into the brief silence. Both women turned to look at her. "At least not physically. Possibly financially."

"Don't worry luv'," Polly said. "Evening ain't over yet."

"Polly," Rose said, struggling to reign in the conversation before it could go too far off tangent. "We're not here for you. We're looking for your uncle."

"Adam?" Surprise was etched on her face, quickly wiped away by suspicion. "What you want with him?"

"Just a quick word," Juliet said. Her voice sounded so painfully posh in this run-down pub that even one of the most heavily drunk men at the bar turned to look.

"Well, I ain't seen him." She said, her eyes tracking across to the men's toilet door, and then back again. "Ain't seen him for weeks."

"You're a terrible liar," Rose said and motioned to Juliet to follow her to the men's toilet. Juliet's eyes widened in alarm, but she tagged along.

"Oi, 'ang on. You can't go in there." Polly was running around the bar, her heeled boots skidding on the slippery tiled floor, she was within a few feet of grabbing Rose, when one of the drunks from the bar staggered in front of her.

"Eh, you.... You's that Polly ain't yer. Polly what's on the internet.... Can I have a selfie," the drunken man struggled to get his phone out, half falling into Polly's arms who nearly collapsed under his dead weight.

"For fuck's sake," she said, doing a slow dance across the room, trying to rid herself of this sudden fan attack.

"Quick," Rose said indicating the men's toilet. "In here."

"If you're sure," Juliet responded with a look of appalled horror.

The two burst into the small room and froze.

Adam stood leaning against the back wall of the sole toilet compartment, the door open, his trousers around his ankles. Also around his ankles was a young man who knelt before him with Adam's cock deep inside his mouth. Both men shared an almost comical look of surprise at the appearance of Rose and Juliet.

"Fuck me, are you the police?" the young man said, jumping to his feet, and wiping at the corners of his mouth. "I didn't ask for money, I swear."

"Relax," Adam sneered. "They aren't the police."

"No, we're not," Rose said, very quickly, wondering how her life had taken such a turn to leave her in a toilet witnessing a man receiving fellatio from another.

"What the fuck do you want?" Adam said, pulling up his trousers, although he appeared to be taking his time about tucking his privates out of sight.

"Mr Russel. It's about a review that you've written on Jacque Noir's cookery book," Juliet said, as though they were in a boardroom discussing a recent PowerPoint presentation.

"Seriously? You're here to complain about a review of mine? There is this thing called email."

"Yes, I am aware, except that… this is rather urgent, and I was hoping that you would…"

"Change my review?" Adam laughed aloud. "Not a chance. I owe that French fucker and this is payback."

"What did he promise you," Rose said, aiming her question at the young man who was now pressed back against the bathroom sink as though the wall might in some way absorb him if he pushed hard enough.

The young man took a moment to realise, as did the other two, that Rose had addressed him. He looked hesitantly at Adam, but found no support or help there, so looked blankly back at Rose.

"I don't really want to get involved in this," he said. "Whatever this is."

"Was it a job?"

The young man's eyes widened in surprise. Bullseye.

"You won't get it. Whatever he's promising you. It'll never happen."

"Why don't you two just fuck off," Adam said, his confidence ebbing, some strain appearing in his voice. He seemed to know where this was going.

The young man picked up on it as well, glancing at Adam as though seeing him for the first time.

"It was a job; in the paper he works at." His face was going slowly red as though realising how foolish this all sounded.

"Adam works freelance for the paper, he has as much pull in the world of media as I do," Rose said, realising the young man probably had no idea who she was.

"Don't believe her," Adam said. "She's a crazy woman."

"Am I now?"

The young man was looking troubled though clearly, he did believe Rose.

"Don't feel bad," she said, keeping an eye on Adam in case he made a run for it. "He does this to a lot of men. Mostly young men. Makes them do all sorts of things they don't really want to do and promises the world in return. It's what he does. It's his thing."

Everyone was looking at Adam for a long hard moment, a moment that had Adam take a half step backwards, his arms half-raised in defence. Then with a frustrated gesture, the younger man spat on the floor, glared at Adam, and stormed from the room, the door banging shut behind him. Beyond, Rose caught sight of two men trying to pry the drunken man off Polly. They had nearly succeeded. Rose didn't have long.

"What now?" Adam said. "You getting on your knees?"

"I don't think I'm your type," Rose said.

"Then what? All you've done is ruin my evening, you think that's going to make me change my review?"

Rose walked the short distance to Adam, standing just a few centimetres away, trying to ignore the pervading smells of the small room. Smells that screamed for attention.

"Did you hear what I just said about you? You know where I got that from?" Rose said.

"Let me guess? Jacque gave you some interesting pillow talk, if he was ever long enough at your pillow to talk."

Rose ignored the jibe.

"Yes, he did, but what's more interesting is Juliet here. She's just commissioned a biography on Jacque Noir. Haven't you Juliet?"

Juliet was silent for a second; clearly trying to remember all those seminars she had been to where they discussed difficult meetings and how to deal with them. Rose was pretty sure this scenario never came up during workshopping.

"Yes, yes I am," Juliet said eventually, and then understanding the game she added, "And I will be the one who decides on the details of his life story, and how those details should be... Moderated."

Adam stared at her for a long moment before taking out a cigarette and placing it unlit into his mouth. He seemed to be wrestling with his next words until finally, he was able to speak.

"Alright, you got me by the balls, that much is clear, but I can't write a good review of Jacque's book, I just can't."

"Why not?"

"It's shit. None of the recipes work, what the fuck was he thinking?" Adam seemed to be genuinely perplexed and Rose noticed that Juliet turned a funny shade of purple when he said it. Adam clearly wasn't lying.

"Okay," Rose said. "Can you at least write something neutral, something that suggests if changes were made a second edition might be better?"

Adam thought about it for a moment. Then nodded.

"I can do that, but do I have your word about the biography? I am never mentioned. Not ever!"

"Of course," Juliet said in her most offended voice. Remarkable when Rose considered she was being offended about not keeping her word on the content of a biography that didn't exist and probably never would.

"Then I'll make the changes, I'll phone it in now. It's going to press tomorrow... But you know that don't you. That's why you're here!"

"Yes, we do know that," Rose said, trying to channel the shorter one from Cagney and Lacey. Her tough moment was ruined when the door behind her was yanked open and Polly, in total disarray, leapt in.

"You two," She yelled and both women almost jumped out of their skins. "I want you out of this fucking pub, now!"

"It's alright Polly," Adam said. "I've sorted it out."

"I still want them out."

"It's okay," Rose said. "We were leaving anyway."

And leave they did, as rapidly as heels on a dirty stone floor would allow. Outside in the cold air, neither one of them stopped until they had rounded at least two street corners. Only then did they come to a standstill, looked at each other, and burst out laughing.

"Well, I must say," Rose said. "I always imagined a night on the town with Juliet Raphael being slightly different from all this."

"Yes, quite," Juliet said, and Rose could see she was shaking slightly. "I feel like we should high-five or something. Is that appropriate do you think?"

"I think we should just get in a cab and call it quits."

"Quite right," Juliet said with a nod.

After a brief moment to see where they actually were, they made their way back to the main street and after a few minutes, managed the good fortune of finding a cab that was free and heading back into the city.

"Okay," Rose said as the cab propelled them back to roughly where they had started. "I guess now all we need to do is get Jacque to alter the cookbook, but of course, the problem with that is…"

"Oh God Jacque," Juliet shouted loud enough to make the cab driver jump, and once again interrupting Rose from spilling the Noir Brothers' deepest secret. "I've just remembered he's at my office. Possibly. He may have gone home by now. Do you want to come back with me?"

"Ah, no, no thank you," Rose said. Twice now she had reached the edge of telling Juliet everything about the Noir Brothers and been stopped. She considered this a warning from the universe to quit while she was ahead. After a day like today, all she really wanted was her bed, a good night's rest. Maybe then, with a fresh brain, she could find a way to tackle this problem that was her ex-husband.

Later, when she finally reached her bed and lay down, she turned to the empty pillow beside her and thought about Adam's offhanded remarks. He had been right, dead right, and yet here she was, still fighting Jacque's corner with the flimsy excuse that he was the father of her child.

As she drifted into sleep, Rose wondered how long she would continue to feed the fire of that excuse; how long she could believe it herself.

Chapter 15

Tina

Tina stared at her phone and wondered vaguely if there was a text message equivalent of Tourette's syndrome. It was the only explanation she could think of for the bizarre collection of words Juliet had just sent. Something about witnessing a blowjob in a Gent's toilet and using it to suppress a negative book review. The fact that it ended with *Rose sends her love* only added to the surreal nature of the whole thing.

To be on the safe side, Tina wrote back that she was glad Juliet's evening had worked out for the best and *love to Rose back*. She added a kiss and some random Emoticons to muddy the waters a bit and make it look as though she understood what was going on.

She felt though, in many ways, that whatever was going on, it would make little difference to their current dilemma. Far as Tina could see, the chances of them coming through this mess unscathed and solvent was something akin to an avocado surviving a poetry slam with a group of passionate vegans (that is to say, all vegans).

The last few days with Juliet had been trying beyond belief, she knew her sister was in trouble, and by definition, so was Tina, or at least her chance at steady employment, but the comings and goings of late had left her reconsidering her loyalties. She even considered the vague possibility of getting a proper job. Albeit that Tina didn't really know of any proper jobs she could apply for; never having actually had a proper job in her entire life.

That's not to say she hadn't kept herself busy. At fifty years of age, forty-seven to anyone who asked, anyone male that is, she was fully experienced in many of the values of life. From school, where she had failed to shine at any particular subject, except pottery, she left to discover a cruel and unjust world. One that didn't really like nice people, like Tina, and also, in the main, didn't like her pottery. She had made this voyage of self-discovery at age twenty-one, by creating her own clay works and trying to sell them at Greenwich Sunday market. She made exactly one pound, which had been given to her by an old woman who thought Tina was collecting for the blind.

"Such brave souls," the old woman said. "Creating pottery even though they don't actually know what good pottery is supposed to look like."

Deducting the cost of the clay, the kiln, and the day rate for the market stall in Greenwich, which had put all of the other expenses in the shade, she made a financial loss that would have embarrassed a 1970's British car manufacturer. From that point onwards, she had worked for her father.

Sir John, or to his friends, Sir John, had employed her at first as a sort of non-entity in charge of not very much. Yes, Tina had some duties and tasks to perform, small matters of paperwork that pertained to Sir John's ridiculously extensive property portfolio, and the occasional guest to entertain when and if any appointments should overrun and cause embarrassing delays.

In these moments, Tina became quite the dab hand at energetic small talk and perfected the art of Insistent-Tea; which is a hot drink that can never be refused if the correct manipulation is applied. Mostly though, she found that people could be persuaded to talk about themselves at great length, and forget about the pressings of time, if only the right questions were asked, and if one stayed silent long enough to hear the answers.

Tina became so proficient at the task of entertaining her father's appointments, that soon he began to actually trust her to get the job done, and to become a substantial part of his business day. This progressed over the years until Tina had taken on the day-to-day running of the office and effectively became the office manager. Albeit the office contained just her and her father. Most of the heavy lifting for the rental fees and sales of banked land was taken on by solicitors and accountants; people who, for the most part, knew what they were doing. It was simply a matter for Tina to make sure the relevant paperwork was signed and returned on time.

It was a job which could be as diversely interesting as it could be dull, a little bit like life. Sadly, this all came to an abrupt end when the volatile British property market took one of its regular nosedives. Her father, being a canny businessman, saw it coming and shed a great deal of his portfolio at the right moment, making him a lot of money and a lot of other people very sad. The real loser though was Tina who had a lot less paperwork to process, and significantly fewer guests to entertain.

Her office duties had then migrated towards making sure the cleaner was doing her job, that flowers in the lobby were always fresh, and that magazines on the waiting tables never went unread. Tina wasn't on the border of being bored, but she could see the mountains of monotony on a clear day, and it worried her. Although she did very little about it for several years.

Juliet's decision to open her own literary agency came as a welcome opportunity.

"Your sister wants money to get some kind arty agency off the ground," her father said to her over luncheon one winter's day. "All well and good, but she's no head for business, so I'm going to send you to look after her. Try and keep her feet on the ground, if you can. Juliet's good with words, but her mind is far too often in the clouds. Just like your mother. May she rest in peace."

Mostly, he was right. Tina started at the office to find bills needed paying and office supplies hadn't been scheduled for delivery because they were still waiting for an order number. A mess, compounded by the presence of Clive who thought business people should permanently be at lunch.

"Perhaps in the acting world," Tina said, "being out of the office on a regular basis has its advantages, but in *other* worlds, it doesn't work."

Clive had poked his tongue out at her and then tickled her from behind, which she always hated. At least Juliet saw sense, and although she acted as though she resented her father for gifting Tina on her, she was clearly relieved when all the day-to-day office problems evaporated like early morning mist once Tina took charge of it all. Although Juliet, in her independent way, liked to think it was her powerhouse of enthusiasm that got things done, and Tina, who was never a fan of praise, was willing enough to go along with this pretence.

This had set the precedence for their working life together. Tina did all the stuff that needed doing, and Juliet pretended she did it. It was an odd relationship, but in the main, it worked. Although of late, Tina wondered how long it could continue. She could manage the office for as long as it existed, but judging by the current business income versus its modest outgoings, that really could only be a matter of months. Perhaps even weeks if Jacque's book didn't do well.

Like most people, or perhaps more accurately, most women, Tina had been charmed when she first met Jacque on that apocryphal afternoon lunch with Juliet and Clive. The very opening of the agency and the start of a grand adventure for them all. The Noir Brothers had taken control of the restaurant from their father at that point, and Jacque, always resplendent in his perfect chef whites was there to entertain the customers with his off-colour jokes, flirting and good-natured generosity.

Tina had though, over the years, come to know the man in greater depth, begun to see the darker side of his narcissistic personality. And there had been that widely reported affair with a young kitchen maid, or waitress, or whatever it was she had been doing. Mainly Jacque, if the stories were to be believed.

And then the Clive thing had happened and brought with it the implosion of Tina's world. All these divorces and family feuds left a fractured mess of Tina's existence. Some days, she really resented the actions of all those who had plucked the wings off her life and pined for the days when all she really had to worry about was when the next bit of gossip was likely to be uttered in her earshot.

Juliet never had time for gossip, which was a crying shame as sisters who never gossiped about other women seemed to be in some way shirking feminine responsibilities. Doubly painful considering that Tina had a lot of gossip to share. Red hot stuff that came straight from the actual source. In the case of famous jockeys, literally the horse's mouth.

In the days of Juliet's rise to success, her little office in Islington had been the unlikely landing spot for untold numbers of celebrities. They weren't actual Triple-A Hollywood stars, more your supporting Oscar winners and sports personalities, a term that Tina came to learn was an Oxymoron in the truest definition of the word. There were also politicians, few in number, but ex-cabinet members nevertheless, and the odd Lord, with the emphasis on the word *odd*.

Tina had used the years of experience she gained from working with her father to meet and greet Juliet's clients. Try to put them at ease, despite the somewhat lacklustre condition of their office. She would offer a drink as soon as they arrived, a drink the celebrity in question would nearly always like, no matter how obscure, or how difficult it had been to source the ingredients. Research, Tina had learned in those early years entertaining her father's busy executives, whose patience could be measured in nanoseconds, was the secret to it all.

In this relaxed condition of having their favourite drink offered in such an unexpected fashion, Tina would use her softly spoken interrogation skills, her conversational weapons, to find out just about anything she wanted. Had she been working for the Sunday newspapers, or rather, if the Sunday newspapers had been even the slightest bit aware of Tina and her specific skill set, she would probably have made a small fortune.

However, for Tina, the real goal was collecting the gossip for herself. It was a hobby. One that she used to while away those dull days in the office when there was nothing much to do, except attend to the daily post, make sure the bills were paid, and keep Juliet focused on her schedule. And occasionally undo whatever complex fuckup Juliet had managed to inflict on her laptop.

Things that Tina could comfortably manage in her sleep.

This had been Tina's life; office manager for her sister, and gossip hunter to the stars. A life that she had enjoyed immensely; had refined to the point of perfection.

Tina had become aware of it ending, the gradual erosion of visiting talent, the lack of necessity to order obscure fruits to make exotic drinks that often tasted vile, the bleak-looking gaps in the appointment calendar. All had pointed to a slowdown, which had begun just after that nasty business with Clive.

She didn't really blame him, well, not now, not with the passage of time, but it was a shame that Tina had to get her gossip from supermarket magazines, just like most people on the planet. She hated that change the most.

Into this void, she had floundered for a while, first becoming involved with the homeless of Islington, and her regular coffee and sandwich supply runs to those she met on her lunch break. Some work in soup kitchens at the weekend was also fulfilling, but it still couldn't completely plug the hole left by all those Celebs telling her all their gossip.

More out of boredom than anything else, Tina had turned to a large pile of unsolicited manuscripts that squatted on a semi-permanent basis beside her desk. The Slush Pile, as it was known, a grand stack of A4 brown envelopes that sat unloved and unread, sometimes for months, in the corner of their office. Most of them would contain novels that were unsuitable for Juliet to represent because she specialised in autobiographies. However, Tina didn't blame the authors for trying their luck, or even for not researching the needs of this particular literary agency before they posted off their hopes and dreams in a dull brown envelope.

In some ways, Tina felt sorry for them and in that moment of boredom, when she began reading that first novel from the Slush Pile, she became involved. At last finding a way to fill the void in her soul left by the dearth of Celebs in her life.

It started with a romance novel that Tina attempted to read. More of a novella really, the author appearing to have lost sight of the plot and ended the book early, presumably out of desperation. The book was an unlikely construction of love and cosy happiness, tinged with some unexpected, but rather pedestrian tragedy, something akin to an episode of Lassie, only minus the dog.

The submission included a stamped addressed return envelope, a rarity from people wanting a reply, or ever again expecting to see the master copy of their work. Tina, feeling she had something to say to this writer about the structure of the book, drafted a letter, printed it out and popped it in the envelope, along with the manuscript, and returned it via the post office. In the letter, she gave some basic feedback; suggestions on perhaps adding a little sex to the story, nothing too graphic, but just enough for the implied reader to get the implied idea that all this hardship the couple were going through was at least worth the implied effort. Once Tina had sent it off, she thought nothing more about it.

A short time later, another brown envelope arrived with the familiar tidy scrawl for the address. Her interest peeked; Tina opened it straight away instead of consigning it to the sometime-never-pile next to her desk. Inside she found a new, reworked manuscript, this time, with her suggestions taken to heart. Or at least taken to one bodily organ or another. The sex scenes, which Tina read over an afternoon doughnut and a herbal tea, left her eyebrows stuck for some time in the position of profoundly shocked. When she finished, a brief walk down by the Thames in the cool fresh air was needed to calm her down a little.

Tina took some time to think about her next reply to this writer. She even decided to do a little research on the internet as to the best way of giving good feedback. She didn't bother Googling *how to write* as she herself had no interest in doing so, but she was an avid reader who devoured books of all sorts in a steady stream, so felt that she was more than qualified to give a writer feedback on writing. Although this time, she wanted to be a little more careful in what she wished for.

Her next letter thanked the author for the changes, and then discussed, at a nonspecific level, how perhaps some of the sex scenes could be tamed a little in order to be more... *Palatable*. Repeated naming of bodily parts, their size, and the order in which they were used was perhaps one area that Tina felt could be toned down. A little!

She sent the letter off and waited. While she waited, Tina opened another brown envelope in search of another letter to write; another bit of imparted wisdom she could give from reader to writer. Finding a novel that was worthy of a reply was a more laborious task than she imagined. That very first one she had pulled from the pile at random, had been a pretty good read, aside from the problems she identified, and somewhat naively, Tina had assumed that all manuscripts writers submitted to agencies would be, at least, at this basic level of readability.

Sadly, this proved not to be the case. Appalled, she waded through the next manuscript; an unfinished fantasy novel of just five chapters, none of which were sequential. Fragmented though it was, the story did hold a certain vague coherence that interested Tina, and in places, was very funny. To this gentleman, a retired taxman from Bracknell, she sent a note stating simply that he should finish the novel in its entirety before resubmitting. Tina also warned that fantasy, even with a humorous undertone (the author's own description that came some way towards the bottom of a rambling five-page introduction letter) could be considered a hard sell.

Once Tina had found an envelope and enough stamps to pay for its return, she sealed her suggestions inside and put it in her Post Out tray, and realised the process was actually giving her a lift. A soft vibrancy of her soul she normally felt while helping at the soup kitchen or giving out coffee to the homeless.

It was at this point she realised how similar writers were to homeless people. Both were a desperate group of people, living hand to mouth, with little hope and isolated from humanity, but right under everyone's nose. They were the silent witness to our social order, and apart from the tap-tap-tap thing that writers did to fill the hours of endless silence, they were essentially people lost to society.

This insight constituted the first baby steps of Tina in her journey to helping writing talent realise its potential. Much better her than Juliet, who once labelled senders of unsolicited manuscripts as; *'irritating fuckers with very little grasp of the English language'*, which Tina considered a little harsh.

In all, it was a rough house for ordinary everyday people trying to become that strange animal, a writer. Tina didn't envy them, but she did enjoy trying to help them. In a way, reading through their rambling plots, and two-dimensional characters was relaxing, almost cathartic in exorcising the demons of all those boring biographies she had been complicit in bringing into the world.

Tonight, however, she was reading a book that had minimal appeal to anyone and appeared to have been written by a ten-year-old with only a vague grasp of diction and grammar. It also featured several plots from recent Hollywood films, possibly more; it was difficult to tell, as Tina didn't go to the cinema very often. The book was called, *Terror, Mars, Disaster*, although she still wasn't too sure if that was the title or a summary. The author's name was written in bold caps directly under the title.

RON BROWN.

Tina had been talking to Ron on the short walk back to his car, and more out of keeping the conversation light and chatty, rather than anything else, she'd made the mistake of mentioning that sometimes she read novels from Juliet's Slush Pile. Before the foggy breath of her words had time to evaporate under the harsh light of a lamppost, Ron had whipped out his phone and emailed his book to her.

Now here she was, reading it.

She poured herself another generous glass of red wine and looked at the notes she had made so far. *Needs More Work* were the only polite comments she had managed to think of so far, although she had underlined it three times. In different coloured inks.

Her phone beeped and with relief she saw it wasn't yet another message from Ron asking her what she thought of his book. Instead, it was a slightly more lucid message from Juliet saying she had just dropped off Rose and was now heading for home, but would drop in on the office first. At which point Tina remembered Jacque was by all probability, still at the office! If Jacque had found that bottle of vodka she had filed under P (for Potentially Awkward Moments) which he might, considering he knew it was there, then by now he would be very drunk. This meant Juliet was walking into a situation that was worrying on many different levels.

Charming and smarmy Jacque might be when sober, when drunk, he tended to be very hands-on, and they really didn't need Jacque at the awards ceremony with a black eye, or worse still, not there at all because Juliet had vetoed the idea of being his plus-one. Or just killed him.

Jacque drunk was also not the ideal person to broach the suggestion of taking Juliet to the awards ceremony. That *suggestion* needed subtlety, it needed careful handling. It needed many different complicated things, none of which was a drunken Frenchman with arms that acted as if their DNA had been spliced in from an octopus. If Juliet met Jacque now and he suggested being her date, it was not likely to end well, and right now, crap client though he was, he was their only client, and as such could not be lost to bad tempers.

In one fluid movement, Tina propelled herself off the sofa and quickly threw on some jeans and a warm top, found her hat, coat, scarf, and boots. Then she picked up her bag to look for her purse, keys, and phone. Then she checked everything in the flat that should be off was off and everything that was on should be on, and then stood for a moment trying to remember where it was she had wanted to go.

Juliet! Right.

As Tina reached the door to leave, another possibility occurred to her. Jacque drunk might be more than both she and Juliet could tackle. With this thought in mind, Tina retreated back to her bedroom and from the back of one cupboard picked out a recent purchase. She checked the batteries by turning it on, jumped a little at the noise it made, before popping the device into her bag and exiting her flat at speed.

Don't worry Juliet, she thought as she hailed a cab. I'm coming to your rescue.

And mine… And mine!

Chapter 16

Juliet

Juliet was feeling pretty pleased with herself as she rode the cab back towards her office. Occasionally she muttered the words she had used to bend Adam Russell to her will, causing the cab driver to look curiously in her direction and then decide he really didn't want to know.

Even though most of the vocal strong-arm stuff had been done by Rose, Juliet still felt pretty good about the whole thing. She was in such a great mood, she decided to check her emails and discovered one that squarely torpedoed her moment of good cheer. Predictably it was an email from Emma, which talked in a chatty, matter of fact way, about publishing plans being scaled back from the previous scaling back.

At this rate, the book run would conceivably scale back into negative numbers; which would require the printers to print fewer books than had ever existed in actual print.

Juliet barked a command at the cab driver for a detour to her office and then had to bark it again as the cab driver had assumed she was still muttering to herself and ignored her. By force of habit, she updated Tina on her change of plans in case her sister had failed to fix her furiously fucked-up laptop. There was no reply, so Juliet assumed Tina had somehow managed to unfuck it.

This was just the sort of existential business crisis that Juliet hoped to avoid by becoming a literary agent. If she wanted real pressure and actual work that affected anything of any worth, would she not have got a job in a proper industry?

At university, publishing had seemed the obvious career choice, right from the moment Juliet realised she didn't want to be a writer, and that stark realisation arrived the morning after she slept with one.

He was a much older man with a reputation that was nearly as big as his surprisingly agile and erect penis. Something she got to see shortly after accepting his invitation to read one of his early draft copies. On the way up to the grandest hotel suite the young Juliet had ever seen, she did briefly wonder if *draft copy* was a euphemism for sex, or if he did actually have a draft copy of something that he wanted to show her. Three seconds after the door closed, his trousers were around his ankles, and Juliet was happy to see that euphemisms were still alive and well, and waddling people into sex at every possible chance.

She had fancied the pants of this man the moment he started reading from his book, one of her favourite modern-day novels, a Booker prize-winner that was still surprisingly readable and full of characters the younger and more naïve Juliet self-identified with. Hearing him bring life to fictional characters she felt she knew so well proved to be an ear-gasmic experience in itself. When he looked directly into her eyes while reading out one of the more tragic passages of a book that was mostly tragic from start to finish, it had proved a tipping point for her aspirations to bed this man. ASAP!

At the end of the reading, with a little deft footwork, Juliet manoeuvred around his somewhat ancient PA and proceeded to attain the man's attention with some Gold Standard Flirting. This appeared to work and in a surprisingly short amount of time, she found herself standing in his hotel suite staring at his cock.

For an old man, one who wheezed a little when he had to get on and off the bed, he still had it in him to ring Juliet's bell.

Twice.

In a row!

Although she did have to help out the second time by going on top, which she wasn't worried about as her figure was trim from all the swimming she had been addicted to while attending the college of her choice. Later that night, she awoke to find him not waiting on the pillow beside her, wanting perhaps to pleasure her again, and if possible again after that, but sitting quietly at a desk in the next room, tapping away at a coffee-stained laptop.

He was so intent on his writing that a single kiss on his neck nearly shot him through the roof. He hadn't been angry, in fact he laughed, pulled her round to him, and she enjoyed the feeling of being naked on his lap, here in this impressive hotel suite, in the middle of the night. There was, however, no lovemaking, no exciting sex on a squeaky hotel chair, just a kiss, and a quiet explanation that he had an idea and really wanted to get it down before it could escape into the ether of forgotten thoughts.

Juliet had taken the hint and walked away, wondering if his eyes followed her pert naked behind as she made her way to the bathroom. In one of the many mirrors that adorned this room, she saw his eyes; his sole attention was once again on the glowing screen as his fingers tapped away at the keyboard in a rhythmicity-focused fashion.

When Juliet awoke the next morning, she found him still at the keyboard, still working, and so she showered and dressed without bothering him. As they parted, half-hearted arrangements to meet again were made, *perhaps* after his next evening reading. To her surprise, he kept that arrangement, meeting her for an evening meal in one of the many exclusive Italian restaurants that adorned Oxford city centre.

Later that evening, they made love and it was, once again, in Juliet's limited experience, mind-melting, but again, when she awoke in the night, he was once more at his laptop, tapping away.

She asked him over breakfast the next day, if he ever switched off, ever relaxed, and he had said simply *I do* then tapped his head and added, *but this doesn't*.

"But don't you get bored with all that…" Juliet made tapping gestures on an invisible keyboard.

"Yeah sure, but …", he mimicked her typing in the air, "is the only way I know to finish writing a book."

A day later they said their goodbyes, she to return to her life as a student, albeit with a tall-tale to tell her fellow dorm mates, and he towards America, following a never-ending publicity trail. As she watched him being bundled into a car by impatient PR people, Juliet realised, she simply didn't have the commitment to be a writer. In truth, she didn't have the talent either, something that had been pointed out by her teacher in creative writing studies, who previously Juliet considered to be a bitch and wrong about everything.

The next day, she looked through the University coursebook and made a decision to jump from creative writing towards a course that would land her a career as close to this art form as possible, without the awful responsibility of having to actually create anything.

Publishing!

From that moment onwards, she never looked back, and never regretted the decision. Although she was disappointed the writer who brought her to this tremendous epiphany, amongst other tremendous things, never bothered to mention Juliet in his autobiography.

Juliet's cab pulled to a stop outside her office, which she was glad to see was free of homeless people. Why they kept congregating around her door was a mystery, she never gave them any money.

"Wait here," she said to the driver. "I need to get my laptop, I'll just be a jiffy."

The cab driver said, *right you are*, or *al'right love*, or something along those lines. Juliet just heard some guttural tones that she automatically tuned out. Part of her enhanced upper-class social DNA was the ability to hear the servants without actually listening to them.

Out of the cab, the cold evening air bit into Juliet's unprotected neck, and she made a mental note to also collect her hat and scarf. She glanced up at her office window and saw the lights glared into the night. Tina would hear about that in the morning. Electricity wasn't free and this was a business that had to pay for itself. She entered through the main door in a whirl of frenzy, grabbing her scarf and hat off the peg as she opened the door to her office and almost jumped backwards out of the office at the sight in front of her.

Jacque sat slumped in her office chair, feet on her desk, asleep and snoring loudly. On the floor next to him was an empty bottle of vodka, all pretty standard stuff for Jacque Noir these days, but the thing that immediately grabbed Juliet's attention was the four-letter-word written on his forehead in what appeared to be black marker pen.

Juliet walked towards the slumbering man and leant inwards to read the capital letters. Her eyes widened with alarm as she realised what the letters said and how much she would have to put in Tina's swear jar if she were to ever utter this word.

"What the actual fuck?" She said, unfortunately a little too loud.

A single eye flicked open, took a moment to focus on her face, and then trained hungrily downwards to Juliet's breasts.

"Ah, the beautiful Juliet," Jacque slurred. "At last we are alone."

He tried to reach for her, but Juliet stepped back out of the way, and the wheels on the office chair did the rest, depositing the drunken man on her floor, his head resting just a few inches away from the toe of her shoe.

"For fuck's sake Jacque," Juliet said with a true understanding of the word exasperation. "I've just had a really good evening and…"

She thought about the toilet and witnessing a blowjob and then blackmailing a man who was clearly a sex pest, and decided that good was probably not the best adjective in this case.

"Well, not a *good* evening per se, a fairly bizarre evening to be frank, but it was an evening, despite its level of bizarreness where I was able to get shit sorted out. Shit that I would like noted belongs to you."

"I fear my sweet Juliet that Jacque Noir is too drunk to understand your English. You are speaking English, aren't you?"

Juliet gave a heavy sigh. This was useless; the man was as drunk as a politician before a leadership challenge.

"Look, don't worry about it tonight, I have a cab downstairs, let's get you into that and I can drop you off home." Juliet tried not to think what the cab driver would say when she returned with a laptop *and* a drunken

Frenchman.

"No wait, wait," Jacque crawled to the window and used the frame to lever himself upright. "You have not yet heard Jacque Noir's plan to help you."

"No, I haven't, and to be honest, if I can get through this evening without that dubious pleasure, I am going to join at least one major religion as a show of gratitude."

"Again, this is English you are speaking?"

"We are taking you home!"

"No, no, listen to this... Jacque Noir has something that will bring a smile to your face."

Despite her best efforts, Juliet felt her eye track downwards towards Jacque's crotch and was relieved to see that nothing was on display.

"I beg your pardon?"

"I said, Jacque Noir has something that will..."

"Yes, yes, yes. I heard you, why does everyone keep repeating everything."

Jacque staggered away from the window with the unhurried ease of a toddler learning his first few steps. He collapsed in the chair opposite the desk. In this clear light, the four-letter word on his forehead once again screamed at Juliet's attention.

"Perhaps," Jacque said, "it is because you keep saying *I beg your pardon*. Typical of the English not say what they mean and use too many words to say it. We French get by with *Pardon*, even the Germans feel no need to say nothing more than *Wie Bitte*. Yet the English carry on and on as though they are in love with the sound of their own voices."

"Unlike the French?"

"Exactement," Jacque said and passed out cold while sitting upright in the chair.

"Unbelievable," Juliet muttered walking over to the slumbering man. "Come on Jacque let's get you home."

Juliet braced herself on the desk and linked arms under Jacque's armpits in an attempt to lift him, her head became locked in his neck and her body writhed all too close to areas that she swore never to go anywhere near. As she struggled with the man, he regained a semblance of consciousness.

"What are you doing, Juliet? I thought you wanted only the business arrangement with Jacque Noir."

"I do," Juliet said through gritted teeth, straining to lift him out of the chair and possibly her life. "Trust me I do, but..."

Jacque's dead weight defeated her and she released him back to the chair, sitting back on the desk in front of him trying to work out her next move.

"But you cannot resist the Noir. I understand, you are only human."

Juliet mentally walked herself through a variety of replies, most of which would need a considerable contribution to Tina's swear jar, then decided the man was too drunk to waste profanities on. Or indeed, money.

"Right this very moment, Jacque, I just really need you out of my life so I can go home to bed."

The word bed seemed to stir the man, and he sat upright, now alert. He sat like that for some time, before he spoke.

"I have to tell you something important, something that will change your life forever."

"I somehow doubt this, but okay, tell me."

There was a prolonged silence before Jacque spoke.

"I have forgotten what I was about to say."

"Unbelievable," Juliet said through teeth that had freed themselves up in order to be once again gritted. "While you're thinking about it, can you tell me what that is on your face?"

"What about my face?"

For a second Juliet thought of telling him, but he was so drunk she didn't know if he would understand her, and if he did, she wasn't sure how angry he would get. Some of the furniture in that office had yet to be paid for. If he was going to throw a temper tantrum because of what some person unknown, although she had a good idea who, had drawn on his face, she would rather it be somewhere else.

"I have remembered what I want to say," Jacque said, his face lighting up with the joy of actually being able to get his brain to do something useful while being soaked in alcohol.

In drunken fits and bursts, Jacque began to explain his plan of attending the awards ceremony as her Plus-One, an idea that at first horrified Juliet until she thought about it carefully, then it terrified her. She cast her mind back to a time just after his divorce, when the two of them had, for various contrived reasons, ended up sharing a limousine back from a prestigious dinner at which Jacque had, surprise, surprise, got hammered. On the brief ride back, he had made a pass at her, the sort of pass an England full-back would make if they were 45-0 down to Wales and in the last 30 seconds of the match. Memories of an eel-like tongue and arms of an octopus still haunted her to this day.

"Jacque, let me be clear, I would rather be a drugs mule and get strip-searched in Peru than ever share another limo with you, ever again, in my entire life."

A hint of recollection drifted idly through Jacque's expression. He stared at thin air for a second before compounding all his previous errors by saying; "Oh, was that you?"

"Unbelievable."

"Juliet, please, it was a bad time for me, I was vulnerable."

"Not as much as my tonsils."

"Can you not forget this? Place it in the past for the greater good," He pleaded. "Besides, most women would give their right arm for an evening with me."

At the time, Juliet distinctly remembered that of all her anatomy, the least of Jacque's interest had been placed in her right arm. She thought of mentioning that, but honestly, what was the point? The man was an utter misogynistic twat. Instead, Juliet explained the basics of business to him, that she just wanted him to do his job and write a decent book of recipes that actually worked and would then sell books, preferably in large amounts. She could use it to attract more business and perhaps go back to biographies, where she felt her talents were better served. Cookery books, Juliet decided, were simply not worth all this bother.

Towards the end of her explanation, Jacque fell asleep and out of frustration, Juliet stalked away to the window, where she peered out to make sure the cab had not wandered off. The black roof was directly below her window; with the driver now standing out on the pavement having a cheeky cigarette. She waved to him and he motioned to his invisible watch that maybe she should come back so he could get on with his evening.

Juliet retreated from the window and perched once more on the desk just as Jacque revived both himself and the previous conversation.

"Jacque Noir has already created a cookery book that is a masterpiece of Noir secrets."

"No, you have not."

"How can this be true?"

Juliet gave Jacque a brief tour of her day, leaving out the dangly bits in the men's toilets, the encounter with Clive, and sharing some of the adventures with his ex-wife Rose. Mostly, she just gave him the highlights, or in this case, the lowlights.

"Negative reviews? What of it? Do you know what my father said of food critics? Those who can do, those who can't teach and if you can't even do that then.... Then.... What was the last bit?"

Lord preserve me, thought Juliet as she glanced at her watch and realised it was too late to rethink her life choices.

"The point is," Juliet said. "I have bought us time; time you need to use in order to improve the recipes in the book, you know, to the point where they actually create food people can eat."

"Jacque Noir cannot believe his public would turn against him. Do they not love me? The British housewives, they were crazy for Jacque whenever he is on the morning TV."

"Well yes there was a small fan base that mobbed you, but what happened afterwards…" Juliet shuddered at the memory of Jacque organising a group of OAP fans from autograph hunters outside the BBC, marching them down to Trafalgar Square, and displaying their love for the simple things in life by stripping off and skinny dipping in the freezing fountains. All performed in front of a somewhat surprised Mounted Police officer, not to mention several tourists, who YouTube'd the whole event to the world.

"Jacque Noir was simply trying to engage with his fan base, your idea, if he remembers accurately."

"Oh, now you can remember accurately! Do you also remember that most of your impromptu naked splashers had to be treated for hypothermia?" In fact, although Juliet was loathed to admit it, the publicity for this had been stellar. It even helped secure the book deal, which in truth, Juliet had struggled to find any interest for up to that point. The aftermath though came with various online debates and even a few questions asked in the House of Commons about the treatment by the media of vulnerably aged adults.

Shit storm didn't even cover it. By then though, the publisher had issued the book contract and wheels were in motion. Wobbly wheels. Wheels that threatened to come off the track at any moment. But, largely, still in motion. Albeit, very slowly.

"Jacque Noir remembers everything. It is all locked in here," Jacque said, trying to tap the side of his head and missing twice. "Once details and facts enter the mind of Noir, they stay locked... Forever, Julia."

"Juli-ET!"

"This publisher, this reviewer, none of them know what they are talking about. Juliet, how can you believe them? Does Jacque Noir look the sort of man who…? Who would…? Who would…"?

"…walk around with *Cunt* written on his forehead?"

There was a long silence while Jacque visibly digested this suggestion.

"Well, Jacque Noir was going to say something else, but he can't remember what it was, so your suggestion will suffice." He sat back. "You know, since those Brexit days, you British, especially you Juliet, have become very fond of extreme language."

Probably, Juliet thought, because we are living in extreme times. Just how extreme she was just about to find out when, without warning, Jacque stood up and walked towards her, grabbing her by the shoulders, ostensibly it seemed, to keep himself upright.

"Jacque Noir will rise to your challenge, he will write more recipes, even ones for those fucking vegans you keep going on about, but only if you agree to be his date for the show tomorrow evening."

"Not happening, not even in your wildest dreams, which I am assuming are very wild."

"No, listen to Jacque Noir. He is talking here, and he has a brilliant idea. Truly wondrous. Even you, my foul talking sweetheart, will like it."

At which point Juliet had to endure Jacque's drunken rant on how if they went to the awards ceremony together, it would start some gossip, that would give the book a bit of buzz, and maybe, just maybe, boost the sales figures. Inexplicably, Juliet realised he actually was on to something. If the pre-orders went up, she might be able to negotiate some time for a few rewrites, maybe even get the scale back on the first print run figure reversed.

Really, it all made sense. In a fucked-up kind of way.

"Okay," Juliet said, "if I agree to this, will you promise that no hanky panky will take place in the limo or anywhere else?"

"Hanky panky? Oh, you English, even your words for the sweet lovemaking are boring beyond belief. How did your ancestors ever find it in themselves to breed with each other?"

"Probably nothing on the TV that night. Your word Jacque, please. And I want you to swear it as though you actually mean it, even if you probably won't remember a word of this tomorrow."

Jacque moved his hands upwards from her shoulders, grabbing her head with a frighteningly firm grip. The effort seemed to cause him some dizziness and he stood there, Juliet's head in both hands, steadying himself with his face a few inches from her own, breathing a brewery full of fumes straight into her mouth.

"Jacque Noir swears that he will…"

"Step away from that woman, you swine!"

Out of the corner of her eye, Juliet saw Tina rush into the room, some kind of small black box in her hand, a box her sister shoved roughly upwards between Jacque's legs. There was a barely audible clicking noise as Tina pressed a switch on the box followed by the unmistakable sound of a sparking electrical discharge somewhere down near the surprised man's testicles.

Jacque's body spasmed in front of Juliet, his head flipping momentarily backwards, before slamming forwards at considerable speed and head-butting her straight on the nose.

The last thing Juliet could remember seeing was blood, lots of blood, covering every single surface, and she had the horrible feeling it was all hers.

Chapter 17

Pascal

In the grey light of an unpalatably early and damp Friday morning, Pascal sat with his espresso staring directly back at him. Its inky black surface absorbing the dark mood emanating from the slightly hungover figure staring into its cold contents. For a moment, the Frenchman wondered; if he stared long enough into the abyss of strong coffee, would it eventually stare back?

He glanced out of the window if only to escape the emotionless unflinching gaze of his coffee. Juliet's office window was still darkened and there had been no sign of Tina. With the awards ceremony taking place later this evening, it was likely they were not going to bother coming into the office. Or maybe they knew Pascal had drawn that rude word on his brother's forehead and were avoiding him. The actual reason for Juliet's absence didn't matter. The end result was another missed opportunity to tell her the truth.

Back to gazing at the coffee then! Better than the alternative of gazing at his phone that lay next to the cold cup, a phone with a message he'd read once with something akin to relief.

The message, a short piece of text written by Candy from somewhere, *stateside,* announced in a curt and polite manner her intention to divorce him. So like her to phrase it in such a way that it sounded vaguely unpleasant but ultimately good for one's health. Akin to an oral hygiene visit, or having an operation to remove wisdom teeth. Perhaps that was indeed the ideal analogy for divorce; undergoing pain and suffering to rid yourself of a part that no longer did the job it should. No longer held the promise of happiness or fulfilment. Or wisdom.

Pascal didn't bother to reply, in fact, the message said, *don't bother replying, the papers will be posted to your lawyer.* He was tempted to write back, *in this country they are called solicitors,* but he knew he wouldn't. Had he been Jacque, maybe he would have, but as his father observed many times, Pascal took after their mother and was a very different man from his brother.

Never had that been more apparent than when they first arrived in London and Jacque became his father's shadow, while Pascal spent much of his time consoling their mother, whose integration into British society and its strange customs came at a cost of Ariel's shredded nerves.

Their arrival in London had been chaotic and seemingly on the edge of failure from day one. The proposed restaurant that Miguel thought he secured in a much sought after location of Soho, fell through at the last moment. Someone offered more money and they lost the deal. It was as simple as that! This introduction into the niceties of UK property markets was one of several disasters to greet family Noir in those early weeks.

The restaurant was not only to be their business, their future, a legacy for the brothers, but also their home. It had a four-bedroom apartment over the top, more than enough room for the two boys and the parents, plus office space. It had been ideal, and it vanished from their grasp before they had time to clear passport control at Heathrow airport.

Virtually homeless, they resorted to staying in a grotty looking West End Bed and Breakfast for six long weeks, during which time it rained almost continuously and Ariel began to cry nearly every day. Their possessions, such as they had decided to bring with them, were diverted to a storage facility, where their mere existence created a weekly invoice and a constant reminder that things were not going to plan.

Weaker men might have folded under such pressure, they might have chucked it all in, they might have agreed with the scolding grandparents that too much had been risked on the word of an Estate Agent. Miguel though was made of sterner stuff. He and Jacque would set off at first light every day, hunting for the ideal property, the place that would be their future. Every evening returning home empty-handed and a little wiser as to the exorbitant prices London's property attracted.

During this time, Pascal took his mother to art galleries to soothe her rattled mind. Highly strung as she was, as most creative people can be, she could be calmed in these oases of culture, balanced to the vibrations of disappointment that echoed around their damp B&B rooms by art and beauty.

"Does the sun never shine on this godforsaken island?" She said one cold morning, wrapped in her scarf, a brown cigarillo clasped loosely between two fingers. Pascal's battle to find her places she could stand and smoke without getting soaked in the day-long rain was part of his daily fiasco.

Even in moments like today, while he sat in his nearly bankrupt café and stared at his cold espresso and down the barrel of divorce, not to mention a hangover, Pascal could not help but smile at the memory of how beautiful a woman his mother had been. Even in those moments of sullen regret she had at leaving Paris, she remained radiant.

Ariel was, to anyone who met her for more than a few minutes, a woman of exceptional beauty, of radiant power; a woman who possessed a dark humour, and moods that were darker still. She also practised an unforgiving attitude to those who displeased her, an exacting personality trait that was merciless when invoked. Under the typically bad weather of a late summer London, those darker moods had been to the fore and Pascal wondered how long it would be before she simply gave in to the temptation of returning to France.

A miracle had occurred before this question needed to be answered. A chain restaurant, dealing with something that resembled Pizza to anyone except an Italian, had gone out of business. They left behind debts and jobless kitchen staff, and more opportunistically, property in some rather prime locations. One particularly large restaurant was in Islington. Not exactly Soho, not even really the West End, but it was the era of the Blairs and a time when the streets of Islington were changing from greasy-spoon sandwich shops to softly lit cafés with a selection of baked products that looked and tasted French to anyone who wasn't French.

The fly in the ointment had been the flat attached to the property, which consisted of just two bedrooms and a tiny living room and a kitchenette area whose dimensions made Ariel wonder if one day she would meet herself coming back the other way. Of the two bedrooms, one was so small it could only be fit for a single Noir son, and only if that son didn't mind having a tiny single bed, a minuscule wardrobe and zero room left over.

Jacque, of course, had come to the rescue with a solution that served everyone's needs, especially his own. He would live somewhere nearby, in his own place. He would have to be paid a little more to cover costs, but Jacque would be willing to do this in order for his father and his mother to realise their dream. Ariel had been appalled. Despite the fact that Jacque had not lived for any length of time in the family home for the last ten years, she still thought of her boys as being her boys.

"Don't worry ma mère," Jacque had said. "I won't be far; besides, Pascal will still be here."

At that moment, Pascal realised Jacque had managed to find a way to maximise his own personal circumstances at the cost of Pascal's.

Opening the restaurant and moving into the flat had posed problems all of their own, not least turning a Pizza restaurant that seemed to be a homage to Formica furniture into something a little classier, and with what little money that remained in the Noir account. Some of the original staff had been kept on, mostly the pretty ones Pascal noted, but this was the domain of Jacque, for all his faults, he was a very effective *people-person*, at least when he wanted to be. None of the kitchen staff survived the cull, not even the ugly ones, and this was mostly down to Ariel and her exacting standards.

All candidates were asked to cook something to impress the Noir mother and be accepted into the business, few had passed her stringent taste test. One unfortunate soul, who attended his *audition* dressed in spotless chef whites and carrying a pack of knives that were conspicuously new and unused, produced a fish dish that Ariel only had to sniff at from a distance, in order to formulate her rejection.

"Monsieur," she said in answer to the unfortunate man's statement that his dream had always been to be a top chef. "I think you must find a different dream."

Eventually, though, they found enough staff who could both cook and at the same time keep their levels of terror for Ariel at bay.

"Monsieur," she had said to one successful candidate. "Is this excellent? Noh?" And as the poor unfortunate tried to slink away, she said; "where are you going? You have promise. Cook it again, this time cook it such a way that I actually would want to eat it."

Their restaurant became famed in catering circles as a tough place to work, but a place where, if you could manage to stay there for longer than a month without being fired, or walking out, or having a nervous breakdown, it would look great on your CV. Over the years and despite the heated atmosphere, Pascal had seen many unsolicited applications for kitchen staff appear on his father's desk, more than they could ever hope to accommodate.

Not that Restaurant Noir had been an overnight success. The opening night had been a damp squib of epic proportions. Miguel worked hard to pull in some kind of celebrity presence for the grand opening, but his contact base in London was minimal, and people from Paris refused to visit England just to eat French food. Eventually, he had settled for inviting the local Mayor of Islington, a woman who cancelled at the last minute citing security concerns. Later they would learn her husband had been arrested in a brothel and she was firefighting the local press. The cancelled dinner date didn't even get a mention in the paper, much to Miguel's disgust.

Despite taking on bankrupt premises and buying in second-hand cookers from auction rooms, the Noir finances were at rock bottom. Within a month of the opening, there was an after-work discussion, 2 am talks that took place after all the staff had left the premises. Talks that went on into the early hours of the morning, with thoughts on redundancies, of cutting costs.

Jacque argued the difficulties of serving a potential twenty tables if he did not have sufficient front of house staff. Ariel and Pascal countered that they did not have enough staff to cook for twenty tables; less kitchen staff would mean nothing more than abject failure. Miguel's voice had carried through the static, reminding them all that so far, their busiest night had seen just ten customers spread over five tables. His own suggestion to sack the bar staff had been met with the rampant scorn of their mother.

"That would only save us two wage packets, and all of that saving would be absorbed by having you behind the bar." Besides, she had countered, that Miguel still needed to wear his chef whites, if only to create the illusion he did something of worth in the kitchen.

This comment ended when Miguel slammed an angry hand down on the table and declared they simply needed to find more customers. An argument that no one could counter, or solve. They retired to bed, with Ariel's last words ringing in their ears.

"It is simple. If we cannot find a solution, we must return to Paris!"

They continued for a week or more with depressingly empty tables and fridges full of food that would go off and be thrown away. It carried on this way until Jacque, typically, rescued them all using just his impeccable charm.

One evening, out of the blue, after being missing all day, he appeared in Restaurant Noir with a young actress on his arm. She had a face everyone recognised, a face from a popular long-running TV show. A face the other guests knew and were delighted to suddenly find themselves brushing shoulders with stardom.

The young starlet had in fact been rather tiresome, demanding a vegan dinner cooked to exacting specifications, and then leaving most of it on the plate. At the same time, she ran the bar staff ragged with constant demands for complicated cocktails. All the time she was either tapping messages into her phone or making loud calls, at one point she even asked for an extension lead to be brought to her table so that she could charge her phone. A request that Jacque oversaw himself, as his father had retired to the living room upstairs to avoid this unappetising spectacle, keeping his wife company who had retired from the kitchen to avoid hearing, for the umpteenth time, the previously innocuous word; avocado.

Then something wonderful happened.

As final curtains fell across various West End Theatres, actors, often still wearing trace amounts of makeup around their faces, began to stagger through the door. Most of those paste-smeared faces were easily recognisable. Faces from films, TV, magazines and newspapers. By 11 pm, the place was half-full of famous faces, making the restaurant look like an impromptu awards ceremony, albeit for actors who were nominated, but unlikely to win.

As a flurry of food orders began to pile in, Pascal had rushed outside to find his mother standing in the back alleyway of the restaurant, swearing in French about the rain, while she tried to light her cigarillo. Pascal explained about the sudden influx of Celebs and that some were ordering French food as though they actually knew what it was, and they were on their various phones and requesting more of their friends to join them.

His mother had sworn a single French word, and then ran to the kitchen door and peered through the rounded window into the restaurant beyond. When she, at last, retreated from the view, a grim look of satisfaction played across her classically beautiful French features.

"Mon peuple," she said, sweeping her dark mane of hair back into a neat ponytail and then covering it with a hairnet. "Tonight, we cook. We cook as we have never cooked before. Bon Chance!"

And cook they did. Into the night and early morning, producing meal after meal. Delights of Paris, of France. The actors who spilt in through the restaurant doors in a seemingly endless stream were refined, well-travelled, they knew precisely what they wanted. And there was an air about their orders, as though they wanted to see if the genuine-looking French menu could live up to its boasts.

At the end of it all, when coffee and brandy and various desserts had been served for the one-hundredth last time, the crowd began to thin, until all that remained was Jacque and the young actress. As she left, she kissed him on the cheek in front of a flurry of flashing paparazzi who had appeared outside the restaurant with impressive hyena-like skills. Jacque was asked some questions from the curious photographers, who made notes of his answers before they too vanished into the shadows of the night.

Back inside, Pascal and his mother had stepped wearily into the main seating area and stared at the havoc that was being cleared away by Miguel and Jacque.

"Did," Ariel's voice faltered, her face drained, her eyes hopeful, almost close to tears. "Did they pay? Did anyone pay?"

Jacque took the cigarette out of his mouth and placed it on a saucer, and from his pockets, he produced receipt after receipt. MasterCard, Amex, Visa, and a fist full of brown fifty-pound notes.

"Oui Mama, they paid. They all paid."

The next day, Jacque's photo with the young actress caused a few minor ripples in the gossip columns of some newspapers. A boyfriend even came calling to find out what was going on, but Jacque charmed him, defused him, and even over-charged him for a very expensive lunch. TV crews caught the two men talking and more gossip ensued. It was as though a secret publicity machine had begun working privately for the Noir family, generating interest and gossip, and an ever-growing book of dinner reservations.

Restaurant Noir was a hit, and not only with celebrities. Food critics came calling and Noir food was judged to be wonderfully authentically French. Ariel curled her lip into a cynical smile when she read this.

"These morons, would they know authentic French food if it spat in their faces?"

"Those who can, do," His father said. "Those who can't, teach. And those who can't even do that, well, they become critics."

Eventually, of course, the West End acting crowd had drifted away, a few still visited, keen to find somewhere quiet and away from the fans to get a meal after their performance. In the main though, it became a novelty to see a star in their restaurant, no longer normality, as the transient nature of the acting population found other, fresher watering holes. By then though, the reputation of Restaurant Noir as a place to eat, and see perhaps a famous face or two, had been etched into the minds of the public, and anyone turning up without a booking was liable to leave disappointed, no matter the day of the week.

Every evening was a busy time for them all. Pascal and Ariel creating the food, Jacque and Miguel making sure the portions that were being delivered were in line with a desire to make a profit.

"Will you have me make a fish dish without fish?" Ariel once screamed at Jacque, causing a nearby waitress to drop a tray of plates.

"Noh mama, but we pay for fish by the kilo, let us sell it in the same way." Jacque was dressed in his chef whites, as he always was, standing in the kitchen, watching and sometimes helping, but mostly waiting to be called out front to receive compliments directly from the customer. A job neither Pascal nor Ariel cared to indulge in.

"Small portions are not a problem," Miguel said, defending his son's opinion as had become the norm. "No one ever goes to a French restaurant because they are hungry."

For a time, they surfed high on the continued wave of success this dalliance with stardom had given them. Prizes came their way. Michelin stars. Recommendations in all the right travel guides. Even people from France, curious to see what all the fuss was about, ventured over to be disappointed at how genuinely delightful the food tasted.

Years passed in the blink of an eye with barely time to acknowledge that Jacque was now married to Rose, and their first child had started school. No time at all to look back, to see clearly how many hours they were putting in, how much work they accomplished in a six-day week; lunchtimes, evenings and into the early morning. Barely time to take a breath. Scarcely any time at all to notice Ariel's nasty winter cough had failed to go away and developed into something more.

From the first mention of lung cancer to a diagnosis of a disease that had spread throughout her body, to the moment when they stood beside her bed and watched the thin woman minus her crown of jet-black hair, slide from life to death was a unit of time that Pascal could never measure. Not even now, looking back, trying to remember the month when his mother first coughed up blood, to the moment the doctor told them they should say their goodbyes.

There was no goodbye. His mother had one last operation, one last chance and it failed. She never awoke from the anaesthetic, slipping like the Princess she was from sleep and pain with as much dignity as death will ever allow. Their goodbyes were to a woman with closed eyes who could no longer hear their words.

They buried her on a cold, cloudless day in November. A quiet funeral. Family only. At the memorial, hundreds attended. Hundreds cried for a woman they had only ever met through the food she had created. No one cried more than Miguel, a man whose heart had been ripped in two by the hands of death.

Both brothers saw this, saw the man who had been their strength and inspiration, sag in on himself and die a little that day. At the sight of his grim face watching their mother's coffin slide away for cremation, Pascal had known this man would never be the same.

Neither of the brothers was surprised when their father, some weeks later after spending all his time in the flat above the restaurant, announced he would retire and return to France. By then, the restaurant had been closed for several weeks, and debt had built up, staff had left, but Jacque had a plan.

Jacque always had a plan.

In truth, Pascal knew that Rose had put together the plan or the details of it. She saw finance as a puzzle to be solved, and her solution was liked by the most important people of all; bankers. In fact, even Rose would later admit they got lucky. Right place, right time. The era of easy money and loans to be grabbed without worry, a time that would soon change, but for now, in the middle of the first decade of the new century, they obtained enough finance to buy out their father's share and begin running the restaurant as their own.

It could have so easily been their undoing, but another bit of luck, a favour of a favour called in by Jacque, led to a junior cabinet advisor becoming one of the first of a new breed of regular patrons. Her visit to Restaurant Noir led to recommendations being made to colleagues in Westminster and suddenly they played host to diners who arrived in dark cars carrying red cases, with bodyguards sitting in the shadows.

Sirs, Dames and Lords perused through their menu, all aficionados of real French food, and with a taste for expensive wine. All with sizeable taxpayer-funded expense accounts to burn. Another moment in time that was about to change, but for now, once again, Restaurant Noir was in the right place at the right time to reap the rewards.

Inevitably, as with those fickle actors, their pull with the political elite waned, but they retained a customer base that consisted of almost exclusively rich people, allowing the brothers to change their menu to suit. Allowing Jacque to create a wine cellar he had previously only dreamed of accumulating, travelling abroad to personally try out the wares and to sleep with women out of sight of Rose.

Eventually, the unfettered expenses of MP's became a major scandal with a leaked hard drive of account details picked over by a major newspaper, and the endless roll of money into the restaurant's coffers came to a shuddering stop. Governmental customers, it would seem, even highly paid ones weren't so keen on spending their own money on expensive food that still left them hungry.

Restaurant Noir even featured in this minor scandal, being one of the top five restaurants in the country to appear on expense claim forms of Britain's venerable parliamentarians. Jacque though, typically, played this to his advantage, managed to get on TV to defend their high bills, took samples of food to be tried by the breakfast hosts, and generally charmed his way into the hearts and minds of the UK population.

Their audience changed again, the menu went slightly down market, to Pascal's internal distaste, and the workload increased as he found himself cooking for larger crowds, more servings than he had ever seen in his life. But no matter how busy they were, he maintained his oath to his mother, to cook the best food ever tasted by their customers.

Every single day.

Six days a week.

In the end, it became a prison of his own construct that tortured his soul. Until he reached a point where it nearly broke him.

Every day Pascal came down from the flat above, where he lived with Candy, to stand in the kitchen and say, as he always did, *today I will make food that will make you proud mama.* And every day, he did just that, toiling at his maximum, doing his duty to be the son he believed she wanted him to be. Gutting, peeling, carving, cooking as though it were an art form that could only be accomplished through total dedication, as though he could always feel the shadow of a ghost beside him.

It was this pressure, this hopeless quest for perfection every single night while producing more food than an average motorway service station, that led to Pascal's drinking. His life was a train that ran out of control. Careering down a hill, sticking to the tracks for now, but threatening to throw itself off the mountainside at every steep corner that life placed before him. One such corner appeared in the form of his inability to be a man in the arms of a demanding and unsympathetic wife. Pascal dealt with this using a quick-fix mentality, something he learnt from Jacque. In trying to solve the problem of why his sexual appetite had vanished, he avoided thinking about it at all by simply swallowing a small blue pill when required.

One evening, Jacque, searching Pascal's desk for a pen, had happened upon his brother's Viagra hidden at the back of a drawer. He had the packet in his hand, looking at it with vague incomprehension of seeing the name on the label when Pascal walked in.

It had been a busy night with demanding customers, many of them of such an advanced age, the waiters joked as to who wouldn't make it as far as dessert. The whole evening was the result of another of Jacque's TV stunts that had gone wrong. On the back of taking OAP's to Trafalgar Square for an impromptu pole dance in the fountains, which led to several suffering hyperthermia. The OAP dinner that Pascal struggled to cook for, to find food that could be eaten by customers with a diminished sense of the present and a sparse collection of teeth, had been Jacque's idea of paying a public penance.

An act of Twitter-Attrition.

For Pascal, it felt as though he paid the penance, while Jacque hid from his older fans in the back office, for fear of another costly gaffe, both in terms of publicity and in terms of takings. The whole dinner was on the house for thirty residents of a retirement home in Oxfordshire whose OAPs had been among those to bathe naked under the presumably perplexed single eye of Nelson.

This incident had created interest in Noir food though, and in the cookbook project that Jacque had been trying to get off the ground for over a year. A book that Pascal had been asked to contribute to, which both men knew was a lie. Only Pascal knew the recipes well enough to actually commit them to paper, and while he railed against writing a book that would turn Jacque into an even bigger lie, all the money they had borrowed in times of good credit still needed to be paid back. The restaurant made money, but the overheads were high, and mostly they lived on the edge of a serrated knife. The book was a lifeline and they both knew it.

All of this was foremost in Pascal's mind. The worry, the stress, a vivid hate for cooking, the thing he had loved so much, a thing that consumed him with a negative emotion so strong he could almost taste it. And now, he felt less of a man than he should, in front of a woman who he didn't love, or even liked very much. All of this was a building fury, a burning fire that raged higher still when he strode through the office door and saw Jacque sitting there with a familiar packet of blue pills in his hand and a questioning look on his face.

Of course, Jacque being the way he was, and knowing Pascal as he did, had defused the situation with ease. Pascal could remember that feeling of rage evaporating away on the back of Jacque's easy smile and comforting words. Words he could no longer remember, but words that were not patronising, or laden with false sympathy, but words of a brother who loved him.

Jacque asked questions, of course, and Pascal mostly nodded and gave monosyllable answers, and they cracked open a bottle of brandy to dilute the tense aura of embarrassment that filled the room. Soon they were drunk, and twenty years younger, and coming up with crazy ideas. Selling the restaurant and moving back to France, selling the restaurant and buying a boat and cooking their way around the world. Selling the restaurant and becoming a boy-band, or in this case, a middle-aged-bloke-band. Soon they became so drunk, their target shifted to something nearer, to the freebie gulping and swallowing OAP's that lapped hungrily at their profit margin.

A menu had been prepared. Seasonal, mostly British dishes that Pascal shuddered to cook, but with some small French influences, he found the meat and veg could be forced to taste of something more than feathers and dirt. Then one joker in the crowd of OAP's had found the regular restaurant menu and demanded to know why he couldn't have lobster. He demanded it so loud, it reached the ears of the two drunken brothers, who rose to the challenge and cooked their belligerent guest his heart's desire. Even Jacque leant a hand in the process, staining his usually unblemished tunic. As the sauce was being stirred, Pascal found his brother crushing one or two of the blue pills, then adding it to the bubbling mixture.

"Noh." Pascal had said and began to prepare a new sauce.

Jacque talked him round, persuaded him the OAP deserved a little comeuppance for taking advantage of the situation. They sent out the meal, both retiring to the office to get even drunker than they already were. Both creating ever more bizarre scenarios surrounding the old man who had eaten the Viagra sauced Lobster and the imagined surprise of his wife when they got home to bed that very night!

The next day, hungover and regretful, Pascal was in the kitchen, arguing with Candy. She had found Pascal reading an article about Juliet, and an old wound had opened.

"It is not just about Juliet," He had shouted, they were both shouting at this point. Most mornings they either shouted or ignored each other. "It is also about my brother. He is writing a book for her. I should take an interest."

"Yeah sure," Candy had said with a look somewhere between defeat and tears. "Take an interest. Great way to put it."

The phone had rung and Pascal had snatched at it, unwilling to spend yet more of his day arguing with Candy. Jacque was on the other end, he talked slowly and quietly, he told Pascal not to overreact, to remain calm, and not to overthink anything. Then he told him the man who had been served Viagra flavoured lobster had died quietly in the night. Jacque had found out after ringing the old people's home to inquire if everyone was happy with the evening. The nurse, who had apparently gushed down the phone at him, mentioned the death almost as an additional unimportant piece of information. Before that, she had been keen to tell him how happy everyone had been, how much they were looking forward to it next year (*hint hint*) and could she have an autographed copy of the book when it came out. Oh, and by the way, one of their elderly *guests* had passed last night, and how happy the wife had been for her husband that he had been indulged with his order of Lobster on his final evening on Earth!

Jacque implored his brother to keep his head, to keep on being the dark and moody man he was, but to never tell anyone ever what had happened. By then, Candy had left for her office job somewhere in Soho, doing some kind of fashion editorial work that Pascal had no interest in. He had the flat to himself. He had time to brood, to think, as much as his hangover would allow, on his part in a man's death. An old man admittedly. A belligerent old man. But still, one that had the right to live a few more years without having his life cut short by a prank from two drunken cooks who should have known better.

From that point onwards, everything had happened at speed.

Pascal refused to talk or even meet with Jacque again. He did not want to be subjected to the man's silver tongue; he did not want to hear the old man would probably have died anyway. He simply wanted to confess, but he knew that would destroy more lives than his own, so he decided to live a life of penance.

Pascal turned his back on cooking, his first true love, opened a small café that never served food, and hoped he could simply exist here while waiting to grow old and die.

When the estate agent had suggested the premises opposite Juliet's office, his mind had turned to another option, to perhaps being with Juliet, as he grew old in his splendid fortress of solitude. By then, with mounting emotional pressures, his marriage had entered the final stages of open warfare, and he was unsurprised when he returned home to the flat after signing the lease on his new café, to find Candy had left.

As Pascal stood here now, in the café that had changed his life, he looked towards the darkness of Juliet's office and thought about the widow, the woman of the old man whose life he had so unfairly ended.

He realised with a burning knife in his soul, that he must see this old woman, the wife of the man he had killed...

He must see her. Apologise. Confess!

Beg her forgiveness.

Seek contrition from the widow of the man he had murdered.

Before Pascal could talk himself out of the decision, his coat was on and he was striding purposefully through the cold air towards Angel tube station and a future of his own making. A future that hopefully would not feature a prison sentence of significant duration, and a future that included Juliet waiting for him when he was released.

If nothing else, once he had been arrested, he wouldn't have to worry so much about that bloody cookery book.

Chapter 18

Jacque

In comparison to Pascal's hangover, Jacque's own alcohol-induced migraine was awful. Although technically, he wasn't truly sober enough to be hungover. Having drunk so much the previous day, throughout the entire day, ending with Tina's hidden supply of vodka in the late evening, Jacque was still holding a fair amount of alcohol in his bloodstream.

Indeed it seemed to Jacque more accurate to consider how much blood was in his alcohol-stream.

A shower had not helped. Not even a little bit. The hot water cutting out halfway through, along with the lights, as the electric company, having not received any money recently or a response to final demands, had chosen that exact moment to withdraw their services.

He dried himself on a damp towel in the encroaching cold of the gradually freezing bathroom, taking time to wipe at a mysterious black stain on his forehead. Where had that come from? He should never drink vodka, it only led to craziness and situations of utter embarrassment.

Though in Jacque's bitter experience, this was the first time it had led to a high voltage current being applied to his testicles.

Jacque shifted painfully on a restaurant chair in the now barren serving area and tried without success to find a sitting position that did not bring tears to his eyes. He still wasn't sure why Tina had felt the need to taser him in the gonads, and even after her lengthy explanation he was none the wiser, although he had passed out several times while she was talking, so there was that.

Vaguely he remembered being carried back to his flat by Tina and a loud man in a cheap suit who drove a Jaguar that smelt of stale cigarette smoke. There was also half a memory of a taxi driver who kept wheezing and collapsing, but Jacque had no idea at all how he fitted into the evening.

He awoke at midday, the winter sunshine making a rare appearance to shine straight into his pain-ridden eyes. For a moment, while shielding his gaze from this instrument of torture, he wondered where on earth he had ended up. Not an unusual situation for Jacque, having ended the night in one bed or another, he would often have those first moments of waking when he thought, *where the fuck am I?*

Internally, Jacque refrained from referring to himself in the third person.

This time, however, he knew after just a few moments where the fuck he was, and also, how much pain he was in. He was back at Restaurant Noir and he was in fucking agony.

Every path these days seemed to lead back here, to this place, to this pain, if not physical, then existential. (Jacque waited a moment for his head to stop hurting after thinking of the word, *existential*.) And no matter how he fought to free himself of this place, to carve out another life for himself, all roads led to this place of doom. This failed restaurant. This albatross around his neck. This place that had killed his mother.

Yes, in reality her smoking had brought cancer to her lungs, but this place, this restaurant that he founded with his father, that he built from the ground up, one customer at a time, this place of stress and pain, had been the reason she smoked so much. The reason she had died so early in life. The reason she had left this world before she could figure out a way to love her eldest son.

There had always been a distance between Jacque and Ariel. It began with the arrival of Pascal, or maybe further back, with Jacque spending the majority of his time with his father and his grandfather. Out fishing, hunting, travelling around vineyards searching for a wine no one had yet discovered. Jacque never stopped loving his mother, but somewhere along the line, he felt that she stopped loving him.

And then she died, and any repatriation, any path back to a place where they could once again be mother and son had been lost. Forever. All to capture their father's elusive dream of being a beloved chef in a city that mostly only cared about money.

Jacque remembered clearly the day when Miguel wanted to give up. Early on in their grand adventure, when everything was going wrong, when money was running out and they had yet to find the right place. It had almost been too much for his father, and one bleak morning he stood in the rain, looking with despair at those grey English skylines of grey English buildings, and sobbed, and apologised to Jacque, and told him they needed to return to France.

Call it quits.

Jacque knew this wasn't an option. All their money had been spent getting this far, to return home defeated would mean getting real jobs and working for other people. It would mean never having the chance to control their own destiny. It meant pain and suffering for family Noir, and Jacque was determined this would never happen.

From that day onwards, Jacque took his father each morning to a small café, bought him a French paper and what almost passed for coffee. He left him there while he went on his mission to find a place the Noir family could call their own.

Fortune smiled on him at that desperate point when he read a headline about a pizza chain closing, and without a second thought, he tracked down the company handling the bankruptcy. Taking a taxi he could ill afford, Jacque arrived at their offices just as they were heading out the door at the end of the day, but his charm had come to the rescue, and there and then, he planted the seeds of what would become Restaurant Noir.

Sitting here now, resting his elbows on a table without a tablecloth, in a restaurant without people, Jacque questioned why he had put so much effort into this emptiness. It's true that nothing lasts forever, not his marriage, not his mother, not even it would seem his business, but he had hoped Restaurant Noir would last long enough for him to sell the damn thing and make his money back.

It had all looked so bleak when they first opened. A high-class French restaurant with too big a seating area, demanding too many staff, situated in Islington, which in the early part of the new century was still morphing itself towards the gentrification of people with real spending power. The opening night had been a disaster, and each night afterwards pointed towards a short future for the Noir family in this place and time.

By then the internet was becoming a thing of actual use, AOL was the place to start, and Alta Vista had not yet heard of the all-encompassing dominance of Google. The World Wide Web was still pretty basic, mostly porn and online chatting to people who were usually not who they said they were, but for a few far-seeing visionaries such as Jacque, it was a valuable tool.

For weeks, he researched famous local people with the aim of encouraging them to dine at Restaurant Noir, perhaps with the incentive of a free meal, but he couldn't find anyone with the ability to pull in other high-spending customers. It soon became apparent to him that in London, one needed a star to create excitement. To create a buzz!

In its basic form, the internet only helped him so far in the pursuit of his quarry. Facebook had yet to rear its invasive head, Twitter was still something only birds did and cyberstalking was a passion dreamed of by many, but remained in its infancy.

Jacque embraced this potential and began the hunt for his golden egg-laying goose in the theatres of London's West End.

After a few false starts, one where the celebrity he was trying to persuade hit him with a handbag, and another where her personal security removed him, somewhat forcibly, from the venue, he eventually came across the ideal person. A minor star in a galaxy of talent, but popular with tabloids and fans. A recent TV Soap actress now turned to treading the boards, with an eye on an eventual Hollywood film.

Her acting name had been appropriated from France, as an apparent homage to her hereditary being 1/64th French, a point Jacque used as his opening into a conversation with her while asking for an autograph at the end of a performance. A performance he had not actually seen, but he had read the review in Time Out, so he was ready to pad out the encounter with vague compliments of her acting ability and relevance to the moment.

He also said, that such a role, which apparently included seven sex scenes and a brief bit of flogging by her onstage lover, must leave her feeling exhausted. And perhaps, a little hungry? Oh, and by the way, he owned a restaurant not far from here. And it was French, which apparently was something that resonated with her.

The whole spiel, delivered with Jacque's effortless charm, along with a cab he had waiting to swing the deal, had led to her accepting his offer, in the way stars do when they follow the whim of the moment. That night, she dined at Restaurant Noir, invited her circle of acting luvvies and the rest was catering lore. A legend that helped put the Noir family in the spotlight.

It was the beginning of a moment in time.

Jacque remembered how the young soap star had driven away at the end of the night, alone in her taxi, but before she left, whispered her address in his ear. Later that night, he enjoyed several hours with her, re-enacting some of the more adventures sex scenes from her theatrical production. Although, in truth, at the time he had to admit in being more interested in her flat, with its big loft windows and exposed brickwork. On returning to his own bed, with a sleeping Rose, he decided that a flat such as the one where he had just been unfaithful, would be just the sort of place he should share with the woman on the pillow next to him. A woman he planned to marry, even though she had no idea of this intention.

For a while, it all worked out and Jacque managed to have it all.

The flat with the exposed bricks eventually became his. Rose became, for a time, his wife, and he sired a daughter whose mixed-race parentage gifted her with looks that defined beauty and a temperament that defied understanding. He created the success that was Restaurant Noir, and after his mother passed, he held that success as his birthright, sharing it with the only other human he truly trusted, Pascal, his loyal, if somewhat intense brother.

Somewhere in amongst all of this success, all of these good times, things had become…

Complicated.

Rose; married to her career.

His daughter; more interested in horses and poetry than spending time with her father.

Polly and Adam Russel.

Juliet and that damned book.

Candy and the blue pills.

Pascal and the Lobster of Death!

In the silence of broken dreams, Jacque looked at the dark, bleakly untidy restaurant and wondered what impending life there was left for him to live.

And what it amounted to, if anything.

On the table in front of him sat a cup of coffee, mixed with rum to fortify his mind ahead of a business meeting. One he had learned about via an urgently beeping text message from Rose. Next to the cup, a newspaper lay open to the book review section where there was a small photo of him, naked and in a fountain, surrounded by old naked women.

The headline above read; *Lacklustre Recipes from the Go-Go Dancing Chef.*

A tabloid name he had yet to live down. The review would also require some living down. It wasn't bad, not as bad as he feared, and considering it had been written by Adam Russel, he had expected much worse. It was not though, by any shade of the imagination, a great review. Anyone reading this *probably* wouldn't cancel a pre-order of the book, but everyone else would think twice, thrice, or four times before bothering to order it, or worse yet, wait for the summer sales.

He folded the newspaper and tossed it onto the floor, topping up his coffee with a generous helping of rum.

"A little early for that isn't it?"

Rose stood in the shadow of the kitchen door, her thin silhouette for a moment bringing back memories of his mother, standing there, judging him. Then Rose moved into the light, her dark complexion as flawless as ever, her figure as wanton as he recalled. How had he allowed this woman to slip away from him?

"The appointment is in an hour," she said, putting the cap back on the bottle and returning it to a shelf behind the bar. "Any chance you can have a shower?"

"I have had a shower."

"Maybe another one?" Rose said with a wrinkle of her nose.

Jacque stood and limped to the light switch on the wall.

"Why are you limping?"

"I drunk too much vodka."

"And that gave you a limp?"

"Apparently."

Jacque flicked the light switch off and on a few times to demonstrate the lack of electricity.

"Things are clearly going from bad to worse," Rose said with a sad smile.

"Tell me something I don't know."

"Okay, I will."

Rose began to outline the state of his finances. Since Pascal had left

Restaurant Noir, the business had suffered a number of setbacks. Despite recruiting a chef from Paris, Restaurant Noir had been incapable of serving the food it had once proudly produced. The Parisian had quit three days after starting, saying he was an artist and couldn't create food of worth to such an extreme workload, and anyway, these English were heathens who did not know the meaning of good food. This scenario repeated itself several times, each time the bar was lowered for the next hopeful replacement. Eventually, the bar became so low, a small fire broke out in the kitchen and guests had to be evacuated. Worse still, it hadn't even made the papers.

At which point Jacque called it quits, closed up the doors, and looked towards other means of earning a living. The book had seemed to be the obvious starting point. Get that out in the world, increase his public profile, then use that to create a chain of restaurants that served French food. Maybe not Noir food, but something that at least appeared to be French. At least to the English.

For a time, it had appeared like the best of the worst solutions on offer to Jacque.

Rose's assessment of his financial status was sadly a reflection of how badly his choice of solution was performing. It was also a reflection on how badly he had become addicted to drinking, and to frequenting bars that opened late and offered entertainment that was both expensive and hardly likely to increase the respect of his public. Rose outlined how large amounts of money spent on drink, cabs, late-night bars, strippers, and of course gambling, had drained his bank account to near-zero. Hence the lack of Direct Debit bill payments and the lack of electricity.

"They call themselves exotic dancers," Jacque said, moving painfully around Rose to get at the brandy bottle. This involved more than a single wince of pain.

"Oh, I don't doubt it, on your credit card statements it just says, *services rendered*, which is something I am not going to dwell on."

"Good, because it is none of your business."

Jacque didn't need to turn and look at Rose to know her reaction to his stinging rebuttal. He could feel the ice-cold stare penetrating through the back of his neck.

"No," she said. "But your... drinking... and all the other stuff... that is my business. Especially if it affects our daughter's future!"

Suspecting a longer speech, Jacque poured himself a large measure but Rose picked up the cup and threw the contents down the sink.

"Come on, I'll tell you the rest on the way to see Sir Geoffrey. And... What is that black mark on your forehead?"

"I have no idea."

"Not doing the third person thing this morning?"

"I am too tired."

"Maybe drag it back out when you're with Sir Geoffrey? I get the idea he's a bit of a fan and it would be good to give him the full..."

"Performance?"

Rose sighed and appeared to mentally give in and change tactics. Without warning, he found his arms being put into his jacket and he was forced out the door and into the waiting cab. On the journey over, she told him more of his financial woe, while attacking the black mark with an endless supply of wet wipes.

At least his flat had now been sold, tragic though this news was to him; it would mean some money coming into his account when eventually the contracts were swapped. Not today, obviously, and not soon enough to get the electricity connected. All of that would take time, but at least he would soon be solvent.

"But only," Rose stressed. "If you reduce your outgoings, and by outgoings, I mean…"

"Strippers, booze and anything else that might be remotely fun."

"To be blunt, yes. It is your choice, Jacque, but maybe you could also think about Yvonne and what she will inherit in the future."

"When I was her age, there was no inheritance for me. Hard work got me to where I am today."

"Walking with an unexplained limp, smelling vaguely of fish, and unable to pay your bills?"

A defeatist argument to which Jacque had no smart comeback. Besides which, they had arrived outside the luxurious offices of Sir Geoffrey.

"Twenty-two pounds fifty," the driver said.

"I'll get this shall I?" Rose said somewhat pointedly.

They were ushered inside by a tall blonde assistant who was dressed in a pencil skirt so tight that it barely allowed her to walk on unrealistically high heels. It was all so blatantly sexual that even Jacque found himself looking the other way.

"Ah, *the* Jacque Noir," Sir Geoffrey said as they entered his office. "It is good to finally meet you. The pleasure really is all mine."

Now, this was more like it. A man of prominent stature and worth, cosying up before him was just the sort of life Jacque had envisaged for himself. The life of a celebrity where he could be famous for just being himself, and not have to actually do anything strenuous, like cooking. Or writing a fucking book.

"I have taken the liberty of creating a small kitchen area in my office," Sir Geoffrey said, dramatically pulling a white sheet off an island kitchen unit, complete with burners, sink and a small oven. "I do hope this will be adequate for you."

Rose looked as confused as Jacque, but at least she could still speak.

"I think there may have been a misunderstanding," Rose said carefully. "We are just here to talk about creating a chain of Noir Restaurants across the country and…"

"Yes, yes of course, although my own team have been showing some negative numbers during focus feedbacks."

"I hadn't heard much about this," Rose said.

While the two talked, Jacque wandered over to the island kitchen, exploring the ingredients, and chancing on a bottle of cooking sherry. He poured a large measure into a mixing cup and downed it in one.

"Yes," Sir Geoffrey said in that irritatingly condescending manner that only titled people seemed to manage. "Apparently, the scars of the mess that was and is Brexit make it difficult to get any traction amongst the public for all things European, including it would seem, the French. Once we move outside this wonderful metropolis, the problems are exaggerated tenfold."

"Okay, that's clearly a problem; however, our business plan does guarantee a way forward in order to…"

"Yes, yes, I am sure it does. All of this can be talked about in great detail, but first, I do wonder if Jacque would be so kind as to indulge me with a small sample of his cooking?"

Jacque stirred from his sherry-glazed mood and looked from the expectant face of Sir Geoffrey to the somewhat more panic-stricken face of Rose. She was silently shaking her head.

"Thing is Sir Geoffrey," she said. "We don't really have enough time to…"

"No," Jacque said, loudly, almost confidently. "If Sir Geoffrey wants Jacque Noir to cook, then Jacque Noir will cook for him. It will only be a starter of course, as even Noir cannot create exuberant dishes with such basic equipment."

Sir Geoffrey blanched somewhat at the suggestion that anything he owned could be described as *basic*, but his polite upper-class smile soon returned to his polite upper-class face as Jacque began to pull ingredients from the selection in front of him.

"Jacque," Rose said, "I'm not sure this is a good…"

"Be quiet my dear," Jacque said, heating a pan and throwing some sherry into it to create a few dramatic flames. "Genius at work."

A short amount of cooking time later and Jacque took a great deal of enjoyment from the look on Rose's face as two security guards manhandled them out of the building and onto the street.

The tall cyborg secretary handed Rose back her business card.

"Sir Geoffrey says he no longer has any need to contact you," she said, before clacking back off on her infeasible heels, the security guards falling in behind like well-trained Rottweilers.

Rose stared at her card, then at Jacque, her face a very large question mark.

"What the actual fuck just happened?"

Jacque, despite his pain, despite the place he now found his life to be, smiled, recalling those wonderful first few moments after Sir Geoffrey had tasted a starter specially prepared for him on the little island kitchen. That moment of panic in the man's eyes had been profound, the moment when he realised there was something not quite right with the food, and that moment of terror when he knew, without a doubt, he would not make it to the toilet before the inevitable happened.

"The man projectile vomited your starter all over his expensive Chinese sculptures."

This had been the icing on the cake for Jacque, or in this case, the vomit on the pottery. The recipe he had freestyled had been something taught to him by his father, a special recipe for customers who were being a little too friendly with the waitress or a little too aggressive with the bar staff. His father called it *the starter that ends badly*. Jacque had never made it himself, until today, but he was glad to know he still remembered the exact proportions of vinegar to orange to mushroom to milk. It was one of the few recipes he remembered by heart.

"He was never going to give us the money," Jacque said. "We both know that. He just wanted a dancing Frenchman in his office. Well, he was the one who danced."

The fleeting moment of joy left him, crowded out by the worries of his world.

"And now," he said. "I need a drink."

"Jacque, don't you realise what you've done? Even if he wouldn't give us the money, someone would, but now…"

Now he would be blackballed, a pariah in the world of serious finance, and he could care less.

He walked away from Rose, from the faded joy of making a posh man cough his guts up into a hand-carved paper bin. Behind him, he heard Rose's fading cries of protest, but she didn't follow, and soon he was alone in the street, walking without aim, but knowing exactly where he was going.

After an age of waiting for green men to change, and dodging whistleblowing Lycra-clad bike riders, Jacque arrived at a place where he could be himself. Where he could be comfortable. Where he would no longer be judged.

He nodded to the bouncer on the door of the Pearl Toothed Alligator, who gave him a half-smile in return. Inside the music of this dank and dangerously familiar strip bar was its usual overwhelming beat of techno and yesteryear pop songs. Loud music that drove thoughts from his head as the sight of naked flesh under flashing lights and strong expensive alcohol combined to relieve him of the images of failure that crowded in his mind.

He felt his phone buzz. A single message from Rose told him not to forget the awards ceremony later this evening.

Jacque switched off the phone and threw it on the table of his regular booth. Ordering a bottle of vodka, he dismissed those women who asked him to pay for dances, and instead focused on getting as drunk as he possibly could in as short a time as possible.

Chapter 19

Ron

In contrast to the hangovers of Brothers Noir, Ron awoke feeling refreshed, almost renewed. Incredible when he considered himself to be an 8-hours-a-night man, who, without these hours of constant uninterrupted slumber, would grumble and moan the whole day long. However, his previous night's sleep had been anything but uninterrupted, having been roused from his bed in the middle of the night by Tina's frantic phone call. The sound of alarm in her voice had rocketed Ron out of his bed without a moment's thought.

This lack of thought, momentary or otherwise, resulted in Ron standing beside his car, in his pyjamas, realising his keys were still inside his flat. A rather embarrassing wait followed while he stood outside his neighbour's flat as she rummaged around in every drawer she possessed until she found the spare key to his front door. His neighbour was also his landlady; a short imposing woman who had a tendency to start sentences with the words, *those fucking blacks* and let loose with apocryphal tales of immigrants getting so much more than the Daily Mail thought they deserved. A verbal diarrhoea that Ron tried his best to ignore, or accidentally agree with.

To say she wasn't best pleased to be woken in the middle of the night by his request for a spare key, was an understatement that came underlined with various swear words Ron had only ever heard at football matches. And then, only at Millwall.

However, this accidental delay did give him pause to dwell thoughtfully on the bit in Tina's phone call where she kept sobbing, in a panic-stricken way, about the unexpected effects of using a high-powered Taser. She also mentioned something about a lot of blood, and if he saw a 24-hour shop open on his way over, could he buy some plasters, some cotton wool and a carton of milk. This sort of drama, Ron deduced while waiting for the spare key to disdainfully materialise, was not the sort that he should attend in his pyjamas.

Back in his flat, Ron dressed and this time made sure he had all he needed (phone, wallet, keys) and set off again. By this time, it was just after 11 pm, and traffic on a Thursday night from the East End of London into Islington was reasonably light. He arrived to find Juliet standing next to a black cab and talking with two policemen. Mostly, they were listening, with an expression of distinct scepticism. An attitude not improved, it had to be said, by Juliet's belligerent swearing and bloodstained appearance.

"I told you; this is not what it fuckin' looks like." She had protested in a nasal whine, although, realistically, to both the police officers and Ron, what it did look like was a bloody and bruised Juliet rummaging through a cab in a way that made them think she might possibly be robbing it!

Ron had managed to intervene at this point, explained the emergency phone call to the police officers, while wisely leaving out the bit about the Taser, which he hadn't really understood anyway. By way of changing the conversation, he asked the two policemen if they were interested in some free samples of LED torches usually only sold to industry. In fact, they were and Ron allowed them to take away several packs, free, for evaluation. At which point another call came in that sounded far more interesting than a posh woman with a nosebleed apparently robbing a cab.

"Found the fuckin' thing," Juliet announced, holding up an asthma inhaler pump, as the police car zoomed off, blue lights flashing. Having found the object she had apparently been looking for, Juliet hobbled back up the stairs to the office.

"Why do you need..." Ron attempted to ask, thinking perhaps he should.

"Ron, just don'. Just don' talk to me," Juliet said, her voice somewhat muffled by several wads of kitchen roll that she had pressed to her nose. A tactic that still left blood dribbling down her chin and onto her clothes.

Ron took in the demonic sight and decided that not talking to Juliet right now was probably for the best. She was bad enough at a lunch date, there was really no telling how she would react while nursing what appeared to be a badly broken nose. He followed Juliet up the stairs at a safe distance, entering the office and freezing as the sheer chaos that engulfed the room, engulfed him.

"What the fuck happened here?" He said as he surveyed rampant bloodstains that appeared to cover just about every available surface in the room. There was even some on the ceiling, with little rivets of blood dripping down the window, landing on the radiator and fizzing slightly at the hot touch. Ron had seen extreme horror films that used less blood than this.

On the floor were two men, one older man wearing a stained white suit who groaned and held on to his testicles while rocking in pain, and another man dressed in jeans and T-shirt who sat slumped against the wall, cradling a tyre iron and gasping for breath.

"This," Tina said, rushing up to him. "Was all the result of a simple misunderstanding."

She snatched the inhaler from Juliet and administered it to the spluttering man with the tyre iron, who Ron could now see was wearing a Taxi Driver badge around his neck.

"Can you please just get him breathing," Juliet was almost screaming, albeit in a nasally way. "He is not allowed to die until he has taken me to the hospital in his fucking cab."

"Fuck... That..." The cab driver wheezed, staggering to his feet. "I'm... Going... Home."

So saying, he took a double dose from his inhaler and left the room with as much speed as he could wheeze, snatching a fifty-pound note from Tina as he went. He didn't offer any change.

Ron looked at Tina with what he hoped would be his best neutral face, the one he kept in reserve for when someone imparted embarrassing personal information he probably didn't want to know. He hoped she would provide some kind of further detail that would explain all this chaos, preferably something beyond her previous explanation of; *a simple misunderstanding*. She didn't. Instead, Tina gave Ron a list of things that needed to be done.

Get Jacque and Juliet into the car.

Take the former to his flat, the latter to hospital.

Also, try and find a herbal tea on the way to calm Tina's nerves.

This last request brought a tirade of complaints from Juliet, who was beginning to pale somewhat and had sat down with complaints of dizziness.

"Your nerves wouldn't need calming down," Juliet said, her voice ebbing somewhat. "If you hadn't have gone all Bruce Lee with my only client."

"I'm not sure Bruce Lee ever used a Taser," Tina unwisely corrected, and then had to endure a torrent of abuse about pedantic corrections and pointed questions on why Tina owned a Taser anyway. Things didn't improve when in the middle of the rant, Tina reached over and rattled her swear box at Juliet. The next few words turned the air a darker shade of blue, with various suggestions on where Tina could shove the swear box, approximately how far, and how often.

At this point, Ron decided to make a tactical retreat to his Jag.

Once at the car, he covered the back seat with a picnic blanket he kept for sunny days on the road. Having seen Jacque's piss-stained trousers and Juliet's horrific blood dripping nose, he was keen to protect his leather upholstery. The blanket was just going to have to take one for the team.

After that, it had been the no small matter of transferring a shaking, moaning and barely coherent Frenchman, who was the apparently well-known chef called Jacque, from the office to the Jag. They then went back for the still swearing, but somewhat subdued Juliet, and sat her next to Jacque. After a short drive to Jacque's flat, they carried the now slumbering man up to his room, dumped him on his bed and stripped off his clothes, before throwing them in a washing machine.

They both then found a sink to wash their hands in Dettol. Several times.

According to his Jag's GPS, the nearest casualty was the London

Free, so back they went to East London, and then spent the better part of an hour trying to find a parking space. Eventually, they stood in front of an A&E duty nurse who was so shocked at Juliet's appearance, she found a cubicle straight away and instructed Juliet to lay down and wait for a doctor. As a seasoned A&E nurse, she also paid no attention to Tina's explanation as to how the injury occurred and summoned the police to interview Ron, just in case.

When the police eventually turned up, things started to look a little tense and Ron really didn't like the way the short female police officer kept fingering the trigger on her taser every time she looked in his direction. At least the taller male police officer smiled at him, although that was a little confusing given the context.

"Good evening, I am officer Patel, and this is officer Eccles, and we've been sent here to establish how Juliet Raffle received her injuries," the female police officer said, ignoring the muffled '*Raph-ae-l for fuck's sake*' that came from a woozy Juliet on the tale end of a pain-killing injection.

Fortunately for Ron, Tina was able to defuse the situation by telling the truth, a tale so bizarre, the two officers clearly had no idea what to make of it all.

Ron had listened to Tina's story from outside the cubical, peering in through a small gap in the examination room's partition curtain. It certainly did sound a rum-do and he wondered, not for the first time, if he was doing the right thing getting involved with Tina and her chaos attracting sister. At which point Ron remembered that officially he wasn't involved with Tina, and so decided not to worry about the details that Tina elaborated to the police officers. Stuff that was worrying in the extreme.

As Tina suggested to Ron on his arrival at the office, this had all been a simple misunderstanding.

She had entered the office, somewhat flustered because the escalators at the Angel tube station had broken down (again), and while staggering along Essex Road, a drunk had thrown up on her shoes. To say that she did not arrive in the best of moods would probably have been the understatement of the night, although as Ron listened on, he heard at least three more statements that could easily have also been contenders for understatement of the night.

"And then I rushed into the office," Tina explained to the now raptly attentive police officers. "I saw... Well. I saw something dreadful, or at least I thought it was dreadful, but turns out, it was something else."

"Something Non-dreadful?" the infeasibly tall officer Eccles suggested in a slow meandering voice as he attempted to write down what Tina was saying in his notebook.

"Not even a fucking word," Juliet muttered from her bed, the pain killers were mercifully rendering her barely conscious.

"You lay still, Juliet, don't try and talk. Don't talk at all, if possible," Tina said, tucking Juliet in and fluffing her sister's pillows to cover her ears before continuing with the story.

Tina's initial impression had been that considering Jacque's reputation for being a womanising misogynistic perverted lying Frenchman, Juliet was in danger of being ravaged.

"You can't say Frenchman," the much shorter officer Patel said. "In this context, it's not politically correct."

"Oh," Tina said, "I don't listen much to Radio 4 so I don't know what's socially acceptable these days. What about the other stuff?"

"Womanising... Misogynistic... Perverted..." listed officer Eccles.

"Oh, those words are fine," officer Patel said.

"...Words are fine," officer Eccles muttered while writing in his book.

"Peter, we've talked about this, you don't need to write down everything I say."

"... Everything I say..."

"Peter."

"Oh, right, sorry, Zaina."

"Anyway, as I was saying," officer Patel continued with a withering look at officer Eccles, "as Jacque Noir is a middle-aged white male, it is socially acceptable to say pretty much anything about him. Just so long as it doesn't refer to his country of origin because that would be racist."

"Oh, that is a relief," Tina said, although, from the sound of her voice, Ron was pretty sure she had no idea what had just been said to her. He would explain it to her later, being a middle-aged working-class white-male, Ron was pretty experienced when it came to the unadulterated hate that poured forth from progressive liberals in his general direction.

"Sorry," officer Eccles said. "Did you say your sister was being... Ravaged."

"I said it may have looked as though there was a prospect that she could be in danger of possibly being ravaged."

"Right," he made a note, but his puzzled expression deepened. "And would you say the ravaging was... Consensual?"

"Peter? What are you talking about?" Officer Patel had started to look slightly embarrassed by the lowly IQ of the hulking man standing next to her.

"I don't know... It's this word ravaging, Zaina; I'm not really sure what it means."

The uniformed woman sighed, pulled her colleague's ear close to her mouth and whispered, with Ron leaning in close, as did Tina, to catch every private word.

"You remember the Christmas party?"

"Yeah, what about it?"

"The photocopy room?" She suggestively raised her eyebrows, and after a few seconds, the penny seemed to drop in her partner's mind. Albeit, a very slow, gravity-defying drop of a particularly light penny.

"Oh," he said, eventually. "That's ravaging, is it? Right. Got it."

"Sorry, Mrs..." officer Patel said, a slight tinge of red on her cheeks.

"Ms Raphael!"

"Sorry, *Ms* Raphael. Please continue."

And Tina did, laying out the rest of her story in such graphic terms that Ron's night time stomach (e.g. an empty one) turned over several times. Essentially though, on entering the office, and seeing Jacque holding Juliet firmly by the head, Tina had assumed that an unsolicited and non-consensual ravaging was indeed in progress. At this point, she took out her Taser, rammed it between the unfortunate Frenchman's legs, and pulled the trigger.

"Don't write Frenchman down, Peter... No, just... just don't do it." She turned to Tina. "So, this Taser, why do you have one?"

"That's a very interesting story," Tina said, scotching Ron's plans to sneak away and buy something warm from the vending machine in the entrance hall. It sold tomato soup for a pound, plus there was a chocolate dispenser next to it, but no matter how tempting all those calories were, Ron really needed to find out why Tina owned a Taser. If only for his own personal future safety. Predictably, Tina's ownership of a weapon of mass testicular destruction was the result of yet another simple misunderstanding.

Out on one of her regular lunchtime walks, Tina had passed The Islington Business Design Centre, a vast hangar type building that sat just off Upper Street and housed many diverse and often short-lived start-up companies. Most dealt with various forms of internet research that only ever made money if you were selling to people on the wrong side of the law. The centre also hosted various different trade fairs inside its cavernous interior and on this particular day, Tina had passed by and seen a lot of Chinese people standing outside in the courtyard, having a smoke. Assuming they were marketing some kind of takeaway service, she had ignored the casual racist slur and popped in with the prospect of claiming some free samples, a few freebie prawn-balls, that sort of thing.

"Not for me of course," she explained, "for the homeless people in the area."

"Right," officer Patel said without conviction. Ron had to agree with her, it did sound like a weak excuse for bagging some free nosh.

Inside the trade fair, however, Tina had discovered the exhibition was not food related, but an extravaganza of high-tech personal security. So embarrassed had Tina been at her prawn ball related bigotry, she immediately tried to find some personal security gadget to purchase to soothe her socially maladjusted assumptions. Preferably one that was cheap enough to mollify her conscience but without causing her credit card to melt. Finding something that fitted these tight criteria, or indeed a gadget whose function she understood, had been a bit of a challenge. Eventually, Tina found a stand where a pretty young girl, dressed for some reason as a sailor, albeit with a micro skirt, was tasering the life out of a crash test dummy.

The Taser had been over two hundred pounds, but by then Tina had reached the end of her lunch break, and her imperialist driven guilt was beginning to peak, so she paid with a credit card her father mostly paid and went on her way. Later that night, after playing with it for a bit, much to the cat's disgust, she dropped the Taser into a cupboard and pretty much forgot about it. That was until she realised Juliet was about to have an accidental late-night encounter with a highly inebriated Jacque Noir!

"Would you say," officer Patel asked slowly. "That Jacque Noir posed a clear and present danger to your sister? One that might also lead to her living in fear of being... Ravaged, or otherwise experiencing unwanted attention of a sexual nature?"

"Well," Tina said hesitatingly. "I'm not totally sure. Did I mention he's French?"

"Yes, you did, but as I've explained, we can't really use that in an official report."

"Then I would say, my answer could be a yes, but probably tinged with a no, that might be something of a maybe if I were to think about it."

Officer Patel clearly decided it was time to give up.

"Alright, listen, I am satisfied that your sister's injuries are of an accidental nature, but I will officially log this chat back at the station... Well, most of it... But if you think of anything else, let me know." She finished without warning, exiting through the examination room curtain in a swift movement that left her nose to greasy nose with Ron.

Ron took a step back from the encounter. "I was just on my way to the vending machine," he said and started searching his pockets for loose change. The police officer looked on aghast as Ron's hands rummaged randomly about in his trousers.

"Well, sir!" She said, her voice not attempting to disguise the contempt she felt for him and underlining this by fingering her Taser once again in a suggestive manner. "We've reviewed the situation, and I can say that we no longer need to talk to you."

"Okay."

"But if we do need to talk to you in the future, then we will… Be talking to you… In the future."

"Yeah," her partner said, appearing beside her. "And no more ravaging."

"Peter!"

"What?"

"We are leaving!"

"Right you are Zaina, have a nice evening sir," the police officer said before snapping a salute at Ron and walking off down the corridor with his partner loudly and mercilessly berating him for the salute.

"It's a force of habit, Zaina."

"Five years, Peter. You've been out the army five years."

Ron watched them go, listening to their bickering, waiting until they were safely out of sight, before making a run for the vending machine. After the excitement of Tina's story, he needed as many calories as he could consume without choking. The machine turned out to be a bit of a fucker about what sort of coins it would accept, and it was some time before Ron had force-fed the machine his limited small change supply and then force-fed himself enough chocolate to feel like his old self.

While he was trying to cool the soup down to a temperature that didn't incinerate his lips, Juliet was visited by an exhausted duty doctor who unceremoniously reset her broken nose bones with one flick of his fingers. Despite being two floors down and several fire doors away, Ron still heard the screams.

Much later, after painkillers had been dispensed and release papers had been processed, the three of them made their way back to Juliet's flat. By this time, the shocks of the evening had taken their toll on Juliet and she slept like a baby under Ron's blanket, on the back seat of his Jag.

Once Juliet was safely tucked up in bed, Tina had insisted Ron stay the night just in case they needed to take her sister back to the hospital, and he would be handy to help carry her. Ron had hoped that spending the night was a euphemism for... Well... Having sex. Tina soon squashed that hope by creating a bed out of Juliet's rather elegant leather sofa and then retiring to the spare room where the soft click of her door lock announced that ravaging of any sort would not be happening tonight.

Despite the uncomfortable sofa, the lack of sex, and the trauma of being almost interviewed by the police for a crime that hadn't really occurred, Ron slept like a log. He woke to the smell of coffee and the sound of Radio Two in the kitchen. For a while, he was content to just remain on the sofa and enjoy Tina's off-key attempts at Abba, and the smell of whatever she was burning for breakfast. In this early waking state, he even allowed himself to idly wonder if married life with Tina would be as heavenly as this.

"What the fuck are you doing here?" Juliet's nasally voice crashed into Ron's dreams.

"I... I ... I...," he said, unable realistically to think of a single word that wouldn't make Juliet angrier than she already was.

"You can say that again," Juliet snapped, her nasal whine amplified by the massive bandage over her nose and an even bigger plaster that straddled her face, pretty much obscuring her nose entirely.

Without looking in his direction again, Juliet stormed off in the direction of the kitchen, a wince crossing her face as she took each step. Through the servicing hatch, Ron could hear Tina's morning greeting being batted aside by Juliet's demands to know why Ron, or as she put it, *that fat slug*, had spent the night on her nearly new and very expensive leather sofa. All of which made Ron thankful that he had decided to sleep with his pants on.

Valiantly Tina tried to defend him, but this too was knocked out of the park by Juliet, whose nasal injury didn't seem to be holding her back when it came to shouting obscenities. The most venomous of which often preceded his name.

"What do you mean," Juliet said in reference to the lie Tina had just told in an effort to explain Ron's appearance at the office. "Fucking Ron just fucking turned up at the right fucking time? Are you suggesting Ron is fucking psychic? Because I'm not even sure the man is fucking sentient!"

At which point Ron decided this was probably as good a time as any to visit the bathroom. That and the fact he had just discovered his morning erection and didn't want Juliet to find him in a state of excitement on her sofa. Or really, anywhere at all for that matter. While in there, he decided it would be best to have a quick shower, and this allowed him to leave the window open a while longer and get rid of the smells his visit to the loo had created. Living with a woman was a minefield of things to remember.

A short time later, he emerged, clean and dressed, and mercifully flaccid. He found Juliet sitting in an armchair sipping coffee as best she could with a large white plaster the size and shape of New Zealand on her face. He was hoping that Tina would be here, but from the badly sung Slade he could hear, she was still in the kitchen, and by the smell, still burning food.

"I'm supposed to tell you when you *finally* got out of the shower," Juliet said, through clenched teeth, "that this rather expensive cup, containing very expensive coffee, is for you."

"Right," Ron said, edging into the room, hugging the wall to stay as far from Juliet as possible, before dropping down onto the opposite end of the sofa. "Thank you, that's very nice of…"

"…And I was supposed to not spit in it while you were not here."

Ron paused with the cup at his lips.

"And did you?"

"Find out," Juliet said, shaking her head in a confrontational way, one that caused Ron to become mesmerised once again by the giant nose plaster.

Ron chose to believe that people of Juliet's class and status were genetically incapable of spitting at anything, least of all in someone's coffee, besides which, it smelt … Roasty. He wanted to comment on how good it tasted, but under Juliet's intense glaring, he found it hard to find any coherent words that could be collected into a coherent sentence.

"You two playing nicely," Tina said, her head popping through the serving hatch in a very disconcerting way.

"Oh yes," Juliet snarled and Ron settled for just waving his mug at Tina in what he hoped would be translated as a discrete SOS or at the very least, a secret message that said please come and rescue me. That didn't happen and Ron found himself being stared at, while desperately thinking of some direction he could take the conversation without referencing Juliet's nose.

"How's the nose?" He said when he realised the alternative was just sitting here in an awkward silence.

Juliet glared at him, giving him a full view of the large white cotton wad that covered her face and most of her central forehead. The wad itself was slightly bloodstained at the nostrils but held securely in place by two large flesh coloured surgical tapes that were spread out under her eyes and across her cheekbones. Eyes that had turned various different shades of yellow and blue to indicate she would soon have two very remarkable shiners.

"How the fuck," Juliet eventually managed to stutter, "do you think it is?"

"Right," Ron said, wondering if he should just make a run for it. "I wonder what's taking Tina so long with that breakfast."

"Oh, I can solve that mystery for you; it would seem my sister believes you are so hungry that the entire contents of my fridge should be cooked for your eating pleasure."

"Really?"

"Yes, fucking really! She is currently frying, baking, and grilling anything that can be fried, baked or fucking grilled."

"She really shouldn't have bothered."

"No," Juliet said through teeth that were now audibly grinding together. "She really shouldn't!"

The awkward silence descended on the room again, dropping with all the finality of an executioner's axe, but with none of the positive upsides.

After yet another exposure to Tina's singing (a rendition of Paint it Black, of which she apparently knew only half the words), Ron made another unwise stab into the dark and dangerous land of conversing with Juliet.

"Not sure if Tina mentioned it, but I'm a bit of a writer myself."

"Define; *a bit*?"

"Well, I've got this great idea for a story, been working on it while I'm stuck in traffic jams on the North Circular."

"And has this idea progressed beyond the fetid brain tissue that plays unfortunate host to your mind?"

"You what?"

"I said, have you actually gotten around to writing anything down?"

"Oh yeah, I sent Tina a copy last night." Silence! "Maybe she will tell you about it." Silence punctuated by the sound of grinding teeth. "Over breakfast, you know, tempt you into representing my story."

Ron watched Juliet's eyes narrow, or what he could see of her eyes from beneath the bandages and bruises. There definitely was a hardening of her expression though to a point where he was reminded of the legend of Medusa. He wondered briefly if being turned to stone for all time would really be that bad.

"And did Tina mention," Juliet said, between deep breaths. "That I only deal with autobiographies?"

"She mentioned something about your agency needing to diversify into fiction?"

"Did she now?"

The tone of voice brought Ron's enthusiasm to a sudden halt, his emotional airbags deploying automatically. He waited for the imaginary bag-powder to disperse before wondering if he could make it to the front door before she could kill him with a glare.

"Seems to be a lot of stuff that Tina does of which I am unaware. But this will change, oh yes; things are going to change."

Juliet settled into some further mutterings, which Ron began to realise were probably fuelled by all the painkillers she had been fed the night before. He wondered vaguely how much of this conversation she would remember, and with that thought in mind, decided to venture further into this clearly unwanted conversational area.

"I'm going to call it... Pigs. Disaster area. Mars." Ron said.

After a protracted silence, filled with the higher off-key notes of Staying Alive from the kitchen, Juliet took a careful sip from her coffee and then shook her head in a pragmatically confused way.

"Is that the title or the synopsis," she eventually managed to say.

"A bit of both really."

"Of course it is."

"What do you think?"

Juliet blinked at him. Twice. "What do I think?"

"Yeah, what do you think?" Ron said, finding new confidence in securing a conversation that had stopped Juliet being constantly sarcastic to him. "I mean, I *think*, it could make us both a great deal of money."

"And I *think*..." Juliet's voice rose to an angry height, before she calmed herself and smiled, the effort causing her some obvious pain. "What I think Ron, is this is clearly a fascinating idea, Ron, full of exciting elements, Ron..."

"You really think so."

Juliet held up a hand. "Let me finish, please. However, I do feel, Ron, that some of these exciting elements are not actually visible at this time and so, at this critical juncture of this project's inception, we need to slide it across to the backburner and let it simmer for a while."

"Simmer?" Ron said. "How long for?"

"Until hell freezes fucking OVER!" Juliet screamed, holding on to her nose with one hand presumably to make sure it didn't fall off.

The scream brought back the disembodied head of Tina, whose reproachful expression calmed the room. Slightly.

"Breakfast will be ready in just a jiffy," she said with a warning look at Juliet that Ron could not decipher, but one that did actually make Juliet sit back and calm down.

After a few moments had passed, during which time Ron decided not to make any further attempts at conversation, Juliet spoke quietly and softly, again apparently to avoid her nose detaching itself from her face.

"You like Tina?"

"Yes, I ..."

"I don't approve."

"Maybe if you just gave me a second chance?" Ron watched Juliet's reaction. He knew she was of a particular class that made giving second chances almost obligatory, but he wasn't sure that applied in his case. "I mean, I really don't get much chance to be with women like Tina?"

"What sort of woman is that?"

"Classy. Kind. Nice."

"No other nice kind classy women in your world, Ron?"

Ron gave a sad smile as he thought about the world he lived in, the world he worked in. Most of the time he just seemed to be talking to men, managers always seemed to be men, and if they were women, they weren't interested in him. If they were interested in him, it was probably an indication that they had problems, or kids, or problems with their kids.

"Beats me why some women have kids in the first place." He said, then realised with growing panic that he'd said that bit out loud.

"Probably because," Juliet said in a slow lazy voice that reminded Ron of a Lioness closing for the kill, "it's the 21st century and women have the right to bear children even if you don't approve."

"Where is that breakfast?" Ron said, starting to feel the panic rising in him.

"Here I am, here I am," Tina said, bursting through the kitchen door with a large wicker tray loaded down with what looked to be most of a farmyard in a grilled format. "Come and get it while it's hot."

As the tray passed him, Ron estimated that most of the meat was so badly burnt, it would probably remain hot for the rest of the day, but he wasn't going to let an excuse like that stop him escaping this conversation from hell. Or consuming a large breakfast.

He launched his way to the dining table, reaching it with a thud, just as Tina set the tray down and began forking most of the contents onto Ron's plate.

"Come on Jools, you have to eat something, we probably won't get another chance to eat before the awards ceremony, and you know they don't give you much food there."

"Awards ceremony," Juliet said with a quietly mocking tone. "You can't possibly be expecting me to go looking like this?"

She waved her hands at the bruised eyes and a white cotton wad that had become slightly more bloodstained in her last rant at Ron.

"You have to Jools. I was talking to Emma this morning, and she says you are strongly rumoured to be the winner of Biography Agent of the year."

"Emma said this?"

"Yes," Tina said, a cautious smile on her face. "Why?"

"Because Emma, in the grand scheme of things, is not what I would call a reliable source of information, or indeed a person able to find her own arse, in the dark, with both hands."

"Not really much of an arse to find," Tina said, and Ron was amazed to see that Juliet smiled at this. Almost!

"Tina, I know you mean well," Juliet said. "But I can't possibly go to the awards ceremony with this… *Thing* on my face."

She pointed at the wad of white cotton that made her look like a Sesame Street version of a John Merrick.

"Oh, that's not a problem, Jools," Tina said, stepping forward, grabbing a loose end of the surgical tape on Juliet's face, and yanking it off in one pull.

Ron just had time to stuff a sausage in his mouth and two fingers in his ears before Juliet's scream began echoing around the flat.

Chapter 20

Barry the Bouncer

"Where the fuck is Jacque?" Enquired a frantic nasally voice. One that was both a lot posher and a lot more female than Barry had come to expect outside the Pearl Toothed Alligator. Especially at this time on a Friday night, or really at any time of the day or night.

Stirred from his cigarette break, Barry the Bouncer glanced behind him and found an unlikely group pressing against the window of the strip club. One woman was cupping her hands against the glass, presumably in an effort to defeat the mirrored surface and get a peek inside. She was wasting her time. The management had spent a lot of money installing windows that would protect the privacy of their patrons. Although why they bothered, Barry had no idea.

Most of the men sitting in the strip club were single, friendless, and without any semblance of family, and most of them would, without a doubt, die that way. However, there was the odd (with the emphasis on this particular word) married man dropping by now and then, and Barry would concede that in this case, it was handy to have windows through which enquiring wives could not peer.

"Can I help you?" Barry asked, more out of curiosity than any real desire to help anyone whose voice made her sound like an actual member of the Royal Family.

The strange group moved as one away from the mirror windows and into the light of the entrance door and Barry started to wonder just what the fuck was going on. There were three women and one obese man, all dressed as though they had just stepped off a James Bond film set. Albeit, Barry mused, a parody version. The man wore a poorly fitting tuxedo, two of the women were dressed in evening gowns that spoke of money and class, while a third woman, slightly younger, and much darker-skinned and who Barry noted seemed to be with the group, but not willingly, wore red leather jeans and a red leather jacket. An outfit at dress-sense odds with the others.

"We're looking for a... Friend of ours...." The posh voiced woman said, before glancing up and down the dark empty street for reasons that were not entirely clear. Her next words were in a lowered tone of voice. "A... Jacque Noir."

"Is that right?" Barry said, taking a puff of his cigarette and being careful to blow it away from her face. He was, after all, a gentleman at heart, even if professionally he hit people on a regular basis.

"Yes," the woman said, and paused, as though waiting for Barry to say something profound, which he didn't. "You see, he's a... Frenchman."

She added a knowing look at this word, a motion of her face that seemed to cause her considerable pain. As she moved further into the light Barry noticed for the first time a discrete but clearly visible plaster that covered her nose, along with two stunning shiners that someone had attempted to cover with some heavy-duty makeup. Once again, Barry wondered what the fuck was going on. This was all getting a little too weird for his liking.

"Very probably," Barry said. "But we don't give out information about our clientele. Company policy."

"Okay, that's understandable…" A larger woman standing behind the nose plaster woman said. "But this man, he's a friend of ours and we just need to know if he is in…"

"I'm sorry, but we don't give out information about our clientele. It's company…"

"Policy," interrupted the woman with the black-eyes. "Yes, we've got that bit… Could you then maybe pop in and ask him to come and chat with us? It really is very…"

"No," Barry said, slowly and clearly, casting aside his cigarette in case trouble should start. None of them looked like trouble, but these days, who could tell? "If I go in there to chat with your friend, who may or may not be in there, then I would be, by implication, admitting that he was in there, which I can't do because we…"

"…Don't give information on your clientele. Please, could you stop saying the same fucking thing over and over again?"

"You what?"

"Juliet," the larger woman hissed, grabbing the smaller woman by the arm. "That's a pound?"

"What?"

"You swore Juliet, that's a pound for the jar."

"Seriously Tina?"

Barry watched the two women stare at each other before the one called Juliet reached into her tiny handbag and pulled out a pound coin, which the one called Tina snatched from her hand.

"Ladies," the fat man said, moving from the shadows. He vaguely resembled a penguin that had been stuffed by a particularly inept taxidermist. "Let me deal with this."

He stepped forward with a hand outstretched and as they shook, Barry felt a familiar bit of crinkly paper being pressed into his palm. He glanced down and saw a neatly folded twenty. Looking back up, Barry realised he recognised the penguin.

"Ron? Is that you? Sorry mate, I didn't recognise you in that get-up. In you go, mate." Barry detached the pink rope from its tattered looking brass pole and ushered the man through.

"Right, thanks," Ron said, his cheeks glowing a dull red as he hurried through, trying not to look at any of the women behind him. The door to the club opened and loud music assaulted their ears for a moment, along with a blast of heat that Barry tried to absorb before the door slammed shut. He just had time to put the rope back as the women all tried to rush in behind Ron.

"For fuck's sake ladies, you're not going in."

A sullen silence fell over the women, with black-eyed Juliet turning to swear-jar Tina and saying; "So you're not charging him then?"

"Wouldn't it be possible," Tina said, ignoring the sullen woman beside her. "Just to pop in for a moment, just in case Ron needs a hand?"

"No, it wouldn't," Barry said in the hope it would end the matter. It didn't.

"Hi," the tall good-looking woman in red leather said, stepping forward with a handshake and a smile. The smile was warm, but the handshake contained zero money. Not a great start to their conversation.

"I'm Rose."

"Pleased to meet you, Rose. You looking for work?"

"Oddly enough, no," Rose said after a short pause during which her complexion went several shades of scarlet.

"That's a shame, you've got the looks."

"Thank you… I think. What I wanted to explain is that our friend Jacque is also my ex-husband and…"

"Oh, is he," Barry said with a small smile. The look on Rose's face was one of someone who felt she had perhaps ventured down entirely the wrong blind alleyway.

"But we have an amicable relationship…"

"You don't say."

"I do, in fact… Say that. But the important thing here is that Jacque is supposed to be attending a very prestigious awards ceremony and…"

"You don't say."

"…And… And he really needs to be there. It is vital for his career. And really, his survival as a human being."

As this story reached new and improbable heights, Barry sighed and pulled out another cigarette. If this Rose had punched him, that might have been interesting, but now, it was just ex-wives with tall stories, and that was boringly normal.

"You don't say," Barry said in a monotone as he exhaled smoke into the night air, wondering when these people would go away so he could sneak away for a kebab. If he left it much later, he'd run into the commuter crowd, all drunked up from their Friday night binge drink.

In this semiretirement of his life, Barry's main desire was just to have a quiet night, man the door, get through the shift without having some drunk puke on his shoes, or having to call an ambulance because one of the leerier punters had fallen down the stairs… Again!

Just get through the night with as minimal trouble as possible, and maybe thump someone once in a while just to break up the monotony. That's all he wanted from life. Mostly.

The one called Rose had just reached the end of her long rambling explanation as to why it was so crucial for Jacque to attend the awards ceremony. Something about books and money, and not going broke, and an expensive finishing school that still needed paying. Barry could sympathise with some of this, but it had to be said, on the majority, he was leaning more towards…

"Honestly luv', I couldn't give a fuck."

The larger woman called Tina glared at him and Barry patted his trouser pockets as though looking for loose change.

"Catch me next time," He said with a smile that made Tina move half a step back. "Ladies, interesting though this has been, I do really need you all to be somewhere else."

"Somewhere else?" Tina said.

"Anywhere else."

"But what about Ron," Tina countered. "What if…"

"Ron will either get your friend, or he won't, either way, you lot out here are bad for business." Barry imagined the reaction of punters rolling up and seeing two women in ball gowns and another in red leather arguing with the doorman of a strip club. No, this had to end now.

"So, off you go into the night, ladies, and with my best wishes."

"Look," Rose stood directly in front of him wearing a solemn expression that Barry tried to take seriously. "This is clearly a problem of communication, and we simply need to find a solution, so… umm?"

"Barry."

"Right, Barry, thank you. Barry. So what will it take, in your view, to find the ideal solution to this problem that will be satisfying to all parties?"

"Fifty quid."

"Fifty," the bruised face of Juliet lit up with indignation. "But Ron gave you twenty."

"What do you think this is? Equal opportunities? Besides... Ron's a regular. He gets a discount."

"Is he now?" Tina said her face an unhappy mask.

"So much for customer confidentiality," Rose said. "Shall we call it thirty and we won't tell Ron about your little slip."

She offered three ten-pound notes, waving them under his nose. He took and folded them into his pocket in a practised motion. Unhooking the rope, he let her through, putting it back just in time to stop the other two women from rushing forward.

Rose slipped through the door, the street once again lighting up to the sound of techno and a blast of warm air. Barry so wanted to be in there, sitting on the bog, reading his racing paper.

"Okay ladies, you go find somewhere to wait now while your friend gets your other friend."

"Oh, come on," Juliet said. "We've paid you thirty pounds. Surely that counts for something, even if it is standing out here on this puke stained pavement breathing in your second-hand cigarette smoke while all around us..."

"...Alright, alright. For fuck's sake. You can wait here for five minutes."

"Thank you," Tina said. From Juliet, he only heard the sound of teeth grinding.

For a long moment, they stood there in awkward silence, a customer letting himself out, becoming the embarrassing focal point of their attention, before slinking off down the street. The sound of a phone ringing arrived as a welcome relief.

Juliet fished in her bag and pulled out the phone.

"Oh God," she said, looking at the display with an expression somewhere between fear and disappointment. "It's Emma... Oh hi, Emma. No, we are on the way, just a bit of trouble getting a cab... No, we're fine, no need to send a car. No, no need. Yes, yes, I do understand that we can't be late and... Yes, we will... Right. See you soon and..."

Juliet looked at the display and from the look on her face, Barry realised she had been hung up on. She placed the phone in her bag and another awkward silence ensued.

"Very cold for this time of year," Tina said, while Juliet settled back into grinding her teeth.

"Ah it's not so bad," Barry said, studying the teeth grinding Juliet; this beleaguered looking woman in her stunning evening gown. He felt like he knew here from somewhere, which was impossible until he realised where he recognised the face and tied it in with the name.

"Juliet? Juliet Raphael?" He asked, a little hesitantly, which was unusual in his game, to be hesitant about anything.

She looked at him darkly for a long moment before giving a short nod.

"I thought it was you, I've read about you..."

"Oh, in probably every tabloid that's ever been earning money from my misery." She said in such a way that Barry expected her to finish the sentence by spitting on his shoes. "Let me just shortcut the next part of this conversation; no, I never realised my husband was gay, and yes it was a shock to find him shagging our builder in the middle of a half-constructed conservatory. And finally, on this subject, I give zero fucks as I have put the past behind me and moved on to the future. That do you, Barry?"

Barry stood for a moment, waiting for the hurricane that had just bypassed his ears to settle into a tropical storm, before ebbing away into a silent rain shower, broken only by a local pub erupting into spontaneous cheering. That's a goal for West Ham, thought Barry, or I'm a Dutchman.

"To be honest, Ms Raphael," Barry said. "I was about to say I saw your photograph in a writing magazine."

This at least got a reaction from the simmering Juliet that was markedly different from the confrontational anger he had endured since she arrived here.

"Writing magazine? Why would you be reading a writing magazine?"

Barry tried not to be offended by the remark, but some kind of non-vocal reaction must have passed over his face as he could see the instant regret in her expression.

"Not that I'm suggesting that…"

"No, course not."

"I mean, writers come from all walks of…"

"Yeah, they do."

"And so, when I said…"

"Yeah got it." Barry folded his arms and looked down his nose at her in what he hoped was his most intimidating glare. "All that stuff about your husband? I had no idea."

"Great, so I've just outed myself."

"What do you write," Tina said, presumably to steer the conversation away from gay husbands and opportunistic builders. She managed it with a smile that seemed almost genuine.

"Film scripts. Well, when I say scripts, I've only written one. It's semi-autobiographical and…"

"We don't deal with film scripts," Juliet snapped, almost childishly.

Barry pulled the collar up on his jacket, flicked away the stub of his dead cigarette and pulled another one from the packet. He had three left and four hours to work. He didn't need to be a mathematician to see this formula was leading him down a path towards stress and unhappiness. This black-eyed beauty with the nose plaster wasn't helping much either.

"What my sister means," Tina said quickly. "Is that we don't normally deal with film scripts, but we are always looking for original material to represent."

"I didn't mean any of that."

"Yes, you did, now shut up!"

"You interested or not?" Barry asked pondering on the wisdom of entering any further into this rabbit hole of a conversation.

"Yes."

"No!"

"She means yes," Tina said.

"Oh, go on then. It's not like we have anywhere important to be." Juliet said and glared at her sister, at Barry, at the little pink rope he stood behind. She finished with a frosty glare that was directed at the club windows but was probably meant for Jacque Noir, who, Barry knew for a fact was sitting rat-faced in the corner of the club, probably asleep with Ron and Rose trying to wake him.

Jacque Noir was one of Barry's favourite regulars. Not that he actually did favourites, not really, but he did like the punters who were less trouble than the ones who were constant trouble, and he always had time for ones that tipped. Bouncer work wasn't especially well paid, you got a decent living out of it if you were prepared to put in the hours, but it was, literally, agro, and some days, that was more difficult to deal with than others. Customers like Jacque Noir made the job not so much bearable, because even non-hassle customers could be a hassle once they had a drink, but at least less complicated than the job needed to be.

Jacque had turned up at the Pearl Toothed Alligator some years ago, a small party of Japanese businessmen in tow, apparently customers at his restaurant in Islington. Barry had looked up Restaurant Noir on the office computer using The Google but had stopped reading when he saw it was pricey and French. He wasn't a fan of French food. If he was going to eat exotic food, he wanted it to be Thai or Indian or Chinese or even Korean. French was just like English food in Barry's viewpoint, only with more garlic.

The group that Jacque brought with him had been reasonably trouble-free, although they weren't happy the Saki ran out so quickly, but who keeps more than three bottles behind the bar? After that, they started to get a bit too touchy-feely with some of the dancers and needed to be turfed out, but even this they seemed to enjoy, as though being bounced out of a London strip club by an actual London bouncer was something one simply had to do while visiting London.

After that, whenever Jacque had a group of men in his restaurant, and occasionally women, who needed to continue the party on a little longer, then the Pearl Toothed Alligator was more than happy to accommodate them. And charge them double for drinks and dances.

At some point though, something had changed. Barry didn't ask what, he knew better than to poke his nose into the actual lives of his punters. Who needed that sort of involvement? In his experience, you just ended up with a middle-aged man crying his eyes out about some breakup, or lack of a breakup, or breakups that had happened, but then reversed themselves. The complex formula of human relationships appeared to Barry to be a never-ending myriad of fucked-up-ness.

So, when Jacque turned up one lunchtime, on his own, face longer than a horse, and drinking heavily, but showing no interest in private dances, Barry just treated it as a change in customer behaviour and decided to keep an eye on Jacque in case he started a fight.

He never did.

Mostly the Frenchman came to the club about the same time each day, just after two in the afternoon. Dropping into a horseshoe booth off to the side of the main stage, and sitting there, watching the dancers with dead eyes while drinking from a bottle of gin that was often the first of many to be consumed that evening.

Today had been something similar. Jacque had appeared, walking today, instead of getting out of a cab, and his mood, which of late had never been great, was darker still. Barry waved him through, and then followed him inside to see him slump in the usual seat and order the usual bottle. Satisfied that he was not going to be a problem, Barry had focused his attention towards a young man in his twenties who seemed to be taking the lyrics of *I touch myself* a little too literally.

Many hours had passed since Jacque had arrived, and as far as Barry knew, Jacque was still sitting in the same horseshoe booth. He'd ordered some food, a frozen pizza, the only food they did, which they cooked in a microwave, and which Jacque had stared at for several minutes, before bursting out laughing.

No one knew why. No one asked.

Jacque had consumed a lot of booze. Barry knew that for sure, and he wondered if Ron and Rose were even able to talk to him. Or if perhaps they were just trying to get him into a state where they could hope to talk to him and he would understand something they said. That task was going to need a lot of coffee.

Not wanting to get involved with his customers had been Barry's golden rule, but he was curious what these two women had to do with a washed-up restaurant owner with a drinking problem. He was on the verge of asking but decided against it. If trouble kicked off between him and these two women, he'd never hear the last of it from his brother. He decided in the end, to accept their invitation, lacklustre though it was, to tell them about his script.

"It's about this footballer who has anger management issues," Barry explained to the two shivering women in front of him. "In my script, he gets a job working in a cinema and he tries to deal with his temper. But stuff happens, people are killed. It's very dramatic."

He'd been writing in his break times, a spin-off from the reading group he had started with the dancers and bar staff of The Pearl Toothed Alligator. A group which just happened, like most good things. Barry regarded good things as stuff that you didn't know existed until it became a part of your life. A part of your life that you didn't want to live without.

The reading group started exactly like that. One evening, when the place was dead and lonely, Barry settled his boredom by reading a book someone had left on the bar one evening. It was a crime story, some book about a journalist knowing the identity of a killer but not telling the police so he could follow the man and get a live scoop on the next murder. He read it in less than a week, it was a page-turner that he enjoyed more than he thought he would, and it kept his mind off fags and gambling.

One evening he came back from his break and found Alesia, one of the more senior dancers reading the book, and they ended up talking about the plot. Some other people came into the room, dancers, bar staff, cleaners, and a few stayed, interested enough in the conversation to join in. At some point, someone, maybe it had been Barry, he couldn't recall, had suggested they all read this book to the end and then discuss it when the club was quiet. You know, just for something to do.

It had seemed like a strange thing to do, create a book club in a strip joint, but the truth was, there could be a lot of downtime for dancers and others who worked there, time that was often filled with playing games on phones, smoking, or bitching about someone or other. Reading a book and talking about it, it sounded… Cool. Almost exciting. Something that made the Pearl Toothed Alligator seem less of a place to dislike.

The group, such as it was, had started on this first book, then discussed it, which in those early days of the groups was just really an argument about the ending. But then, remarkably, they moved on to other books. Somewhere in amongst these discussions of reading, Barry started to get ideas himself, ideas of characters and stories, until one day, he found himself at the office computer painfully pecking out his ideas on the grim dirt-encrusted keyboard, one finger at a time.

A month or so of pecking at the keyboard and he had a film script.

And no idea what to do with it.

"And although the bloke in my story tries his best to keep his temper throughout the film," Barry said, trying his best to explain the ideas he had committed to paper, but when verbalised sounded a little less credible. "He is constantly engaged by twists of fate into acts of extreme, terrifying, and often graphic violence."

Barry flicked away his dog end and looked back at the listening women, both of whom were staring at him with wide and alarmed expressions.

"And..." Tina said. "What's it called?"

"Man of Violence."

"Of course it is," Juliet said, her head shaking at some indisputable wrong the universe was currently doing to her.

The doors behind Barry burst open and Jacque Noir fell through, literally, landing face-first on the soiled red carpet. Barry bent to help him up, but Jacque was on his feet and moving erratically towards Juliet, a broad smile on his face.

"*Ma Cherie*," he said. "Juliet, at last you have seen in me..."

His sentence cut off midway as the fresh air appeared to hit him in full and he staggered off to the curb, where he began regurgitating his frozen pizza and most of the gin.

Rose and Ron appeared through the doors and froze when they saw Jacque by the road, vomiting for France.

"Well," Tina said. "At least you guys got him out."

"Yes," Juliet said. "Well done, what managed to convince him? Awards leading to money and women? The threat of Bankruptcy? That someone might think French food isn't filling?"

"Actually," Rose said, her gaze avoiding Juliet's searching look. "Ron managed to crack it."

Barry watched as everyone's head, apart from Jacque's, which was still busy praying to the double yellows, span to look at a deeply reddening Ron.

"Ron?" Juliet and Tina said in shocked harmony. Barry had to fight the urge to join in with them.

"Yes," Rose said, glancing at her phone with some alarm on her face, before walking rapidly away down the street. "I'll let Ron explain about it."

"Rose, where are you going?" Tina asked in a shocked voice of abandonment.

"Pascal sent me an urgent message. He's been... He's got himself... Let's just say, he has an emergency and I need to help him. Sorry, I have to go."

Without further explanation, she fled down the road, blind to Juliet lamenting after her that no one else had a car. She turned to look at the assembled group, who in turn, looked to Barry.

Barry pulled his phone out with a sigh and made a call to his cousin in a cab office near Brick Lane. Within a few minutes, a car pulled up outside the club. Standard bouncer tactic, once you had the troublemakers outside, clear them off the street and away from the door as quickly as possible. That way they became someone else's problem, which was a problem Barry could always appreciate the beauty of; if but from a distance.

As he helped the group into the car, securing a plastic bag on Jacque's lap, Tina pressed some paper into his hand, and Barry smiled his thanks at her. It was only when the cab had left that he realised it was a business card and not a ten-pound note. He almost threw it away in disgust, but at the last second noticed the email address and realised she was inviting him to send the script.

At least, he hoped so.

A little later that evening, when the punters had dropped to single figures and the girls were mostly gossiping outback under a cloud of blue smoke, Barry fired up the office computer, and on the third try, managed to attach his script to an email and send it to Tina Raphael.

Well, there goes nothing, he thought, then pulled out his phone to see his brother had been trying to call him. Harry never sent text messages; Barry often wondered if he knew how, but had never found a polite way to ask. Or at least a way that would not result in a trip to the dentist.

He dialled his brother's number.

"Okay, Harry? Yeah mate, a break about now would be great… No… nothing's happening… Been very quiet."

Barry hung up the phone and made a silent oath that he would never tell his brother about the events of this evening, or even about his writing.

And he definitely wouldn't ever mention the book club.

Chapter 21

Rose

Rose hugged Pascal as soon as he emerged through the police station doors.

"Oh my God, are you okay?" She said, her mind racing back to all those terrible prison stories she had read in The Observer.

"The coffee was dreadful," Pascal said, shaking his dark mane in the cold night air. "When they say crime does not pay, I think it is this cup of lukewarm milky muck they are talking about."

Rose paused for a moment, unsure if this was French for humour. Despite being married to a Frenchman, and enduring many visits to grandparents' homes for summer holidays, she still had no idea how French humour actually worked. Or indeed, if such a rare and fragile flower even existed.

The text message she received from Pascal as she was exiting the Pearl Toothed Alligator had been an example of this.

It simply said; *Being held by the Transport police in Marylebone Station for trafficking coke.*

Rose had thought that foraging in a strip club for her ex-husband had been surreal enough, but Pascal's message had rather incredibly dwarfed the bizarreness of the whole situation. On arrival at Marylebone transport police station, a building she didn't even know existed, she discovered the truth was even weirder and at the same time, somewhat disappointing.

Trafficking coke turned out to be nothing to do with drug smuggling from the home counties into London, but an incident involving an actual can of Coke, which a careless owner had refused to put in the bin. At that point, Pascal promptly returned the can to the owner, and at the same time accidentally assaulted him with it.

"I did not assault him," Pascal said as they worked their way from the police station towards the hideously expensive car park where Rose had been forced by circumstances to leave her car. "I made the rightful owner aware of his responsibilities towards the can after he had finished consuming its unpalatable contents."

This, according to the policeman Rose spoke to, had included bouncing the can off the offending teenager's head.

"Very civic-minded of you, but what were you doing on a train from Oxford in the first place?"

"That is a story that is too dark to tell."

"Oh, for fuck's sake Pascal." Rose exploded and Pascal stopped in surprise. "You cannot keep hiding behind; *this is too dark to tell*. Come on man. Tell me what the fuck is going on?"

"Very well, if you insist, I will tell you, but do not say I have not tried to warn you of my story's darkness."

As they walked through the streets, finding a convenient Pret a Manger to sit and drink (despairingly in Pascal's case) a rather lacklustre latte, Pascal outlined the events of his day. Events that, Rose had to agree, were pretty dark. Typically, for Pascal, he delivered all the relevant information at the speed of sucking pate up a straw.

"You remember," Pascal said to her, lowering his voice, even though the only other person in the place was a bored barista busily cleaning something that needed cleaning with the noisiest appliance he could possibly find. "You remember why I left Restaurant Noir?"

"Well," Rose said hesitantly. "I only really recall when it happened. Just after that OAP Christmas special. I seem to remember these were some of the OAP's Jacque had taken down to Trafalgar to dance naked in the…"

"Please," Pascal held out a hand, his face that of someone finding a dog turd wrapped in a fifty-pound note. "Say nothing more about the events of that day, and the actions of the man who I am ashamed to say is my brother. A man who has…"

"Pascal! Listen, I am parked in a very expensive carpark, even for London, so if you could possibly stick to the point?"

"Oui, of course." Pascal looked away, as though searching the empty café for inspiration. "There was a man at the OAP dinner… He… He died."

"Which man? Was it in the papers?"

"Noh! The restaurant was never linked to the death… Despite… Despite…" Pascal tailed off leaving Rose wondering if his hesitant storytelling left her time to get something to eat. She was just about to tuck into a microwaved lasagne at home when Tina called for the first emergency of the evening, finding Jacque before the award ceremony started. In the club, she'd been tempted to snaffle the remaining bits of a cold pizza that Jacque had ordered and not eaten, but then Jacque was on the move, thanks to some unwise promises from Ron.

Then Pascal sent his cryptic text message and she had rushed to him. Food kept appearing in front of her, before being taken away again courtesy of someone or other and their problems. Often a Noir Brother, or a victim of their actions. All of which left her starving and very short on patience.

"Pascal, if this was all covered up, then I'm unlikely to have heard about it."

"Yes, that dark chapter of Restaurant Noir was erased from history by my brother, a man who is beyond the description of words, but if I were to do this, then I would call him a…"

"Pascal!"

"Excusez-moi. I will tell the story to you. I will tell you everything."

"Yes please Pascal," Rose said, and then adopted a softer tone. "Look, I've always known something was wrong, we all did and …"

"All?" Pascal's face was the definition of paranoia.

"Well, you know, me, Yvonne, Juliet, Tina, Candy probably."

Pascal slumped in his seat.

"My guilt has been etched for all to see. Like a bleeding scar on my soul."

"I wouldn't go that far," Rose said, wondering at the man's seemingly unlimited capacity for the dramatic. "But maybe if you just told me what happened. Perhaps using short words and maybe sticking to the point?"

"You are right Rose; you are so very right. The time has come for me to be honest, to bear my guilt to the world, to be forthcoming with the facts, to make a stand against the lies and half-truths that have blighted…"

"Pascal!"

"Oui. Of course. The facts."

Pascal at last began the story, outlining how the restaurant's success had become his cross to bear, how cooking high-quality food for so many people each night had drained his soul, how this had an effect on his life. On his private life. On his marriage.

He stopped there and looked at Rose with a tilted head and a knowing look that seemed to suggest that she should be getting more from his story than simple words could imply.

"You are talking about... The arguments you had with Candy? That's not exactly a secret Pascal."

Most family get-togethers had been filled with either Candy and Pascal sniping at each other, or painfully ignoring each other. In amongst Jacque's endless affairs, it added an extra level of awkwardness to family gatherings that were already a minefield of non-permissive conversations.

"Noh! More than just the arguments, or petty behaviours and mood swings, or even the unwelcome interventions and unhelpful suggestions."

Rose got the feeling Pascal was now exclusively talking about Candy, and though she had never actually warmed to Pascal's American bride, too brash and in your face for her liking, she did have a certain sympathy with the woman. Pascal's dark moods were legendary and just meeting him for dinner was like turning up for a game of Russian roulette with a gun loader who couldn't count.

"Pascal, what exactly are we talking about here?" Rose asked, still a little uncertain what Pascal was hinting at in what appeared to be the vaguest of forms.

Pascal's expression turned from pain to embarrassment as he struggled to find the right words, which in his case, would probably not be anything below the level of a suggested metaphor. Rose tried to think of some way to coax the information out of him, but her focus became distracted by a cake selection in the distance, just behind Pascal's heaving shoulders.

"I am talking about..." Pascal said. "Well... You know."

"If I knew, I wouldn't have said, *what are we talking about.*"

Pascal let out an explosive breath. "We are talking... We are talking about... The bedroom." He finished by giving a complex set of hand motions that appeared to make no sense whatsoever.

"Right," Rose said, both concerned and wondering how stale the chocolate brownies were. "So you and Candy were having problems..."

Pascal did another bout of energetic hand movements.

"Oh, so just Candy... No! No... Just... Just you. Oh. Oh, I see!"

Pascal's face was a perfect portrait of personal pain.

"It had never happened to me before. I was under so much pressure. I just looked for a solution."

"Solution? Do you mean... Viagra? That's nothing to be ashamed of Pascal."

"I am not sure Candy would agree with you."

He had a point. Candy did like a good fuck; Rose knew this because Candy liked to tell her about it. In fact, Candy liked to tell everyone about her sex life, including anyone who read her blog.

Pascal continued his story. Now they were over the speed bump of impotence-laden embarrassment, he became more animated in his need to tell her everything. Rose was grateful that he had at last begun to get on with the story but slightly disappointed that no natural break in the narrative appeared in which she could grab something to eat.

Pascal had bought Viagra from a website to avoid the humiliation of a clinically trained doctor's opinion and then hid the pills in a drawer at work to avoid the ever-snooping Candy. Which would have been fine, if Jacque had not found them.

"Of course, he recognised the Viagra logo on the pill straight away."

Did he now? Rose thought but kept quiet. She didn't want to interrupt Pascal while he was in full flow on the Viagra issue, so as to speak. Although she was unprepared for the next part.

"You did what with the pills?" She said, somewhat surprised that she was still capable of being aghast at the actions of brothers Noir.

"We were drunk."

"And being drunk gave you the right to mess about with someone's food?"

"Please Rose; you cannot torture me any more than I torture myself every day."

Of this at least, Rose was in agreement. However, she still found herself shocked as Pascal explained that finely crushed Viagra mixed in with a sauce served with a lobster had killed an old man who ate it.

"How can you be sure the sauce killed him?"

"He had a heart attack that very night. The old people's home told Jacque when they rang him the next day. They wanted him to know that this old man died happily and that everyone was so glad he had such a lovely last meal at Restaurant Noir before he passed."

Pascal's head collapsed into his hands, and Rose wondered for a brief moment of terror if he was going to start sobbing. He didn't. Tossing his mane of black hair back out of his face, he stared at Rose, a broken man.

"I did not know what to say. What to do. I wanted to confess, but I could not…. Jacque said that… Well, let us just say, he had many arguments that made sense at the time, and yet now…"

Yeah, that would be so like Jacque to cover this up. Rose seethed. The man was a walking hashtag for irresponsible behaviour. At last, though, things were becoming more transparent. Why the Noir brothers had split at the height of their fame, just when Jacque was finding some traction for the idea of launching a chain of Noir Restaurants across the UK.

They had been on the verge of having everything, and now Jacque was broke, and Pascal not far behind him. On top of all that, it looked like Juliet's agency was going to be collateral damage in this whole debacle.

"Once I left, the restaurant could not continue." Pascal darted a look over his shoulder, like a spy smuggling nuclear codes to people who probably shouldn't have them. "Rose, what I am about to tell you, it is the darkest secret of Restaurant Noir. Something that has been closely guarded. Never spoken off outside of family circles. Even you Rose do not know…"

"You did all the cooking and Jacque just watched?"

"Merde," Pascal exploded with such emotional force, the barista behind the counter was forced to look up, briefly, from his iPhone. "How can you know this?"

"Everyone knew." At least Rose assumed everyone knew. Pascal did the cooking. Yes, Jacque played the part of a master chef, with his chef whites, and his grand talk of ingredients, but it was an open secret to anyone who actually worked in the kitchens of Restaurant Noir that Pascal, and before him, his mother, were the actual creative power. Sure, Jacque, and before him, Miguel, were the brains, the people who kept the finances on track, came up with the ever-changing menu, and made sure the cooks were not being overly generous with the portions and reducing the profit margin. The actual cooking, though, that was not their domain, and never had been.

"Everyone?"

"Well, the inner circle. Candy for sure, Yvonne, probably. All of the staff. How could they not know?" All too loyal to let the truth slip, even after they left. Fortunately, Polly had not worked there long enough to figure it out, otherwise it would definitely have been part of her kiss and tell. Rose assumed the same applied to Adam, although after reviewing Jacque's recipe book, he probably had his suspicions.

"And... And Juliet?"

"Probably not. She does seem to lead a rather... insular lifestyle. Although after the beating the press gave her over Clive, who can blame her."

"Juliet is an innocent soul in this world of liars and charlatans."

Rose thought about Juliet in the toilet of the pub last night, negotiating with Adam who had been mid-way through getting a blow job, and also how she spoke to Emma, or indeed how she confronted the frightening bloke outside the strip club. Innocent was not really the word she would have used and it wasn't the word she had expected Pascal to use. As far as Rose knew, Pascal and Juliet rarely talked even though he had opened up a café directly opposite Juliet's office and of course tended to sit next to her whenever Juliet attended a Noir celebration.

And every now and again, Rose had noticed Pascal staring at Juliet for periods of time longer than might be considered polite and...

"Oh my God," Rose said, the light of understanding for a moment brighter than her desperate need for food. "You fancy Juliet. You do, don't you?"

"Please, are we 12-year-olds? I do not *fancy* Juliet... I ..."

Rose waited for as long as she could, which in her current hungered state was about three Nanoseconds.

"What, Pascal, what? Tell me. For God's sake, just spit it out."

"I love her, I love her, is this what you want from me? The truth you say you want? Then yes," Pascal sat back and gave what appeared to be his best stoic expression. "I love this woman. I always have."

"Bloody hell."

Now the giant chasm of admitting his love for Juliet had been breached and making the Viagra speedbump look in reflection like a non-event, Pascal spoke in uncharacteristic rapid fire. Sometimes breaking into French, always waving his arms around, at one point slapping himself in the face to fully convey to Rose the true force of his feelings for Juliet Raphael.

He needn't have bothered. As Rose sat and listened to the man listing Juliet's physical features, and comparing them to this sunset and that flower, and a whimsical metaphor towards elegant long-legged fishing birds, she could see he was a man besotted. Although she had to admit, he had hidden it well, even though, in retrospect, it was all a little obvious. That convenient coincidence that led Pascal to open a café just opposite Juliet's office, just before his wife left him and not long after Juliet's divorce to Clive. The fact that Pascal was always a little less dark when she was around. That he was always a little sharp with anyone who had anything negative to say about the woman. All of this now made complete sense.

Except for one tiny detail.

"But, with you both being single, why didn't you just ask her out?"

"Have you not been listening to a word I have said? A man died, Rose, in my restaurant because of my foolish actions."

"Oh right, yeah, the dead old guy." In the rush of information, she was getting about his love for Juliet, she had almost forgotten about the death of an OAP. "But still, you know, if you're not going to actually confess, would it matter all that much?"

Pascal gave her an intense look that seemed to indicate that it did matter. Then he sighed, deeply and darkly.

"There is more. Much more. Before Jacque and I split, he had signed the publisher's contract to write this cursed book of recipes."

A unique name for a cookbook thought Rose but said nothing.

"Of course, Jacque would not write it, would not do anything that bored him, instead, he forced me to do it, saying it would be good for us both and... Well, you know how he is when he wants his own way."

Oh yes, Rose knew about that all right.

A silence stretched between them, Rose remembering all the manipulation she had endured while living with the very definition of a narcissistic husband. Substitute brother for husband and no doubt Pascal was remembering a lifetime of the same.

"You know," she said into the echoing past that stagnated the air between them. "He can cook. I saw him do that this afternoon."

"Of course he can cook. He is a Noir! It is in our blood to cook, but like my father, he finds the grandeur of customer applause more gratifying than the actual hard work of culinary creation." Pascal finished that rant with a small amount of spittle building on his upper lip.

"I'm sure!" Rose said, trying to beat down her maternal instinct to wipe away the spittle. "But what he cooked today, something with mushrooms? It actually made the man who ate it projectile vomit everywhere."

"He cooked the Devil's Brew? Why? This is a dish we used to get rid of only the most awful customers."

"Really? You did that? That's awful."

"Perhaps. But at least none of those died."

Small mercies thought Rose.

"He cooked it for a man today that wanted to fund Jacque's restaurant chain. At least, we thought he did but turned out he just wanted to meet Jacque and have a private cooking session."

Pascal's laugh barked out in the silence of the café. "Fame is a capricious mistress. I can remember when my grandfather…"

"Yeah, Pascal, not to be rude, but we seem to have gone off-topic again and the clock is still ticking at my carpark. Just tell me, why didn't you simply tell Juliet that you love her?"

"Because Jacque blackmailed me. He said the dead old man would become common knowledge, and then my use of Viagra would be in the papers, and I panicked, and I agreed to his demands to write the book."

"So you did write the book?"

Pascal nodded, head in hands, staring into his unsatisfying cold latte. He spoke quietly now, almost ashamed, outlining that although Jacque could have written it himself, he was too lazy, so Pascal decided he would make his brother work for his fame, and Pascal wrote a cookery book that was precisely wrong. Recipes that from first glance looked fine, and yet, created food that was at best, unpalatable.

"I hoped that Jacque would at least try some recipes, see the problems, and then work out how to fix them. But of course…"

Pascal didn't need to finish the sentence. Rose had known Jacque long enough to realise that once he had the book, he was just going to hand it over to the publishers without even glancing at it, and then take the money.

"When that happened, when I realised what he was doing, I was wracked with guilt, not for him of course."

"Oh, for Juliet! Of course, She was the agent on a duff book and she didn't know it."

"Poor Juliet, she is an innocent of this world. Her lips are like that of a delicate…"

"Yeah, yeah, we've covered this Pascal. But why didn't you just tell Juliet?"

Like all things Pascal, or indeed Noir family-related, the answer was a complex one. At first, he thought that it wouldn't matter too much, that Juliet had so many high-flying clients that it would just be a minor embarrassment. And then, through chatting to Tina, he soon learned the truth, that Juliet had only one client of worth, that all her business plans were dependent on the success of Jacque's book, and that if it were to fail, then her agency would fail too.

"By then it was too late and I no longer knew how to explain my own actions." Pascal looked now close to breaking point.

Rose desperately hoped he wouldn't cry. While she adored men who were in touch with their emotions, and encouraged the feminine side in all men, the reality of a crying man, especially in public, even with only one barista as a witness, was potentially mortifying.

"I did go to her office last night. Briefly. I had decided to confess everything, the book, the death, my love."

"In that order?"

"I don't know. Is it important?"

"Probably not. Carry on. What happened when you went to her office?"

"When I got there, I found Jacque drunk and asleep at her desk, and just like that," Pascal clicked his fingers in frustration. "I lost my nerve. I left the office with nothing."

"Right," Rose said, remembering something Juliet said earlier in the car. "You didn't happen to write a rude word on his forehead, did you?"

Pascal snapped her a guilty look and then nodded.

"But it was a good thing that he was there, it made me realise, beyond all doubt, that before I could confess my love to Juliet, I must first make peace with all my sins."

"How do you mean?"

"I realised that I could never be with Juliet if I did not first clear my conscience of the disaster that was a Viagra spiced lobster."

Rose forced herself not to laugh.

"And that's why you went to Oxford today?"

"Oui, I went to visit," he paused for dramatic effect. "The widow of the man I killed."

Pascal had set off from his café earlier in the day, determined to find the widow, confess his part in her husband's death and, at last, to rest. His first stumbling block had been the UK rail service.

The effects of a new timetable, having being introduced some two years earlier, was still being felt in the everyday reliability of the trains. Or the lack therein. On his arrival at Marylebone, he could see only a tangle of red letters on the train announcement board indicating delays and cancellations. Eventually, he managed to secure a ticket, at great expense, find a train that was actually there and a seat that wasn't occupied by someone's bag.

Pascal then lamented, at great length, the surreal nature of the British, a population who could be offended by a hashtag, milk being poured in the cup before the tea, and imaginary EU laws that never existed, yet when it came to public transport, were happy to accept a service that registered as less than mediocre on the world's seismograph for life-satisfaction. And pay through the nose for the pleasure of using it.

Rose thought about her own experience with European public transport, of French ticket officers who claimed only to speak French and Italian trains that seemed to run a timetable based around a need-to-know basis; with the actual travellers not qualifying for such information. However, she refrained from dutifully rising to the challenge of defending the underfunded and over privatised mess that was UK railways, and instead mentioned to Pascal that the café they now sat in closed at 8.

Pascal got the hint and began another bout of his tale.

Banbury was his earlier destination, and apparently the home of a railway station that Pascal described as one of the bleakest places he had ever visited, although it was unclear to Rose if he had ever visited Milton Keynes. From there he took a cab to the old people's home, which was apparently in the middle of nowhere and cost him twenty pounds for the journey, and several years off the life of his soul while listening to the opinions of the cab driver on Brexit.

His destination had been Dale View Retirement home, which sat at the top of a valley, just outside the main town, poking out from the side of a quiet country road and looking down on the unmistakable beauty that is Constable Country. Rose had been to the area. Once. Taking Yvonne on a family picnic. One. A day the young teenager had described as a day from hell, with particular reference to the poor quality of mobile reception. A city girl at heart, Rose had enjoyed the views and the fresh air, but at the end of the day, she had been keen to escape the countryside smell, which seemed to be processed shit, and also the large cows that were a little too friendly for her liking. In truth, she preferred her farmyard to be in a carton and at only 1.5% fat.

If Pascal had time to admire the beauty of the retirement home's view, he did not mention it. On arrival, he had asked at reception if he could see the woman who had been married to the man Pascal believed he had killed, with the totally unfunny Viagra spiced Lobster.

Mrs Hornby was the name Pascal asked for, but that lead to blank faces until of course, someone mentioned her first name, Beth, and all became clear. This led to another rant from Pascal about overfamiliar usage of first names and the English obsession with friendliness being incompatible with their unfounded suspicion towards anyone who spoke with a foreign accent. He then digressed into a rant about Brexit, one that Rose forestalled by tapping him on the back of the hand and then pointing to her watch.

Reading between the heavily laden metaphors of Pascal's story, Rose gauged that Beth had been somewhat enthralled to see the Noir brother turning up to personally see her.

"She was so kind to me," Pascal said, his eyes misting up to the point where Rose wanted to hug him, but she also wanted that chocolate brownie, so her emotions were somewhat conflicted at this point. "She took me into her room so that we could talk."

And probably so she could isolate him away from the other inmates and claim her visitor prize for herself, thought Rose.

In the room had been photos of Beth's husband. Dotted about the place in little silver frames. Mixed in with these had been photos of children, some recent ones that he presumed were grandchildren, and in amongst those memories that were not his to enjoy, emotions had boiled over.

"You cried," Rose said, trying not to sound appalled at the thought of Pascal randomly wandering into a retirement home and blubbering his eyes out.

"There was too much sentiment. I thought of this poor man whose life I had cut short..."

"Didn't you say he was 96?"

"Perhaps not cut short, but ended... Earlier than it should."

"Oh no. Pascal, did you confess to Beth? His widow?" Her eyes were already picturing the tabloid headlines, and also trying to imagine how much the lawsuit would cost. If the Noir brothers thought they were broke now, they had a shock coming to them.

However, all was not lost. In his deep state of traumatic emotional shock, Pascal had mainly spoken French to Beth, who had, of course, not understood a thing. Instead, she did what the English do best in these situations, and made him a cup of tea.

"After my confession, I felt free, drained of my guilt."

"Even though you spoke in French and conceivably she hadn't understood a word you said?"

"It is, as you English say, the thought that counts."

"Well possibly, but Pascal, what happened next?" The barista had started to pack away the pastries in preparation for closing. He hadn't reached the chocolate brownie section yet, but it was only a matter of time.

"Then," Pascal said, sitting up straight and smoothing his hair back, which immediately fell over his face again. He looked at Rose with an air of renewed energy. "Then, everything changed."

While sitting in silence, Beth filled the uncomfortable void with small talk. She talked, sadly, and in a way, romantically, about the day her husband died peacefully in his sleep. Of course, this had roused the almost but not quite dormant guilt in Pascal, who once again tried to confess, this time in a language that Beth might actually be able to understand.

"Beth," he said, struggling to find the correct English words. "I think your husband died because the lobster I gave him was… Not cooked correctly."

Which Rose thought was an interesting euphemism both for a confession and for adding a dose of erectile dysfunction medication to food. At that point, however, Beth had dropped her own bombshell. One that changed everything.

"Oh, no! Bob didn't eat the lobster; he's never eaten shellfish in his life… Apart from whelks. But that's not really shellfish is it?"

At which point Pascal attempted a rant on the lack of basic knowledge in England not only on seafood but the world in general. One that Rose beat down by waving a stern finger under his nose.

"No, Pascal, no. Back to the point. Back to the point."

Her husband had, according to Beth, a rather acquired sense of humour. One that only she and perhaps one or two of her less politically correct grandchildren found amusing. He had apparently ordered the lobster after a dare from one of his rivals in the care home and had become forceful about the order because of the long-running rivalry between himself and this other man for… Reasons! Once the lobster arrived, Bob had given it to Beth to eat and tucked back into his turkey with all the trimmings.

"Trimmings that I sweated blood to produce as you English like them, which is, apparently, boiled to death and soaked in enough salt to preserve a corpse."

"Pascal, I swear to God, if you do not stick to the point, I will beat you to death with my expensive iPhone." Rose exhaled with the true feeling of the famished.

"You English, since that debacle that was Brexit, you are all very violent people."

"Something to bear in mind if you deviate again from this conversation. Now... Beth ate the lobster... But... But she was fine."

"Oui, although she said it made her feel a bit funny... Downstairs."

"Downstairs?"

"Oui." Pascal raised his eyebrows and looked pointedly towards Rose's lap.

"Oh? Oh!"

"She asked me for the recipe."

With the revelation that Beth's husband had in fact died of natural causes, mostly that of being old, and not been killed by an anti-erectile dysfunction lobster sauce, Pascal wanted nothing more than to race back to London and confront Jacque.

His brother must have known that Beth's husband had not eaten the lobster, Jacque worked front-of-house, he must have known. Pascal needed to get back and expose his brother's lies.

Beth, however, had other ideas, and she wasn't going to let her captured guest go without a fight. She suggested, rather forcibly for a frail old woman, that Pascal cook something special for the old people's lunch. There were only eight of them, most being on a day trip to a lunchtime theatre production that Beth had not fancied.

"I can only watch so much culture in any one year." She explained, towing Pascal by the hand to the kitchen and introducing him to a stunned group of kitchen staff.

"Oh Pascal," Rose said. "Did you explain to her that you don't cook anymore?"

"I tried, but for some reason, she could not hear me. I think maybe her hearing aid was not working correctly."

Rose nodded knowingly. Her mother had, in her final years, also possessed a hearing aid that seemed to have an unreliable battery. One that would shut down when her daughter said anything her mother wasn't receptive to hearing. Mostly stuff about Jacque.

"You cooked? Wow!"

"Wow, indeed Rose. I cooked. Simple fair, just a lunchtime menu, but I cannot do this in your English half measures. When I cook, I cook for the food. For the moment of taste. I cook for real. I can do nothing else. I am a... A chef!"

Pascal described to her the meal he had created from the basic meagre ingredients he found in the retirement home larder. Bouncing the catering staff around the kitchen too, by the sound of it, in his efforts to create a *modest lunch*. As he spoke about the cooking process, a diversion that Rose allowed, there was a light in his eyes, a lifting of his head, an almost physical elation of his soul. Something that she had not seen from Pascal since his mother had died. A glint in the back of his story was the suggestion that, perhaps, while he was cooking, creating, being the man he was born to be, he had been...

Happy.

After the meal, after he had sat in the old people's main room and sung some songs that he did not know the words to, but mainly they seemed to be about the war, he bid Beth goodbye and got into his cab. The shock of the lobster revelation still pinged about his brain, but the joy he'd felt from cooking filled his heart, a conflicting tapestry of emotions that brought a tear to his eye as he described it again to Rose.

Beth had tapped on his cab window just before he left, and when Pascal wound it down, she said to him; *this woman, this Juliet you keep talking about, you should tell her you love her.* And then with a sad smile on her face, she added; *none of us is getting any younger. There's no time to waste.*

The cab returned Pascal to the train station, costing this time fifteen pounds, and he had crossed to his platform with a head full of ideas. A mounting plan. A moment perhaps of madness, but a moment he had to follow to the end, or die trying.

He would return to London; he would confront his lying brother. He would find Juliet. He would tell her he loved her. He would open a new restaurant. He would live the man he wanted to be. The life he was born to live. That of a French chef. The future beckoned to him like an alluring creature singing a siren song from the rocks of a better life.

Rose, listening intently, decided not to mention that siren songs traditionally lured men to their doom. Pascal was on a roll and now wasn't the time to inhibit the flow with facts. A tad of verboseness could be accepted from the man. So long as he eventually got to the fucking point.

When Pascal arrived at the Banbury platform, he found his train was delayed forty minutes. When the train finally arrived, it was packed with no seats available. This turned out to be less of a problem though, as it only got as far as Oxford before the driver announced the train had broken down. Another hour passed before a replacement turned up and Pascal was once again heading for London.

At least this time he got a seat. Unfortunately, he was next to a teenager who had a runny nose and no hanky. After listening to him sniff for the entire ninety-minute journey, (which should have lasted only fifty, but was apparently still quicker than usual), Pascal had snapped and given the young man some, presumably unwanted, advice on nasal cavity hygiene. They arrived at Marylebone about then, and as the teenager left, he compounded his cardinal sniffing sins by leaving an empty can of Coke on his chair, which Pascal advised him to throw in the bin, and to be sure this would happen, returned it to the teenager by lobbing it across the crowded compartment.

Regrettably, it turned out the can hadn't been totally empty, spraying several disgusted commuters, and the teenager hadn't heard Pascal due to his earbuds playing music just below the pain threshold. The can bounced squarely off the young man's head and it was more or less at this point when British Transport Police turned up.

"Fortunately, they are not going to press charges," Rose interjected. Having reviewed the footage, and spoken to a number of passengers who all seemed to be referring to Pascal as the *coke can hero*, even those who had been soaked in sticky soda, the police had decided to let it go. Probably because they had more pressing matters on their hands, like an upcoming football crowd that would be coming through the station a few hours later, and they would probably need the cell places.

"Then I am free," Pascal said, standing dramatically. "Free to confront Jacque, and then free to tell Juliet that I love her. We must go now. Where is this monster who is my brother? Where is he hiding?"

"Actually, Jacque will be at the awards ceremony right about now. He's.... Ummm... He's there with Juliet." She refrained from telling Pascal that his brother was technically Juliet's Plus-One for the event. The evening was complicated enough as it was.

"That is wonderful. Both of them in the same place at the same time.

It will save time. We must go there straight away so that I may rise to the calling of my destiny."

"Great," Rose said, feeling both swept up in the moment, and excluded at the same time. "Listen, I can drop you off, but I'll have to leave you to it, I need to pick up Yvonne from Ballet practice and I'm already late."

And also, Rose felt as though she'd had her fill with sorting out the Noir Brothers' lives, and loves, and all the stuff in-between. Besides, she could still hear the silent call of her cold lasagne, alone, at home, in her fridge.

"Before we go," Rose said, "do you think I can just grab that chocolate brownie?"

"Noh! Love and destiny cannot be denied for a moment longer. We leave now."

"But…"

"Now!"

Without further delay, Pascal grabbed Rose by the hand and dragged her from the café.

On the way to the carpark, Rose pinned her hopes on stumbling across a chocolate vending machine. Maybe one that stocked Yorkies.

It didn't happen.

Chapter 22

Juliet

Juliet sat upright and with a confident smile glued to her injured face. She allowed this confidence to be bolstered by the expensive evening gown she wore and shoes that had cost more than a package holiday to Tenerife. Shoes she had loved at first sight, but whose love had become tarnished after having worn them for several stress-filled hours. A pale representation of the happy future she had foreseen for the two of them, three if you counted both shoes separately. Now she mentally referred to these former feet-hugging lovers as *those bastard things*, although she was careful not to say it aloud as Tina sat next to her, painfully sober and ready with her swear box.

Tina had got the jar out of her handbag just after they sat at their allocated table at the glitzy venue, even though it was clearly inappropriate to jangle it in the middle of an awards ceremony every time someone swore. Especially if they were, at that moment in time, giving an acceptance speech. The first few times Tina had done this, a number of people had laughed, in a good-natured way, but this laughter had soon morphed into muted smiles, which had withered into polite grimaces as the joke wore quickly away to irritation.

Despite this, or perhaps because of the onslaught of the many, many negative life experiences that had occurred to Juliet in these last twenty-four hours, Juliet remained upright and confident.

A smile of relaxed optimism stapled to her face.

It was all she had left. There were, in her opinion, very few options left on the table. Particularly as what was physically on the table was Jacque's head, slumped face down in a drunken stupor, brought on by filling his recently emptied stomach with as much alcohol as he could find. Jacque's snores were at least relaxing; in a strange rhythmic fashion. Like the sound of dry windscreen wipers scratching across rain-free glass in the utter silence that accompanies the critical seconds after a near-fatal car crash.

Throughout her life, Juliet had suffered many difficult situations, many, although by no means all, had been man related. When *#MeToo* had popped on the scene, with women everywhere saying, yes, they too had encountered men with personal boundary issues, Juliet had just wanted to say *Duh!*

This invasion of her personal world by unwanted forces, unwanted men, and occasionally women, had been part of her life for as long as Juliet could remember. Her earliest memories of the first such incident dating back to a time in Spain, in her father's private chalet, swimming every morning as she liked to do, and finding the statuesque and handsomely rugged pool-cleaner down on the roof of the outdoor shower, minus his trousers. Juliet's mother had been in the shower but afterwards, after he had been sacked and set packing, Juliet wondered how often the pool man had seen her naked in the shower. The thought, that single incident of betrayed trust, had affected her more than she cared to admit. An uncomfortable initiation into the cold realities of life and one that certainly had not been helped with her future dealings with men of all ages, races, and looks.

In Juliet's experience, it was the good-looking ones you needed to really watch out for. They had a particularly entitled view of themselves and very often they had the charm to go with the good looks. They were the type who liked to chase, in fact, Juliet was convinced they enjoyed the hunt more than the capture, the intimacy, or even the sex.

These types of men were difficult to refuse, often failing to take a clear no for an answer. Sadly, in Juliet's experience, their good looks and charm often lifted them above the suspicion of their activities. After all, good-looking men can have whomever they want, why would they grope a woman in a lift, or spike her drink, or find a way to get her alone when they could have anyone they want, whenever they wanted.

At this point in the thought flow, Juliet would always see two eyes peering through a roof, gazing at the innocent naked teenager that she had been.

As a woman with a certain level of beauty above the average, Juliet fought a constant war on two fronts; against the unruly attention of men whose attention she did not crave, and against the impulse to believe that not all men were made this way.

Clive had not been made that way. He had treated her like a Princess, and then, of course, she had found out that he too, on occasion, liked to be a Princess as well. This hadn't helped her outlook on men in general and midway through the divorce proceedings she had, against her better nature and own self advise, sought out therapy to deal with such long-standing and often career prohibiting issues. And also, rather depressingly from Juliet's point of view, to find a cure for her lapsing voice.

Initially, Juliet had sought out a therapist who looked like those psychologists she always saw in Hollywood films; tall fit types with a mop of dark curly hair, spectacles to prove undisputable levels of caring intelligence, but with a glint of something raw and unpredictable behind the bifocal glasses. Juliet figured if she was going to be bored by condescending advice on her life choices, she might as well have some eye candy to look at.

She ended up with a woman in her late 70's who spoke with such a strong German accent she could almost be mistaken for a parody of someone trying to speak English with a fake German accent. Hilda Mayer came from South Germany, expressed very little opinion on Juliet's gay husband, but was livid about the pool cleaner story. Mayer traced pretty much everything back to this event, claiming that every single negative foible of Juliet's personality sprung from that one traumatic point in time.

"It is as though," she explained in her thick accent that Juliet always strained to understand. "You were raped that day. Raped by his eyes. Your loss of the voice… Can you remember it happening before this time?"

There are moments when a flash of understanding is an understatement, and yet, here was that moment when Juliet realised her vocal problems, the voice that came and went with embarrassing frequency, had never actually been a problem before that day in Spain. Before she stood staring up at two small holes in a shower room ceiling.

"We have much work to be doing." Mayer had said and that very day they had worked through a lot of deeply personal stuff.

In future sessions there would be tears, there would be laughter, there would even be times when Juliet wondered if the therapy was doing anything useful at all. Until one day a crisis at work occurred and Tina had rushed in with some throat lozenges, and Juliet had wondered why, because her voice was just fine.

Tina had cried when Juliet put down the phone, and for a while, Juliet had cried with her. Decades of finding her voice coming and going like a ghost ship in the fog had finally been conquered. She need not fear it any more. She was whole again.

If only it were that easy, Juliet thought, staring at the Frenchman asleep on the table, his face squashed into a strange shape by a serviette half blocking his mouth. The blockage caused his unconscious drunken mumblings to be even less coherent than usual, and perhaps that was for the best.

Juliet had not attempted to speak for the last thirty minutes, no one around the table had either. Both Tina and Ron were focused, intensely, on the coffee and biscuits in front of them. Even though both had clearly finished drinking the coffee some time ago, and the biscuits were no more than a few sparse crumbs on the plate.

If she were to speak, Juliet was sure her voice would once again be a painful rasp. A stage whisper; an old man who smoked twenty-a-day and somehow managed to avoid dying of cancer. And she was livid about it all.

After all that therapy, all that hard work, all of that personal plunging into areas of her past that she would have preferred never to have dipped a toe, let alone jump emotionally naked, after all that, it had been for nought. Juliet felt as though she had taken two steps forward, only to take one giant step back, and then be hit by a speeding lorry. One that failed to notice her until it had driven her failing corpse several miles back down the road of unremarkable personal progress.

All of that work. All of it. Reversed by Jacque Noir and his ability to fuck things up as though it were an Olympic sport.

The evening had got off to a splendid start when on their arrival at the venue, Jacque had fallen out of their cab, literally, thumping down on the pavement with such a noise as to attract the attention of every Paparazzi in the area. At that moment, they'd all been happy getting photos of a young soap starlet who apparently decided that formal evening gown meant strapless, short, and showy. Juliet had watched the starlet's smile turn upside down as she lost her faithful followers of snapping photographers to the Buster Keaton escapades of Juliet's own personal Plus-One for the evening.

It was more or less at this point she realised the gamble to get some publicity for Jacque's book was more risk-laden than she had allowed herself to comprehend. In the same way that mountaineers quickly appreciate a rapidly fraying rope is unlikely to be a funny story they will share around a warm fireside. The plummeting feeling inside her stomach was suitable for this metaphor, as was the feeling of the air rushing past her ears as she'd picked Jacque of the pavement and stumbled inside, only to have him dash off to the toilets, knocking a tray of drinks over on his way.

As disasters go, this attempt to revive her flagging career had been pretty comprehensive, and in such totality, Juliet might have had time to admire the true meaning of chaos, if she hadn't been so squarely sailing into the eye of that storm. The situation had rather improbably proved that it could get so much worse, when Emma clacked up to her on equally expensive heels to ask, in a somewhat restrained way, what the fuck was going on.

"So, right, here's the thing Juliet, Jacque appears to be a little... Well, I don't want to cast aspirations, but he does seem... You know..." Emma wobbled her head as if to mime someone whose motor functions had recently deserted them for reasons that were unclear.

"You can...say... *drunk*," Juliet said, through her teeth, her voice now less than a raspy squeak. "It won't make... situation... worse."

"So... Right... Here's the thing Juliet..." Emma began, then spotted Jacque coming out of the toilet and fled towards the relative safety of other people. She mouthed; *we need to chat to you about this* as she retreated.

After that initial disastrous entrance, Juliet at least felt comfortable that things couldn't possibly get any worse. That she had been wrong on a seismic scale was perhaps one of the reasons that Tina and Ron were now studying their empty coffee cups so intently and failing to meet Juliet's gaze.

Their table for the evening sat towards the back of the hall, appropriately in a corner where the fire extinguishers were kept. About as far from the stage as they could possibly be without sitting in the lavatory, or perhaps the carpark.

At first glance, Juliet realised the position of the table meant neither she nor Jacque were likely to have won a single award. They were there tonight strictly as nominees and happy-clappers. Despite Tina arguing that Juliet was reading too much into the situation, her arch-rival in the literary world, Melody Smyth, had bagged the award for best biography agent. An award that Emma had assured, beyond a shadow of a doubt, that she, Juliet Raphael, *Literary Agent to the Stars*, would be winning. The fact that Juliet and Melody were old enemies that dated back to Uni, was the shitty icing on a particularly shitty cake.

At the University Juliet attended, Melody had been one of the wealthiest and most entitled people she had ever met. All wrapped up in the passion for upholding the right to be offended, not only at anything and everything but also on behalf of people that were often not themselves actually offended by whatever ineffectual thing that had been said or done. In the University debating club, Juliet liked to argue the counterpoint that Melody should perhaps stop being such an empty-headed, knee-jerk, social-justice-warrior. It was an outburst that cemented the lifelong feud between the two women, and a quote the press got hold of when digging around in Juliet's past during the long period of Clive's outing. A quote that had dogged many of Juliet's radio interviews when launching books. A quote that Melody had paraphrased that very evening while accepting her award.

"And finally, I'd just like to say, that if I, Melody Smyth, an empty-headed, knee-jerk, *feminist*, can achieve this, then anyone can." Melody had said, then beamed a smile in Juliet's direction and in doing so, with this deliberate misrepresentation of what Juliet had actually said, banged a final nail into the coffin that now entombed her career.

It got a big laugh, an even bigger round of applause, which Juliet seethed over. The laughter, more than the substituted dishonest word, haunted Juliet the most. Even after a toilet break, she could still hear it clearly in her head. A toilet break that brought no solace as Juliet found Tina waiting by the sinks when she emerged from her cubicle with some motivational words of comfort. In mid-pep-talk, Juliet silenced her sister by pointing out that she had paid nearly five hundred pounds for the dress and shoes, in the expectation of winning an award that was supposed to save her career.

"And, not only did I not win the award, but it went to that bloody awful Melody..."

At which point, Melody had opened the door to the cubicle next to the one in which Juliet had sat quietly crying, and trounced up to the sinks, proving that she actually did possess dark powers purchased by selling her soul.

"Oh, darling." Melody blew air kisses on either side of Juliet's head.

"Melody, yes, hi, I was just saying to Tina, great win, great. Really. Great. Was just saying to my sister, Tina, how it was Ummm..."

"Great?" Tina suggested.

"I was saying, how great it is to see a strong woman winning by talent ability and belief in herself. Really... Great. Absolutely... Great." Juliet wobbled to an end of the sentence, her voice little more than a kitten mewing.

"You go, girl," Tina said with unexpected enthusiasm, raising her arms like a cheerleader.

"Oh, darling, your poor voice," Melody said, taking time to apply some lipstick, before disappearing out of the toilet, award held loosely in one hand.

Outside, the two sisters tottered back towards their table on their implausibly high heels. Juliet's cheeks burned red at Melody's closing remark on her voice. There seemed to be no way to rescue this evening, her career, or even her ability to talk. In her moment of pain, she turned some of the anger towards her sister.

"*You go girl?*" Juliet said, sparing a moment's precarious balance to glare at Tina.

"I wanted to say something nice," Tina said in her defence. "But you'd used up all the platitudes. Anyway, judging by the amount of cleavage Melody was showing, it's easy to see how she landed that award."

"What are you… Talking about?" Juliet seethed; it wasn't easy to seethe and walk in high heels. She grabbed a glass of wine from a passing waiter and used it to recharge her speaking abilities. "She's the agent for a prize-winning biography, and anyway, five of the judges were women."

Tina's passing comment that it just goes to show that you can never tell *who's gay or not*, with a knowing look, had done little to improve Juliet's dark mood. A mood that was painted a whole different shade of black at the sight of Ron still sitting at the table, picking through the remains of the biscuit crumbs.

"Oh God. Nipple rubbing Ron is still here. Why is he still here? And how can he still be hungry, he ate all his dinner and Jacque's."

"Poor love," Tina said, "I'll have to make him a sandwich when we get home. And Ron is still here because I asked him to wait for me. Please don't be mean to him Jools, he's feeling especially emotional tonight."

"Please don't tell me he's going to cry again. What's wrong with the man?"

"He's an open well of sentiment."

"Really? Because I thought he was a bigoted emotionally retarded misogynistic salesman."

"I think he's cute."

To which Juliet had no comment to make and presumed this hidden cuteness Ron possessed had nothing to do with the belching and farting he had subjected them to during and after dinner. One particularly loud buttock trembler had contained such vigour, Juliet had reasoned that if her own body expelled gas at such volume the force would have propelled her through the roof of the hall and sailed her into low orbit above London. Which considering the way the evening was progressing, might have been for the best.

As they approached the table, Tina's phone beeped and she checked it, a smile lighting up her face.

"Oh, it's Ron, he says he misses me."

"We've been gone, literally, five minutes."

"I know, and in that time he's sent me loads of messages. Isn't that romantic?" Tina put away her phone and looked to Juliet for assurance. "That is being romantic, right?"

Juliet thought it sounded more like the embryonic actions of a stalker. One that was only a date or two away from working out which bit of his garden to bury her in. She held her council though, partly because her voice still hadn't recovered enough and she didn't want to waste it talking about Ron, and partly because she was going to need Tina's help in getting Jacque out of the venue.

Jacque was still slumped face down on the table. Still snoring. Waiters had begun clearing the table, but the plate pinned down under his drooling mouth was being tactfully ignored.

"Our lucky winner hasn't stirred," Ron said as they got back. "Been sleeping like a lamb."

"Lucky winner?" Juliet said, incredulous that her incredulity could become any more incredulous.

"Yeah," Ron said, retrieving the award that Jacque had collected at the end of the evening; a wooden spatula, embossed in gold and mounted on a shiny black plastic block. The block contained a brass plaque, with Jacque's name engraved in italics. "Credit where credit's due, I don't like the man, not because he's French, but because… You know… But he deserves a good drink for winning something."

For a moment, Ron tilted the award backwards and forwards in his hands, looking at it from various angles.

"All I can say is," Ron said. "He must be one hell of a porn star."

Being surround by older males of the publishing industry who had mostly chosen very young and beautiful women to be their Plus-Ones, and older women of the same industry who had brought with them very young and handsome men, Ron had appeared to persuade himself the awards ceremony was for the Adult Entertainment Industry. A point of view that once established had proved for both Juliet and Tina, impossible to reverse. Even more so after Ron had started drinking from the free bar.

"That," Juliet said, sliding into her seat so that at least her feet could have a break from the drama of the evening. "Is a wooden spatula. Not… Whatever the hell you think it is."

"Really," Ron said, viewing the award now with evident disappointment. "I thought it was some kind of French variation on the theme."

A theme Juliet felt in no hurry to explore.

"It's a wooden spatula that Jacque *won* for writing the worst cookbook of the year. It's a booby prize, Ron. Please let me know if I am talking too fast."

A slow light of realisation crept across Ron's face, in the same way, the Earth creeps around the Sun, fast when measured in miles per hour, unbelievably deadly slow when viewed from a distance.

"I did wonder," Ron said. "Why people booed when he gave his acceptance speech."

When it came to the last award of the evening, the infamous Wooden Spatula, Jacque had not taken the sound of his name being announced with anything approaching good grace. He had in fact not reacted at all, simply staring up at the stage as though he expected a punchline, that someone would whip out the proper award, and present him with that. As the laughter began to ripple around the room, before lapsing itself into an embarrassed silence, and the last of the slow clapping faded away, the presenter had asked if Jacque was willing to be a good sport and come up and collect the Wooden Spatula.

Eventually, after what had felt to Juliet to be a little longer than eternity, Jacque had stirred from his chair, walking in fits and bursts of a drunken man, stumbling up the stairs, to yet more embarrassed laughter. He ultimately collected the award by snatching it from the presenter's hand with a petulant motion that almost span himself off the stage.

His acceptance speech had been pretty colourful. Some of it Juliet hadn't heard because she put her fingers in her ears around the three-minute mark. Others, deciding they too could live without this diatribe of self-pity and insults, had left for the toilet, or the bar, or anywhere really, fairly early into Jacque's rambles.

At the juddering end of a speech that tailed off as Jacque lost focus on what he was saying, there had been a small amount of muted applause, during which time Emma materialised next to Juliet at their table. She didn't stay long, just long enough to let Juliet know that in light of recent developments she would probably advise her head of marketing to cancel the launch of Jacque's recipe book.

And then Emma had jaunted away, and with her, Juliet felt, went any chance of ever resurrecting her career. And now, after the ceremony had finished, and Jacque had got spectacularly drunk, Juliet was tempted to just leave the man there, face down in his own crushed ego. However, she was a professional, and so long as he remained her client, which would probably be at least until Monday when her business folded, she would do her best for him. Her best, she decided, would be to get him in a cab, send him safely home and never speak to him ever again in her entire life.

Even this last act of contrition proved complicated on a scale that only Jacque Noir could invoke. Simply moving him had turned to farce when Jacque slipped from her grasp and slid under the table.

At least it woke him up.

"If it is not too much trouble," he slurred, "could one of you English idiots help me? There appears to be some kind of grease on the floor that prevents me from standing."

One of the floor managers from the hall appeared at Juliet's side, a concerned, but non-judgmental look on his face. He spoke a few polite words, mostly a short request that Jacque be taken to a private room until his car could be summoned. Juliet was both relieved by the offer to get out of the public glare but also mortified by the thought that Jacque's embarrassment had reached such heights of discomfort they now needed to be quarantined.

"Ron, can you help me?" Juliet said, hating the fact that she needed to ask this man for anything at all.

"Sure, babe."

Juliet ignored his inability to use her name. Now wasn't the time to fight that particular battle.

With Ron lifting the bulk of Jacque's weight off the floor, Juliet and Tina were left in charge of faffing around behind him, saying things like, *are you sure you can manage.* And, *let me get the door.* At last, they reached the privacy of the private room and placed the once more unconscious Jacque in a chair, which he immediately slid off and onto the floor.

The room had clearly been used sometime earlier as a reception area to which Juliet had not been invited. Presumably because this is where the winners were informed of their impending win. At one end was a short bar containing many empty wine bottles and a few that were not completely drained. Juliet decided to attempt to raise the ghost of her voice with alcohol, and at the same time, perhaps, buffer her mind from any future disasters this evening might hold.

"There was some curtain cord outside," Ron said to Tina. "Fetch that and we can tie him to the chair, and then we can use that to carry him down to the cab."

Tina left and Ron once again manhandled Jacque from the floor, bracing him against the bar in front of Juliet while he waited for Tina to return with a rope.

To tie Juliet's client to a chair.

To stop him from sliding to the floor because he was so drunk.

Surreal appeared to have clocked out for the rest of the evening, leaving the tail end of its shift to be covered by a close relative called bizarre. Juliet wondered who took the shift after that? Complete fuck up? Unparalleled disaster? Or maybe the world would just end and all this madness could be forgotten in a fiery ball of flame.

As Jacque regained consciousness while pinned to the bar in front of her by Ron, Juliet realised she would probably not be so lucky as to experience the end of the world.

"Ah my wonderful literary agent," Jacque said, momentarily regaining consciousness, but apparently unaware that Ron was the only reason he didn't fall over. "How are you feeling?"

"How… am I…. Feeling." Juliet rasped, her anger and despair finishing off the last vestiges of her voice.

"Oh, have you lost your little voice again? Let me see if this helps."

Before Juliet could react, Jacque reached across the bar, grabbed her around the back of her head, and lunged in for a kiss that was deeply evasive, in every definition of the word.

She pulled back, slapping him around the face. The slap didn't appear to affect Jacque at all, in fact, he smiled.

"And now I see you are breathless from the passion of being kissed by Jacque Noir."

"No… I am… Breathless…. Because I couldn't breathe…" Which did have some truth to it, mostly because her throat had been blocked by Jacque's persistent tongue. If she could have said as much, it would have been accompanied by various words that would have seen Tina's swear box bulging at the seams.

"Oui, oui, Jacque Noir understands it is the excitement of being so close to Noir."

Juliet gave a glare over the Frenchman's shoulder at Ron, who was still struggling to hold Jacque upright against the bar. Preoccupied as he was, he didn't see the intensity of her glare; otherwise, he probably would have turned to stone. On the cab ride from the strip joint to the end of her world at the award ceremony, Ron had admitted to *perhaps* giving Jacque the impression that Juliet wanted to shag him, and then tried to defend this by saying it had been the only way to get Jacque out of the strip club. Jacque had been sleeping through Ron's confession and even now was still apparently suffering under the delusion that Juliet desired him, a desire she had hidden so well for so long and had invited him to this awards ceremony simply to act on that hidden desire.

Juliet's only hope of remaining unmolested appeared to be finding a way to get Jacque home, or at bay for long enough so that eventually he passed out from all the booze he had drunk and forgot about what Ron had said to him in the strip club. Tina appeared to answer her silent call for a physically restrained Jacque by running dramatically into the room, holding a length of curtain tie back. She held it stretched between both hands, her face strained and serious, for the moment looking like a ninja in an evening gown.

"Ron. I've got the rope," she said and waved it a bit as though to prove its existence, which given the surreal nature of the moment, was probably for the best.

"Great stuff luv'," Ron said, heaving Jacque away from the bar and dragging him to the chair. "Get ready to tie him to the chair when I put him in it."

"Okay, no problem," Tina said in a tone of voice that seemed to indicate that none of this was out of the ordinary.

"Why fight it?" Jacque continued his desire laden charm still directed at Juliet. "Can you not see that we are meant to be together?"

"Your book… Your presence in my life… Cost me my reputation… My business," Juliet said, taking a swig of wine from a half-empty bottle to keep her voice from crashing completely.

"Oui," Jacque said with an oomph as Ron slammed him down in the chair and held his shoulders so Tina could wrap the rope around his upper body. "But apart from these trivial points, what objections can you possibly have to not be with a man such as Jacque Noir?"

Having tied him to the chair, Ron and Tina were finding that just the one curtain drape wasn't going to do the job. After a couple of frantic signs from Ron, which at first Tina completely misunderstood, she slipped off her tights and used those to tie Jacque's legs to the chair.

"We are Jacque and Juliet," Jacque was saying. "Like the book, we are destined to be together."

"You mean Romeo and Juliet… It… Was… A play."

"Was it? I only remember the Dire Straits version… Anyway, you cannot deny, Juliet, that we are meant to be together forever."

"Forever!"

"Well… At least a few nights, perhaps more if you are lucky."

Juliet felt her voice eat itself as the stress levels in her reached an unsurpassed high. She opened her mouth to express something, anything, with what was left of her vocal cords, but nothing except a dull rasp came out.

"Ah, a woman without a voice," Jacque said, noticing a half-empty bottle of red on a table within reaching distance and grabbing it with a feat of impossible drunken coordination. "What a tragic concept. Would it help your voice if I identified the important times you should speak and then gave you permission?"

"Everything… I say…" Juliet said, forcing her voice into a herculean effort to overcome the trauma. "Is important."

"I had forgotten," Jacque said. "This particular female version of logic."

"You really… are," Juliet said and took a long drink straight from a bottle of pink wine that tasted of summer and fewer problems than she had in this one room right now. "The most arrogant man… I have ever met."

"Mon chéri, what you call arrogance is mere…"

"… Unmitigated… Conceit?"

"Confidence."

Having tied Jacque's shins to the chair legs, Tina was now busy tying his thighs to the seat of the chair, while Ron had taken off his tie and was using that to secure Jacque's arms to restrict his access to low-hanging wine bottles.

"And the confidence that men possess," Jacque said, apparently under the impression that Juliet gave a damn what he thought. "Is like... Is like... Shoes to women."

"Uncomfortable? Liable to break under pressure?" Juliet took another slug of summery wine, it really was helping to restore her voice, and remove her emotional pain. "Oh wait, I know, expensive but rarely able to give any lasting pleasure."

"Noh, noh, noh my prickly bundle of sexuality. For men, confidence is..." Jacque said *confidence* with such enthusiasm, it forced the chair back on two legs. Ron dived to the back to hold it but was badly angled and unable to push the chair upright. Instinctively, Tina knelt in front of Jacque, pushing all her weight down on his thighs. The chair righted itself, Ron red and ruddy-faced to the rear, Tina, face down in Jacque's lap. The Frenchman rocked for a moment, as though unsure what had just happened, and then slowly became aware of Tina's head in his lap.

"Well, I must say the evening is starting to improve," he said as Tina looked up at him from between his legs. "And for some reason, I am reminded of Paris. Now, where was I?"

"Debasing the entire female race... With pointless... Platitudes?" Juliet suggested.

"Ah. Oui of course."

Ron helped Tina up and they both retreated to a small table to get their breath back, with the assistance of a glass of much-needed red wine.

"You see confidence is something only a man can successfully wear," Jacque said, killing any hope that he had actually finished speaking. "A woman with confidence is shunned by society and so she has no choice. She must become a man, and you know what happens then?"

"She gets paid more? Gets to drive her own car?" Juliet guessed, wondering if she could find another bottle or two of this voice recuperating summery wine. "Oh, I know… Does she never have to worry about piss on the bathroom floor?"

"Noh! When a woman has confidence," Jacque said. "She becomes bitter and unloved and unattractive to men."

"Sign me the fuck up!"

"And so instead runs to a man of confidence, to shelter under his… Confidence. And the woman. She no longer has to be bitter or twisted or buy lots of wine and live alone in a house with lots of cats." Jacque said, at last appearing to run out of steam. "Does that answer your question?"

"I'm pretty sure I never actually asked you a question."

"Oh, mon chéri, let me tell you this one important thing," Jacque said, and the room froze, all eyes on the man tied to the chair, the silence hanging in the air, waiting to hear if all of this would start to make sense. Jacque's head falling forward to rest his chin on his chest, accompanied by soft snoring, destroyed this illusion forever.

"Great, he's asleep," Juliet said, putting down the bottle. If it came to losing her voice or being able to walk in a straight line in heels, she would have to choose the latter to survive the day. "Tina, come with me."

She walked towards the door, grabbing Tina by the hand and yanking her out of a moment that looked as though she and Ron would kiss. For a second, Ron failed to notice Tina had moved and sat with his eyes closed, puckering up and kissing thin air.

"Oh well done, sis', I missed getting a kiss from Ron by an inch."

"You can thank me later. Meanwhile, we need to find a cab to get Jacque out of here before any more embarrassing photos can be taken by the press."

"I think that ship has long since sailed."

"I don't care," Juliet said. "I want him out of here, and more to that, I want me out of here so that I can go home and have that nervous breakdown I've been promising myself all evening."

She towed Tina's protesting form from the private room, ignoring a soft voice in the background that would only have been Ron saying; *I'll just wait here, shall I?*

Great, Juliet thought. If the evening had a lower point than its absolute low point, then feeling guilty about leaving Ron alone with Jacque had to be it.

Chapter 23

Jacque

Laughter. Loud. Raw. Inescapable.

A chilling sound that even alcohol failed to obliterate. A haunting legacy of an instant when Jacque realised, perhaps for the first time, that everything was gone.

Ruined.

Perhaps, forever.

As the last vestiges of unconsciousness painfully slipped away, he remained slumped and defeated, starkly awake, head resting on chest, his mind still replaying those moments of utter humiliation. An unending, palatable prism of pain that speared deep into his psyche; that echoing sound of a room laughing not with him, but at him. Seeing him as a fool and not just acting one. The clown mask pulled away to reveal a less attractive, less funny, less perfect version of Jacque Noir beneath.

Why had he left the comforting embrace of the Pearl Toothed Alligator? Had he not been content to lay in his own congealed pool of gin flavoured misery? Rose had disturbed his transcendence to oblivion with frantic appeals for him to attend the award ceremony, for one last attempt at digging him out of a hole he nurtured so willingly. He had rejected all of his ex-wife's arguments, but the fat man, the one calling himself Ron, had persuaded him with tales of a wild and wanton Juliet, waiting outside, waiting for him. For Jacque! Why had he believed these lies? Was his ego so vulnerable, so weakened that fabrications from an obvious idiot could persuade him?

The memory of laughter invaded his thoughts again, causing him to question who was the obvious idiot. This laughter, this sharp tearing of the soul, this venomous sound of shame; this was the unmistakable echo of all future doors of unspecified opportunity slamming shut in his face. It was a noise he had run from his whole life, but in the end, it had caught him up, tracked him down, and taken him to the ruin of everything he wished to achieve. Everything he had dared dream possible. Leaving him alone in this room, sitting on a chair, afraid to open his eyes.

Afraid to face the future.

Afraid even of the present.

When his name had been called for the Wooden Spatula Award, he had assumed it was a joke and laughed, heartily. Loud and drunk. He had thrown up his arms to the muted amusement around him, prepared to show that he too could take a joke; even if it was aimed at him in some spiteful vindictive way that he could not fathom. He simply assumed it was yet another example of the famous English humour, which Jacque found to be similar to French humour, only minus any redeeming qualities that might possibly make it funny.

Through the laughter, Jacque had detected a slow clap, one set of hands at first, hands he could not see, but somehow, he knew they belonged to Adam Russel. Those hands were alone for just a short time, soon others joined, and then a beckoning hand from the stage host had become more frantic, and a small lackey had been sent to fetch Jacque, underlining the horrifying truth.

The award for the worst cookbook had really and truly been given to him. To Jacque Noir! To a member of the Noir family.

Distantly, as he staggered to his feet, and numbly made his way to the stage, he saw in the crowd the ghost of his mother, dressed in kitchen whites, smoking, her hair piled high and beautiful. Jet black and fading into the darkness around her. Her eyes stared and as he stumbled up the stairs to the podium, she said something, something only he could hear, but something that chilled him to his core.

Honte! Shame!

And then that dreadful spotlight was on him, blinding him, removing the faces of those whose laughter had stilted, slowed, until silence followed, leaving Jacque room to make his acceptance speech. The crowd now had a taste for his blood, and anything he said would be a lavish crust of gore for the spectacle of his professional demise.

Here and now, in the present that was his drunken shame, sitting in this private room on a chair that for some reason he could not stand up from, his eyes still closed, his head still supported by his chest, a version of the speech he should have given flowed fluently through his mind.

The speech he wanted to give, in that moment of spontaneity, should have drawn from his experience of being in the limelight, of being front-of-house, of being Jacque Noir. He had in his mind a series of pointed remarks to turn the laughter from him to the committee members who had elected to give him this shameful award. He had in mind to mention, one by one, their individual failures, in detail. Humorous detail, of course. Then... Then he would have worked his way into that crowd of slow clappers, and laughers, dissecting the mockers, the heretics of Noir with a combination of witty remarks, well-timed jokes and, yes, a restrained humility. It would have been a speech of such cutting facetiousness that he would be carried into the annals of speech giving legend.

The speech he gave, however, in that moment of the imperfect present, was far away from the speech he imagined he should say. In the end, he lacked the wit and humour to carry it off, his voice slurring from too much booze, his mind reeling from the fact that he needed to defend himself at all, his body almost caving to the stress of the fuck of a day he had experienced. All this combined to defeat his grand gesture, his moment of response.

As he began his slow, rambling, off the cuff acceptance speech, Jacque assumed the room's laughter was on his side, supporting him in his fight for justice. He soon realised his meanderings were the main focus of laughter, along with his inability to find a conversational point that he could stick with, his failure to remember the actual names of people he wanted to insult, and his eventual loss of control that would turn the air blue with his frustration. Insults that he soon discovered held little weight when he constantly referred to his intended targets as, *that bloke with the ears*, or *that woman with the spikey hair*! Fairly soon the boos started, and with every passing stumble of an insult, they grew voluminous in their need to silence him.

There was an attempt to take the microphone from him, but Jacque batted that away, a little too enthusiastically, the host of the event staggering under a mistimed slap to his face and falling off the stage. His fall was broken by the small table of hors d'oeuvre, and Jacque tried to think of a witty joke about landing on the starters, but in the middle of saying it, he forgot what he found funny about it in the first place. Eventually, Jacque staggered off stage to utter silence, the award held limply in one hand, security arriving to presumably make sure he didn't try to go back on again.

When it became clear the host was neither dead nor injured, the audience once again began their soft, slow clap. At least those that were still present did; most had fled the scene, heading for the bar or the toilets, no longer having the stomach to see Jacque rip himself apart in a moment of true professional suicide.

At the table, Ron had been the only one to greet him, inexplicably shaking Jacque by the hand and congratulating him. Jacque had been too numb to correct Ron or even remark at the man's stupidity. His gaze was also focused on the stone-like-mask that Juliet now wore. A mask that refused to look at him as he sat down next to her. Even Tina would not meet his eye. All in all, the next three bottles of wine on the table seemed like the only sensible solution.

Unwilling to think any more about this recent past, Jacque opened his eyes and stared for a moment at the small unfamiliar private room he now found himself in, and then at the chair that he was tied to.

"Why am I tied to a chair?" He said and then realised that aside from himself, the room was empty, although there seemed to be someone in the toilet. If the noises were anything to go by it was in all likelihood Ron. This Jacque confirmed as his sense of smell began to come back online. His mind shrank away from the images conjured up by Ron's toilet groaning and the odour emanating through the closed door and focused instead on the mystery of why he had been tied to a chair.

Jacque Noir was no stranger to the more expression-full displays of passion when making love to a woman, but he had to admit, when he was tied up and awaiting sex, there was usually someone else in the room with him. Often someone that was doing something imaginative to him.

Right now, there was no one. There was plenty of alcohol, in half-empty bottles around the place, but all of them out of his restrained reach. Jacque vented his rage by straining at the bonds that secured his arms to the chair, and almost straight away Ron's knots gave up the ghost and Jacque was free.

With a maniacal laugh, he swept a bottle from the table and drank the remains in one go. Whoever had attempted to thwart Jacque Noir in whatever he had been doing, had failed. He was free. Free to pursue whatever it was that he had been doing. He tried to think for a moment what that might be, but nothing came to mind, so he reached out for another bottle, but found it out of reach. An attempt to stand brought to his attention a pair of woman's tights securing his legs to the chair.

The knots on these were trickier to untie, almost impossible. After a few frustrating minutes, Jacque finally managed to undo enough to free himself, the effort leaving him off balance and he fell on a heap to the floor.

"And with one bound," Jacque said breathlessly, with his face pressed down into the carpet. "Noir is free."

Now he really did need a drink, but something other than wine. He got painfully to his feet and stumbled around the room until he found a bottle of peach brandy. This was strong enough to burn his throat and bring tears to his already red eyes, but it helped with the physical pain, even if it did little for his ongoing emotional trauma. Turning, he caught sight of himself in a mirror that ran the length of the wall behind the bar. A tortured soul looked back, a man who had reached the very end of the end, and knew there were no more ends to be had. This was the actual end of everything, and it was a frightening final destination.

Jacque placed the bottle back on the bar and cradled his face in both hands. There had to be a way out of this, there had to be a way to…

A woman's handbag on the table caught his eye. An expensive woman's purse! Juliet's! It had to be. Then it was not Ron in the toilet. It was Juliet and… Well, from the noises being made and the smells emanating out from the door, she clearly had some digestive issues, but Jacque, in this moment of desperation, forced himself to see beyond that… He would have to see beyond that if he was to find somewhere to sleep tonight. Juliet had a flat, one that presumably had electricity, if he could seduce her, then he would at least get through the night without sleeping on a park bench, and tomorrow…

Jacque marvelled at his own survival instincts. Juliet had rebuffed him so many times he had given up trying to seduce a woman impervious to his charm. But now… Now he needed to try again, try to find a way for her to fall for him, to be seduced by him. How though?

As he walked away from the bar, his foot slipped on a patch of wine, and in drunken over-compensation, he found himself spinning round in a lazy circle, like a stripper around her pole. The image caught his imagination and to Jacque's drunk and dysfunctional mind, a plan began to unfold. He would seduce Juliet by stripping off, waiting for her, naked and defenceless, and she would be tempted either by his rugged sex appeal or feel the need to mother him. Either way, it was a win-win scenario. Plus, it was damned hot in this room and his head was spinning, and he really felt the need to be less encumbered by clothes that stank of booze and puke.

His jacket came off after a short struggle and having freed himself, eventually, Jacque considered his next move. Experimentally, he kicked off one shoe. It flew through the air, taking a German bottle of wine with it, both crashing to the floor, the shoe looking more damaged than the bottle. He was getting in the mood now, humming one of the often-played tunes at The Pearl Toothed Alligator, Jacque kicked off the other shoe and watched it sail off into a dark corner of this abandoned room. The belt of his trousers went next. Not willingly by any means, first fighting his drunken attempts to undo it, then his yanking attempts to clear it of every loop on his trousers. Finally, he threw it to one side, undid the button and zipper, and dropped his trousers to his ankles.

Removing the trousers proved problematic, as did keeping his balance as he tried to ply the leg of the trousers over his socks. After a couple of aborted hops around the room, he grabbed hold of a chair and used it to steady his balance. At last stabilised for the moment, Jacque bent over to free himself from the restriction of the now snake-like grip his trousers had around his ankles.

He was still, somewhat breathlessly, holding on to the chair while bending almost double to finally free his legs from the clinging material, when the toilet door behind him opened, and a large man rushed out, slamming into his behind with great force.

For a moment time stood still, Jacque bent over the chair, trousers round his ankles, trying to work out why a large fat man was standing directly behind him and not a slim and nimble Juliet. A glance in the direction of the mirror behind the bar confirmed the person directly behind him was Ron. Directly behind, as in, with Jacque's bum rammed into Ron's groin for reasons that were entirely unclear. It worried him greatly because his bum was guarded only by the thin material that was a leopard-skin posing pouch.

His lucky posing pouch. He had worn it today specially to bring him good fortune. When he got home, if he ever did, the first thing he would do was burn it.

"What the hell are you doing bent over outside a toilet door," Ron said, his hands now gripping Jacque's waist in an apparent effort not to tumble the two of them over.

Jacque didn't have an immediate answer to this question. The short version, that it had been a seduction plan that he now doubted would ever have worked, seemed to be a non-starter. He decided on an even shorter version of the truth.

"I was trying to get my trousers off and... And I ran out of breath."

"Well, if you ask me that makes no sense at all!"

"I did not ask you." Jacque tried to straighten up and move away from Ron's over-friendly grip. He was alarmed when Ron shuffled along with him, step for step.

"What are you doing?" Jacque said with a building sense of alarm. "Let me go you gripping pervert."

"Oi, don't you call me a pervert, I've got kids," Ron said inexplicably. "And anyhow, I can't let go, your thong thingy has got caught in my flies. I'm sort of attached to you by my trousers."

"You are what?" Jacque felt himself break out in a cold sweat.

"I said..."

"I heard what you said," Jacque could feel panic giving way to a rising tide of hysteria flooding through his body. It felt vaguely like being sober. "And it is not a thong, it is a leopard skin posing pouch. An item that was created for me by a French fashion designer whom you have no doubt never heard of."

"It looks like a thong."

"You are seeing it from the wrong angle."

"Honestly, I'd rather not be seeing it at all."

"Then free me you moron and your idiotic wishes will come true."

Ron pulled his hips backwards in an attempt to free himself, but this tightened the posing pouch's already lethal grip around Jacque's testicular area, an area still extremely sore from Tina's Taser session.

Jacque let out a muffled cry of pain as Ron jiggled his hips, trying to free himself, the gyration forced Jacque's own hips to follow this bizarre dance, or risk extreme gonad pain. For a second they performed a hideous version of Twerking; Ron pulling back, Jacque slamming his arse unwillingly back into Ron's groin when the limit of posing pouch elastic had been reached.

"You have to free me," Jacque panted, out of breath and in a state of mental shock. "If the paparazzi find me like this, I am finished."

He ignored for a moment the events of earlier this evening that had probably trashed his career for the rest of his life. Still, if there was a photo he wished never to see, it was that of Ron attached to his arse by the unyielding elastic of his underwear.

In desperation, Jacque reached down to strip off the offending garment, realising that being left stark bollock naked was infinitely superior when faced with the onslaught of continual buggery by an obnoxious salesman. This move of desperation was defeated when he found the tassels on the front of his posing pouch had become entangled with the buttons on his shirt.

"Ron, listen, this is very serious, you need to untangle the elastic from your zipper, do you understand? You have to do it now."

"I can try," Ron's voice was filled with doubt and uncertainty, underlined when he added; "problem is, I've got me driving glasses on and I really need me reading glasses."

"Then put your fucking reading glasses on, you imbecilic cu…"

"… I left 'em at home."

"Please, just try," Jacque pleaded.

"Okay, okay, let me just see if I can…"

Jacque felt the unwanted intrusion of Ron's fingers moving around a part of his body that he usually reserved only for his most adventurous lovers. Certainly, he never envisaged this being a middle-aged, balding salesman. He began to wriggle painfully around as Ron probed deeper into the problem.

"Hold still man," Ron said, puffing with exertion. "What's the matter with you?"

"Your hands are cold," Jacque wined, a little louder than he would have liked.

A short sharp female scream from the doorway announced the unseen arrival of Juliet, who stood there, eyes wide, mouth open, and an expression of utter incredulity on her face.

"This isn't what it looks like," Jacque screamed, uncomfortably aware that Ron echoed his words at precisely the same time. He tried again to free himself, pulling forwards and causing Ron to hump him a couple of times until the elastic stopped elasticising.

"What the actual fuck?" Juliet said, clearly surprised that she could still talk.

"Please help me, Juliet," Jacque pleaded. "I am at the mercy of the Paparazzi if I am found like this. They will ridicule me; I will be finished."

"Honestly, I think that ship to the island of celebrity obscurity has long since sailed," Juliet said. "Would anyone care to explain to me what's going on? Apart from the obvious."

"Fucked if I know," Ron said. "I came out the Carsey and bumped into the Frenchy here who was bent over outside the door with his trousers round his ankles. And now me zipper got stuck in his thong...."

"It is a posing pouch you imbecile."

"And now here we are," Ron said, finishing the explanation with a shrug of his shoulders that seemed to suggest this sort of thing could happen to anyone. At any time.

"Please Juliet, please, you must help me."

"I think you'll find that I don't." Juliet turned to the door and stopped. Jacque held his breath. "But I suppose the way the evening has gone so far; this is par for the course."

She walked over to the two men and gingerly poked at Ron's zipper with less than enthusiastic fingers. After what appeared to be some very deep breaths, she retrieved her reading glasses from her handbag and turned to the task.

"My God, your hands are freezing as well," Jacque said. "What is it with you English, do you have no blood in your veins? Do the gallons of piss-weak tea you drink have no warming effect at all?"

"Oh, I am sorry Jacque," Juliet said as she probed about in his underwear. "If I had known I was about to commit myself to exploratory surgery on your thong I would have pre-warmed my hands first."

Posing pouch Jacque mentally screamed, wisely deciding to keep this rebuke to himself. He was desperate to be free and didn't want to disturb Juliet's concentration. The tightness around his recently electrocuted scrotum was reaching a level of alarming tension, one that he would like to come to an end as quickly as possible.

"I am probably going to regret asking this," Juliet said as she worked her fingers around his now goosebump covered behind. "But is there an intelligible reason why you were bent over outside a toilet with your trousers round your ankles?"

"It is, as you English say, complicated."

"Oh, right, I'll ask Clive about this when I next see him then. He'll probably know."

Jacque felt his soul die a little at these words. Oh great, now Juliet thought he was gay. So much for his chance to seduce her and grab a bed for the night. The way things were looking, he was going to end up sleeping on the street, or worse still, at a Travel Lodge.

"Please, just free me," he pleaded. Could this evening literally get any worse? Juliet's next words confirmed to him that in fact, yes, they could.

"I think I've nearly freed your thong from Ron's zipper, which is a sentence I never ever thought I would say, there is just this last bit, which is caught on something hard in Ron's trousers ..." Her words faded away as Jacque felt the fumbling at his backside came to a sudden halt and saw Juliet stiffen beside him. He looked back to see her face was once again shocked and appalled.

"Ron..." Juliet said in a faltering voice that threatened to crack and fail with every following word. "Have you... Do you have... By any chance... An erection?"

"A bit," Ron said.

"Free me," Jacque shouted, now filled with utter panic. "Free me now. Now. Free me."

"I think," Ron said, apparently by way of an explanation. "It's because your hands are cold."

A shrill scream from the doorway announced the presence of Tina, hands covering her face, but her wide eyes told a similar story of shock and dismay.

"This isn't what it looks like," Jacque once more protested, dismayed to hear both Juliet and Ron now echoing these words in a perfect chorus.

"For fuck's sake Juliet," Tina said, then realising what she had just said, retrieved her swear jar and popped a pound coin in the slot, then after a moment's thought, found several pound coins and put them in the jar. "I leave you alone with my boyfriend for three fucking minutes and you turn him fucking gay?"

"Tina, this isn't the time for your particular brand of logic," Juliet said. "I've no real idea why, but this one's thong…"

"*Posing pouch* for Christ's sake, why is this so difficult to remember?"

"This one's *posing pouch* is stuck in this one's zipper." Juliet pointed from Jacque to Ron. Clearly, she wasn't taking chances with Tina's creative thinking process.

"Because?" Tina asked.

"It's complicated," the three chorused.

"Wow," Tina said. "I only thought that happened in Enid Blyton books. Anyway, not to want to add further complications to… Whatever is happening here, but I met Pascal downstairs and…"

"Pascal is here," Jacque said with a groan. "Why, why now?"

His brother had consistently avoided him for nearly a year, and now he was here when Jacque least wanted to see him. That was so typical of Pascal.

"Yes, and he told me about… Well, he told me this stuff, about stuff, that is supposed to explain stuff, but you know," Tina said, still looking at where Ron and Jacque were joined at the hip. "Pascal speaks so quickly, and that accent of his is barely understandable, lovely though it sounds... Anyway, to be honest, I am not totally sure I got the full nuance of the situation. Or really, any of the facts."

"Tina, what are you talking about," Juliet said, her voice starting to recover itself after the revelation of Ron's healthy prostate gland.

"It's probably best if Pascal explains himself," she said, and opened the door to the private room, despite the howls of protest from Juliet and Jacque. "Come in Pascal, although I should warn you, the situation is a little... Complicated."

"Juliet," Pascal said, sweeping dramatically into the room. "I am here now to declare my love for... What the fuck?"

The room dropped into silence, broken only by Tina rattling her swear jar under Pascal's nose. Pascal considered it for a moment, then took a five-pound note from his wallet and stuffed it into the slot.

"You shouldn't worry, Pascal," Tina said, pushing the blue note further in. "Apparently, this isn't what it looks like."

"The hell it is," Pascal said, staring directly at the scene with a look of someone who just found his new puppy had shit in his favourite slippers. "My God Jacque, I knew your tastes for the sexual were Avantgarde, but even I did not realise you engaged in such public displays of sexual gratification."

"I have already said; this is not what it looks like." Jacque protested in the vain hope that someone would eventually believe him.

"Yes of course brother, I am sure there is a perfectly rational explanation for why you have a fat businessman with his hands up your bum."

"I'm just holding onto me flies," Ron said, in what Jacque decided was an unhelpfully high-pitched voice.

Unexpectedly, Jacque let out a yell of pain as Juliet once more began frantic tugs at his underwear.

"Juliet, could you please remember that my skin is attached to my body."

"I am trying my best," Juliet said, then paused dramatically with her probing. "Okay, I think I have it, Ron, when I say now, I want you to pull off."

"You want me to do what?"

"You want him to do what?" Jacque said, no longer caring that his own voice had reached the same high-pitched panic as Ron's.

"Anyway," Pascal said, clearly having decided to carry on with what he was saying despite the surreal nature of events playing out before his eyes. "I am here today, brother, to expose you."

Everyone turned their attention to Pascal.

"I mean... I mean, as a liar and a fraud, not a social deviant, this is well known and no one cares."

"Go away brother," Jacque pleaded, squirming again at Juliet's less than feminine touch. "No one will believe your lies."

"I come here not with lies, but armed with the sword of truth."

"He was like this downstairs," Tina said. "You have to listen carefully to the next bit because it's very complex and a little bit on the long side."

"Complicated and moody is what Pascal does best," Jacque said through gritted teeth of pain. "He gets these moods from our mother. You remind me of her Juliet. Very complicated personality."

"You leave Mama out of this," Pascal said, his fists balled up and slamming them with frustration into his own thighs, for a second he looked like a very tall toddler. "Is it any wonder she was a little... Unpredictable? The way you and Papa acted, never lifting a finger in the kitchen to help. Is it any wonder I had to write that cookery book for you?"

"Ah, excuse me," a female voice from the door said. "Officer Eccles and myself, Officer Patel have received some complaints from the staff about the behaviour in this room and… What the fuck is going on?"

Jacque looked up to see a surprised looking female police officer walk in, followed by a tall male police officer. The male police officer's eyes narrowed when he recognised Ron.

"Oi you," officer Eccles said. "I told you, no more ravaging."

"Ron, I need you to pull off …. NOW," Juliet said and both police officers took a visible step back.

Ron gently lifted himself up on his toes, and then moved backwards in an improbable pastiche of a ballet dancer, at last freeing the tortured Frenchman. Jacque stood carefully and hesitantly, beginning to enjoy the wonderful release of blood flowing back into his gonads as the elastic loosened and areas that were threatening to drop off slowly came back to life.

Jacque pulled up his trousers, trying not to meet the eye of anyone in the room. Particularly the police officers. For a second he thought he had entered a never-ending circle of hell reserved for people who spent too long with the English. Worse still, the whole experience had left him shockingly sober.

"Seriously," officer Patel asked, her eyes still wide with shock. "What is going on?"

"Shall I call it in?" Her partner asked, reaching nervously for his radio.

"Call what in? Suspected buggery in the VIP suite? No, don't Peter, that was a joke."

"Thing is," Tina said. "This isn't what it looks like."

"Oh well, in that case, we'll be on our way then," officer Eccles said with a smile and a salute. He turned a perfect about-turn and prepared to march from the room.

"Peter, I think we need to take another look into this, don't you?"

"Right you are Zaina," officer Eccles said, turning back from the door and whipping out his notebook. He licked his pencil and glared at the various people in the room, or at least, any that would meet his gaze, which wasn't Jacque, who moved from bottle to bottle as Juliet's voice asked the question he hoped would go unasked tonight.

"Sorry, Pascal, did you just say that you had to write the cookery book for Jacque?"

"It is true Juliet, I created a book for Jacque, but I sought revenge on him for a dark deed that I have recently found out did not happen…"

"This I the bit I didn't really understand," Tina said.

"I created recipes for the book that were exactly wrong, I knew if Jacque checked them, he would see this, he may not cook, but he is a Noir, and it is in the blood of every Noir to cook, to create, to be the best, to carry on a tradition handed down…"

"Probably best," Tina said. "If you just stick to the core story for now Pascal."

"Oui, Tina, you are right," Pascal said, sweeping his hair from his eyes. "But even I did not realise how lazy Jacque had become, and the book, with its wrong recipes, is now the one that exists for all to see and is a constant torment to my soul. Juliet, can you ever forgive me?"

"Me?" Juliet said, with eyes now even wider than when she first saw Ron bouncing about on Jacque's thong. "Well, I still have no real idea what's going on here, but as your fake recipe book seems to have trashed my agency and bankrupted my business, I think the answer is probably veering towards a no."

Pascal's face was a portrait of pain and emotion.

"But Juliet, I had good reasons, please, listen to me."

And Jacque, who knew this was likely to be a very long story, found himself a nice bottle of French red, one more suited for the summer, but at this point in life, he was pretty sure he gave zero fucks. He drained the contents as Pascal told his sorry tale of deceit, death, and Viagra spiced lobsters.

At one point in the story, namely the death of the old man, officer Eccles became very alert and said '*murder*' as though he was on the stage of Oliver Twist, to which his partner clipped him round the ear and told him to be quiet so she could hear the end of the story. In the end, once Pascal had explained everything, as far as it could all be explained, the entire room's attention shifted, eye by eye until Jacque became aware of everyone staring at him.

"What?" He said. "You think it is easy working with this human mood indicator? I did what I needed to do. You would probably have done the same."

"No," Pascal said. "That is where you are wrong because you would never be capable of doing this."

To Jacque's compounded horror, Pascal took Juliet by the shoulders, dragged her forwards on her tottering heels, and kissed her, passionately, deeply, and with raw emotion.

"Well that was unexpected," Juliet said when they separated and she had the breath to speak. "Although surprisingly nice, all things considered."

"Juliet, I love you," Pascal said, almost shaking her with the intensity of his words. "I have always loved you. That is why I opened my café across the street from your office just so I could glimpse you from day to day. Did you never wonder?"

"I did think it was a bit of a coincidence."

Pascal pulled her upwards again, kissing her again with such passion that everyone in the room felt obliged to look away. Apart from Jacque who was already staring at the bottom of another rapidly emptying wine bottle.

"Wow," Juliet said when this second kiss finally ended. "Do all your stories end like this?"

"Our story has not ended," Pascal said and Jacque let out a groan of pain from being forced to hear such unpleasant clichés. "I want now to declare my love for you, to take you away from all of this, and to tell you how I want to share my life with you."

"Okay, I guess we'd best see if there is a Starbucks still open."

"No," Pascal said, placing Juliet lightly back on the floor. "I have another idea, but first…"

Pascal walked away from Juliet towards Jacque who attempted to cower behind the bar, but Pascal loomed over him anyway. How was it this man was so tall and he was so short? How was that a fair division of genes?

"I came for revenge," Pascal said. In the background, the policeman started to eagerly write down Pascal's words, but his partner snatched the pencil from him.

"I came for revenge, but now, as I see you here, humiliated, defeated, stripped of everything you held dear, I know there is little more for me to do. Your ego has been your end, brother. I believe that this goes back to when we were young and you would never let me…"

"Oh merde," Jacque said. "If you really want to have your revenge on me then yes, please do tell me all these dull, painful stories from our childhood that only you can apparently remember."

Jacque looked up to see if Pascal was going to hit him, and for a moment, it looked as though he might. Then, surprisingly, his brother just smiled.

"I no longer need revenge, brother, but I also no longer need you in my life." Pascal turned and walked towards the nearest table. "I doubt I will see you again, but if I do, I will, of course, give you my spare change."

He picked up a bottle of German wine and placed it on the bar before his brother.

"Here have this. Soon the bitter aftertaste will be like honey to your withered lying tongue." He said, turning again and walking away, tall and confident. "These will be the last words I ever say to you, Jacque. Adieu... Brother."

Pascal lightly took hold of Juliet's hand and swept a hand out to indicate the door through which the pair vanished, hand in hand, their dramatic aura leaving the room frozen in a moment of contemplative silence.

"Well," officer Patel said searching for a hanky so she could wipe a small tear away from the corner of her eye. "It does not appear as though any actual crime has been committed, so we will leave you to it. If you'll excuse me, I just need to ... Go and...."

She walked hurriedly from the room, blowing her nose and sobbing openly into her hanky.

Officer Eccles remained in the room for a long moment, as though he wasn't sure what to do. In the end, he settled for pointing accusingly at Ron.

"And you," he said.

"No more ravaging?"

"That's right sir," officer Eccles said and snapped a perfect salute. "Have a nice evening everyone."

He left, behind him an awkward silence filling a room of broken dreams. Through his drunken stupor, Jacque became aware of Tina and Ron whispering in the background. Hesitantly they stood in front of him.

"Ah well," Tina said. "We've had a super time, Jacque, but we're going to push off home now."

She nudged Ron, who suddenly came back to life.

"Right, yes, it was… Interesting. Bye then."

And then Jacque was alone. Jacque Noir, the man who was never alone, never without a companion, never without a smile or a joke, stood isolated from humanity. Worse still, he stood at a small bar of a private reception room reserved for winners only and knowing he was a loser. The final irony. One that had him drain every single bottle in the room until eventually the caretaker found him in a pool of his own vomit and kicked him out onto the street.

Without money, or a will to call for help, and realising anyway there was no one left to call, Jacque walked the long way home to Restaurant Noir. Here he spent the night drinking in the small flat above the darkened dead restaurant.

In that isolated drunken moment, Jacque went down to his well-stocked wine cellar, his pride and joy, the place he had invested so much of his life to create the perfect companion to the food that Pascal crafted. Here, he began opening and drinking bottle after bottle. Very soon, Jacque became swallowed whole by his own desolation.

Chapter 24

Juliet

Juliet arrived for her lunchtime meeting with Rose a little later than planned. Not something she made a habit of, but since the earthquake in her life that had been the awards ceremony, she had found in herself a change.

Not a dramatic one, but just enough.

A little bit every day.

She wouldn't go so far as to say she was an entirely different person, she remained intolerant of fuckwits, and people called Ron, but she did feel, in many ways, a little more relaxed about life. Almost as though she had been able to travel back in time, get in touch with her younger self, and feed on that youthful confidence and optimism of life.

Her lunchtime meeting was, as could be considered the *norm* these days, at a small and relatively undiscovered café near Covent Garden. One that today contained fewer people than usual, probably because August in London was bereft of the larger slice of its commuter traffic. This city in summer became a different beast; a tranquil creature. One where Tube lines were suddenly not the claustrophobic affair they usually were and seats at cafés could actually be found without having to sell a kidney to secure one.

Rose waved to her from a table, pointing to her watch with a knowing smile. Rose seemed to like this new version of Juliet and as she flounced up to the table, her white summer dress billowed around her, the small straps and low cut showing off her new tan, Juliet found herself in agreement.

None of this actually happened overnight. It didn't even happen after several nights on a magical island that had been Juliet and Pascal's final destination after leaving the awards ceremony together.

Fuerteventura.

A destination that had not exactly been chosen by either of them, but selected by fate. Once Pascal had declared his love to her, in front of his utterly defeated and somewhat drunken brother, Juliet had expected Pascal to whisk her back to his place and consummate the moment, so as to say.

Instead, he asked the cab driver to go directly to Juliet's flat, which at first riled her as she wasn't sure if the sheets were clean, but she decided to just go with the flow. It seemed at the time the moment to do such things, to do crazy stuff. Even if her flat was piled high with bloody nose bandages and even if the bathroom still smelt of Ron.

Going with the flow, however, hadn't taken into account how crazy and dramatic Pascal could be. On arrival at her flat, he asked Juliet to fetch her passport and a toothbrush, and dramatically told her they would need little else. Before she could get comfortable with the way going with the flow had turned into being swept away by a rushing wave, they were headed for the airport. Once there, he booked seats on the first available flight out of the country, one that fortunately took them to a place where they didn't need any inoculations.

Of course, *next available* was actually *first thing next morning*, and they spent, what Juliet would later describe to Rose as a very anticlimactic evening in an airport pub, drinking cider and eating their body weight in fried bacon sandwiches. This enforced wait though did give them a moment's breath. After the passion of his speech, there were things to say, to clarify. Things they needed to agree on.

Rules of engagement.

Rules to be respected.

The first was Pascal's insistence they have separate rooms at whatever hotel they found at Fuerteventura. Locked on a plane and looking down at the ocean below, Juliet wasn't sure how she felt about the prospect of having unbridled sex removed from the menu of future delights. However, she respected his decision, and arriving dog tired and in desperate need of a shower, she was rather glad in hindsight to have the bed to herself.

The next day they had taken a small toy train, a tractor really with wagons following uneasily behind it, to the vast, long beaches on the edge of Corralejo. Here, under the warm winter Canary Island sun, they had walked between the families and nudists, surfers and bird spotters, ignoring them all as Juliet and Pascal talked, and talked, and talked.

At one point, they came across a small café on the beach and sat, taking lunch together as though it was something they did every day. It was here they agreed, for a moment at least, to talk about something other than themselves. At which point, the subject of Jacque's award had come up and, in a rush, Juliet remembered the book deal and Pascal's sabotage bomb he had dropped into the room on Friday night.

She had been walking along a beach talking about feelings and all this time her business could possibly be saved. From Pascal she coaxed any information he might have on how the book could be fixed; and if possible, made great. Juliet was delighted when Pascal said the process of unfucking the fucked-up cookbook would be simple, and something he could do in a few hours.

"Can you also make it vegan-friendly?" Juliet had asked, her head spinning from the thought of solvency being so profoundly snatched from the jaws of bankruptcy.

"Ah Juliet, I love you, and I am a genius in the kitchen, but I am not a miracle worker," Pascal had said, which disappointed her until she realised, he was actually making a joke!

After lunch, they had taken a cab back to the hotel, and once there, Juliet secured a laptop from a surprised receptionist and sent a request to Emma to schedule an emergency Skype meeting. Juliet suggested, through the vaguest of lies, that the cookbook received by the publisher had in fact been a draft copy sent in error. She then hoped Emma would be so keen to salvage something from this disaster that she would overlook the improbability of this explanation.

From Tina, whose messages were suspiciously quiet, Juliet asked for the publisher draft of the cookbook and tried not to think too much about what might be going on between her and Ron. After a short delay, an email that contained a dozen questions and about as many emoticons appeared in her inbox, along with the original Word Document.

A few emails back and forth, both to Tina and Emma, revealed the book's publishing date had been, as Emma had foreshadowed, *permanently stalled*; publisher speak for, *cancelled*. Emma though was delighted to hear Juliet was working on a *solution that satisfied all parties*; Emma speak for, *thank fuck for that*.

After that, it was simply a case of sitting Pascal in front of the laptop and providing him with endless espressos and refusing to allow him to leave the room until every single recipe had been corrected, improved, and where possible, made vegan-friendly. Then she pulled off her masterstroke and sent it directly to Adam Russel, with a note saying this book was now co-authored by Brothers Noir and that Adam had an exclusive 24-hour preview window if he wanted it.

The next day, a somewhat flustered Emma got back in touch to say a glowing review of the book had kick-started public interest and the publishing date was now *no longer stalled*; publisher speak for, *ready and willing to make money*.

"Right, so, thing is, are you sure you want to credit the Brothers Noir for the book?" Emma said through a stuttering Skype connection. "You do mean, the two of them? I thought they didn't get on very well of late and right now Jacque is…"

"Pascal says the recipes are the property of Family Noir, so they need to be shared with his brother," Juliet said, not really understanding this part herself, but she was more than willing to go along with it just to get the bloody book out the door.

"Right, so, thing is, have you seen the newspapers? Because Jacque is…"

"No, English newspapers are gloriously absent from the hotel we are in. To be honest, I haven't heard the word Brexit in nearly two days, it's marvellous."

"Right, so thing is Juliet, Jacque is in hospital," Emma said, her expression on the pixelated image looking poorly adapted to delivering bad news of this flavour.

After Emma disconnected, Juliet closed the laptop and walked urgently away until she found Pascal, sitting by the pool, his top a crumpled heap next to him, the soft hairs of his chest alluring and now, sadly, unreachable.

They flew back to the UK on the next flight, Juliet watching the island drop away beneath them, wondering again on the justice of spending a romantic two days on a paradisiacal island, but not actually getting to have sex. And of course, it had to be Jacque that cock-blocked her plans.

Things did not get any easier when they touched down at Heathrow and were met by Ron, in his Jag, and a worried-looking Tina.

Tina had been the one to find Jacque, concerned after twenty-four hours of no one having seen or heard from him. She eventually phoned Ron when she received a worrying lack of response from the doorbell or the intercom outside Restaurant Noir. Ron turned up, in his Jag, and between the two of them, they attempted to find a way inside. Their attempts didn't go brilliantly, with Ron breaking his arm trying to batter down the side door. He didn't actually break his arm on the door, but tripped on the run-up and fell down some cellar stairs.

Once the ambulance crew turned up and sorted Ron's arm out, one of the first responders had the wit to ask what they had been doing in the first place. Hearing Tina's genuine concerns, they summoned the police, who finally managed to break down the door, and not a moment too soon.

They found Jacque comatose on the floor of his bathroom, suffering from the effects of alcohol poisoning. Another few hours and he might not have been so lucky. By the time Juliet and Pascal arrived at the hospital, he was out of danger, but still in the ICU, where he would remain for several days. During that time, Pascal rarely left the hospital, rarely left the floor where his brother was being treated. Rarely left his side. Talking in low voices with doctors who all used the phrase *could have been worse, much worse,* over and over again.

Those dark moments in the hospital felt a million miles away from Juliet as she sat now in the sun with Rose, and ordered a cream cake and chatted about life and the chaos of love.

Through Rose's unfettered help with the aftereffects of that legendary awards ceremony evening, they had once again become firm friends. It was a rare day the two of them did not meet, and in some way reference one of their adventurous moments, like a couple of school kids, talking about the day they had played hooky or caught one of the teachers rubbing one out in the storeroom cupboard.

"Nice cake?" Rose asked.

"Better than a blow job in a pub toilet," Juliet responded and watched Rose nearly choke on her vanilla latte.

When Jacque had recovered enough of his health to be transferred down to a regular ward, Pascal had continued to sit beside his bed for hours at a time. Often the two would sit quietly staring at nothing, but sometimes they would talk, often arguing so loud a matron threatened to throw them both out on the street. Eventually though, in this enforced area of calm, the two brothers began working through the sort of shit they probably should have worked through years before. Juliet stayed out of their way as much as she could, while still staying determinedly within Pascal's orbit. There was a time and a place for romance, and here, beside his brother's hospital bed, was not it.

In the weeks that followed, with the book becoming a success, and Jacque being quietly transferred from hospital to a swish rehab centre paid for by the publisher, there opened up a moment for Pascal and Juliet. A moment for them to continue a conversation they had started in a beach café, in what felt like a different lifetime.

Gradually, without any real sense of urgency, their lives became ordered, became once more something they could enjoy and not worry about. Juliet's business slowly inched its way back to solvency, based alone on the number of books that Noir Bros Recipes were now selling. It became an unexpected summer blockbuster, and a lifeline for *Juliet Raphael - Literary Agent* (but no longer to the stars) and even more unexpectedly, for Brothers Noir.

Pascal, having rediscovered his cooking mojo at the old people's home, was keen to restart Restaurant Noir, but even with the unexpected revenues from the book, Rose pronounced the place too big and too much in debt to salvage. The lease to the premises in Islington was sold on, as was Jacque's flat, which at least left the brothers with something in the way of money.

Just not very much.

It looked for a moment as though Brothers Noir would become the only famous chefs who didn't work in the restaurant business. A moot point that had not passed unnoticed on Emma's irony radar and the publisher had taken the unusual step of becoming the loan guarantee for the brothers to open a new restaurant. Emma didn't capitulate quietly to this deal and Juliet, as the brothers' agent; she had to practically sell their souls to Emma to secure her help. The final deal involved two more books, one of which would be exclusively vegan.

"Fucking vegans," Pascal had said when he heard, and then quietly paid into Tina's swear box without complaint.

There was also another catch.

As the first book was branded *Brothers Noir*, then the restaurant also needed to be Brothers Noir (plural). A sticking point that Juliet had dreaded mentioning to Pascal, but he surprised her.

"I will work with him, yes, of course, he is my brother," Pascal said. "But I don't know if I will ever like him."

Which Juliet decided was the best she could hope for from these unpredictable men and decided, once more, to go with the flow. In truth, she quite liked this spontaneous new lifestyle that being with Pascal had revealed. It was, at times, disconcertingly different from anything she had ever known, but she was learning, slowly, that this may not be a bad thing. Often it occurred to Juliet that in some way, Pascal had, during one long star-filled night on that magical island, secretly removed the stick from her arse.

Looking back, she had to admit, that stick had been a major stopping point for any kind of personal joy. Although from the sidelong looks she still obtained from various men, even if the stick was gone, the arse remained true to form.

With Pascal's agreement to work with Jacque, Rose went about finding an alternative property with surprising speed. Not the infeasibly large premises that Restaurant Noir had been, but an off-side-street cubby hole of a restaurant that wasn't *too* far from Soho (as the black cab flew) and seated a maximum of ten people around five tiny tables.

Juliet remembered how hesitant both Rose and she had been to show Pascal how small the place was, expecting a landslide of volatile French remarks. Instead, he had smiled, laughed even, then hugged them both, and said, *you found for me, perfection.* Which they both took at face value and never discussed it with him again.

Brothers Noir opened in early August; just four months after the original had closed. By then the book was doing very well and their finances, far from being secured, were at least above the waterline. There was the minor point of Emma still having her hooks into them all for the remaining books, and possibly for the remaining years of their lives, but the ends had very much justified the means.

Jacque emerged from rehab, not exactly a changed man, he still referred to himself in the third party, and still created a certain amount of chaos by merely existing, but he was a muted form of the original persona. Quieter, not so self-centred. Almost a fractured version of the man Juliet once knew, even given to moments of self-reflection where pain would pass visibly across his unfocused gaze, perhaps moments where he recalled the loud laughter in one desperate night of his life.

Pascal and Jacque, having buried the hatchet, and not in either of their heads as Juliet had feared, now ran the business as it should be run, with Pascal cooking and Jacque entertaining the guests, and sometimes, although rarely, also cooking.

Jacque's face when he had seen the tiny venue and the limited seating area had been a picture of pure defeat, but he shrugged it off, turned up for work every day, sober, and attended his Alcoholics Anonymous meetings on a regular basis. He still needed watching and the staff were informed never to let him clear a table, never to let him near an open bottle, never to let him open a bottle himself.

It would be, Juliet realised a constant battle.

The fact that Jacque continued to have such a destabilising effect on her life, both irked her, and in a strange way, comforted her. He was a part of Pascal's family, and she wanted to be a part of this man's life and for better or worse, sickness and in health, wacky family problems, and all, she accepted Pascal into her heart with open arms.

At some point, after the initial drama of the hospital, while Jacque was in rehab, Juliet and Pascal had the chance to take up where they left off in the island sun. The conversation they had in that small beach bar felt like it belonged to a different universe and they struggled at first to rekindle the magic that had been lost in amongst the stuff of life. But find it they did, gradually, through their own persistence, coming towards each other from the point of mutual attraction. Eventually, they were back on that island again, if not physically, at least in that state of mind.

Spring that year turned into a damp squib, with the wettest May on record, followed by what looked to be an equally lacklustre June. Despite this, or perhaps because of it, on the day Pascal signed the lease on the new restaurant, he whisked her away again. A little more refined this time. He gave her a day's notice to pack a weekend bag, be ready at six on a Friday, and less than an hour late, he turned up in a hire car and drove them to Portland Bill where they stayed in a hotel that overlooked a foggy English Channel.

One morning, through the swirling mists, a bit of Chesil beach revealed itself, stretching away into the yonder distance, a thin line of gravelly sand and stones separating an inlet waterway from the sea. Much in the same way, she and Pascal had been separated by events and the actions of others.

On a windy headway in Weymouth, with both of them practically shouting at each other to be heard above the roar of crashing waves, she asked him, as delicately as she could, why they still slept in separate rooms and why they had not yet actually had sex.

In truth, despite her conviction that Pascal was not gay, she felt the spectre of Clive floating above her, and it came as no surprise to hear that Pascal felt the ghost of Candy floating above him. On that stony beach, he confessed about his problems with Candy, about the issues in the bedroom, and despite the wind, and the sand, and a group of shell collecting children who stood and stared, Juliet took Pascal's face in her hands and kissed him for the longest time.

It was, of course, his fear. His lack of performance. His perceived need for Viagra that had knocked over the house of cards that was Restaurant Noir. So much trauma that it couldn't easily be washed from his mind. It presented a high fence over which Pascal's steed flinched at jumping through the fear of failure.

To which Juliet had simply said; *we will never know unless we try*.

That night, after a fish meal at a local restaurant that Pascal tolerated, although not quietly, they retired to their lofty hotel room and attempted to coax Pascal's steed over that fence. After a few false starts, some angst, and a little bit of alcohol, things started to look up.

So much success with this problem was had, that Juliet woke the next day just after 11 am, and feeling as though she had recently run a marathon. She wasn't inclined, however, to refuse a rematch that took them up to a late lunch.

Returning to London the next day there was time to talk as the car became snared in the weekend getaway traffic of Londoners returning to their nest. They should date, Pascal had suggested, although the word *suggest* would in other people's minds promote the illusion of choice. Pascal clearly felt it was important they did things correctly. Not get distracted, or seduced into thinking they needed to make up for lost time. Instead, they would date as normal couples did by going to the cinema, having dinner, and doing romantic walks in the park on a Sunday. To Juliet, these suggestions sounded idyllic.

That's not to say Pascal didn't still suffer from his legendary dark moods, but at least when that happened, when he burnt something in the kitchen that had an improbably long and complicated French name, then Juliet would put him back into a good mood, simply by fucking his brains out.

Sometime later, she revealed much of this, although not all of it, to Rose. Juliet was hesitant about mentioning her good luck with love and romance, considering how Rose's marriage to a Noir Brother turned out. However, Rose seemed receptive to the whole thing, even going as far as to mention that Jacque liked the idea of his brother seeing someone worthy of a Noir.

"Jacque said that?"

"Words to that effect."

"Right!"

Rose placed her empty cup down and checked her watch.

"Speaking of the devil himself, I need to leave, I promised to meet Jacque and go through some paperwork with him."

"Really? You're still doing stuff for him."

"Oh, not much really, you know, just stuff about the flat, tying up loose ends and that sort of thing, boring tax stuff that I won't bore you with because, you know, it's boring."

Juliet couldn't help noticing that Rose had a strange tint of red about her face and that she was rambling as though she wanted to avoid saying something revealing. Almost as if she were…

"No! Rose!" Juliet said as realisation dawned on her. "Tell me I'm wrong!"

Rose stopped fussing with her handbag and sighed, placing it down on the table and staring at Juliet for a long time. Eventually, she spoke while uncharacteristically failing to make eye contact.

"We are enjoying each other's company again," she said, slowly and evenly. "Off the booze and not chasing women, Jacque reminds me now of why I married him."

"But you haven't forgotten why you divorced him."

"Oh no… No." Rose chewed her lip for a second. "Look, it's just something I'm going with at the moment, see where it leads. I haven't really told anyone because I don't want to confuse Yvonne."

"Assuming she would notice."

Yvonne had taken over Pascal's café as the lease had proved impossible to be sold on to anyone who would want to pay the going price. In the absence of anything happening with the business, Yvonne had quietly turned the café into a hip little place where Millennials could meet and share their very long and angst-driven poetry, or singing a sad cover version of a song that sounded much sadder when accompanied by a poorly tuned ukulele. Often these youngsters would just sit and stare at their phones, but together, with newly installed free Wi-Fi and vegan chocolate brownies that Yvonne created from a recipe in the Noir Brothers cookbook.

Yvonne was actually making a success of the place, relatively speaking. She wasn't making a massive profit, but her business approach was much better than anything Pascal had ever achieved. In the absence of a buyer for the lease, Rose had agreed to continue funding the basic overheads.

"She's not got bored of it all yet?" Juliet asked. From listening to her parents talk about her, you would think Yvonne had the attention span of a lobotomised goldfish.

"Doesn't seem to be, no, but still, you know, I want to keep this…. whatever *this* is between Jacque and me… quiet just for now."

They said their goodbyes and agreed to meet the following week; updates from both would be required. This was their private club. The Noir Brothers survivors club. For hardy women only.

Juliet took a slow stroll in the summer sun to ease away her lunch, enjoying the sound of the falling water at Trafalgar square despite the traffic and the tourists. She was supposed to be back at the office right now, but she felt there was no real rush to get back, a few more clients had surfaced once the Noir book had been declared a success, but they weren't exactly forming a queue to see her. Besides, back at the office, Tina would have some dreary novel or other she wanted Juliet to look at.

Yes, Juliet had to concede that Tina had chanced upon some interesting writers, using the old fashioned but little-used method of developing said talent, and their books. Working with writers to make their efforts worthy of publishing.

But still. Fiction? Juliet shook her head.

Who reads novels these days?

At the same time, Juliet, despite herself, was getting a little bit excited about Barry the bouncer's script. Tina had, without Juliet's knowledge, passed the script on to Clive, who had used his contacts to get it into the right hands. Progress from that point had been a frantic affair of transatlantic calls, a video conference, and a Hollywood contract turning up by courier before anyone knew what was happening.

Now the script looked to be an actual thing that would actually happen and actually be turned into an actual film. Names were floated past her by email each day; Jason Stratham, Vinnie Jones, David Leitch. Names that had her tapping Google for insight and coming away none the wiser, although Barry and Tina always got excited.

Juliet did hope, however, that if Barry's script did ever become a film, and he became a famous writer, he would forget their very first meeting outside the Pearl Toothed Alligator or at very least, never mention it in any subsequent interviews.

All of this drama and the eager Tina awaited her arrival at the office, and honestly, this new Juliet didn't care for it on a day such as this.

There was also the spectre of Ron to deal with. Despite everything, she failed to warm to him, but since he broke his arm saving Jacque's life, he could do no wrong in Tina's eyes. The fact that he hadn't really rescued him, just broken his arm falling down some steps, and as such, subsequently delayed Jacque's rescue, seemed to be neither here nor there. The injury had cemented his hero status in her sister's eyes forever.

There was a trip planned soon. One to Paris; Ron and Tina alone for the weekend. Juliet did hope there wasn't a plan for a wedding proposal in there somewhere. Having Ron as a brother-in-law did not bear thinking about, especially as she still didn't like to consider breathing the same air with this man.

Today though, trials and tribulations of work, of books she didn't really like reading and Hollywood contracts she didn't really understand, and of course, her sister dating a man who rubbed his nipples in public and spoke like Political Correctness was a disease you could be inoculated against, all felt vaguely unimportant. In truth, in that moment of summer sun and a faint breeze in the air, none of it mattered to Juliet.

Around her the cacophony of London carried on as it did every day, the smells and sounds though, they felt new, enhanced, a strength of life infused into the moments all around her. Even the air she breathed, polluted though it was, tasted fresh and easy.

It tasted free of worry.

None of the other stuff mattered. Not today. Not right now.

Right now, she was focused on enjoying being with Pascal, enjoying getting to know the man behind the moods. They weren't in each other's pockets, (or joined at the hip as they would sometimes joke when neither Jacque nor Ron were around) but they were still finding their feet in their newly emerging careers and this newly emerging relationship. Both of them rising phoenix-like from failed moments in their lives. Lives altered beyond recognition.

As she walked the steps up onto the Golden Jubilee Bridge, with the London Eye dominating the view over the River Thames, she spotted Pascal, leaning against the rail running along the bridge. His white cotton shirt and untameable hair blowing in the breeze, his expression, despite the swirling crowds around him, relaxed and at ease. He looked up as Juliet threaded her way through the throngs of picture-taking tourists and waved, his face splitting into a smile that lit up Juliet's day.

They were still taking things easy, seeing each other when they could and enjoying getting to know each other's foibles and strengths. Discovering the beauty of them. The moment of sharing. Juliet enjoyed this old-fashioned courting and Pascal's insistence that even though they were both no longer spring chickens, they should not forsake the romance of their first months together.

She had no idea where the future was taking them, or indeed if there was a future for them to be together. For the moment, she was willing to just go with the flow.

Juliet was willing, quite simply, to be dating by the book.

The End

Other Works of Fiction

By

Paul Ekert

Ordinary Monsters

A crime novel that you won't want to put down.

In Rallow New Town, a killer has awakened, driven by a need to silence years of repressed guilt. He stabs a pregnant woman to death while her daughter looks on and the police begin a desperate hunt to catch him before he can strike again.

Jon Baptist, a journalist in dire need of a career boost, accidentally uncovers the identity of the murderer but tells no one. Jon wants to be there when he kills again. He wants the ultimate scoop. But with time running out, who will he sacrifice to get it?

Next Best Prophecy

A comedy-fantasy novel

Errena; a Princess looking to evade marrying the next idiot prince to knock on the castle door. Draag; a Barbarian warrior looking to rescue/kidnap the Princess. Garrad; a young Knight looking to stay alive while helping the Barbarian. Amorck; an evil Sorcerer who wants to rule over everyone and everything forever.

Peter; an ordinary man transported from Earth to their magical world by a mispronounced spell. Everyone thinks Peter is a Living Legend destined to rid the world of an Ancient Evil,
or a great source of power to be exploited at the cost of his own life. Peter thinks, and hopes, they have the wrong man, but persuading anyone of this might just turn out to be a little bit tricky and very deadly.

Next Best Prophecy, a novel set in a rich and diverse fantasy landscape.

Escape there today.

A Darker Truth: Anthology 1

A collection of Short Stories from the darker side of comedy

A man with 13 seconds to live; a war being fought against time; a drug addict getting cocky; a betrayed spouse seeking redemption in the arms of a prostitute; an author finding that for him, reality is slowly breaking down. Welcome to 'A Darker Truth', a collection of short stories by award-winning writer Paul Ekert, that takes you to the darker side of human emotions.

A Darker Truth collects together seven original short stories written by Paul Ekert over the last few decades. Anyone familiar with his writing, both on the page and the stage, will know he has a tendency to dwell on the darker side of life and that his humour, when it does make an appearance, lurks somewhere around pitch black. The stories in A Darker Truth are no exception.

Being Darkly Humorous

Ten Short Darkly Comedic Dramas for Small Production Companies

Ten plays collected in one handy book and aimed specifically at small theatre companies with low budgets. The majority of these plays have been performed in various venues around the world; including the Henley Fringe, the Oxford Fringe, and the Camden Fringe, to name but a few.

Yes, these plays are very fringe friendly and usually work if you pick four that can be performed by the same actors. Pick any four. They all go down well; they all get a laugh.

Speaking of which, all the plays are of a specific dark humour, for which I make no apology.

www.PaulEkert.com

Printed in Great Britain
by Amazon